Missives
The Eternal Quest

D. K. Barnes

ISBN 978-1-63814-618-6 (Paperback)
ISBN 978-1-63814-620-9 (Hardcover)
ISBN 978-1-63814-619-3 (Digital)

Covenant Books, Inc.
11661 Hwy 707
Murrells Inlet, SC 29576
www.covenantbooks.com

A special thanks to Paul and Karen Hood, proprietors of the Frosty Treat in Licking, MO.

1

Broken Trust

"**H**ang on, newbie! We're gonna fly!"

An old sedan leaned hard around a sharp turn, quickly gaining speed. The warm western night sent noisy breezes rushing through windows. Diala bent forward, brushing a hand through disheveled hair. She clumsily fumbled with the steering wheel, struggling to maintain control. She blatantly ignored any measure of danger, choosing rather to test the edge of madness. Her eyes were wide and glassy—a consequence of four crinkled cans at her feet. The old car's nearly worn tires eerily whined as she weaved back and forth across the centerline. Oncomers, startled by her darting headlights, frantically lurched to the shoulder, creating a chorus of blaring horns. She threw her arm out the window and mockingly shook a fist, freely offering a string of vulgarities. With no more cars in sight, she haltingly rapped with a CD's racy lyrics, keeping the beat with a nodding head and taps on the wheel.

"Don't tell me ya didn't get a kick outta that, LaRana! Wow, what a blast! Get me another can then grab hold on somethin'! I'm gonna hit it again!"

A young girl held tight to the passenger door, terrified by the danger rushing by at arm's length. Her whole body tensed, widened eyes filled with fear. LaRana quickly glanced to the back where the enticing cooler hauntingly rested on the seat. In a panic, she swiftly reached for her second can then lifted Diala's fifth. Her shaky hand danced over the tab till a fast pull brought a sudden spray. She handed it to the driver then popped her own, nervously taking a healthy drink when Diala again veered across the centerline then quickly swayed back, barely missing a deep ditch. Beer sloshed to her lap, sending cold, oozy suds seeping through her jeans. With growing fright, she slapped the dash, screaming at the top of her voice.

"Seriously? This is crazy! Slow down! You're gonna kill us!"

"Hey, chill, and don't be such a dufus! We might as well have some fun. Live for the day, the thrill of the moment! This is what life is all about!"

LaRana's hands began to tremble. A quiet, early evening cruise rapidly grew to a perilous nightmare. Anticipation of excitement became a terrifying journey to the brink of disaster. She chanced riding with a tough girl to help gain acceptance with the in-group at her new school, another new school. A burning desire to be hip quickly changed to a heart-throbbing struggle for survival.

A few minutes passed with Diala dramatically celebrating each swig. She jerked the wheel from side to side, sending an old pickup reeling to a shallow ditch. Tires eerily squealed when the car tilted dangerously around a sharp curve. LaRana stiffened and clutched the armrest. The wild-eyed driver yelled a cowboy's yahoo while pumping a triumphant fist.

"Yeah! Whadda a rush! Jus' like a video game…but a 'hole buncha' times more thrillin'!"

"Hey! Let's cool it! We'd better back off! You're getting drunk! I don't want to end up in somebody's back seat," blurted LaRana with a shaky voice and toss of the half-full can through the window.

Diala tapped the wheel in rhythm with a bobbing head. She guzzled the last of the feel-good then slammed the empty to the floor before jeeringly saluting an elderly couple crossing an intersection. Along with screeching tires and thrumming engine came her piercing voice, chastising the panic-stricken rider.

"Gads! Are you fer real? Ya gotta be new round here. Wow, you're really green! Haven't 'eard of me, I guess. I'm da queen o' da road! I own it!"

Gusting breezes whipped through the window, making a loud vortex swirling with a throaty sound. The stout smell of beer intensified, churning LaRana's stomach. A quick glance at the bug-eyed driver brought an overwhelming fear chasing all other thoughts. Sweat beads found her forehead. Her hand choked the door, nervous feet pressed hard to the floor. She desperately wanted to stop and get out but couldn't muster sufficient courage to tell the nearly crazed driver.

Wind sounded like a train in a tunnel as Diala raced under a bridge bordering a residential complex. The road straightened for over a mile, inviting a stomp on the pedal. As speed grew, houses blurred, and the road shrank. She took a deep breath, rubbed her eyes, and again labored to steady the wheel. The passenger-side mirror smashed into a mailbox, sending shattered glass into the terrified rider's face.

LaRana felt the stinging scratches. Reeling in fear, she frantically grasped Diala's shoulder, shouting hysterically, "Slow this thing down! This is crazy!"

"Are ya kiddin'? Lay off! Ya ain' seen nutton' yet!"

The brash driver shuffled in the seat, spat out the window, and firmly grasped the wheel with both hands. She nervously blinked her eyes, desperately trying to focus. The car strained, turning hard around each bend.

LaRana's heart leaped to her throat, anxious eyes widened. Her hands quivered, frantically trying to grasp anything more solid than the door. She ached to vent fear but could no longer bring forth any words. Her whole body tensed.

Suddenly, the shrill sound of a siren broke through the rushing air. Flashing lights sent red and blue waves whirling window to window. Diala defiantly floored the pedal, offering another string of choice words. The car leaped forward, sending startled traffic careening to the shoulder. Her rant turned to a declaration of defiance.

"C'mon, coppers! Give it yer bes' shot!"

LaRana gulped hard with nerves sitting on a razor's edge. She wanted to scream but nearly choked. A small dog scampered across the road. Diala didn't flinch. She kept the pedal down. A telling bump with a mournful yelp proclaimed its doom. LaRana suddenly realized the canine's demise might not be the only one.

Another cruiser with flashing lights sat by the road near a sharp turn. Without hesitation, Diala yanked the steering wheel, sending the car skidding across the passing lane. Another tug sent the car sideways. Like a wayward missile, it tore across the road, bounced over the ditch, and hurtled head-on into a craggy embankment. Airbags left hidden rests, barely lessening the blow. Heads bounced off steel and glass. Clamor of the chase disappeared, leaving only woeful groans and hissing steam rising above a smashed radiator. Two bodies sat slumped and dazed. In moments, light streaks filled the windows as three officers surrounded the car.

LaRana slowly lifted her bruised head, gently swiping a hand across a beer-streaked shirt. In slow motion and slight quivering, she raised the other hand to a thin cut over the right eye. A fine trickle of blood seeped down her face through still trembling fingers. All within her vision grew blurry. Voices outside were muffled and vague. She sensed swirling in a void with everything around gradually receding into the distance. Several dizzy moments passed before a patrolman yanked on the door.

LaRana took a long, deep breath. *Oh, what have I done? What's going to happen now? What's Mom going to say?*

She sank in the seat, wanting out but a little more than staying in, safely hidden from the outside world. Her day that started with misery had only grown worse.

Diala threw her head back then forward, gagging with each breath. With a deep gurgle, she puked, sending a frothy glop down the airbag and into her lap. She moaned intensely, struggling to regain a sense of presence.

LaRana, choking at the stench, turned to the opening door, feeling a sudden need for fresh air. Each small movement magnified the pain in her knees. She deeply sighed then glanced up and saw an officer and a badge.

Another officer. Another badge.

Recollection flashed back to an encounter with the law a few months before. She agonizingly realized life was narrowing to nothing more than replays.

"Try to relax. Don't get out too quick. The ambulance will be here soon," came his stern voice. The officer leaned in. His slightly startled look brought a reminder of similar ones in the past, some from passersby, a few from teachers, but most from peers. The accident quickly grew beyond the agony of the body to the ache of the heart, lending an odd credibility to the present stare.

Yeah, badge! That's right! I'm different! I shouldn't be surprised. People never change no matter where I go.

A few onlookers quickly gathered. Some wriggled through the gathering crowd, trying to get close, but officers moved them back. With considerable effort, LaRana swung her legs toward the open door. Her feet hit the ground, and pain hit her knees. Slightly groggy, she took a deep breath, grateful to be in one piece. She gingerly rose from the seat and stepped outside, feeling the stares of both the curious and condemning. Whispers were hissing snakes, eyes of judgment stinging arrows. She burned to shout them back to the darkness from which they came but realized she already was enough of a spectacle.

The sound of a siren rose above the murmurs as an ambulance wove around a growing line of cars. Within moments, two paramedics stood by the crumpled car. One took LaRana to the rear of the ambulance, carefully cleaning and bandaging the cut above her eye. She continued the examination with nothing but short, direct questions.

"Anything else? Any pain?"

"Not much," came a fib. "My knees are a little bruised, but nothing more than that."

"Well, count yourself lucky. I believe you're going to be okay."

Lucky? Okay? Sorry, lady, but I don't feel either one.

An officer gingerly escorted her toward a cruiser. A question, received once before, again touched her ears. "Do I have permission to test your blood for alcohol content?"

Her heart began to race, but she reluctantly consented. She felt tarnished, dangling just above the bottom of insignificance. With the PBT done, the officer slightly smiled then looked directly into her eyes.

"Close," he stated emphatically.

The pronouncement brought no comfort. Close, she knew well; over, waited in the wings. Though several more of the curious joined the scene, she was alone. Marooned on an island with nothing to latch onto, no solace for a drifting soul. No matter where she looked, all doors were closed. The darkness of night paled against the darkness of life. A loud outburst turned her head toward the wreckage.

Diala had regained a good measure of coherence. Though balance was somewhat lessened, her blatant defiance had not subsided. Verbal abuse ran nearly nonstop. She laughed when asked to take the PBT. The officer's expression revealed the results. With a shake of the tester's head, a patrolman led her to the walk test. The bedraggled driver had nothing nice to say. She wobbled to the line then failed to stay on it for more than two steps. She shrugged her shoulders and spit toward the crowd. Cuffs soon held her hands but not her mouth. She continued to curse everybody in sight, officers, paramedics, and bystanders. No one was spared.

LaRana peered at the mangled car, suddenly realizing things could be worse, at least physically. With attention riveted on Diala, she stood between the ambulance and the cruiser, aching and ashamed, longing to wind back the clock to turn down Diala's invite to a good time. All she wanted was a friend and a group to belong to. She sorely concluded whatever she searched for had again eluded her grasp. One more effort to fit in had been dashed. One more anxious desire to be significant and popular disappeared into the blackness of night. The "where to now" question rose once again, but "nowhere" was the only place that answered.

Diala's lurid defiance persisted till the closing of a cruiser's door. Moments slowly crept before LaRana was placed in the back of the other cruiser. Sore and exhausted, she shut her eyes and melted into the seat. The gathering of the curious finally began to leave at the wrecker's arrival. Within moments, two patrolmen gained the cruiser's front seat.

LaRana gently leaned back, oddly welcoming the near silence. The rear seat held a strange feeling of comfort and security. The troopers' voices seemed loud at first till slowly fading. She tried to picture what would happen in the next few hours, then the next few months. Trying desperately to find answers, she drew nothing but a blank. Her vision of the future went no further than the next curve in the road. The engine's throaty hum orchestrated her passage down the highway of failure.

She peeked over the seat, wistfully viewing beyond the bend, yearning to gaze upon a scene of peace and happiness, but saw only night's blackness. She quickly closed her eyes, shivering at lingering thoughts of a troubled past. They were full of holes, voids punched by rejection and neglect. Out of the darkness came a vision of her father, but he offered neither help nor sympathy. He was as distant as the stars.

In a moment of uncertainty, a memory resurrected, a haunting memory refusing to stay buried.

*****

"Mommy, why doesn't Daddy ever hold me or hug me? I try to climb into his lap so he can read to me, but he pushes me away. Did I do something wrong?"

Hannah stood calmly in the tense atmosphere. She glanced at the bedroom door where Allon brazenly passed through after ignoring LaRana. While the scene was added to the many before, this was his most blatant. Her body slightly quivered, precariously standing between the greatest delight and the greatest disappointment of her life. Anger fought composure. Emotions waffled. Nerves ran on edge. She looked into to the face of her sadly puzzled daughter.

"No, LaRana, you didn't do anything wrong. Daddy has just been…out of sorts. He has a…lot on his mind. There are some things he's…uh, trying to work out."

Hannah beamed while ruffling the silky hair of her precious four-year-old whose eyes of innocence ripped her heart. A young, tender face sought comfort, but Hannah could find no soothing answers. She offered a smile of assurance, recalling her own childhood. Papa provided the food, Mama the love. Far too well, she knew the dilemma racing through LaRana's mind. Was her daughter on the same path? It seemed life was allowing her to go so far but no further. She tried to be consoling in the midst of haunting thoughts.

"Now, don't worry, my love. I'll try my best to make things better for you. I'm sure everything will work out okay." While keeping a reassuring smile, she felt lessened at her persistent lack of conviction.

Hannah gently set LaRana on the couch and placed a new book in her hands. She softly patted her head and hugged her while trying to collect thoughts. The warmth of the caress was pleasant with the growing chill of her mate waiting but a few steps away.

"You'll like this book. It has a lot of funny pictures. We'll look at them together. I'll be back in a little while. I need to talk with your daddy."

With a sigh, she calmly eased across the floor then briefly paused, looking back at LaRana slowly turning pages. The vision of innocence was short-lived. She reluctantly turned to confront her rapidly growing remorse. Trying to muster strength, she entered the bedroom and quietly shut the door, unsure what Allon would say or do.

He stood near the mirror, combing his hair, preparing for another night away from home, another night of drink, another night to disregard those seeking a normal family, a family traveling together on the same road. With a quick glance at Hannah, he tossed the comb on the dresser, donning a light jacket. She gently put a hand on his shoulder, but he abruptly brushed it off, starkly declaring his state of mind.

"Leave me alone! I'm going out. Don't know when I'll be back if I come back at all."

He quickly turned around, intently peering at her. His face, once tenderly aglow, now held an aura of remorse mixed with a touch of disdain. His embrace, once cherished and freely given, had all but disappeared. There was no reluctance to reject her desires. He stepped back, glaring with cold eyes. In the spur of the moment, he revealed his heart.

"You're a good woman, but I'm just not cut out for this family routine. If we had a boy instead of, well…maybe things would be different. I'm really not comfortable around LaRana. Good or bad, that's the way it is!"

"She's only four! She desperately needs a father to care for her, spend time with her, love her."

"Love? I'm sorry, but it just ain't in me right now. Maybe someday…"

"Someday! Someday! Don't you think…someday…might be a little too late?"

"If it is…it is! You'll give her what she needs till then, if there is a then."

Hannah tried vainly to quell anger. "Now is the important time! Someday is a day that rarely ever comes! Now is a time that can't be recovered!"

He took a couple of steps toward the door. Hannah quickly moved in front of Allon and peered into his face. His eyes no longer held the sparkle of days gone by. The young, dashing man who captured her teen emotions now turned a cold shoulder. The distance between had grown, and it seemed he was boarding a train that doesn't return. She anxiously wanted to say something, to turn back the clock, to magically create a common desire for a harmonious home. She sought her mate's assurance, but he said nothing. A stark realization burst into mind. She wanted to shake it but couldn't.

Allon snatched a rather thick wallet from the dresser then slid it into his back pocket. He paused and gazed into Hannah's eyes, seemingly wanting to speak but no words came. With burning defiance, he turned away and left the bedroom, leaving her leaning against the doorframe. He briskly started across the family room only to hesitate for but a moment when LaRana rose to her feet and reached out her arms. She stood near the end of the couch, her eyes imploring no more than a token of care. Any token.

None came.

He boldly walked past without a word, a touch, or a kiss, nothing but a slight glance from callous eyes. The door slammed shut, leaving a hollow sound slowly ebbing into silence. LaRana stared at the door, eagerly hoping to see it open and a father whisk her to his arms.

13

Closed it remained.

Confusion danced in misting eyes. She sped to the door, grabbed the knob, and then paused. She turned back as her mother drew near, dropping to her knees. Hannah seethed inside, some toward her mate, but mostly at herself.

What did I do? Why did this happen? Why does he despise his precious daughter?

LaRana quickly leaped to her mother's open arms, arms offering refuge from the storm of rejection. With an expression beyond sad, LaRana longingly looked up. Her fretful questions tore through Hannah.

"Mommy, Daddy was loud. I heard what he said. Why am I not good enough? Am I ugly or bad? Why does he hate me?"

"Oh, he doesn't hate you," she lied, gently lowering her to the floor. "I wish I had answers for both of us, my love. Maybe the time will come when he will realize he has a beautiful daughter and how much we wish for a peaceful home. Till then, we must stay together, close together. No matter what comes, remember, you are my delight, the shining star of my life."

LaRana clung to the only constant in swirling depths of confusion. "Mommy, I love you. Please don't leave me."

Hannah wilted. The four walls seemed to collapse. Her only reason for living was by her side, torn and confused. She braced to keep from falling and failed to stem welling tears. She softly caressed LaRana's hair then kissed her forehead.

"Never, my joy, never on this earth, will I leave you."

The evening slowly passed with Hannah trying to fill the void of a disappearing husband and father. She read to LaRana who relaxed on the couch with her head calmly nestled on her shoulder. LaRana suddenly put a finger on the page. She quickly looked at Hannah with excited eyes.

"Mommy, I like this picture. Isn't that a…mountain?"

"Yes, it is. The story is about two kids going up the mountain to see a beautiful double rainbow."

"Gee, that would be some real fun. Can I go up a mountain someday…with you and Daddy?"

Hannah struggled to hold tears. She smiled as her joy took the book in her hands. She patiently waited till LaRana returned it to again rest on her shoulder. Each new page brought a change in the story, but she couldn't see a portal to change life's cruel pages. A myriad of thoughts came and went, some wishful, some dreaded. She gently ran her fingers through LaRana's silky dark hair, looking deep into the past, recalling the forever words on a magical road now becoming a path to heartache and failure.

The nagging dilemma returned.

She struggled to balance a hasty, ill-conceived marriage with the complete joy it brought: shattered expectation against fulfilled desire. She delicately stood poised between light and dark, between the mountain and the abyss. She vividly remembered her mother's concern when she broke the decision to wed. *Don't marry on emotions, she said. Think past the moment, she said.* What seemed so right at eighteen now tore at every fiber of her being.

Oh, Mama! If only I had listened. I wouldn't have an uncaring mate. But neither would I have LaRana.

Hannah took a long, deep breath and then returned to the book. She met LaRana's loving smile with one of her own. With her pride once again softly nestled against her shoulder, she continued to read with her heart and mind in different places. She finally relaxed as LaRana yawned then giggled at the funny story. The pleasant sound of her laughter brought Hannah's purpose back into focus. A touch of warmth came through the cold.

With LaRana absorbed in pictures, Hannah's memory visited the past. She had seen many kids grapple with cold and broken homes—several she grew up with. Many found deceptive comfort in the seedy side of life. Most found only crushed dreams and failure. Never thinking such desperation could befall her; she now wallowed in the same situation. Her heart began to race while her resolve gained strength.

LaRana is not going to lack love and direction! Here is my life and my delight no matter the circumstance that comes our way.

LaRana fell sound asleep two pages before the story's end. Hannah set the book aside, rose, and gently carried her to the bedroom. With her pride snuggly tucked in, she returned to the family room where the cold and barren stillness waited to once again engulf her, bringing a sharp awareness of the void taunting her mind. With LaRana in bed, the room appeared to darken, and eerie shadows slowly crept toward her then around her. Maybe, she decided, a novel's words would resolve the mixture of thoughts and the pain they carried. She pulled a book from the shelf, settled on the couch, and snuggled a throw over her legs. A long sigh tore through the deafening quietness.

Time passed. Pages turned. Anguish remained.

As much as she tried to find an angel of harmony, the demon of chaos would not go away but doggedly followed her every move and thought. Adoration for Allon turned to a wearisome burden. Efforts to knit a family unraveled to a breaking point.

She pulled the throw around her shoulders, laid her head on the pillow, and shut her eyes only to find sleep elusive. The more she pondered the past, the moments of bliss, the missteps, the expectations, the despairs, she found no solace for the present anxiety. Life became a stale novel where she knew the end by the third chapter.

Shortly before midnight, a knock on the door grabbed her attention. Startled, she cautiously crossed the floor and peeked through the viewer, unsure who stood on the other side. She tilted back, perplexed yet wondering.

Two policemen.

*****

LaRana gently leaned back in the seat. She shuddered at the thought of her mother's reaction. The last thing she wanted was to grieve her more. The patrol cruiser turned onto the main highway with the engine's drone numbing any sense of presence. She rubbed sore knees then gently touched the bandage over her eye. A sudden, sharp sting brought a wince. Reality painfully set in. She wondered if this was the bottom of despair then pondered if there was a bottom.

LaRana, what are you doing here? Look at yourself! You're an absolute mess!

She was suspended in a void, hating days to come only slightly less than those gone by. The officers in front seemed as daunting warriors guiding a chariot of horses to an unknown destiny. Her resolve collapsed. She slammed hard on the brakes of life and gazed in all directions.

"There's nothing behind and nothing ahead. Is this where I belong? Trapped somewhere between misery and hopelessness?" she mumbled, gazing at the darkness of the seat.

An officer looked back. "What's that?"

LaRana was startled. "Nothing, just…nothing."

She sagged as if her bones gave way but continued to let misery freely run. *Here I am…nowhere, a nobody. Why can't I be like…like…somebody else…anybody else?*

She melted into the seat, desperately trying to quell tears. The engine's persistent thrum summoned distant memories. A painful reminder of Allon's uncaring face, turning away in an unforgettable moment, brought mist to her eyes. In a heartbeat, another face crossed her vision, a face with eyes piercing yet saddened, loving yet bewildered. Her heart now hurt more than her knees.

Mom, I'm so sorry…so sorry.

*****

The late evening hour found a mostly clear sky, common for a fading summer in Pallon Ridge. The peaceful, western town of a little more than twenty-seven thousand nestled in a wide valley below a large, rugged mountain range. The usual random sound of distant critters could barely be heard. All was peaceful in a clean, modest residential section not far from the vale's lake. Well-kept houses, some of the wealthy, some of the less affluent, sat on the gentle arc of a wide, freshly paved street. Decorative lights rested on poles like tall sentries, creating a host of haunting shadows.

The usual light breeze fell to a dead calm, leaving a feathery mist hanging like gentle thoughts. The eerie but peaceful silence was broken only by sporadic chants from whip-poor-wills at the edge of small tree groves. The hour was late. Windows yet lit, quickly began to darken.

Nothing moved but a couple of curious dogs till three vague figures turned onto the clean, wide lane. They paused and then quickly split to each side while the unwary turned in for the night.

In but a few moments, the stillness was splintered by clamorous sounds of trash bins, metal cans, and glass bottles smashing on concrete and asphalt. Just over a minute, two boys arrived at the street's end, leaving a sea of trash in their wake. They breathed hard then paused and fisted each other in celebration, gazing over the debris-laden path as if victorious in battle. Lights quickly returned with curious heads popping from windows. Several angry shouts and colorful words raced above cluttered lawns and driveways.

With beaming smiles, the boys scurried back from the lights. "Wow! What a blast! Hey, where's Bernie?" asked Darien with a puzzled look.

They scanned the inglorious deed, unable to locate their accomplice. With sudden concern, they peered into the shadows, seeing nothing till the sound of breaking glass turned their eyes to a nearby car. As quick as a thought, thieving hands grasped an iPad and pistol. A stocky lad sped across the grass, quickly approaching his stunned comrades.

"What the heck do you think you're doing, Bernie?" said Jalen angrily, holding both hands in the air in disbelief. His heart quickened at the unexpected theft.

Bernie held his prizes like cherished possessions. "Now what does it look like? I know a guy who'll gladly pay for these. Might as well get a little green along with the fun."

"That's stealing!" blurted Jalen angrily. Sweat beaded his brow. The thought a humorous prank had suddenly turned criminal stoked his wrath. He took another step forward and raised a fist, ready to take out his frustration.

"You think?" came the arrogant reply. "So what? Chill, man."

"Put 'em back!"

"Put 'em back? Put 'em…are you serious?" Bernie's eyes quickly steeled. "I guess you want me to fix the window too. And maybe… tidy up the lawns. Get a grip, dude."

"Hey, we'd better get out a' here," blurted Darien. "Never know how close the fuzz might be."

Jalen ignored the warning, continuing to rail on Bernie. "We didn't come here to steal!" He shoved him back then shoved him again. Bernie held his ground, remaining defiant.

"Well, tough. Hey, ease up, bro. Things change. Can't pass an easy pick like this. A little cash comes in handy when I need a shot in the arm. Hey, how 'bout this, man. I won't tell anybody, and you don't tell anybody. All's cool, right?"

With several more shoves and louder words, they argued for too long. They finally paused to watch as residents adorned in various attire burst from quickly lit houses. They crept back into deep shadow, keeping quiet till Jalen again exploded. He resumed venting his wrath. Suddenly, wailing sirens and flashing beacons lit both ends of the cluttered street.

"Ah, blast it! We gotta get outta here," said Bernie, bolting toward an alley, but quicker feet prevailed as an officer took him down. Two more officers bracketed the boys who cringed at glaring lights and convicting eyes.

They stood as a stone, suddenly racked with shame. An officer got out of the car and calmly approached. Jalen looked into a familiar face, a face deep in disappointment. Mike Monroe, his former baseball coach, reached for a set of cuffs. Burning inside, Jalen shuffled his feet and dropped his head in utter disgrace. The thrill of the prank was gone. Shame replaced euphoria. He ached to turn back the clock.

"Well, boys, got nothin' better to do?" came the officer's sarcastic query. "There must be something else to do on a nice Friday evening. Well, now, Jalen Strade, of all people…never thought I'd see you in a situation like this. And you, Bernie, I'm guessing this iPad and gun has your prints on them. It appears you've taken a big step. I hoped you had learned from your last ordeal."

The cuffed vandals dejectedly crawled into back seats of anguish while an officer met with shocked residents gathered along the street. The cruisers' doors shut with condemning thuds. Jalen caught his breath at the sudden silence. The view from inside the cruiser thrust him toward a yawning gulf. The pulsing lights were swirling hammers, bouncing off houses and hovering trees, driving nails of guilt with each burst.

A man started to pick up scattered boxes when an officer raised his hand. "Just move what is needed to get your cars out. Most likely, these lads will gladly volunteer to clean it up in the morning."

Officer Monroe entered the cruiser with a quick glance to the back, a glance Jalen deemed an arrow spiraling directly at him. He couldn't remember feeling so small. With swirling lights mercifully turned off, a lonely darkness welcomed his accusing thoughts while silence became a deafening assault. The fleeting levity of a jester's dash vanished in the dread of an unsure path. Fear and humiliation brought a stabbing regret of an ill-devised deed.

What am I doing? Why?

Reasons streamed from the gloom, quickly popping into mind like biting gnats. Fun. Control. Look tough. All drastically paled against the last word.

Revenge.

Getting back at neglect, he tried to brush off years of anger in a swift moment. He stared at the carnage then turned his head as though in a flash it would all disappear. He suddenly realized his rage, hopefully diminished in the rush of the moment, was still firmly entrenched. His anger wasn't vented at the residents but to one solitary soul.

Jalen's thoughts rambled, and he slumped in the cold seat. He glanced at Officer Monroe as he slowly drove past a few, still angry people, wondering what thoughts were running through his mind. He had been his coach, his mentor, and his friend. Now his friend was his arrestor. He wasn't sure he could feel any lower. But he found a way. His mind turned to the one whom he loved the most.

Mom's face filled his vision. His cuffs screamed he broke a bond, a mother's trust with a son's vow, a trust now shattered by a moment of recklessness. A queasy feeling visited his stomach.

What will Mom say? Dad? No telling. At least he'll know I still exist.

The patrol cars quietly passed by familiar stores, favorite places to eat, and the baseball park near the high school. With classes starting on Monday, he wondered how his friends would greet him. He wondered if he would be suspended from the baseball team. Pleasant memories of each raced through his mind. For reasons obvious, everything was suddenly different. He now felt disconnected from usual surroundings. He kicked himself even harder.

Shortly before midnight, three pairs of slumped shoulders trudged through the station's entry. The few staff remaining curiously eyed the trio. Jalen felt considerably lessened as he neared an ominous cell. The turn of a key, the creek of the door, the clink of its closing sent unnerving chills down his spine. He had never viewed the world from inside the iron barrier. It was just a little more despairing than life. Time seemed to pause while thoughts began to nag.

Words dropped like a judge's gavel. Separation. Conviction. Dishonor. Disgrace. At last came his mother's reaction…heartache.

That one cut deeper than all.

He leaned back with self-blame yet in high gear. He scanned the room till his eyes paused at the small waiting room where a girl sat with a female officer. She was visually different than most girls in Pallon Ridge. Her head drooped, and she slouched on the well-worn bench, longingly staring at the floor. Her wrinkled, blood splattered clothes well matched a bandage over the right eye. With dark, bedraggled hair, she appeared to be languishing at the back end of hard times, oblivious to anything around her, no sense of presence, no look of regret, nothing but a lost, empty stare.

Wow, and I thought I had a bad night.

He briefly set aside thoughts on his predicament. He kept his gaze till a lady, he guessed somewhere in the midthirties, entered and hurriedly approached the counter. With little said, she was ushered to the dejected girl who still didn't lift her head. As the distraught woman sat by her, he pictured his own mother coming through the door. He winced at the vision of a mother's loving face turning crestfallen by a teenager's callous disregard.

After a short conversation, a female officer led the girl toward another room. For a brief few seconds, she glanced toward Jalen then returned her gaze downward. His eyes followed her. A strange desire to know her plight swept over him. Must be new to the area he guessed. Definitely out of sorts for some reason he concluded.

She's oddly different, yet...

The distraught woman remained in the waiting area. Visibly upset, she paced the floor then sat down only to quickly rise and pace again. Finally, she sat and put her head in her hands. He had never seen anyone in such distress but gave it no more attention as a stocky man approached then reached for the cell's door. The unnerving clink of key to lock lingered far too long. His thoughts quickly returned to his own predicament.

"Officer Monroe wants to meet with you. Your parents should be here soon." With a reluctant sigh, Jalen left the cell giving a final look at the sorrowful woman.

The room became deathly quiet till the entry door opened. A woman, rather tall and slender, briskly walked to the desk. After a brief exchange, the clerk led her to the waiting room where she sat across from the downcast woman. Neither said anything for several moments. Each was absorbed with despairs of her own. After a few quick glances exchanged, the silence was finally broken. Not one to mince words, Jalen's mother nicely but directly spoke.

"Hello, my name is Shelly Strade. Is one of the boys yours?"

The woman was taken aback, wondering who would be interested in her plight. Preferring to be left alone, to keep agonizing sorrow to herself, she slowly lifted her head, uncertain how, or even whether, to reply. Though the moment was awkward, she couldn't keep her anxiety inside.

"One of the...boys? No...my daughter is here. Please forgive me. I'm Hannah Lester. My daughter, LaRana, is only seventeen, and...she...and...she..."

The woman paused and took a deep breath. Her gaze begged for answers. Unable to tightly hold intense agony, the emotional dam finally burst. Tears streamed down her cheeks. A slow sigh and lowered head revealed a deep sadness. Years of anguish, lapping at the rim of life, now spilled without restraint. Shelly rose and moved to her side, gently reaching for a trembling hand.

"I'm so sorry. Unfortunately, it seems we have something in common."

Hannah looked up with reddened eyes. "I apologize for breaking down, but I had always hoped this day would never come."

The gulf between had been crossed, a flicker of light rose in a common darkness, and they spoke for several minutes till LaRana emerged with an officer. Shelly rose with Hannah who quickly wiped her cheeks, struggling to regain some measure of composure. In the commonality of their plight, each understood the discouragement of the other.

LaRana inched toward her mother. They conversed only through eyes. Hannah's were distraught yet loving. LaRana's wallowed in despair and quickly hit the floor.

Shelly broke the awkward moment. "As we talked about, Hannah. I'll see you at the Frosty Treat, Monday morning about nine. We can meet for coffee and get to know each other under, uh, different circumstances."

Hannah nodded with a thin but thankful smile. She conversed with the officer for a few minutes then left with LaRana who still lacked emotion. Shelly closely watched the despondent girl trudging behind her mother.

Quite attractive, but she's so young to test the waters of danger. But here I am with the same plight. Oh, well, another woe for the Strade home.

Hannah and LaRana's disappearance reduced Shelly's thoughts to one...a broken-hearted mother with a confused, searching daughter. She suddenly realized, save the gender, she would leave the station in like manner.

Shelly gathered herself then sat down, ready to face her own trial. Fond memories of Jalen's childhood passed gently through her mind. She revered the early days of oneness of the family and the peace of a warm home. She also knew with time changes always come—some desired, some unwelcome. The unwelcome held the moment at hand. Pondering the current atmosphere, she fretted a crisis of some kind rapidly approached.

A middle-aged lady entered the waiting room. "Your son is with Officer Monroe. Please follow me."

She walked down the hall trying to maintain composure. She entered with some apprehension. Officer Monroe rose to greet her. Jalen fretfully remained seated.

"Mrs. Strade, welcome. I was hoping your husband would be with you."

"He's…not feeling well, but if you need him also, I can call him."

"That won't be necessary for this situation. Jalen and I have been talking. He knows and regrets his behavior. Jalen made a poor judgment, and he agreed. I believe he has the character to be truthful with not only you and me, but more importantly, with himself. I'm releasing him, but I would rather he inform you of my action. I have faith this will be the last incident of such irresponsibility. Do you have any questions?"

"Not at this time, sir."

"If you need to ask at a later time, please feel free to call me. It's late, so I won't keep you any longer."

With goodbyes exchanged, Shelly and Jalen walked down the hall to the main lobby. Their eyes met. Jalen expected the wait till we get back home look, the daggers of indictment. That was fine with him, maybe even slightly hoped for.

None came.

In place of anger was calm, instead of a chasm, a bridge. No panic, no frown, no despair, only love.

Now, he really felt lousy.

Scold me. Tell me I should know better. Get out the old paddle. Do something. Say something. I deserve it.

Shelly briefly spoke to a casually dressed, elderly gentleman while Jalen meekly stood with a hanging head. Swimming in a sea of humiliation, he heard but a few words. With the conversation ended and the exit door shut, they briskly walked toward the Jeep parked no more than a stone's throw from the station. Jalen couldn't recall a longer trek. The only sound was that of feet to pavement, a sound pounding his ears.

Nothing was said as the thump of closing doors brought an unnerving atmosphere. Jalen didn't think quiet could get any louder. He wanted to talk, to scream, but couldn't utter a word. Shelly carefully turned onto the highway before anything was said.

"What was Officer Monroe's pronouncement?" she asked, trying to nicely but directly elevate the moment's impact.

"He gave us two weeks probation with two Saturday mornings of civic cleanup. Tomorrow, or rather today I guess, we'll be cleaning the street we trashed. I'm not sure about Bernie. Age-wise, he's an adult. He took a bigger bite since this wasn't his first charge, plus he was caught stealing."

Silence was the third passenger for several minutes. They passed by darkened houses and businesses appearing cold and lifeless. The same feeling crept over Jalen. He stared out the window, looking for answers, but none came. He was angry at everything entering his mind till overtaken by a sudden, overwhelming sense of separation from the one who had never given him anything but love. A glance at his mother only deepened his dismay. The Jeep became a traveling tomb, a haunting sepulcher for the lonely and lost.

Shelly drove slowly, peering at the few headlights remaining on the early morning road. Each turn led them closer to a dreaded encounter. She bore a sense of failure mixed with a keen awareness Jalen was troubled by his father's neglect, an inner rage for which she had no answers.

She wistfully recalled how they were nearly inseparable during early childhood years. She agonized how circumstances had driven them apart. So many things changed. Loving attitudes, shared desires, a sense of togetherness all gradually eroded over time. The chasm had widened considerably over the past two years. She wondered how this incident would change the situation, for better or worse. The latter was well ahead.

She turned onto the paved lane, splitting a pristine stand of pines. Their modest house sat at the back of a wide clearing with a large lawn to her left. She pictured Jalen and his once-doting dad playing catch and hitting balls. She recalled a very young Jalen running around the bases with his dad frantically chasing, trying to tag him out. She would sit on the porch, watching and listening with a proud heart. In current eyes, she suddenly realized home was no longer an eager anticipation of pleasure to come. Now it seemed no more than an archive of distant memories.

Shelly's vision moved from the pain of today to the anticipation of a better future. "I won't ask why since you don't know yet. I have only one question. Which direction will you go from here? Take your time, but...when you find that answer, let me know with maybe a few words but mostly without words."

Jalen started to speak, but the request hung in his throat. *Without words! Without words? Now what in the world does that mean?*

As they approached the garage, another nettle rose in the churning quagmire of uncertainty. "Why didn't Dad come with you?"

"Well, you know your dad. As you might guess, he was rather angry and decided to stay home. Considering his frame of mind, it was probably a good decision."

"Figures. What's new?"

Confusion swirled in Shelly's eyes. Conflicting thoughts fought to air. Balancing a husband's indifference with a son's needs tore mind and heart. Efforts to bring them together had been futile. She tried to look past the volatile present, searching for serenity in days ahead. All paths were paved with poorly defined solutions crafted by the world. All ended back at the home of failure.

All but one.

Pausing the Jeep at the garage, she reached for the latch of a door ignored for years. A thought shoved long ago in the dark closet of neglect now ascended like a beckoning call. She turned and faced Jalen directly.

"We don't seem to be making much progress. Something has to change. I've been thinking. We haven't been to church much lately... in fact, not for several years...in fact, not for many years. You were quite young, and things were better when we went. Maybe we should start back. What do you think?"

Jalen gazed through the glass at the wooded darkness summoning him to draw closer. He longed to dash into the black, yawning refuge as hated memories raced across his mind. He shrugged his shoulders.

"Ah, well, I don't know. Whatever. Maybe. Probably just you and me. That's the way it always is."

"At least that's a start."

Shelly pushed the button on the rearview mirror. The door took its usual slow time to rise. To Jalen, it seemed no longer a shelter for a vehicle but a gaping portal to a courtroom door. With the Jeep coming to rest, the garage door closed like a beat of a drum. The dull bump on concrete was a judge's gavel signaling a pending condemnation. Jalen reluctantly got out, briefly desiring the cell's coldness to the imminent fire in the house, a house now deemed no more than a hall of inquisition.

Shelly paused at the door, took a deep breath, and went in first. Jalen trudged behind, unsure of the storm waiting inside. He hadn't long to wonder. They stepped into the family room where a figure of fury stood near the fireplace. His fiery eyes hurled spinning knives of anger, his face ready to erupt, barely holding a pounding tirade. He turned and slowly paced back and forth with occasional glances at the door.

"Take it easy, Roland. We need to work this out," said Shelly, trying to diffuse an ugly confrontation.

"Take it easy? Take it easy? This...son of mine is no better than the misfits he runs around with! A vandal no less! What's next... theft, drugs, violence?"

He snapped his head toward Jalen who meekly stood behind Shelly. "Well, what do you think of yourself now? How does it feel to be a common hood? You've certainly brought shame on me. How am I going to answer the snoops at work? And after all I've done for you, this is the thanks I get?"

"This is no way to..." started Shelly before another voice rose, a voice with words long held inside, desperately wanting to be heard, but never able to air.

Till now.

Jalen quickly stepped in front of Shelly. "All you've done for me? Just what is that… Dad? What have you done for me, or for that matter, with me? You act like I don't even live here anymore. You ignore me as if I had the plague. I feel like an unwanted guest."

"I've given you money for school, bought you a good ATV, bought your clothes, fed you. You never seem to lack for anything."

"Money! Money! Is that all there is to being a father? What about time? When have we done anything together since…since… I can't remember? When was the last time we went fishing? How many baseball games did you watch me play in? After the few you came to, you only cut me down on the bad plays I made. Time! You must only have enough for yourself!"

Roland's face reddened. He raised a hand and took a step toward Jalen. Shelly quickly stepped between, unsure of her mate's next move. The air was rife with tension, ready for shattering in a violent explosion. She carefully spoke with a lowered voice.

"Take it easy, Roland. Calm down."

"That's it," said Jalen, bobbing his head but holding his ground. "Take a shot at your punk son! Just maybe you can brag to your precious friends that you took care of business at home!"

Roland paused then slowly lowered his arm, his furious eyes still aglow. Jalen waited for his next move. None came. With a flip of his hand, he loudly stomped off to his room. The slam of the door slowly abated. Only a stunned mother and Roland's heavy breathing shared the room with silence.

Moments passed till Shelly started to follow Jalen. She paused near the bookshelf, gathering composure while turning to Roland. She grasped the side of the shelf, uncertain if she could remain standing. Rage remained on his face. She gazed without flinch, bringing agonizing thoughts to light.

"Did you listen to your own words, how you spoke only of yourself? Whose welfare are you concerned with, yours or Jalen's? He feels he has lost you, that he is nothing more than a fading footnote in your life."

"You know how much I have to work. I don't have the time to mess around with baseball or fishing or whatever!"

"You manage to spend plenty of time in your workshop, or reading the paper, or meeting with your buddies at the bar. Just take a step back and try to see the gulf between you and Jalen. Try to remember when you played catch with him, when you took him fishing at the lake. We can still bring this family closer together. I'm not certain where the right path can be found, but we're going to start back to church. I really think it would be a step in the right direction if you would come with us."

Roland shook his head and mockingly smirked. "Church? You got to be kidding! Of all things! Now, why would I go to church? What a waste of time. I figured you both outgrew that myth."

Shelly stood strong, resolved to her thoughts. Her eyes steeled. "Is it? We don't seem to have an answer to our situation. Just maybe it lies elsewhere."

Missives One

Jariel,

It's been a rather long spell since we've exchanged missives over a common desire. If I rightly recall, our last encounter resulted in two souls coming to our cozy domain. It's been brought to my attention that you and I are striving for the same soul, LaRana by name. Delightful. I do enjoy a stiff challenge from one of heaven's brightest.

I thought my task would be more difficult on this occasion, but fortunately, I do not see much of an opportunity for you. As usual, a young girl with a split home and no safety net seems an easy task.

So sorry, but I must say I had a good night, a very promising night indeed. It looks as though I have all but snared our mutual quarry and, it seems, maybe another along with her. It did my heart good to see such a lovely girl begin her journey to us. I was also pleasantly surprised to see the lad, Jalen, enter the fray. He appears ready to harvest also. I believe I made a good start. Even my master was pleased and lauded me.

We have found neglect to be a very powerful tool. We abound with anticipation when parents neglect the needs, hopes, and desires of those depending most on their love and guidance. We do our best to help parents turn a cold shoulder to their offspring. We also scour the land to find others to meet their needs and desires. As you are aware, we have a large number of humans meeting our approval to influence the neglected. Our collection of misguided souls constantly expands.

A rejected mind and broken heart are excellent for our efforts. It becomes much easier to add them to our grand abode.

I especially swelled with anticipation when charming LaRana took another go at our delicious potion. A few, but fortunately not many, have managed to turn down a second drink, or third, or…well, you understand. I foresee she not only drinks again but will also find it highly irresistible. How marvelous our magnificent brew is so, shall I say, enthralling. It makes those hapless teens think they are grown up and tough.

After all, consider the examples around her. In nearly every aspect of human behavior, there are many who claim allegiance to your Master but glorify our enchanting concoction. In joyful ignorance, they willingly bow to that sparkling god, not thinking, or even caring that it often destroys their lives and homes. It must be quite dismaying to see so many dancing not at the feet of your Master but ours.

It was quite enjoyable to see Jalen's adventure. I frowned for a moment when he had second thoughts on the glorious rush of foolishness. It seems he has a vague notion of what is right, but his companions helped him disregard it. Jalen touched his toes in waters of the seamy life. It only stands to reason he will want more, especially with the family stress.

As you have seen, Roland's neglect finally piqued Jalen's anger. And I know you are aware he, like so many, doesn't believe in you or me. Fantastic. Ah, the thoughts that dwell in a child's head when parents spurn your efforts. As usual, most offspring respond to neglect with about anything but seeking your Master's way of life.

Watching Roland wallow in the depths of drink and indifference greatly encourages me. I believe it's quite possible to collect the whole family.

Oh, let's don't forget Hannah. I almost felt bad to see her in tears trying to raise a daughter alone. Indeed, some mothers have been successful, but the road is treacherous. Escar, my esteemed colleague and excellent servant of our master, helped her make some poor choices when she was a teen. LaRana will be no different. Her father's neglect made our task easy. Hannah may try to fill the void, but good intentions will not be sufficient. When LaRana embraces the vile, Hannah will wallow in despair the rest of her life.

Let's see, LaRana, Jalen, Hannah, and Roland all appear easy to collect. My only concern at the moment is Shelly. The thought to return to church has us a little concerned. We have kept such a detestable notion in darkness for many years. I will work diligently to squelch that disturbing possibility.

I could go on but won't. LaRana and Jalen have experienced enough neglect that their destination to our realm is all but sealed. Sorry for your loss. You seem to struggle with luck.

Esul

*****

Esul,

I just received your missive declaring a premature victory. I was somewhat taken by surprise when I learned you were my foe. I thought back to the many souls we lost to your tenacious efforts. So I give you credit for stubborn pursuit of the Creator's greatest handiwork. The fact you have drawn away many more than I have garnered has caused me great displeasure. However, I highly question your over-confidence on this current challenge.

As you may know, my methods vary little, but we can be quite persuasive with those who truly seek a better life. Helping humans find the decent and righteous often leads them to my Master. Be assured, you will not find it easy to gather LaRana or Jalen.

I have been informed how we tried to turn LaRana's father toward us, and it sorely grieves me to see him doomed to your realm, but his loss has only made me more determined to bring his daughter to ours. And just consider, I may influence others to come with her. In case you didn't notice, both LaRana and Jalen had an aura of shame, whether from regret or getting caught is yet to be determined. My assumption is the former.

I must admit, I am very concerned with LaRana's willingness to imbibe in that dangerous brew. We have lost far too many to that deceptive concoction.

And Shelly, whom your cohorts coveted for a long time, spoke the word that drives you mad. Church. I know, I know, many in your collection used that word from a sense of convenience rather than conviction, but there is still a host of humans who give it high regard. Shelly may well have found it a start to counter your deceit.

How heartening to see her comforting Hannah even though she herself shouldered the pain of a broken trust. For certain, you will try to crush her spirit, but you will fail. You will try to sow bitterness, but I sense an inner strength to challenge your devious efforts.

Jalen's father seems firmly in your grasp for the moment, but the power of the Creator's word may yet change his destiny. You have used selfishness quite effectively, but even he may eventually see through your schemes. It's my hope Jalen's outburst will open his eyes.

Yes, Esul, you often wound me by your progress and numerous victories, but I will never lessen my determination to deny your desire. And be sure to recall the saving of one has, on numerous occasions, led to the saving of many.

Jariel

2

Connection

The first day of school brought the usual chaos of students reuniting with old classmates, discovering the new, and eagerly stuffing lockers. Enthusiastic chatter bounced off walls, creating a nearly incoherent din. A myriad of faces, some joyful, some dejected, filled the halls. Teachers proudly stood by smartly designed rooms. Some appeared indifferent, but most offered pleasant smiles and greetings. Various pictures and crafted images of eagles, the school mascot, proudly graced trophy cases and freshly painted walls.

LaRana meandered down the hall looking for locker numbers hidden by the swirl of excited students. She deftly dodged two boys madly dashing through the throng, bouncing from shoulder to shoulder. A few eyes turned her way; some held curiosity, some indifference, some disdain. A feeling of déjà vu swept over her. She had seen these eyes at other schools, and the anguish of being noticeably different rose again.

With still haunting memories and recalls of frustration, she trudged through the onlookers. She ambled by the science lab where three freshmen coiled back with a prolonged "ooooh." Hated recollections of being ridiculed by classmates flashed like lightning. She had an urge to rush to the door and escape the cruelty of the inconsiderate. With angst still rising, she recalled her mother's words, "You will stay in school no matter what." Envisioning her mother's furrowed brow and piercing eyes, the impulse gradually lessened.

She was briefly distracted by several noisy students nearby but quickly resumed her hunt, peeking over and around the churning crowd. She spotted row 200, but a rather tall, rugged group of boys blocked the locker numbers. Only one course of action came to mind. She squirmed through the mass of bodies and spotted 202 being stuffed with books by an older student with a rather rough appearance. With no hesitation, she boldly nudged by students. Though a little intimidated, she mustered enough spunk to voice objection.

"Hey, that's my locker!"

The boy narrowed his eyes and looked straight at her with a good measure of arrogance then shoved a schedule in her face. "Not today, little…uh, strange girl. See this! 202 is mine! Go get your own!"

She stared at the schedule, lowered her head, and dejectedly backed away, despising the boys' rude laughter. Letting the barb bounce off, she again looked at her schedule. It still showed 202. She stood in the middle of the hall, unsure what to do next. She considered going to the office, going back to locker 202 and facing the rude boy, or going home. The latter was considerably more desirable.

Abruptly pausing near the middle of an intersection, she calmly scanned the halls. Students rushed in all directions. She angrily deliberated on which hall to take, still with 202 in hand. Standing nearly frozen, she wrestled with the dilemma, unaware of a student making his way through a host of stinging comments.

Jalen leisurely walked down the corridor, heading for his locker. Several eyes and a few whispers turned his way. He knew why. *Doesn't take long for news to pass around here.* He continued down the hall with a few remarks catching his ears.

"What in the world are you doing, man?"

"Running with Bernie is a long way from cool."

"Better be more careful next time, bro."

"Hey, what's up? I heard you were in jail this weekend."

"Pretty gutsy, dude. Not smart, but gutsy."

Jalen slowly shook his head with a wry grin but kept his composure, letting the barbs pass. He high-fived and fisted a few teammates. Nearing his locker, he spotted LaRana standing in the intersection looking completely lost. He abruptly stopped and gazed as if dumbfounded.

There's the girl I saw at the station. Wow! What a change!

He eased around students then paused and stared as if no one else was there. She was considerably more attractive than his first vision.

Considerably.

She stood alone with all other students a blur. Her slender frame and radiant, dark russet skin stood out among students of certain ancestry. While admiring her appearance, it was her eyes that captured his attention, twinkling like stars on a moonless night. He barely felt students bumping him.

"Hey, move it, dude!"

"Uh, sorry 'bout that."

He stood awestruck, keeping his vision on LaRana who nervously gazed forward then backward, searching through the frenzied quagmire. Jalen gathered enough courage to silently approach from behind and tap her shoulder. She twitched and spun around, dropping a notebook. A slight blush found her face. Tossing Jalen a glare, she started to pick it up.

Jalen quickly held up his hand then stooped. "Sorry, my bad. Didn't mean to startle you. Allow me to get it. It's always hectic on the first day of school. My name is Jalen, Jalen Strade, and it's my guess you're new here since you're obviously trying to find your locker."

"I am, and I am. I'm LaRana Lester, the newbie as some have said."

Finding an available ear, she abruptly held up her card, frowning and shaking it vigorously.

"I was told and have this proof stating my locker is in Character Hall, number 202. I found it, but some clown had the same card as mine, and...and...uh, you look familiar. Have I seen you somewhere?"

Jalen slowly nodded, slightly grinning. His reply came just above a whisper. He realized enough students already knew of his ill-conceived antic.

"You may have seen me at the same place I saw you. Like, Friday night late, or maybe Saturday morning early. I kinda lost touch with time."

"Oh," came a rather muffled answer from a blushing, lowered head. She glanced from side to side, hoping no one heard. "I was… I…uh…"

"You don't have to explain a thing. I'd like to forget being there myself, except maybe for seeing you."

She snapped her head straight back. "Well now, you sure don't waste any time."

"Sorry, again. Another bad. Didn't mean to be so forward, but I must say you certainly light up this hall, even with the cute bandage over your eye. I might be a little stupid at times, but I sure ain't blind."

She smiled and started to reply when one of the few who knew her rushed by and grabbed her arm. "Come on, LaRana. The office goofed. You're in 402. It's this way. I'll take you to it."

LaRana turned her head, half-stumbling, as the girl pulled her down the hall. "Nice to meet you…uh… Jalen."

"See you at noon," he shouted, unsure she heard. He kept his eyes fixed till she turned the corner and disappeared. Remaining still, he entertained a slight hope she might reappear, longing to see her again. He suddenly realized his voice may have been a little loud and his gaze a little long. Several students around him had quieted and looked his way, some grinning and some frowning.

Suddenly feeling the attention, his faced flushed. He glared their way and got a little testy. "Hey, anyone got a problem?"

One of his teammates broke the moment with a wide grin. "Dude, it's all cool, man. All cool."

He didn't blink an eye as he returned his vision to the corner of the hall where she disappeared. *LaRana. That's a nice name. Now she is attractive, yes, very attractive indeed.*

*****

Early Monday morning rays flooded the Frosty Treat, a café of local renown. Large windows wrapped around well-designed seating areas. The parking lot was over half full. Patrons flowed through the entry with smiles and casual greetings. Hannah was reluctant to meet new people, harboring a fear of others learning her past. She calmly neared the door only to pause. In the midst of pleasant surroundings, tormenting thoughts arose once more.

What am I doing here? I hate being a spectacle. I wonder how many here would welcome us. But…who knows? Oh well, it's worth a shot.

She gathered courage, opened the door, and briskly stepped in. Several turned as she entered. A few held gazes a little longer than others, but her entrance was quickly disregarded. The crowd of mostly regulars eagerly chatted over coffee and rolls, heartily discussing the weekend's happenings. She quietly took a seat in an empty booth by a large, sun-drenched window. After several quick glances at customers, she tried to relax, but unsettled nerves doggedly remained. Constant chatter from nearby tables ran words together, creating a persistent buzz. She tried to grasp muffled conversations, wondering what, or who, they talked about. Slightly ashamed, she abruptly quit listening, suddenly preferring not to know. Her nerves gradually settled as an attractive lady with a cheerful countenance briskly approached the table.

"Good morning. My name is Karen. May I help you?"

"A cup of coffee for now. With cream, please."

"Regular or decaf?"

"Regular, please."

"Yes, ma'am. I'll be right back."

She diligently labored to appear calm, trying to be discreet. Her cautious glances found friendly faces. Chatter came light and easy. She thought how good it must feel to be accepted, to gather with friends in a casual setting.

As in towns before, she was reluctant to allow anyone a glimpse at her life, yet desperately needing someone to talk to. Her anxious eyes darted to patrons then quickly back to the window as if the locals had come to check out an odd newcomer.

Once more.

The pattern of recent years seemed unbreakable, becoming a noose choking all efforts to change. Here she sat—another town, another trial, another maddening reminder that she was an outsider. Nagging thoughts of a troublesome past scolded like an angry mother. She dared another glance only to find no one looking at her. She again grappled with perception of others.

Oh, what are you thinking, Hannah? They're not here to talk about you. They're just good people with normal lives. Ah…normal. What I wouldn't give for normal.

The waitress brought the steaming coffee, gently placing it on the table. "Thank you… Karen."

"You're welcome," came the reply with a smile. "Can I get you anything else?"

"Not for now but thanks. I'm waiting for someone."

Time dragged while waiting for Shelly. Still unsettled, she glanced at her watch then the door wondering if this was another frustration. Meeting new people in previous towns had proven difficult. She sipped on the coffee, uncertain of nearly everything.

She calmly turned and stared at the sun-drenched window reflecting an image of a woman woefully bearing an aura of dismay, near the end of chances, desperately looking for another road. The woman appeared too young for all the miles, yet feeling too old to get up and try again. She wished the woman would give her answers, but no words came. The woman's face revealed a like wish of belonging. She slowly reached her hand for the woman's stretching hand only to quickly pull it back. Sighing deeply, she brushed away the same tear trickling from the woman's eye.

A regretful gaze beyond the window brought a vision of two doors, one wide and open, the other narrow and closed. Once again, mistakes visited her memory, refusing to be forgotten, choosing rather to pummel her as many times in the past. Bitterness and heartache overshadowed the few, bright memories. A hasty marriage became a disaster, and the only remnant remaining was a dearly loved daughter.

There was no other reason to exist.

She carried a burning determination to see LaRana discover the route to a happy future. Closing her eyes, she stepped into a void, desperately reaching for LaRana's hand as she dangled in space. No matter how far she stretched, her hand remained empty. She now stood between dual roads of futility and failure. All other paths were hidden. She slowly shook her head, staring into the cup where steam, like her dreams, leisurely rose then disappeared. Footsteps from behind caused a quick turn.

"Good morning, Hannah."

Shelly's cheerful greeting came with a warm smile and touch on the shoulder. She waved at someone two booths over then slid into the seat across the table.

"How's the coffee?"

"Hi. It's quite good actually."

The waitress gracefully approached. Shelly was ready with her usual order. "A cup of decaf with cream plus a small cinnamon roll for both of us if that's okay with Hannah."

She glanced across the table and received a nod. "Nice to see you, Karen. It seems you have a good crowd again."

Karen scanned the customers. "Well, actually, it's a little more than usual, but we certainly don't mind."

"Karen, I want you to meet Hannah Lester. She recently moved here with her daughter LaRana. I just had to introduce her to the most friendly place to eat in Pallon Ridge."

"I met her a few minutes ago but didn't have enough time to get acquainted. So, Mrs. Lester, welcome to our little, but great city."

"Thank you, Karen. My daughter and I have looked forward to settling down in a pleasant location. Hopefully, we found it."

"Let me know if there's anything else you need. We're a little short-handed this morning. One of our waitresses called in sick, and since school started today, we're without student help."

"Where's Paul? Got him doing dishes?" asked Shelly, wryly grinning.

"Well, actually, he's not here, but...the weather is warm, the wind is down, and one of his buddies came by the house. So...where would you guess he might be?"

"Aha, couldn't be fishing, could it?"

"Left a little before daylight. Oops, I'd better get back to work. Don't want any restless customers. I'll be back with your order in a jiff. Again, it's been a pleasure to meet you, Mrs. Lester."

Hannah smiled and nodded. "Same here."

Karen briskly stepped to another table. Shelly turned attention back to Hannah who finally relaxed.

"Paul and Karen are really nice people. Not only is the food and service good, they're also big on helping students with temporary work. Some need it for college, some current reasons. It gives them a taste of the work world. We've always found the food excellent and the atmosphere friendly. The lady talking to patrons at the table near the mounted fish is Leasa, a pleasant lady with a bubbly and uplifting personality. The man standing by the customer at the counter is David, a gentleman who strives to please and enjoys interaction with customers. A regular group of gentlemen meet here nearly every morning. They're mostly retired or semi-retired. There's several of them sitting near that mounted fish. Some say it's an intellectual assembly of seasoned minds while others call it a bull session of old codgers. One thing is sure, they're decent, solid chaps, the backbone of our city. They know more history of Pallon Ridge than anybody I know. By the way, have you found work yet?"

Hannah's growing confidence now held a touch of apprehension. Shelly noticed the hesitation, and quickly changed the subject. "I trust LaRana's first day at school goes well. Jalen sure wasn't anxious to go. It's his last year, and considering this weekend, I guess he's off to a sluggish start."

Hannah shrugged, uncertain what to reveal. She was reluctant to let anyone into her space, past or present, but Shelly seemed genuine. It was time to trust.

"I hope the fourth time's a charm for LaRana. Her first three schools didn't work out very well."

"It's a good school with quality teachers. I imagine she'll find some nice friends. Can I be so forward as to ask where you and LaRana came from?"

Hannah hesitated and briefly looked away, unsure whether to open windows long closed. For a few moments, she gazed at Shelly then around the room before quietly replying.

"Well, originally, Alabama. I met LaRana's father when I was seventeen. He was white and twenty. Although our seeing each other was met with no small measure of disdain from both races, we tore full steam ahead. We had the answers to all of our questions, or so we thought. We knew everything about each other, or so we thought. We married soon after I turned eighteen. Emotions definitely raced ahead of common sense. There was no tomorrow, only today. I had LaRana a little over a year later. No matter where we went, condemning eyes were all around, but I was so proud of her. She became my port in the storm of life."

"How did you find Pallon Ridge?"

"Well now, let me think. Just where do I start? A new job. Another getaway. Change of climate for LaRana…for me. I guess we wore out the south, so we decided to head west. I'm still chasing a dream, especially for LaRana. It's hard to raise her without a father, not that she really ever had one. That was my second police station. She never seems to find decent friends. I continually fret she'll run away or get pregnant…or worse. When she was four, her father brushed her off one night then died in a bar fight. Her attitude has been erratic ever since. Mood swings dance between angry, pleasant, and I don't care. I had hoped things would be different this time. I guess we're not off to a very good start…again. So here I am, a single, black mom in another new town. Might I ask about your son?"

"Jalen is barely eighteen and on a shaky bridge to adulthood. It's not a short bridge, and he sometimes steps back to about age twelve. Friday was my first, and hopefully last, time at the station. We had a cordial heart-to-heart chat. I left the ball in his court…with some suggestions."

"I trust his father will help him through tough times. How do they get along?"

"Now that's a sticky situation. Not well. In fact, I would say distant, quite distant to be precise. They were nearly inseparable when Jalen was younger, but now they each sort of do their own thing. Friday night's incident was a little tense. His dad was quite upset, but I thought more sorry for himself than Jalen. I feel like I'm being pulled in opposite directions, hanging on to each by a thread."

"I'm really sorry. And here I thought I was by myself on that thread. I mostly work afternoons and evenings as a maid at the hospital. To some, it's a menial job so I rarely talk about it. I had to take it even though the hours aren't good. I would like to be at home when LaRana gets off school, but I haven't been able to get the early shift. I worry about her—too much freedom, not enough personal discipline. I'm sure you know the pressures facing kids these days, especially girls."

Hannah became nervous at her reply as if suddenly it rested on the rim of reality. She stared out the window overcome by unbearable fear. Anguish raced across her face. Shelly sipped on the coffee, giving her space. Hannah turned back with a slow breath.

Rachel quietly set the cup down. "One of my suggestions was to start attending church again. We used to go many years ago, but Roland, Jalen's dad, wouldn't, so we just drifted away. He always says he has work to do, but in reality, he just doesn't want to go. Sometimes, a father at home isn't much better than one not there."

"I suppose. Either way, it isn't easy."

"Jalen and I had hoped to go yesterday, but…things didn't quite work out. I would consider it an honor if you and LaRana would attend with us this coming Sunday. The church is a little more than a mile south of the school. Would you be able to make it?"

"I don't know much about religious things. I haven't been to church in years, many years to be more precise. Mama would take me when she could. I was quite young, not yet in school, and I guess religion didn't take hold. All I can remember is the joyful singing. Most of those I was around as a teenager said church was for dull people, no offense."

"That's okay. I've heard that before. LaRana will meet some good kids there, and you will meet some friendly folks also. Please say yes. It would do my heart good. Plus, I may need the company."

"I've often thought of several possibilities to explore, but church was never one of them. Well, I suppose we need to do something different. Uh…okay, we'll give it a try, although I'm not sure what LaRana will say."

"Great. Maybe we'll both find something to help us. I believe they start at 10:00 a.m. Do you need me to come by? I would be glad to give you a ride."

"Thanks, but that won't be necessary. We live not far from here—three blocks down, turn right, go two blocks, home. I don't drive a fancy car, a clunker actually, but it usually gets us where we need to go. We'll meet you there."

They visited for nearly thirty minutes, sharing a few laughs and heartaches till leaving, calmly walking to the parking lot. Watching Shelly's Jeep disappear around the corner, Hannah juggled emotions. Did Shelly really care? Or was it desperation? Trying to find a positive, she leaned to the former.

A real friend perhaps? That would be pleasantly different. She seems genuine. I'm probably grasping at another straw. But who knows, maybe somehow, this will help LaRana.

*****

Morning classes dragged, but finally the fourth period bell rang for the noon break. Students streamed through the lunchroom entry, most chatting, some quiet. LaRana sat around a table of classmates in a cafeteria nearly full of talkative students. She heartened that three of the apparently well-known girls chose to sit with her. A few of the curious sized her up, but for the moment, fear of rejection and isolation took a back seat. She set aside lingering memories of sitting alone at previous schools. A desire to belong to the in-group deeply burned. She desperately sought acceptance with anyone offering attention, especially the popular crowd.

"What do you do for fun around here?" asked LaRana, opening a carton of milk. "I cruised with a girl named Diala last Friday night. That didn't end so good."

"Diala? Seriously? I heard she had a wreck, but I didn't know who was with her," replied Janene, plopping her knife and fork on the tray. "So you're the one who had guts enough, or was dumb enough, to be with her in a car. She doesn't have all her marbles, but I guess you realize that by now. Other than being a total disaster, she's okay. She flunked a couple of years then got booted from school. She was in and out of juvy like a revolving door. As far as us, we sometimes hang at the mall, cruise a little, or kick around with some guys who like to party."

"Oh, yeah," said Sarona, a sandy-haired girl with a somewhat ruddy complexion, yet still nice-looking. "Things get a little wild sometimes, especially when they bring the sting."

"The sting?"

A devious snicker found Sarona's face. "Yep, beer with a bullet. Makes it a little more, ah, interesting. I heard there's going to be one this Friday right after school."

Laughter raced around the table. LaRana offered a token smile then peered into the tray. Enticing puppets danced in vivid flashes of the past. Forbidden indulgences, twice taken, rekindled a pestering desire to again frolic in their delights. She quickly realized running with these girls could bring pleasure or peril, but compelling hunger for friends chased any possible risk. Besides, she thought, what harm could there be in a little party?

I can take care of myself.

"What's a bullet?" asked LaRana with a slightly puzzled look.

"I could try to explain it, but you just have to experience it to know," said Willow, the most attractive of the three. "Go with us Friday. You'll find out."

"Got that right! Once taken, you can't wait for more!" added Sarona. "Hey, if you don't mind me asking, you're a little, uh, darker, than us. Who's what in your family?"

"Well, Sarona, might you be a little blunt and inconsiderate?" said Janene with a slight frown. "You're about as polite as a wounded sow."

LaRana plopped her fork on the tray. Memories of that question, spoken or visual, were sharp. She served a day of detention at the last school for fighting over her mixed heritage. LaRana had a rush of anger but held it. She peered at Sarona without a blink.

"My mom is African American. My dad…wasn't." She narrowed her eyes. "Does it make any difference to you?"

"No, no, not at all! Sorry if I offended you. Just asking."

LaRana held her gaze, a piercing stare daring further inquiry. Willow noticed the tension and quickly changed the subject. "Hey, did you hear about Orlando and Arlen getting busted for weed?"

"No. Tell us about it," replied Janene.

With an awkward moment now passed, LaRana silently returned to her lunch. With the three girls eagerly sharing the recent gossip, her attention abruptly turned to the food bar. She spotted Jalen inching down the counter, carefully selecting from various offerings. She intently watched him slide a light green tray across the serving shelf. Why, she didn't know, but his presence demanded her attention. She shied away from boys at previous schools because she was different. After all, she reasoned, he was polite earlier in the day.

Hmm, I'd say about six one maybe two, well-muscled, nice brown hair.

One of the ladies behind the counter said something to Jalen who returned a laugh with a headshake. Gathering a napkin and utensils, he glanced around the room till his eyes fell on LaRana. He smiled with a slow nod, pulling a chair by two boys at a corner table. She quickly looked away, realizing her gaze might have been a little long. Her table had silenced. She quickly turned back to a round of sneaky grins.

"Do you know Jalen? You seem quite interested," said Willow with a sly look.

"No, I just met him in the hall this morning…looking for my locker…and, uh…"

"And uh?" interrupted Sarona gleefully. "Now, I could be wrong, but I believe your eyes were fixed on his physique…just maybe?"

LaRana blushed then grinned. "No, well…anyway, he was kind to me when I was looking for my locker. That doesn't mean I'm attracted to him. Personally, I think boys are highly overrated."

"Jalen's a pretty cool guy, a baseball jock," added Janene, giving her cup of applesauce to Sarona. "He's been at a couple of stings, but he sort of like hangs on the edge."

"Yeah, we tried to draw him in…for obvious reasons. But he's a little backward on some things," added Sarona with a slight snicker. "We keep hoping he'll open up at a sting, but he hasn't yet."

"Hey, I gotta get to science class, and I need to make a stop at the office," blurted Janene, scrambling from her chair. "Mr. Somero gets quite cranky when students don't arrive on time. I made it to my senior year without being late. I certainly don't want to break the run."

The girls hastily returned their trays and disappeared down the hall. LaRana quietly sat, resuming her lunch. She leisurely looked around the room, catching several swift glances between unheard comments and mocking smiles. A flash of past visions flooded emotions.

Different school, same crap. Yeah, here I am, creeps...the weird newbie, the odd looker. I was hoping your eyes would stay at the last school. Should have known better.

She intensely wanted to throw her tray at them but decided she had enough trouble hanging over her head. She once again realized connecting with students had limited possibilities. As in times past, loneliness slowly crept over her, suffocating and persistent. Thoughts of a sting summoned a stubborn curiosity, an anticipated reprieve from haughty eyes. A strong urge to enjoy its touted thrill ran ahead of a faint beckoning to let it be. She took a final swallow as Jalen walked to her table and sat down.

"Mind if I have a seat?"

"Not at all, especially since you're already in it."

"I was hoping you wouldn't mind. Looks like you found some new friends," he said with a frown. "Just be careful. I've seen them in action. They can get a little crazy at times."

"Oh? Are you now my protector?" she replied with her own faintly creased brow. She wasn't quite sure how to take Jalen. Perception wavered. Was he hitting on her, or just being nice? Her demeanor remained cautious.

"Just letting you know. I don't want you to wind up back at the station...or maybe somewhere else."

"Mercy, man, you're beginning to sound like my mother. Why do you care? You don't know me."

"No, I don't, but... I would like to. Although, I guess at this point, the only thing we have in common is an official tour of the pokey."

LaRana laughed then relaxed. "I'm not sure how to follow that, but thanks for being kind to me. Being half white, or half black, depending on where I am, I never know how others think of me, but I usually have a good idea."

Jalen leaned closer to her. "Pallon Ridge has come a long way to overcoming prejudice, but a few hardheads are still around, some here as you probably gathered."

"I guess I'm a little too touchy. It really gets old when it happens school after school. I've tried to get used to it, but I'm not getting very far."

Jalen returned a calming smile and looked straight into her eyes. "Well, one thing I can say for sure, newbie LaRana, you definitely got the best of both parents."

"Well, now that's nice of you, different even. It's good to know someone doesn't consider me a freak of nature. Uh, I'd like to stay and chat, but I need to go. Don't want to be late to a class, especially on the first day. The last thing I need is a visit to the office. Thank you for…well, just thank you."

Jalen rose from his chair and slightly bowed. "Tis been a pleasure, my lady. I'll diligently count the moments till I once again behold your beauty, possibly at noonday's royal feast come Tuesday if not afore."

LaRana was pleasantly surprised and joined the genteel exchange. "Well, I do thank you again, and I must say, sire, you are quite…a change from the ordinary."

"Jolly! Your observation I do appreciate, my lady. I'll heartily embrace that as a compliment. Sufficiently pleasant twill my evening be."

LaRana slightly waved a hand with a tilt of her head. "'Twas meant to be, kind gent."

They shared a laugh before LaRana left the table. Jalen carefully watched her put up the tray then leave. He took a deep breath, staring at her graceful walk down the hall. No girl ever stroked his emotions as LaRana. One thing was certain. He wanted to know her better.

Out of the blue, a familiar voice grabbed his attention.

"Now just what do you see in that half-breed," said Brenton with a hearty scowl. He sat with two friends a couple of tables away. "What's up? Ain't regular skirts good enough, or is she all you can get?"

Jalen spun around. "Shut up, punk! She's as nice as anyone else and probably more! And I for one, think she looks pretty, darn good."

Brenton slowly rose and stood defiantly. His two friends glanced at each other then also stood. The few remaining students stopped eating, intently staring at the scene. Brenton's eyes narrowed.

"Ooh. Did I touch a nerve? I heard Diala got busted with another DWI Friday night. She had someone with her. Rumor says it was the new halfer. Be careful, she might be a little wild for your blood."

Jalen sent the chair careening across the floor and took three quick steps toward Brenton who sprung forward with arms raised. Jalen shoved him. Brenton swiftly returned it then made a fist. Jalen slightly crouched, bracing his feet. The room silenced. Tension grew till Brenton's friends stepped between angry eyes and tightened nerves. Nothing more was said as the supervisor quickly approached.

"Break it up, boys! Break it up. Best let it be. Ain't no way to start a new year. I don't want to see this again. I won't be warning you the next time. Now, move on out and keep it cool."

"I'll see you someday, jock. We'll settle this," scowled Brenton.

"Sounds good to me, punk. I can hardly wait. Bring it on!"

Jalen stepped back till the agitator walked away. The cafeteria had become deathly quiet. He shrugged his shoulders, eased his nerves, then trudged toward the hall, kicking and scolding himself for flying off the handle. He saw newcomers get roasted before and not reacted. Why now, he mused? His mother, and for some reason, Officer Monroe, crossed his mind. He slapped his head.

Don't get in trouble again, you big dummy, especially over a girl. You'd best get her out of your head...if you can.

Missives Two

Esul,

Well, I am highly interested in your retort to the actions of our quarries. It appears our prospect and at least three others are finding their way to church. My, it does hearten me to say that. For you know good things happen when searching souls mingle with true believers. It's encouraging to see caring people take an active interest in those who are struggling.

Shelly has put thoughts into action, and lo and behold, she is setting the table for others to discover the narrow but magnificent road to life. Granted, Roland will need more encouragement to open his eyes and heart, but I see a portal for him to also come our way. Need I remind you my Father's word is living and powerful, sharper than any two-edged sword? It perceives the thoughts and intents of the heart. You know of what I write.

You and your vile cronies have hidden the Light from Hannah for a long time, but take a look at what is happening. You often use the pit of despair to firm your grasp, but sometimes it works to our advantage. She is a determined mother deeply concerned about her daughter. Her ardent passion for LaRana's future is unmistakable. While you are a master of deception, I believe she will see through your devious enchantments.

You may have nudged Jalen toward your despicable abode, but his thoughts are drifting in the right direction. Though small in your sight, he took a stand for something right and noble.

Taking such an honorable action must cause you a great measure of irritation. Honor shows respect and concern for others, a trait you so often try to destroy.

And look at LaRana, our main goal. You thought she would be easy to garner. If you noticed, she is thinking about past mistakes. You tried hard to tickle her emotions, entice wayward impulses, but I am quite encouraged she entertained a thought to deny your desire. You know what happens when humans actively determine to resist your master. Does that make you squirm a little?

Since her early days, your cronies have put in her head the lie a split ancestry was a curse. It seems she has found someone to help derail such a notion. And now she is going to church where caring people and the Lord of life will be.

Needless to say, but I must, I am greatly heartened by the circumstances quickly unfolding. So don't add to your collection until the doors are closed.

Jariel

*****

Jariel,

You need not preach to me about the Creator's word. I know how sharp it is. I know what it can do to the human heart. I know the scriptures far better than any of your Master's children. When it touches a human's heart, it pierces me, but I often use His word against our prey. I simply convince them it's only a general guide developed by man.

My master tried to trap your Jesus when He walked the earth. He offered three excellent possessions, but He rejected his offers. His heart was strong. However, such is not so with simple souls. When we offer life's pleasures, humans usually find them most appealing, compelling even.

So our quarry may find the church. They haven't yet honored their commitment. And even if they do, what will they find? Has the havoc we wreaked in your Master's church slipped your mind? Remember, those many years ago, when Escar sowed division in His body of believers. Paul, once an up-and-coming servant of my master, warned those at Corinth against division. That caused us significant annoyance, but after a good while, we overcame unity in your Master's flock.

Church is too big a change for LaRana and Hannah. They have never considered a life of following the Christ as a solution to woes. That will not change. They will not be able to grasp the perception of a spiritual realm or life style. All I need to do is set a few obstacles in their path and any consideration of your Master will be history.

As a gentle reminder, the human mind is my doorway to the soul. I simply put into their thoughts and hearts they could make their own rules, devise their own opinions, live however they wanted to. The pretenders began gathering followers who like a certain brand of your Master's Word. Divide and conquer is a tactic my master employs often. He has given the thought to many who have used it quite effectively. It works well in your Master's flock.

I know you recall Paul telling Timothy some of your Master's converts would have itchy ears, twisting His word to their own desires. Itchy ears no less. I thought it a novel touch. He also warned those at Ephesus about our minions. He even called them savage wolves that wouldn't spare the flock. I took quite a liking to that comparison. Made me proud.

So many use your Master's word as no more than a suggestion, and look what you have today, yes, indeed, discord and even resentment. Many of your so-called children are converted to an organization, not to Him. I loathe to think what would happen if all of your believers were of one mind. But then, we have great confidence such unity will never happen. We are considerably relieved that most humans are proud and stubborn. Helps me rest easy.

While we have been highly successful in dividing your believers, I do fret about the people our common quarry has found. They seem bent on following your Master's word. That presents considerable trepidation for us, but not to worry, a massive number of humans yet remain who like religion their way, to define the Creator by their desires.

There are still those who harken to your Master's plea for unity, but I will not lessen my efforts to collect them. They, in fact, have become my special targets, and I find it especially rewarding when I seize even one of them.

It amazes me how you put such hope in hopeless situations. Have you forgotten the marvelous wiles at our disposal? Destroying decency and morality, sense of family, distorting awareness of right and wrong, and glorifying indulgence...to state but a few. And be certain I will set loose my greatest weapon.

Doubt.

As you so well know, doubt brings a lack of conviction, which leads to disregard, which leads to my master. Those in whom I sow doubt find it easy to consider the Creator and his Son as nothing but myths. And they even consider my master and me a myth. I don't mind that at all. In fact, I prefer it. I love the surprise, or rather, terror in their eyes when they meet us. Yes, doubt has been a trusted friend since Adam and Eve.

I still vividly remember Peter when he tried to walk on the water. My master simply encouraged him to look down. He did, and doubt finished his walk.

We were quite upset when he overcame our other attempts to collect him. He denied your Savior, even cursed when He was taken. He struggled to believe He rose from the grave. Our grasp on him was firm, or so we thought. Yes, we really hated to miss him.

Thomas' doubt could only be allayed by physical contact with your Savior. If the Christ hadn't been near Him, we would have the pleasure of his company now.

Which brings me to the present.

If I can instill doubt and keep your Master's children from His presence, I can make His first commandment worthless. Ah, doubt...such a wonderful state of mind.

And here you are now, grasping at straws, feverishly trying to overcome doubt with stories from a book, be it your Master's precious word. That is a tall order for self-centered humans...

but we don't mind their efforts. Doubt will prevail. It's too daunting a barrier for most.

Roland is a fine example. He began with doubt, progressed to rejection, and is now comfortably, and yes, maybe unwittingly, well on his way to us. He'll put a damper on Shelly's hollow enthusiasm. Each week he denies your Master is another nail in his coffin. And just think, his defiance and lifestyle will eventually lead Jalen to our realm. Indeed, selfishness is another of our most successful traits, and as you know, we have so many. Shelly's so-called new direction will not last. She will get discouraged and give up hope and faith in your Master. She did once before, and she will do it again. There's nothing to prop her up and Roland to tear her down. I must say, just the thought of it makes me feel better. I do look forward to collecting this family.

Hannah? I have gleefully watched her bend to Escar's guidance for some time now, but I am a little concerned about her determination, or even tenacious, love for her daughter. I will make sure such tenacity is limited to LaRana. I have some apprehension that those aggravating churchgoers who have embraced your Master could encourage her.

I have a hand on LaRana's mind, and now, I am going to work on her emotions. Her resolve will crumble. When I destroy her life, I get her mother also. Or who knows, I may work it the other way around. Either way, it's a scenario of life I revel when it comes to pass.

The foundation holding Jalen is very weak, thanks to his father's negligence. He's getting all gushy about LaRana, but when she falls, he will see his father's point of view. It's inevitable he will deny your Master.

Now let's cut to the chase. I simply have too many charms for you to prevail. Humans want instant gratification, and we try hard to oblige. And remember, they have such a desire to belong, usually to those well on their way to us. Since mothers and fathers do not teach their children about your Master, they have little choice but to come to my master. It's been that way for ages. You know this!

Look how many females are willing to do untoward things to be accepted by my preying male servants. My, such a beautiful process it is. Some may ask why they do things that usually destroy their lives. I love those gullible humans' answer, especially teens…everybody else is doing it. That burning desire to be accepted at all costs has opened more doors than even we imagined. Independent thinking is fading. Pressure to conform is rapidly rising. Surely, you must admit, it couldn't get much better for our collection efforts. I almost pity your task to bring souls to your Master. Almost.

It has been said my master is subtle, cunning, and sly. For certain, his ability to persuade is staunchly undeniable. He convinced Eve, and the door was open. It is my intense craving to precisely emulate my master. I'm getting so good at it I must brag on my collection.

So many now walk our broad valley we can barely keep track of the number. It must be quite lonely in your realm. But I know you will keep trying. Although the battle is quite easy most of the time, I do enjoy a good challenge.

Esul

3

Sting and Sing

The last bell on the first Friday was the sound anxious students waited for all week. The sense of freedom, even if short lived, sent students bursting from the doors. Many left with mixed emotions. Some left campus in glee, some left a sanctuary to weather an uncertain weekend in cold homes, and several chose to enjoy the warm afternoon at favorite gathering spots near the school or in remote settings.

LaRana leisurely strolled toward the sidewalk, dreading another return to an empty house and lonely hours before Shelly came home. She stood with longing eyes, watching students, some walking alone, but most with others. Laughter raced up and down the street. She tried to shake the pestering notion she might be the subject of the amusement. Leaving school alone was nothing new.

Many classmates at other schools were cordial till the day ended. Rarely would they include her in social interaction after school. Past rejection allowed anger to grow.

Trying to block out the joyful noise, her thoughts turned to Jalen. She pondered what it would be like to have him walk her home, but the desire quickly faded. He was nice and friendly but nothing more. After all, she was not among the popular girls in school. Not even close. He was one of the most popular guys, and she could see no way to breech the gap.

The thought of the slow trudge home revived the loneliness and relentless desire to belong. To her, that void needed filled, and friends, any friends, were the only resort. She calmly waited at the curb, wrestling with the invitation to a sting. Willow's persistent pressing to join the crowd kept coming to mind. She knew her mother wanted her home, but the call to a great party pulled hard. A blast they said. Where everyone who is anyone is at they said. A faint inkling to run somewhere was easily overtaken by the yearning to be with classmates, to mingle with those who wouldn't label her a nobody. Desire grew while reason waned.

Besides, I can handle myself. At least, they won't be calling me a dufus.

She stood with despair yet growing when a bright red pickup screeched around the corner, quickly stopping at the edge of the lot. Willow frantically waved from the passenger window. LaRana abruptly stopped. Her heart quickened. The persistent desire to belong returned with a vengeance.

Go, don't be a prude. This is your chance. Don't blow it.

"Come on, LaRana. Let's get goin'. It's time to party."

"I don't know. I have some studying I need to get done," she fibbed.

"Study? Ah, you can do that later. C'mon, you won't regret it. We want you to be part of us. You'll be blown away!"

What should I do? Somehow, this doesn't seem right, but...

Her mind's struggle suddenly ended. She threw hasty glances to each side before hopping into the front seat as Willow scooted to the middle. Tires screeched when the pickup whirled around a corner. A speedy right turn at the next street sent two students leaping back to the curb. Willow laughed it off with a rousing "yahoo."

The boy behind the wheel sported a well-trimmed mustache. His mouth held a cigarette, his arm a tattoo, his shirt a declaration: "Hell Bent."

Familiarity swiftly faded in the rearview mirror. LaRana's breath came slow at the precarious step into the unknown. The look on Hannah's face at the police station flashed before her eyes, eyes screaming I love you, eyes imploring caution. The vision quickly disappeared in the presence of new friends and the chance to be accepted. She finally put the battle to rest. Desire for acceptance was the victor. This is what she had searched for. Willow broke her thoughts with a tap on her arm.

"LaRana, meet Jackson, or Jackknife, as we call him. Watch out," she snickered. "He has fast hands and a rugged mouth."

Nods exchanged.

"Willow's been telling me about you. You look a little different, but that's cool, I like different. Whatcha got, babe?" came his chilling query.

Willow giggled, LaRana quivered. She didn't answer. A glance at his eyes, his carriage, said caution should be taken. *What am I getting into?*

The deep recesses of her mind sent a frantic plea. *Stop the truck. Get out. Get out now!*

The urge for home was suddenly strong, but she couldn't summon courage to tell them. Her heart beat faster, but the burning flame of fitting in could not be doused.

Cool it, girl. This comes with the territory. You can take care of yourself. Just go and see what's happening.

Willow blew it off. "Don't pay any attention to the wild dude. Just keep your distance. He has enough gals to mess around with. Other cool guys will be there. Trust me. You'll be glad you came."

LaRana threw a wary glance at Willow. "Trust me" was a phrase embraced only with her mother. A touch of anxiety returned.

With the pickup's limit breaking speed, town quickly vanished. LaRana silently sat, unsure whether she was racing to something or from something. She tried to settle dancing thoughts, some stroking her desire, some stoking her fear. Angst grew as nerves tightened. Though uneasy, she forced a laugh at the crude chatter between Jackknife and Willow. Her classmate's unspoken, yet implied, requirement to join the circle battled a shallow sense of decency. She became more cautious, but a desire to go home remained unspoken.

Two miles from the city limit, Jackknife whirled onto a gravel road and barreled for over a mile to a secluded setting at a dead end. Several boys and girls meandered around the front yard of a large, attractive cabin. LaRana noticed elbows bending from a few. Their tilted glasses of joy juice piqued her curiosity, the blissful nectar of the chosen called to offer its euphoria. Her near stupor was broken when the truck suddenly stopped. Warring thoughts were flashing beacons.

What am I doing? I shouldn't be here. Get out and head for home. Now!

Hang in there. You'll be careful. Just think of all the fun you'll have and all the friends who'll think you're really with it.

Sarona raced toward them. Her wide eyes and animated gestures set a tone of expectations. "Hey, 'bout time you got here. Sorry we didn't wait for ya. The party has left the pad!"

Willow nearly pushed LaRana out of the pickup. She sped to Sarona, exchanging double hand slaps. LaRana cautiously followed at a distance. Her attention turned to two boys bringing beer from the cabin. With a raucous chorus of cheers from all around, they poured a few six-packs into a large kettle. A short but muscular boy gave a victory yell while gleefully lacing it with a large glass of something unknown. LaRana guessed it was the bullet Sarona mentioned in the cafeteria.

A rather tall boy stood poised over the kettle while another stirred the mixture. "We are here today to inaugurate this year's noble event, affectionately known as, and rightfully titled, the Sting. We trust its pleasures shall be enjoyed by all."

With the ceremonial stirring done, the girls loudly giggled while eagerly taking the cups, dipping them into the kettle then lifting them high with a shout.

Time crept while rejoicing soared. Salty language swirled around the ample yard. An old pickup and a car brought a few more anxious partiers. Some LaRana had seen at school, others were new. The crowd at the kettle grew, anxious to leap into the ecstasy of the moment. LaRana stood at the edge, unsure what to do. She had moved little till a nice-looking boy approached. He stopped and lightly bowed.

"And you must be LaRana. I've heard a lot about you. I'm Darnell. Come on and have a sting. It turns a good party into a great one. Don't be shy. I won't bite."

He appeared harmless…reddish hair, a few light freckles, thinly built. LaRana smiled and took his hand. He swayed to and fro as if dancing, holding a cup above his head. A few boys and several girls shouted welcomes with encouragement to take a cup. She relaxed as though belonging at the party, belonging to the group.

Accepted. Felt good.

Her apprehension began to fade in the eager faces gathered nearby. For over an hour, she basked in the dancing and pounding music. The pain of rejection, the fear of loneliness, the agony of ridicule, all disappeared in the thrill of acceptance. Many revelers came by and extended a hearty welcome. They were considerably cordial and outwardly unconcerned about visible differences. Bathed in excitement, she realized what so eagerly had been sought was finally found.

As the party grew louder, suggestive chatter flowed over the lawn. A voice, deep within, screamed caution. Darnell moved to her side and gently grasped her hand. His face was pleasant. His eyes were seeking. She pulled her hand away then emptied another cup.

Willow walked by, noticing her indulgence. "Uh, be careful. Don't polish off too many. You might get a little high."

"Hey, don't worry about me, I can handle it," declared LaRana, trying to sound as tough as those around her.

A few more couples broke into dancing to the music blaring from the cabin porch. A free-spirited sensation swept through her like gentle waves on a sandy shore. A longed-for sense of freedom lifted her spirits. Setting caution aside, she weaved to the music. She felt liberated and joined in the laughter swirling around the icy cooler. A couple of boys wandered by and ruffled her hair.

"Hey, good to meet ya. You're a really cute skirt. Welcome to the blast."

Those were words she longed to hear, words of acceptance, of fitting in. She returned a wide smile. "Glad to be here!"

Arrival.

From the side, Darnell jumped in front of LaRana, and with a deep bow, he took her hand, gently whirling to the music. The trees, the cabin, the revelers all started to spin. She felt unbridled. Her feet glided over the lawn as if gently walking on a billowed cloud. All of life was now.

She suddenly stopped, feeling light-headed. "Whew! I'm getting…a little woozy."

Darnell put an arm around her shoulders. "That's okay. Take your time. We have plenty of it."

She watched partiers go in and come out of the cabin. They all appeared ecstatic, shouting and dancing, wholly unfettered. Boys laughingly fisted each other. Girls, nearly hysterical, giggled like grade-schoolers. Darnell slowly eased her forward till LaRana bent over at the waist then fell to a knee.

"Stop! This…isn't…right. Everything's moving!"

"That's just the sting. Let yourself go! Give in to the excitement!"

She stared at the ground, waiting for it to settle. With both knees and head down, vision began to blur till an image of Hannah crossed her mind. Her face lasted for a few seconds, but her eyes remained, piercing eyes, pleading with concern.

She slowly lifted her head, and eyes began to focus. Rising to her feet, she shoved Darnell then ran toward the forest with what strength remained.

"Hey, what are you doing?" screamed Darnell. "Come on back!"

She tripped over a tray of flowers, sprawling to the turf. With little hesitation, she scrambled to her feet, brushed her arms, and raced down the road. She ran till collapsing by a tree well away from the pounding music and merriment. All became quiet except for a chirping bird not far above.

Breath suddenly came quick and short, and with a heave, she threw up a grayish spume. She felt weary and drained. With a long sigh, she leaned against the tree for what seemed an eternity. Her eyes closed, visions of vile monsters swirled in a taunting frenzy. She desperately reached for them with one hand and fought them with the other. One grabbed her throat when she suddenly awoke with a start. The sun had all but set with twilight quickly approaching. With strength all but gone, she sluggishly gained her feet and headed toward Pallon Ridge. Tears of disgrace mingled with tears of victory.

A two-hour slog down back roads and dimly lit streets left her at a quaint house. She reached the steps, breathing a long, slow sigh of relief. The old Escort was not there. Shelly had yet to come home. She hurried to the door then paused, battling a sense of triumph mixed with embarrassment of going against the in crowd.

Her mind whirled, torn between relief and betrayal of friends, escaping indignity and perhaps, calamity. Troubling questions came fast and hard. Would they turn against her? Would they ridicule her? Would they shun her? She knew they could ignore her and make life even more miserable. Wrestling with the probable consequence, she plummeted into the chasm of loneliness. She stood at a distance watching life's light dim, listening to doors shutting all around.

Entering the house brought urgently sought relief. The old chime clock inched toward eleven. Home's walls offered welcome protection, gently wrapping around her. Hannah wouldn't know where she had been, and LaRana had no intent to tell her. She quickly readied for the well-worn bed, a bed unusually soft, greeting her weary body. She lay for but a few seconds till her skin began to crawl. She squirmed at flashes of Darnell's demanding eyes.

She felt grimy.

Urgently leaping to the floor, she entered the bathroom, quickly turning on the shower. The cool beating spray cleansed both body and mind. She changed to gentle flow, relaxing under its soothing touch. Somewhere within came a singular angelic voice, touching the very depth of her soul.

"I'm proud of you, LaRana."

For once, she reasoned, the limit of danger was severely tested, but this time she prevailed. For a pleasant few moments, she tossed aside the probable hassle, the labeling, or even rejection. Now free of the sting's effects, she laid back the bed's cover. A longed-for peace paved the way to a sound asleep.

*****

"There they are," said Rachel, waving her hands.

An old Ford Escort turned into the church driveway, noisily rumbling to a stop in a closely packed parking lot. LaRana timidly eased from the torn seat, skeptical of the Jesus people she was about to meet. The large building appeared no less than a dark cavern teeming with unknowns. She kept pace with Hannah down the sidewalk splitting an attractive yard adorned with various beds of brightly colored flowers. Recollections of passing by churches were numerous; walking toward one brought a new sensation. What waited inside, she could only guess. Stories from scoffers teased her mind. With no lack of anxiety, she nudged her mother.

"I've heard some creepy things about Jesus freaks…oops, I mean, about people who go to church. I hope they don't go and get all crazy, like, screaming and stuff."

"Oh, I doubt that, but I'm not sure what to expect myself. Let's just be cordial and see what happens."

A large crowd quickly gathered, streaming from side parking lots, chatting and laughing as if actually enjoying each other. Some men wore suits while others were casually clad. Some women wore lavish dresses while others were plainly adorned. A host of blacks, whites, and Hispanics mixed freely with beaming faces and frequent hugs. LaRana nervously wondered how each would behold her. She spotted a middle-aged couple whose skin was hued a little like hers. She wondered how they fit in.

The demon of split ancestry again resurrected.

There's black and white here. Now this could really be awkward. Which one will reject me this time? Probably both!

They spotted Rachel waving her arms near the entry. Hannah waved back and hastened the pace. Anxiety lessened at being in the company of someone she knew. She spritely stepped toward Shelly who gave her a quick embrace.

"It's so good you could come."

Hannah offered a smile. "This is my daughter LaRana. LaRana, Shelly Strade."

"Glad to meet you, ma'am."

"A beautiful young lady, indeed. You should be quite proud of her, Hannah. This is my son Jalen. I believe he and LaRana have already met. Come on in. I want you to meet some really fine people. It's been a good while since I've been here, but I still know several."

Jalen solemnly stood a few feet away. He looked at LaRana then shrugged his shoulders. While juggling mixed emotions of going to church, he was thrilled to see her. Their eyes met, revealing a common apprehension and solace in each other's presence. His first meeting with LaRana brought visions of enjoying her company at a multitude of memorable places. Church was without doubt not among them.

"We're glad to be here," returned Hannah, trying to sound enthusiastic. "I hope we're dressed properly."

"You're just fine. I don't know what has changed if anything, but I do know attire means very little here."

"Pardon my uneasiness, but even at my age, this is a new experience for me and LaRana."

"Let's all try to relax. I believe we'll be met with a courteous welcome. At least that's the way it was years ago."

They cautiously stepped through a lightly decorative glass door into a large foyer. A pleasant couple offered a hearty greeting with a handshake. Displays, rows of pictures, well designed ads for upcoming events, and motivational posters elegantly covered the walls. Conversations were akin to bees around a hive. Small children giggled and dashed among adults. Laughter and warm smiles came easy. LaRana, uncomfortable at best, tried to be as inconspicuous as possible. The phrase, a fish out of water, vividly came to mind. She edged closer behind Hannah.

An attractive, middle-aged woman approached with a wide smile. "Well, Shelly Strade and Jalen. How heartening to see you again. Would you be so kind and introduce these fine-looking ladies?"

Hannah was pleasantly surprised that Shelly and Jalen were welcomed as if they had only missed a few weeks.

"Martha Sand, this is Hannah Lester and her daughter LaRana. They moved to Pallon Ridge a few weeks ago. LaRana's a junior in high school."

Martha offered a hand to each. "We are honored you chose to come our way. I hope you find us warm and friendly. We always like to see visitors. Come, let me show you around."

They began the tour when a pleasant looking woman set a quick pace down the hall. Several young children danced around her, each giggling and grabbing for her hand.

"Belinda, I want you to meet Hannah Lester and her daughter LaRana. They're here with Rachel and Jalen Strade."

Shelly was unsure whether to put out a hand, seeing the woman's hands were occupied. She chose courtesy. Belinda quickly lifted her hand from a young lad's shoulder, heartily received Shelly's then did likewise with Hannah and LaRana.

"It's good to see you again. We've missed you. Jalen was about the age of these rather excited youngsters when I saw him last, and here he is, all grown up." She turned to Hannah and LaRana. "And it certainly is a pleasure to meet you. I would like to talk longer, but I think I need to get these eager young'uns to class. I look forward to seeing you all again. Sorry for the rush, but..."

"Understood," said Martha, putting a gentle hand on a rather active young lad.

Belinda gathered then skillfully led her charges across the foyer then down the hall, carefully dodging adults. Martha paused the tour till the seemingly well-organized teacher and students disappeared around the corner.

"Belinda has touched many lives. She always has a positive outlook, no matter the task."

Martha led them down a wide corridor when several teens eagerly approached. Five were girls LaRana had seen at school. With a little struggle, they moved around the boys. Their eyes beamed at the sight of known yet surprising visitors.

"LaRana! Jalen! It's so cool to see you. You gotta come with us. We're headed for Mr. Cook's class. He's rad. You'll have a blast."

"Well, thank you, Amelia. That's nice of you. It seems you know them both," said Martha with a slight bow.

"Oh, yeah, I have a class with LaRana, and we all know Jalen."

Hannah spotted a familiar face. "Now, I have met this young lady. She graciously waited on me at the Frosty Treat on Thursday evening. It's good to see you, Ashlynn."

"Same here, Mrs. Lester. Let me think…coffee…uh, regular with cream as I recall."

"I am impressed, young lady," replied Hannah with an approving nod. "Now let me think…lead bow on the archery team."

"Now I'm impressed. Good to see you again."

Hannah was pleasantly surprised when the girls gathered around LaRana while the two boys fist greeted Jalen.

Though yet hesitant, LaRana felt a slight warm rush. The girls' sincerity was open and noticeably different than her usual acquaintances. She wasn't quite sure how to act or even how to talk. She wondered how Willow and Sarona would react if they knew she was at church. She couldn't think of any situation that would compel her to tell them.

"Don't fret Mrs. Lester. We'll take good care of her," said Katelyn with a wide grin. "Now Jalen? That's different. The guys will take care of him."

"Yeah, that's right. Just stick close to us, LaRana," added Bridgette. "By the way, can you sing? We have a few that can bring it."

"Well, I do like to sing, but only when I'm alone."

"We can certainly take care of that," said Jessica, sporting a sneaky grin.

LaRana thought she had seen Bridgette before. She gathered enough courage to ask a question. "Did you sing the national anthem at the assembly last week?"

"Yes. I was a little…ah…a lot nervous."

"You sure hid it well. It really sounded good. I definitely heard your pipes, uh… I mean, your voice. It really stood out, smooth yet powerful."

"Well, thank you. I look forward to hearing you sing. Let's head for class. We can talk on the way."

Before the mothers could reply, the gleeful hosts whisked LaRana down the hall. Chatter came nearly nonstop. She swiftly turned her head to the right for Amelia's words then quickly to the left for Jessica's. Katelyn's came a heartbeat later.

"Sorry about that. These kids get a little excited when visitors come our way," came Martha's apology, noticeably framed in pride.

"Oh, that's okay," replied Hannah, peering down the hall, a little hesitant. "They seem to be...quite pleasant."

Amelia led the visitors through the classroom door. Mr. Cook offered a smile and a hand toward Jalen and LaRana. "It's a pleasure to see you both. I have watched you play baseball on several occasions, Jalen. You do seem to have a knack for the game. Any thoughts about continuing baseball after graduation?"

"Well, I would like to, but that opportunity is in the hands of others."

He turned attention to LaRana. "And it is a real pleasure to meet you, young lady. Just a word of warning, don't believe everything these sorta weird guys and gals tell you, especially about me. I sometimes wonder how I ever get along with them. They can be a mess at times."

"Now, now, Mr. Cook. You know us better than that. We're just a very quiet, attentive group," declared Katelyn as if a halo floated over her head.

"Yeah, right."

Though somewhat bewildered by Bible passages and strange questions, LaRana thought the class flew by. Bridgette and Ashlynn politely ushered her to the auditorium. She paused at the entry, perplexed at the scene. The large room buzzed with more greetings, more hugs, more smiles, and more conversation as the crowd mingled before the main service. Several more offered a cordial welcome with a friendly hand till the morning's events began. Silence quickly fell when a few men stepped onto the stage.

LaRana sat with the girls on the left and her mother on the right. She had a strange feeling of connection far different than imagined, far different than felt at the sting. The greetings were not trite but real, given without expectations. She frequently glimpsed at unknown faces in other pews. Most, catching her glance, returned warm smiles. Eyes from black and white took her by surprise. They held no condemnation, beaming without prejudice or visual judgment.

This must be an act or something. This can't be real.

The congregation sang as a whole, blending voices caressed her ears, magnificent tones urging her to join in. She began humming. Amelia heard her efforts. She reached around Bridgette, tapping her on the shoulder.

"Just let 'er rip, LaRana."

LaRana managed a slight smile then half-heartedly sang, unfamiliar with the words. After two songs, she sheepishly turned to Bridgette. "Sorry, I'm messing you all up. I don't know these songs."

"That's okay. You'll get 'em. I can tell your voice is good, really good."

Those sitting nearby welcomed her presence. Several turned and nodded with a smile. She was completely caught off guard. Though hesitant, her spirit was lifted, caught up in the magic of harmony. She had a sudden desire to learn the songs. She again started to sing but paused, oddly compelled to watch and listen.

A young couple with two children of Asian ancestry sat among a small group of Native Americans. It suddenly dawned she was in a cross section of America. It was like she had fallen into a world of illusion while the world of reality waited outside. What was it with these people? What was the reason? She tried to put it into a single word. Though several were tossed about, she finally settled on one.

Joy.

It came abundant and overflowing. It appeared to have no boundary. It swirled from wall to wall, from one to another. Her heart was lifted while her mind yet wallowed in confusion.

As the service unfolded, some things appeared formal but very solemn, especially when Jesus' death on the cross and His resurrection was mentioned. LaRana inwardly scoffed at the impossible scenario. A myth came her thought.

Give me a break! Now that's a weird story. I've heard it before, but I didn't think rational people would believe it. They're really friendly, but they need to get a grip.

The lesson introduced Hannah and LaRana to words never before considered. It was like a discourse given partially in English and partially foreign. They both listened intently as bewilderment mixed with curiosity and skepticism. LaRana wondered how the unearthly comments presented had any connection to reality.

The preacher spoke of a way of life that seemed surreal, a strange contrast to the only life they had known. LaRana squirmed, pondering the distance between the church world and her world. She became keenly aware of the gulf between her and the Jesus people, a gulf of no little expanse. A new sense of being different swept over her, far surpassing the hue of her skin.

With the final prayer, the large crowd began to leave while several paused to talk with regulars and visitors. After exchanging greetings with many unknown but quite pleasant people, Shelly and Hannah stopped near the water cooler and waited for Jalen and LaRana who once again were hijacked by exuberant peers. The wait was not long as the perpetrators soon returned with both.

With nods to friendly faces and handshakes to offered hands, they made their way toward the exit. They reached the lobby when Martha quickly approached with a well-dressed man at her side. LaRana guessed somewhere around forty, maybe less. Martha appeared anxious to make an introduction. Upon seeing the gentleman, Hannah became uncomfortable. She moved near Shelly, hoping the greeting would quickly end.

"Before you leave, I want you to meet Mr. Isaiah Johnson. He teaches one of the adult classes and fills in for the preacher at times. Isaiah, I believe you know Shelly and Jalen Strade. And new to our city is Hannah Lester and her daughter, LaRana."

Hannah wasn't sure why Martha brought Mr. Johnson. Maybe it was because she was black came a thought as she held out her hand. To her surprise, his touch brought a long-absent tingle, one she had all but forgotten. Years of emptiness flooded her mind. Whether from shyness or shame, she briefly dropped her eyes and quickly retracted her hand as he turned to Shelly.

"It's good to see you and Jalen again."

With a handshake to each, he turned back to Hannah. "It's a real delight to meet you, Mrs. Lester, and you, LaRana. I do hope you will again give us the pleasure of your company. Hannah, if I may, I would certainly welcome you and Shelly to my class. We would be delighted if Mr. Lester was able to come with you."

Hannah glanced away, reluctant to reveal a nagging past. "I don't... I'm not...my husband passed away several years ago."

"I'm so sorry. I shouldn't have been so assuming."

"That's okay. LaRana and I try to get along on our own."

"Well, I do hope we see both of you again."

"That also goes for me," said Martha. "And it's a pure joy to see you again, Shelly. And you, young Jalen, my husband Larry and I have enjoyed watching you play baseball. Some of your games were just after our grandson played. His name is Easton, a really good player, and an upcoming all-star if I might say so."

"Yeah, I know Easton. I've watched him play. He can sure smack a baseball."

"Well, thank you. I'll tell him that. We trust you all were pleased to worship our Lord with us."

"Uh, yes, yes we were," replied Hannah, slightly smiling, unsure of the word worship.

The slow walk to the front door found Hannah making several swift and curious glances toward Isaiah as he talked with another man. Each were quickly sent then just as quickly retrieved. She finally returned attention to Martha.

"We enjoyed the morning, especially all the friendly people."

"I agree with Hannah. I actually feel...encouraged," said Shelly with a gleam in her eye.

Stepping outside, they found several people still talking. Their joyous interaction was no less at the leaving than at the coming. LaRana was anxious to get on the road, but the scene of obvious close friendships created a sense of wonder, piquing her curiosity. She wrestled with a growing dilemma.

Is this real or a put on?

With final goodbyes and waving hands, Hannah and LaRana settled in the front seat. The familiar interior of the Escort felt good, but though the setting was the same as when they came, something changed. The departure held several questions, mystifying questions far different than those at the arrival.

The old car sputtered down the road. LaRana kept her gaze out the window, contemplating the puzzling experience. Hannah was silent. Mr. Johnson would not leave her thoughts. She beheld a vision of character and decency, a vision rarely seen since leaving her childhood home. His touch on her hand was still there. She tried to think of other matters, but Isaiah remained. Neither spoke as the calm was broken only by the engine's somewhat erratic hum.

LaRana gazed out the slightly cracked window, struggling to make sense of the morning. She entertained a myriad of feelings, but one stood well above the others.

"Know something, Mom? Even though I certainly didn't understand all they did and said, they treated me like I was one of them, not a mixed-blood spectacle or toy to play with nor one to reject. Amelia, Bridgette, Jessica, Ashlynn, and Katelyn, all were top-drawer rad. They are like…real people. No judgment, no demands, just pretty cool dudes. There must be a catch somewhere."

"Well now, even the older 'dudes' were…uh…cool. I was delighted that Ashlynn was there. Martha and Isaiah… I mean Mr. Johnson…were especially friendly. It sounds like you found your group the same. Think we should go next week?"

"Yeah, I guess so, at least till the other shoe falls."

"Don't trust them?"

"I don't trust anybody but you. But I actually, well, kinda enjoyed being there, especially the music. Those girls can really sing! All the singing was cool. I don't know anything about this Jesus stuff, but I felt good or at least welcome. I didn't see any condemning glares."

LaRana paused then sent a sly look to her mother.

"Besides, I think I saw a strange glow in your eye when you met Isaiah… I mean Mr. Johnson. I lost count of the glances you gave him."

With slightly squinted eyes, Shelly shot a glance at LaRana. "Now look, young lady, don't you get any wild notions about me and anybody. You are my only concern, and it's most probable he is a happily married man."

LaRana burst out laughing. Despite an effort to maintain any measure of decorum, Hannah caved and joined in.

*****

Jalen brought the Jeep from the parking lot while Shelly shook her last hand, gave her last hug. With a final wave, she soon settled in the seat. Pleasant memories of years past surfaced, fond recollections of taking a young Jalen to church when he could barely see above the dashboard. Now, he was driving. She wondered where the years had gone. She couldn't keep from blaming herself for the lost time. Questions began to nag. *Was the return to church too late? Can he avoid the path of his father? Why was Roland so negligent? Why did I follow his lead?*

"Well, what do you think of our Sunday morning? Anything worthwhile strike your fancy?"

Jalen turned left at the light, deftly maneuvering between cars. His thoughts were varied, meandering, and uncertain. Religion was deep and distant. Life's realities, both loved and hated, were close. One thing was clear, the chasm between he and his father became clearer…and wider.

"Oh, it was okay. Saw some friends, or at least some who were friends years ago. Others knew me from school. I've seen a few in the hallways, but I wasn't close to them. Class was, ah, okay. Sure made me think of, well…things I guess I'm supposed to think of. We talked about now and eternity. Pretty heady stuff yet strangely interesting. It was kind of awkward so many dads were there and mine wasn't."

"Now, don't write off your dad yet. Who knows what may happen to get him to change his outlook. As Martha Sand said in class, God works in mysterious ways."

Traffic was light as they continued discussing the morning's events. Jalen turned the Jeep down the driveway, wondering what the afternoon held in store. Would going to church set his dad off on one of his tirades? Since the altercation after his run in with the law, Jalen had a queasy feeling in his stomach each time he turned toward the house.

With the Jeep silent in the garage, they entered and found Roland sitting near the front window, deeply engrossed in the newspaper with his favorite brew resting nearby. The recent cold atmosphere remained, dampening the morning's warm reception at church. The return to reality quickly came.

"About time you got back. I thought maybe you got lost."

Shelly let the dig pass. "We had a great time. We saw several people we hadn't seen in years. A couple of gentlemen asked about you. I said that you might come with us some Sunday morning."

"Huh! Fat chance. But if that ridiculous church stuff makes you happy, I won't stop you. Just make sure Sunday dinner isn't too late."

"Some man named Tom Ardaneo, I believe was his name, asked about you. He knew you from the time he worked at the cement plant several years ago."

Roland gently lowered the paper. "Tom? Now, that's really strange. He was quite the cusser and drinker for years. I can't imagine him going to church."

"People do change. He was very nice and courteous and hoped to see you there."

"Yeah…well…don't count on it. Some people may change, but most don't. Wow, I sure can't see him turning into one of them churchgoers."

"Well, it does give a person something to think about," said Shelly, still trying to create a glint of hope.

Roland finished a hearty swig, set the can on the ledge then glared straight at her. "You can't be serious. Whatever you do, don't hold your breath."

Missives Three

Jariel,

You do seem to be getting lucky. I almost had LaRana. A few more minutes and her soul would be well down our path. Everything went like I anticipated until, for some reason, she rejected my desire. But it's only a temporary setback. That she found joy in meeting your inane flock at church could make my task more difficult, but I will caress her emotions until she breaks. Of that you can be certain. Collecting her has become quite personal.

I will definitely work on Shelly and Hannah. If I can keep their spiritual efforts inside the walls of that despicable edifice, their search for relevance in your Master will soon be rendered worthless. I already have a few in that appalling group whose faith is nothing more than a sacrificial hour painfully endured. You have seen their hearts. You know those of whom I speak.

I do work hard to bring indifference and complacency at home, but I also sow that seed in your precious congregate. Many of your Master's followers want just enough religion to feel comfortable. It's quite satisfying to see so many try to fit Him into their lives. We become concerned when we find those who are fitting their lives into Him. All it takes is planting a thought on who comes first. Works quite well, you must agree.

Shelly thinks she has found a small light in the gathering of your paltry saints, but it will not last. And remember, Roland is still in my grasp. He is the family leader, and if I can maintain his self-centered attitude, his disregard, his rejection of your Master, then it is quite certain Jalen will follow in his father's footsteps. Slay the leader, scatter the sheep, has always been a good strategy. And when Shelly loses Jalen, her weak belief will disappear.

When adversity strikes, the faith of so many in your Savior's flock crumbles like shaken castle walls. Doubt rages like a prairie fire. I only need to help them believe our world, which they can see and touch, is more important than your world, which they can neither see nor touch.

Look what we have done to your Master's sphere of marvelous creation. We have progressed from our enticements being distant and disdained to available at arm's length and glorified.

How, whited foe, can you stand against such power? Your Master's handiwork, pure and unblemished at birth, no longer possesses the integrity or character to withstand my master. We find it rather simple to collect the...simple.

However, if I must resort to extreme circumstances to draw these four into my collection, be assured, I will use whatever it takes. Since we tried violence to erase your fledgling converts at Jerusalem those many years ago, we now look to destroy you from within. And might I say, we have been quite successful. However, I am not above physical resources to be noticed. Beware, I can summon a host of heinous circumstances just using a lack of common sense and carelessness among these heedless humans.

So to be brief, you might as well give up. LaRana, Jalen, and their mothers are mine, and there is no way for you to draw them from my grasp. Sorry to be so blunt, but I rather enjoy it. I hope this missive doesn't cause you considerable anxiety. But I surmise losing so many souls at once must cause a good measure of distress.

Farewell, for now. Stand by and behold as I ply my trade on such glorious and unwitting souls.

Esul

*****

Esul,

I certainly see how you can pitch a tantrum. I sense apprehension in your missive. Why is it when my Master turns the hearts of His creation toward the Light, you tend to get so upset and talk out of your contemptible head?

As you must see, we are pleased Hannah has taken a positive step to brighten not only LaRana's future but also her destiny. I'm sure you must get infuriated to see a single parent seek a better life for her child.

I am quite encouraged by Shelly. We believe she will return to our Master and bring Jalen with her. How magnificent it is to see a mother overcome a father's neglect and lead her offspring to us. You have to agree, two mothers are looking in our direction. If that makes you fret, well, that's life, so to speak.

While a few in that congregation attend for temporal convenience or misplaced motives, many are true believers, excellent ambassadors for my Master. Their influence combined with His Word makes them powerful persuaders, and your hoped-for collection has found them.

I know you will employ whatever devious and sinister tactics you can muster to thwart my Master's progress, but you shall not prevail. You cannot stop the power of our Savior. You cannot prevent His plan for deliverance of the human soul. You cannot prevent the love of the Almighty from flowing like a river of peace.

As adamant as you are that LaRana and Jalen will not find value in spiritual matters, we are just as resolved they find sense and relevance in our Master. You may attack body and spirit, but you will not prevent them from grasping the Mantle of Life. I see within them a determination to find that better life. Although each may stumble and doubt, they will continue to reach upward.

You and your cohorts have made Hannah's life dismal and uncertain far too long. Her heart is strong, her intentions noble, and her love for LaRana undiminished. You will by no means find her easy prey.

Shelly's strength is also a great asset. She has connected once again with those who helped bring brighter days in years gone by. As stated long ago, often the value of something is not appreciated or understood until it is lost then once again found. How uplifting to see love rise above all obstacles, to scatter night for a brighter day, to bring her son to the hands of the Lord.

I could say more, but I surmise you are already squirming in utter distraction at the impotence of your diabolical efforts. I would recommend you take a long walk in the cool rain, but I know such relief is not available in your abode. Sorry for your plight, but that's just the way it is.

Jariel

4

Encounter

To the resounding jubilation of students, a scheduled staff meeting brought an early bell, and the Friday noon sun gradually chased a slight, misty drizzle. LaRana once again left school alone. She threw herself into studies, a little due to necessity, but mostly to relieve her mind of being shut out by the in crowd. With Jalen at baseball practice, she had fewer chances to enjoy his company.

The welcome afternoon found her sitting alone on a school bench, absorbing the rising warmth, pondering what to do with unusual free time. Several students gleefully passed by, a few walked alone but most with friends. Their laughter and playful teasing magnified the loneliness. She pictured herself walking home with Jalen, laughing and joking about events and happenings, even if trivial. With ample time before Shelly's day ended, she decided to head for home and stop at the Frosty Treat where students often gathered after school.

She eased from the bench, flung the satchel over her shoulder, and started down the sidewalk, wondering what the weekend would bring. Conflicting thoughts fought for attention, contrary paths of the church and the street doggedly wrestled for her steps. The street provided familiarity, the church, a puzzling unknown. Doubt was the unknown's companion. Reality rode the street, and it abruptly turned in front of her.

"Hop in, LaRana. We'll take you home," yelled Willow, pulling over to the curb. Sarona eagerly threw the door open. LaRana took a few more steps before stopping.

The street was calling.

LaRana's on-the-edge friends had spoken little to her for two weeks; due, she surmised, to her flight from the sting. An urgent desire to belong once again rose like a sly intruder. The girls' beaming faces were enticing, drawing her close. The two paths to uncertain destinations fought for her choice. It didn't take long to choose.

Hello street.

LaRana peered all around then warily crawled into the back seat, unsure of her decision. Willow sped down the avenue. The girls gave her the silent treatment, looking out the window as if she wasn't there. LaRana was puzzled, glancing at the back of three heads. She was about to speak when the silence was broken.

"Welcome back, LaRana," they said as one with laughter following.

LaRana relaxed, relieved to again be with familiar companions. In the somewhat awkwardness of the moment, she entertained one comforting thought.

She wasn't alone.

Old desires revived. The line between right and wrong again blurred, racing to her mind's deepest recesses. The "I shouldn't be here" took a back seat to "I want to belong." With the welcome came pointed criticism.

"I heard Darnell hit on you at the sting," said Sarona bluntly. "Don't be such a prude. If you want to be around the dudes, you gotta loosen up."

Sarona laughed and ruffled her hair. LaRana managed a smile through a blush. She leaned back in the seat, tossing emotions like fragile eggs, wanting to be accepted by these girls yet remembering new friends at church. They seemed bent on validating their lifestyle by an implied demand that LaRana do the same while the girls at church were freely genuine and demanded nothing. A sudden uneasiness swept over her, a strong urge to get out of the car and not look back.

She shook it off.

Besides, I doubt anything will come of going to church. That Jesus thing is a little hard to swallow. I'll find some friends a little more like me. As long as I'm careful, I can handle whatever comes my way.

They arrived at the Frosty Treat, slowly pulling up behind two cars at the takeout window. Off-color conversation kept rolling. LaRana leaned back, remaining quiet. Willow finally reached the window.

Ashlynn offered a warm welcome. "What can we get for you?"

Willow, still giggling, leaned to the open window. "Two Dr. Peppers, a Pepsi, and a Mtn. Dew. All small."

LaRana thought about meeting Ashlynn at church. Although not a close friend, LaRana thought she was a pleasant girl who seemed to have her head on straight. She was quiet at school, the studious type, never involved in the party scene. She mentioned in a class she needed the work to save for school. She suddenly realized the difference between the girls in the car and Ashlynn was much akin to night and day. Juggling whose character to respect rekindled the battle within.

The short wait brought the usual conversation. Comparison of boys mixed with slangy remarks seemed endless. The girls hadn't changed. LaRana was content to listen, suddenly realizing the thrill of the crude side of life lost much of its allure.

Ashlynn returned with the drinks, took the payment, and gave LaRana a curious look. LaRana lowered her head as if embarrassed. She returned a slim smile with a short wave. In moments, they were back on the street. She wondered why she had a sense of shame. Ashlynn's eyes bored deeply, puzzled eyes offering concern not condemnation. It was a look yet to grace the faces of those in the car.

Though LaRana lived but a few blocks away, Willow took what she referred to as the scenic route. She went back around the school then headed for the strip, a popular cruising street for the night crowd. Little was said for several blocks as they sipped on sodas. LaRana wondered what Jalen would think of her somewhat closeness to these girls. She found herself thinking relationships were a matter of choice. She liked her recent acquaintances at church, but she also liked the carefree manner of those in current company. The middle of the road seemed the right solution.

I can balance them without too much effort. I should be able to get along with both.

At the end of the strip, Willow turned into a restaurant parking lot. She shut off the engine then reached for the iPad. "Hey, take a gaze at my Facebook page. What do you think?"

She handed it to Sarona who held it up. Curious faces looked from the back seat. Janene stared in disbelief. LaRana was startled to silence. Willow was posing in a series of beach photos.

"Wow, gal! These are a little racy, don't you think!" blurted Janene, mimicking a doting mother. "Ain't you concerned these pics will make the rounds at school? And what about your mom? I can't see her smiling at this."

"Nope! I'm a senior, knocking on nineteen and ready to fly. I want those clowns to eat their hearts out. And Mom? She's okay. Tells me she loves me and to be careful, but she doesn't have the slightest idea of what I do. I doubt she even knows how to turn on an iPad. She's a good mom but mostly in name, that's about all. She simply does her thing, and I do mine. My good old dad would have laughed, but that makes no difference, he skipped out long ago.

I've had a lot of comments about how glamorous I look. I've received texts from near and far. One was really cool. He's driving in tonight, and we're going to kick around town. His name is Dawson, a real hunk, let me tell ya. He's a photographer and agent for an up-and-coming advertising agency. Who knows, maybe I'll tickle his fancy. Wouldn't that be something for a little town girl to make it to the big time."

"Seems a little risky to me. Do you think that could be danger-ous?" asked LaRana softly.

"LaRana! Are you for real? Get with it. This is a cool way to meet some rockin' guys, especially those in high places. Besides, he said I really jumped off his screen…and he'd never seen such raw beauty. He sent me his picture. Here, scroll it and take a look. Awesome Dawson, I call him. I can't wait to get in front of his camera."

LaRana found Willow's fantasy quite attractive and entertained a slight touch of jealousy but thought the meeting still uncertain. Sarona landed on Willow's view.

"Getting a possible shot at a modeling career or movie part is nothing to sneeze at. Who knows, if this guy is able to get Willow a look, I think it would be a good move. I'd sure give it a go."

Janene, usually game for anything, was a little less enthusiastic. "I don't know. There's a lot of pressure and other stuff models face other than just a camera. I'd have to think twice about it."

"Well, the way I look at it, the bright lights are calling, and I'm answering. I don't think I have anything to lose, and I look forward to telling you about our evening. Just thought you might be interested. I guess we better get LaRana home."

LaRana patiently listened to Willow's continued rave about a thrilling evening and possible modeling career. There was no doubt; this was a shining moment in her life. Nothing or nobody was going to spoil it. She sat quietly, eager to say more, but reluctant to again be ridiculed. With anticipation still in high gear, she nervously twirled her hair while Sarona and Janene laughed between crude and sarcastic remarks. She suddenly realized she hadn't heard such language from those at church. The difference grew wider. She began to understand Hannah's warning about the chancy life, enticing and magnetic, yet oddly uncertain. Her heart began pulling away, but her mind stayed the course.

As lightning across the sky, an odd but compelling desire raced to her lips, eager to pass, whether from boldness or foolishness she couldn't tell. She hesitated for but a moment. It was as though someone, or something, took control of her tongue.

"Hey, why don't you girls come to church with me this Sunday."

Silence. Puzzled faces. Laughter.

LaRana blushed and eased back in the seat. *Oh, where did that come from? Why in the world would I say something like that? They'll think I'm a real dufus.*

"Church! Now that's a good one. C'mon, don't tell me you go to church," taunted Willow. "Church is for sorry losers and prudes.

They don't have a clue what makes life fun. Wow, LaRana, we need to screw your head on straight."

More laughter. More teasing. LaRana cringed and slowly leaned back, kicking herself yet somehow thinking she did what was right though yet bewildered by the whole church thing.

LaRana, you dummy, you're such a dodo. Can't you keep your mouth closed? Why would I ask them to come to a place I don't even understand? If you ain't careful, they'll shut you out for good.

The scoffing gradually calmed. Willow stopped in front of an old, well-worn house. LaRana stepped out then poked her head back through the window, trying to muster words of warning. She wasn't sure if she was wary or jealous. She knew the reply before blurting forth her thoughts.

"Just be careful, Willow. I don't want you to get messed up with this guy."

"Gads, LaRana! You sound as dumb as my mother. Even she doesn't fret that much. Besides, if he tells me I'm not model material, at least I can say I tried. You just never know where things will go. And remember, this is little ol' Pallon Ridge. It's not often we get a chance to step up to the real scene."

Mirth filled the car as Willow sped away. LaRana watched her disappear around the corner, unsure of conflicting emotions. Envy challenged worry. Wisdom battled folly. Acceptance butted heads with rejection.

Maybe I am a prude. Maybe I am jealous. What's wrong with meeting a cool guy? Could I be just a little envious? Ah, well, they'll probably never speak to me again.

*****

"I'm going to the movies with the girls tonight, Mom. I'll be back by eleven. Is that okay?"

Untouched by the lie, Willow peeked from the bedroom door, anxious to make the eagerly anticipated rendezvous. Her mother nestled in the couch. Her hands held a book, her heart emptiness. The relationship between mom and daughter seemed no more than a free renter at a landlord's boarding house. Willow impatiently waited for the usual warning, which quickly came forth.

"I suppose. Don't be cruising. The crazies are all over town on Friday night. I'll expect you here at eleven. Love you."

"Gotcha. Don't worry about me. You know how careful I am. I'll do my best to be back by then. Love you to."

Willow teased her hair and admired herself in the mirror. She threw several provocative looks, trying to find the most glamorous. The thrill of bright lights, of being admired, posing as a model, whirled in her mind. She read about the love affairs from the tabloids, watched them on the TV and movies. The elite. The celebrities. That's where she craved to be.

Get ready, Awesome. You're in for the time of your life. I'll show you what we country gals are made of.

With a few swift sprays of perfume, she grabbed the iPad and rushed from the house, her heart racing to the beat of quickened steps. She thrilled at the thought of telling the girls of the fantastic, storybook night. This is what she and her friends had talked about, dreamed about. Finding an amazing time with guys from anywhere outside Pallon Ridge was the ultimate achievement of cool. Finding it with a modeling agent of high profile was even better.

The evening grew warm and inviting, and a slight, wispy breeze created a dreamy atmosphere. Her mind was so occupied with anticipation of stardom she nearly rammed an approaching pickup. With each mile, she entertained various scenarios of modeling, each one more moving than the one before.

As thoughts of stardom wildly raced, she gave no thought to speed. She glanced at the dashboard and found her chariot going as fast as her mind. The arrow danced well over the limit. She began to slow down but too late. Someone else noticed. Grumbling at the siren and whirling lights behind, she pulled into a grocery store parking lot. Anger tussled with worry she would miss her magic moment.

A few minutes passed with the officer still in the cruiser. *Come on! Come on! Let's get this over!*

The officer leisurely approached from behind. Her heart began to race. *Blast it! What is she going to do? I gotta get out of this quick.*

The officer leaned forward, making eye contact. "Ma'am, can I see your license? You must be in quite a hurry. You were twenty-one miles above the limit."

"I just realized that. I was thinking about something really important at home and just didn't pay attention to my speed. I'm sorry. I'm a little nervous. This is my first time to get pulled over."

"Thank you. I'll be just a few minutes."

The officer returned to the cruiser for what seemed an eternity. Willow couldn't sit still. Anxious fingers danced on the steering wheel. Precious time crept. The officer finally came to the window with the license.

"We have no record of previous citations. Do you realize your insurance could be higher, and you could eventually lose your license? More importantly, your chances of an accident are much greater."

"I hadn't given it much thought, but I guess I had better in the future."

"I hope so. I'm going to trust you to slow down and think more about driving than other things. Consider this a warning."

"Thank you, officer. Thank you very much. I certainly will be more careful."

"For everybody's safety, be more careful. Regard the limit. You may go."

Willow gradually crossed the parking lot to the next exit. A look in the rearview mirror saw the flashing lights go out. She breathed a sigh of relief. Her mind returned to the anticipated meeting.

"Wow! That was close, but it's also an omen. There's no doubt about it now, this certainly is going to be my lucky night."

She anxiously drove toward Dolan Bridge, her mind twirling with enchanting visions. She couldn't wait for Dawson's adoring eyes, praising her beauty and declaring his awe. She was casually clad as he requested an informal meeting. She turned into the Pallon Ridge Mall feeling like a Hollywood starlet. Her nerves tightened when she stopped under the lights at the far end of the parking lot just outside the concession area. A final shot of perfume topped off a hoped for, amazing first impression.

She took a deep breath then quickly, but nervously, got out and briskly walked to the food court entrance. A good number of patrons still mingled, several shopping, a few eating, while others headed for the exits. She scanned the court but couldn't find anybody resembling the picture on her iPad or the vision in her mind.

She sat down at the designated table. Several minutes passed, then several more, and the crowd dwindled to only a few, most of which sat at lonely tables, much in the manner hers was quickly becoming. She glanced at her watch then anxiously rose and paced the walkway, looking in each direction. She saw no one resembling Dawson. Anxiety slowly crept. Frustration challenged anticipation.

She gruffly returned to the seat, lit a cigarette, and waited. Patience ran on empty. Thoughts of being duped hung in the air with spent smoke. She jumped from the chair, resuming a nervous pacing. Annoyance ran from thoughts to words.

"Well, here I am, people watching at the mall. Rats, what a lousy bore this is. I thought this might be too good to be true. He better not back out. I couldn't stand the jazz. I can just hear the girls now. 'How did it go? Did he think you could model? Was he as good looking as his picture?' Makes me want to puke. Come on, hotshot. I haven't got all night."

She suddenly realized her last words were a little loud. Several patrons glanced her way. She slightly blushed then returned a glare.

"Hey, what are you looking at?"

As curious heads turned back, she shuffled to the table when a stray cat ambled by, stopping near her feet. It softly rubbed against her leg, purring like a long-lost pet. A small, white spot centered on the throat mingled with smoky gray fur. It had the saddest eyes, a look saying "I'm alone and no one cares," an expression screaming "I don't have a home." She scanned all around but no one seemed to be looking for anything.

"Anybody lose at cat?" she half-yelled. Some answered no while others glanced her way but said nothing.

She shrugged her shoulders, returning attention to the feline. Her nerves settled as she gently stroked the visitor, bringing a soft purring. Thinking the rendezvous may have been a prank; she needed someone or something to talk to. The cat's ears were the closest available.

"Oh, such a cute, little kitty. Now where did you come from? How did you get in here? It's my guess you're an orphan. I'd like to take you home but not tonight. Hey, I know, if my plans get screwed up, I might take you home. Mom needs a pet, and I kinda like you myself. Stick around for a few more minutes. I just may need your company if…if…what am I doing…talking to a cat! Relax, Willow. Quit being so stupid! Don't get so uptight! He'll get here. He better get here!"

Time dragged as several more patrons left the mall. She lit another cigarette and glanced around the food court. No Dawson. Twenty minutes late. A few walkers, laden with packages, strolled down the hall, oblivious to her presence. Suddenly, she was startled by a touch on her shoulder. She spun around to find the object of her desire. Dawson looked a little different from the picture but close enough. She was instantly oblivious to anything or anyone. The startled cat scampered under a nearby table and quietly sat on its haunches. It stared at Willow with a gloomy countenance, a pleading look begging for a home.

"Sorry to be late. We came across an accident and had to wait for a while. You look absolutely stunning, even better than your picture," he said, scanning her frame.

He was very polite, clean cut and well dressed. His attire was definitely not purchased at a bargain store. She was immediately impressed. They sat and talked for a few minutes as several young customers noisily entered. She scooted her chair closer to Dawson then opened the iPad and panned to her pictures.

"You wondered if I had more shots of me?" she said proudly. "Will these do?"

"Oh, quite well, I'm sure. You appear to be made for my line of employment. I showed your Facebook pics to my friends and co-workers. Believe me, they were not only impressed but also more than a little jealous. They thought you were quite attractive. You have that certain radiance we're looking for. And coming from a midsize, western town would be a good human-interest story."

Willow's eyes returned to normal. "I don't want to be forward, but what do you do?"

Dawson leaned back. "We take pics of places around the country viewers may like to visit. We spike it up with shots of locals to make the location more attractive, a little folksier as some might say. Many agencies use our pics for advertisements. They've found it helps sales. And it doesn't happen every day, but a few of our ladies have been offered contracts by Hollywood biggies. But before you get ahead of all this, we strongly believe you should finish school. Modeling is a tough business. If you aren't able to make it, you need an education to fall back on. Even if we decide you would fit in to our business tomorrow, we wouldn't think of signing you till school is done. We also prefer your parents be onboard. Understood?"

"Sure. Understood."

"Speaking of parents, are they here? It's important they know what this is all about. Do they know we're meeting here tonight?"

"Uh, well, not really, just Mom, but she doesn't mind. She trusts me."

"I'm not very comfortable without your mom here. I really need to meet her tonight if possible."

"Well, would tomorrow be okay? She's a little under the weather tonight."

"Well… I guess that'll have to do. We can't come to any decisions without her approval. How about noon at your house?"

"Well, I guess okay. We don't live in a very good house."

"That's fine. Maybe if you become part of our company, you can get her a better one."

Visibly excited, she quickly moved the iPad in front of Dawson. Her heart raced when his eyes adored the alluring images. Willow tittered as his fingers moved through the pictures. Dawson's oohs and aahs sent shimmers down her spine. The thrill of the big time was more than she imagined.

"Wow, these are some really intriguing shots. Looking at you in the flesh, it's not hard to see why. Also, can I see some of your friends? I like to know the young ladies you run around with. My friends… the rich ones…may ask about them."

"Sure. I have a few in here…somewhere…ah, here we go." She turned several screens before finding Janene, Sarona, and LaRana.

"These are some of my closest friends, except maybe for this one. Her name is LaRana. She's a little prudish."

"Which one is which?"

She pointed to each, but he took special notice of LaRana. "She appears quite different, but…not bad."

"She's a newbie at school, a halfer as some say. She's only a junior. I don't know much about her. She sometimes hangs around with us but seems…a little…out of the loop…our loop anyway. She told us today she went to church, and even asked us to go. Can you believe it? I always thought she was a little strange but not that far out."

Dawson stared at length. His fingers slowly glided over the pics, gentle and caressing, his breath slowed to nearly nothing. He seemed mesmerized before drawing back his hand with a start.

"Well, church can't be all that bad. We all should be going to church more. I'm guessing these are nice girls. Thanks for bringing them. You have some attractive friends, but none as attractive as you. I believe the buddy I came with would like to meet Janene. She looks like his type. Oh, he's one of the rich dudes, Mercedes Benz no less. I know… Janene…would love to meet him. He's a good guy. Country, as some would say. Well, we're about an hour to closing. What say we go for a cruise around your nice, little town? Although it's dark, I can get a better concept of where you come from. We also need to talk a little more about tomorrow. Plus, we need to find a location to take some pics. However, I do have to get back before too long to polish up for an online meeting early in the morning. Let's just say I have an odd boss."

"Sounds good. There's not a whole lot to see, especially after dark, but maybe we can think of other things," she slyly replied. Her eyes narrowed above a wide grin, revealing an eager expectation.

Dawson looked a little perplexed. "I'm not sure what you mean by other things. At least, I can get to know you better. Can we take your car? I came with a friend, and he had to meet a relative. We agreed to meet back here somewhere around nine thirty."

"Sure. We should be able to get better acquainted by that time."

Dawson seemed pleased. "Yes, that would be beneficial."

She scooted her chair under the table. The abrupt motion sent the cat scurrying across the floor. It stopped and looked back. Disappointment appeared on its face, an aura saying it missed another chance for a home. She smiled at the feline, now sitting with its tail curled around its legs. A "feeling sorry" look prompted a bidding for the stray to come. It leaped to its feet and came straight to her with tail in the air.

"Didn't know you brought a pet."

She looked up at Dawson. "No, not mine. Just a poor stray, but I guess it's like…a new friend. I sorta made a promise to take it home. I'm not usually big on cats, but this one seems to really like me."

Words of comfort came with a stroke of its fur. The cat immediately began to purr. "If you're still around when I get back, I'll take you home. It looks like you could use one."

"Appears to be a nice cat. It'll probably be around when we get back. I doubt it will forget your kind attention. Just a thought, but… maybe…we could use it in some pics tomorrow. I've never had an animal in my lens. Hmm…interesting. I just might be able to work it in somehow."

"That would be nice," said Willow. "Stay around here, whatever your name is. I'll be back in a little while."

Small talk mixed with laughter on the walk to the car. The mall lights quickly faded in the rearview mirror. Willow drove around the downtown area, past business and upscale neighborhoods. Dawson was visibly excited, and talked with little room for Willow to jump in. He spoke about the grind of company business for both agent and client. She listened intently, her mind racing to visions of stardom. His words leaned toward a possible interest in contracting her for small town mag shoots. She could barely contain emotions.

Willow drove by the high school till turning onto a secondary street. She easily chatted, but Dawson gradually grew more silent. He smiled at her stories but said little.

"Are you okay? Did I say something wrong?"

"No, no. I'm just thinking of how you might fit into our plans."

Willow had a quick sigh of relief. She didn't want to make any wrong moves that might dampen the chance of a lifetime.

"Most towns have city parks. My research found this town had an old one. I would like to take some night shots if possible. Do you know if there's an old city park, hopefully with at least a few lights?"

"You bet. It's about two miles from here."

"Could we go to it? I believe I can see enough to evaluate whether we can take some pics of you there, if not tonight then possibly tomorrow. We can take a muted picture under a night-light and…maybe use the same place to enhance the shot. A rustic setting with a mountain background can make for some appealing pics."

"We'll be there in no time."

Aglow with anticipation, she turned at an old abandoned house and sped down a darkened road till reaching an open area where the few remaining lamps dimly glowed, leaving a host of eerie shadows. Dawson sat very still as Willow parked near a light pole.

She turned off the lights and reached for the radio buttons. "Do you want to hear some music while we're here?"

"Not right now. Maybe when we start back."

Visions of stardom swirled; warm emotions swept. She unlatched her seatbelt and turned toward Dawson, patiently waiting for comments or directions.

No response came. No feeling. No passion, nothing but a cold stare. Confused at his reaction, she slightly recoiled.

"I hope I'm not being too forward. We can head back if you need to go."

"No, not at all. I'm… I'm in no hurry. I just needed time to get into the mood I'm comfortable with. It's just my nature. I need to see the lights from various positions. I'm not sure there's enough light to get good pics tonight. Let me snap you under the lights. I can get a better idea whether this is feasible."

"Sounds good to me."

Exiting, they slowly strode toward the nearest light. Dawson suddenly stopped, standing as though entranced. Willow paused then started toward the base when Dawson grabbed her with one arm while dragging her toward the light's edge.

"What are you doing!" yelled Willow. "Let me go! Please, let me go! I'm not one for this kind of game!"

"Game? Yes, I guess you could call it that. My game. It would be good to say nothing more. We're going to take a little walk. Please be nice to me. I really need you to be nice to me. I may let you live if you're nice."

He neared the edge of a shadowed tree grove. Willow wriggled and kicked till she saw a large dagger in Dawson's other hand. Terror set her heart racing. She trembled in despair, screaming with all her might.

"Help! Help! Let me go! Please, let me go!"

"Shut up! Shut up! There's no one to hear you! Just be nice to me! I really need a friend. That's all I want...someone to be my friend."

Intense regret flooded Willow's mind. His strong grasp held tight. His eyes glared demonically. A long-held fantasy quickly became a frightening terror. His voice calmed but determination grew.

"Now, my dear Willow, you wanted to be a shining star, a model. Now...if you're not nice to me, you may get your picture taken, just not in a pose you desire."

In desperation, she swung her leg around Dawson's, tripping him to the ground. The knife flew out of his hand. She broke free and ran for the car. Her hand touched the handle, but Dawson, again brandishing the blade, caught her, spinning her around.

"Why are you running away? I need you here, to be with me. Isn't this what you had your heart set on? To be adored? I can do that if you'll be my friend," he said, slow and deliberate.

His voice grew stern below furrowed brows till briefly pausing. His words were almost pleading. "Why wouldn't you like me? I just wanted you to like me, to be my friend. Maybe you will treat me better next time."

His piercing eyes raced through her. His cold, emotionless stare bored into her soul. A strange sense of eternity flashed before her eyes.

Visions of a glorious career fled in the face of madness. She squirmed, but his grasp held tight. He pulled her toward a shadowed opening in a grove of small trees. Several minutes passed till agonizing screams filled the empty night air, speeding through the stillness to nobody's ears. In the returning quiet, a lone figure with iPad in hand passed calmly under the lights, disappearing into the darkness. In moments, all that could be heard was the mournful call of a lonely owl.

The smoky furred cat was still an orphan.

*****

Saturday noon found spectators from all over the county and beyond streaming into Cavelson Field for the annual Veterans Memorial baseball game between Harris Rock Junior College and stars from Ponderosa League high schools. A few feet over the center field fence, the American flag slowly, but majestically, rippled in a gentle breeze. Lesser flags wavered at the feet of the greater. An entire section was full of veterans, many who served in Korea and Viet Nam.

Jalen stood with his teammates down the third base line. Chills ran down his spine while being in the presence of such heroes. He felt proud to be an American as an honor guard marched toward second base. The crowd stood in silence and homage when two soldiers, a man and a woman, touched patriotic hearts with a stirring performance of the national anthem.

After rousing ovations ended, the Ponderosa all-stars took the field. Jalen scanned the crowd. Hannah and LaRana were missing, helping with a fundraiser for a children's hospital. Shelly sat with the all-star boosters three rows behind the third base dugout. Though comfortably sitting between two others, she was alone. Since given the honor of playing in a high-level game, Jalen looked for one more in the stands. Each game brought the same hopes, always expected, never fulfilled. He chased frustration with unwavering respect and gratitude for Shelly, his anchor, his balm for a rocky road.

The game was one for memory. The high school all-stars rallied with two runs in the last inning to win. Jalen had a double and a home run in four at-bats, garnering attention of college coaches, some gathered behind the plate, and some grouped in a middle row just off the first base line.

After hand slaps and compliments between players, Jalen collected his gear and started for the gate. His shoulders sagged when a familiar figure approached from beyond third base. Mike Monroe drew near with a confident stride. A wave of shame swept over Jalen. He hadn't seen him since his oft-rued incident with the law. He found it difficult to keep his head up.

"Hi, Coach. Thanks a lot for coming. Uh, I, uh, I've been meaning… I want to say… I'm really sorry for the crazy stunt I pulled. It was just plain stupid. I should have known better."

Mike looked straight in Jalen's eyes and offered his hand. "Accepted and put in the past. We all make mistakes. Only those of solid character are strong enough to admit and learn from them. I believe you are one with such character."

Jalen finished the handshake, startled at the officer's declaration. It was given directly, firmly, and sincerely without hesitation. Mike's eyes didn't waver but stayed on Jalen's. He felt smaller yet relieved at the same time, forgiven by a man he admired. He relaxed, once again feeling a little more whole. He looked straight back at the officer.

"I don't know how to thank you enough. I will certainly try my best to live up to that."

"I have no doubt you will…also, nice game. You definitely turned some heads today. Several coaches came, and I believe a pro scout. I'm guessing you were one of the reasons for their presence. I think it would be reasonable to say you are on the first page of prospects. Colleges and pros are looking for shortstops with speed, power, and a strong arm. If you continue to have games like this, you'll most likely be offered a scholarship package from more than one school. Pursue your passion with all you've got. Work hard, keep studying, and keep practicing. You never know what could happen."

"I will, sir. You taught me a lot about playing the game. I appreciate all the help. I couldn't have done as well without you. Again, I apologize for my crazy prank."

Mike once more looked him straight in the eyes. His voice didn't waver. "What prank was that?"

Jalen stood speechless, puzzled by the reply. The officer's eyes remained fixed on his. Trying desperately to find an intelligent answer, he entertained the thought Mike was making fun of him. It suddenly dawned he really put the deed in the past. Each held a firm gaze and handshake till Jalen nodded. An exchange of smiles said the gulf had been spanned, the misdeed buried. With a nettlesome burden relegated to the annals of history, his countenance brightened.

He watched Mike walk to the cruiser, briefly entertaining a desire his father could reach such character. *Ah, Jalen, quit dreaming.* He scanned the crowd leaving the field and spotted Shelly at the gate, smiling as usual.

"Great game, Son. You were quite impressive, at least to me, and I think others also. I spotted a few men with notebooks and speed guns behind home plate. Somebody said others were here also."

"Thanks, Mom. Officer Monroe noticed too. Your support is really important, but I hate to see you sitting by your…well, never mind."

"I wouldn't have missed it for the world. I only wish LaRana could have been here."

"Yeah, me too, but she's doing something more important. I can only admire her for that."

"Good! I'm glad you see that. She seems to be trying hard to fit in at church, and she's also willing to work for good causes. It appears she's learning quicker than most the value in helping others. Well, be careful. I'll see you at home."

The parking lot down the left field line rapidly emptied. Jalen passed the fence, briskly walking toward the Jeep parked alone near the far end. He glanced around wondering where his home run landed, pondering what colleges coaches thought, and questioning if he was good enough. Scenes of an unfolding future rushed to his vision, some of being a college player or even a pro, some of sweaty gym work, some of slices of life in between. They all meandered and overlapped.

"Ah! Quit getting ahead of yourself, you big dummy. You've got enough to take care of today!"

He hummed a pop tune and reached for the door handle when a shrill scream suddenly pierced the air. He paused and scanned the large hay field seeking the source. Nearly a hundred yards past the end of the lot, near a grove of young pines, stood two boys. One was easily recognizable. Brenton. The other he didn't know. Brenton made a short, but quick, move.

Again, a scream.

Jalen quickly tossed his gear into the Jeep and headed for the boys. He saw Brenton kick at something on the ground. He picked up the pace and drew near. His breath nearly stopped as Brenton again thrust his leg forward.

Another scream.

A young boy writhed in pain in front of Brenton. Jalen knew him, a handicapped freshman, short of stature and strength.

"*Cesar!*"

The helpless lad's glasses lay broken. He held his stomach, wallowing in pain. Fear filled his eyes. Tears, mingled with blood, slowly trickled down his cheeks. Brenton hovered over him, taunting him.

"What's the matter, runt? Get up and fight like a man! Come on, where's your guts."

Jalen's heart began to race. He dashed toward Brenton, yelling at the top of his voice. "Leave him alone, jerk!"

Jalen rapidly approached. Brenton spun around. "Well, if it isn't Jalen the Great, the halfer lover."

"Cesar hasn't done anything to you! Maybe you should try somebody your own size!"

Jalen swiftly moved between victim and attackers, keeping his eyes on Brenton. "Cesar, get your glasses."

Brenton took a step toward Cesar, but Jalen stayed between them, slowly picked up the glasses yet watching his adversary. "Here, now go to my Jeep by the ball field. I'll be there as soon as I take care of this problem."

"T'ank 'ou." Still racked with pain, Cesar haltingly moved toward the park as quickly as possible.

Jalen stood defiantly facing Brenton. His nerves settled. "It looks like just you and me, loser. Bring it!"

Brenton nervously laughed. "You can't count very good, hot shot. Open your eyes. I'm not alone. Are you sure you want to do this? I'd hate to see a momma's boy get all messed up, especially with your cute, little uniform on."

Jalen glanced at the other boy who looked unsure of the situation. His eyes darted between the adversaries while slowly moving to the side. Jalen shuffled his feet, trying to keep eyes on both.

Brenton clinched his fists. "Come on, Garon! Talk's over! Let's get this rube! He's been needing this for a long time!"

Brenton leaped forward, wildly swinging fists, some landing, some glancing, some finding only air. Jalen caught Brenton square on the chin, sending him reeling backward. Jalen took a step forward, but Garon grabbed his arms from behind. Brenton pounced and sent a fist to Jalen's stomach then two quick jabs to his face, opening a cut above the eye and another on the cheek.

Jalen dodged a potent swing and lurched backward, tripping Garon. Both fell to the ground. Jalen took Garon's breath with a hard blow to the stomach. Brenton kicked Jalen who groaned and rolled to the side then scrambled to his feet. Garon remained on the ground, writhing in agony, gasping for breath.

"Now, it's just you and me, punk," said Jalen, wiping blood. He glared with steely eyes. "I don't think you can take me!"

Brenton spat blood and lunged in frenzied desperation. He madly swung again, catching Jalen hard in the stomach. Another wild swing missed its target. Jalen calmly shifted to the right and sent his fist to an open face. Brenton staggered backward. With a blow to his stomach and another to his face, he dropped to his knees. He tried to get up but fell back. Blood freely flowed from a slightly tilted nose.

Jalen reached down, grabbing his shirt. "There's a lot more where that came from, punk! Don't even think about picking on Cesar again! I'll find you, and I may not be so gentle the next time! You can mark it down!"

Brenton rocked forward then slowly rose. He stumbled and swiped blood. He waved to Garon, slowly plodding away without a word. Jalen carefully watched till they disappeared through a grove of trees at the end of the open field.

He turned toward the Jeep, painfully realizing Brenton hadn't missed with every swing. Blood seeped from the cuts. His shirt was splotched in red. He wiped his face, smearing the blood, but still managed a wry smile.

"Now this day has been a real roller coaster. It seems like I'm just bent on getting into trouble."

Bruises talked loudly, and he sorely replied to nobody while plodding across the field. "Ouch! That really hurts! Maybe I shouldn't have done this, but at least Cesar got out of there."

He gingerly stepped toward the Jeep, wiping blood on his sleeve. He entertained a myriad of thoughts. Baseball, college, church, LaRana, Mom—all presented choices, all competed for his attention, all except one, the one so desperately wanted. He tried to see in each direction, but vision blurred by pestering uncertainties, the unknowns. The only sure thing was the pain in his face and ache in his stomach.

He gingerly eased into the seat. Cesar sat quietly yet slightly bent over. "How bad is it, Cesar?"

"I 'urt. Are 'ou 'kay?"

"Ah, yeah, I'll be fine. We better head for your house. I'm sure your parents are wondering where you are. Do you still live on Battlefield Drive?"

"'es."

"Buckle up. Let's get you home."

The drive took a little over ten minutes. He pulled into the narrow driveway and cut the engine. Cesar's parents rushed from the door. A few small faces watched from the window. The aching lad sluggishly crawled from the Jeep, melting into anxious arms.

"What happened?" queried the father.

"A couple of scumbags were picking on him for no reason as far as I could tell." Jalen managed a wry grin. "Sorry I couldn't get him here sooner, but I was…uh, slightly detained."

"Thank you very much for helping Cesar. We were worried about him. Come in and let me help with your injuries," offered Cesar's mother.

"That's mighty nice of you, but I need to be going."

"How can we repay you for your kindness?"

Jalen watched as the parents consoled Cesar. A loving connection was obvious. "You already have. It appears Cesar is in the best hands possible. That's all that matters."

After final thanks, handshakes, and farewells, the drive home seemed an eternity. He sorely felt each bump in the road. Blood still slightly trickled as he pulled into the driveway. With a painful, swollen face, his thoughts turned to his mother's reaction. He despised adding to a full plate of frustration. She had enough on her mind, especially with Roland who seemed to withdraw more each passing day.

Jalen brought the Jeep to rest, gently eased out, and trudged toward the door. He entered the front room where Shelly relaxed with a book. With a quick look, she leaped to her feet, sending the book tumbling to the floor.

"My goodness! What happened to you? I wondered where you'd gone. Come to the kitchen and sit down. I'll get something to clean you up."

Jalen plopped on a chair, groaning with each breath. Shelly returned with a pan of water, a washcloth, and a towel. "Just relax if you can. I'll wipe off the blood and patch you up while you tell me about it. Where all do you hurt?"

"Nothing's hurting but my face and stomach."

She listened quietly as Jalen filled in the details between twitches when sore spots were touched. Her countenance baffled him. She was unusually calm. Her eyes revealed little emotion. It bothered Jalen that he may have again grieved his mother, but he still couldn't see any other choices.

"There was no way I could ignore Cesar, and Brenton didn't want to quit. I couldn't see a way out. I know I should turn the other cheek, as the preacher said, but I couldn't turn Cesar's other cheek. I had to help him. Sorry if I did the wrong thing, but I would do it again."

Shelly calmly placed two butterfly bandages on the narrow cuts. "They're not too bad, but we need to get a stitch or two for the one near the eye. These will do till we get to the doc."

"Where's Dad?"

"Where he is far too often."

"I wish I could make things better for you."

"You're doing just fine. I just hope I'm not leaning on you too much."

"Lean all you want. Maybe someday he will…once again see your beauty, inside and out."

She was stone quiet a few moments before carefully scanning her handiwork. Jalen didn't know what to expect. His body racked with pain, but his heart felt good. Though his mind was at peace, he wondered when she was going to let go with a barrage of correction. Her silence set his nerves on edge.

Shelly washed and dried her hands, stepped back, and nodded. "Well, now, you're going to have a real shiner, but I guess you can live with it. Let's head for the clinic as soon as I clean up all this. By the way, that's a good start. A really good start."

Jalen was puzzled. "Good start. To what?"

Shelly smiled and ruffled his hair. "Might I suggest you change your clothes then give LaRana a call to let her know you…are going to look a little different for a few days?"

"Yeah, I guess so," replied Jalen, picking up his cell and slowly plodding to the bedroom.

Shelly spent several minutes cleaning the kitchen. She squeezed the last towel when a phone call begged her attention. "Hello, this is Shelly."

Within seconds, her aura suddenly turned from slight elation to utter shock.

*****

The late Saturday afternoon graced Pallon Ridge with a glorious sunset. The pleasant day lazily spent its hours gently cooling the valley with a wisp of southern breeze. Six hours of fundraising wore

Hannah to a frazzle. She quietly sat reading a book while LaRana poured over homework, tapping a pencil on a clipboard, keeping time with headphone music. Hannah pulled a thin throw over her legs, finally relaxing till startled by the phone's ring. She lowly groused, set her book down, and quickly rose.

"I'll get it. You just keep hitting those books. I don't want to take you away from all that fun."

LaRana wrinkled her nose. "Yeah, right."

Hannah held out the phone. "It's for you. Somebody named Jalen, I believe."

"Funny."

LaRana quickly shut off the music and grasped the phone. She barely said hello then stopped and said no more for well over two minutes. Finally, she got in a few words.

"So let me get this straight. You did really good at the game, talked with Officer Monroe, got in a fight with Brenton, took a hurting lad home, and now you're going to get stitches in your face. Wow, not much use in talking about my day. It would most certainly pale to yours. Well, if you had to fight, I'm glad you're able to talk. Thanks for letting me know about all this. I guess I'll see you tomorrow...if you're still alive."

LaRana silenced the phone, rolling her eyes. "Never a dull day with him around. Wow, baseball and fighting. Ah... I can't imagine what's next."

"Sounds like Jalen had an...uh...interesting day. Hope he's all right."

"He is except for all the wounds. He's getting at least one stitch. Oh, well, back to my boring day's work."

She set the phone on the table and returned to the couch, regaining the earplugs and textbook. For the next several minutes, a calm again fell over the room. Just as both had settled, the phone again rang, breaking the silence.

"I've also got this one," said Hannah, stretching unsuccessfully to reach the phone. She finally rose with a groan.

"Oh, hello Shelly."

She said no more but listened intently. A deep furrow found her brow. Moments of silence passed before she replied with a tone of astonishment.

"That's awful. Do they have any idea who could have done this? Hold for a second. Let me ask LaRana if she knows her."

A puzzled frown crossed her face. She slowly lowered the phone. "LaRana, do you know a girl named Willow?"

LaRana lifted the headphones. "What did you say?"

The question came again, somewhat louder. "Do you know a girl named Willow Fontane?"

LaRana dropped her pencil and quickly sat up. The iPad photos, Willow's racy language, and her reckless desire for adoration rushed to mind. She felt she already knew the answer to her question.

"Yes! I met her at school. Why? Did something happen to her?"

Hannah slowly returned the phone to her ear, nearly at a loss for words. "Shelly, I'll…uh…call you later. Thanks for letting me know."

She gently set the cell on the table then stared at it, deep in thought, trying to find a way to address Shelly's news. She chose the direct approach.

"The body of a girl named Willow Fontane was discovered this morning at the old city park. Did you know her?"

LaRana dropped the headphones then quickly leaped from the couch as her book hit the floor. Her last vision of Willow flashed like a beacon, the picture of her possible killer, the impatience and lack of common sense. Her eyes misted, and her whole body trembled. Emotions twirled. Anger. Fear. Another dart settled in, refusing to go away. Blame. It fell on her shoulders, pressed hard, setting her heart racing.

"She drove me home yesterday. Two other friends were with us. She said she met a guy through Facebook, and she was meeting him last night. I tried to warn her…to get her to think, but…"

LaRana fled to open arms. Tears began to flow. "Oh, Mom. I should have stopped her, somehow talked her out of it. I tried… I really tried, but I should have tried harder. She just made fun of me and wouldn't listen. It's my fault. I should have thought of something else, anything else. Why wouldn't she listen? Why?"

Hannah tenderly patted her back. "That's okay, LaRana, that's okay. It isn't your fault. Don't blame yourself. You tried your best. You did what was right, but not all things turn out right. I'm sure your grandma had the same thoughts about me at times. Often we have a chance to correct a mistake, but sometimes we don't. I've made plenty of my own, but maybe I've been allowed a second chance."

LaRana glanced up. Hannah lightly brushed her tears. "And maybe you also have been given a second chance."

"Mom, I want to go to the funeral if they have one. I doubt very many people will show up. She may not have had good morals or sound judgment, but I did try to talk her out of it... I really did. I don't believe many of the crowd she hung around will be there. I want to see her to the end...and, it's my guess her mother would like to know some people cared."

Hannah proudly looked into LaRana's eyes. Her daughter expressed concern for the feelings of others regardless of circumstances. "Most certainly. I think you should be there, and I would be proud to go along if I wouldn't embarrass you."

LaRana flinched back with widened eyes. "Mom, you will never embarrass me, never! I'm always proud to let people know you're my mom."

The brutal murder shocked Pallon Ridge. Talk spread like wildfire. People from all around the city were caught up in the vicious deed, but most chatter and concern focused on the killer and his whereabouts. Several students knew Willow, but her mother was all but unknown.

Far too few brought food and offered condolences to Mrs. Fontane. A short graveside service was held on a misty, overcast day. A small number of residents, mostly the curious, attended but remained at a distance. Merely four people gathered near a plain casket below a canvas tent at the far side of the cemetery. Willow's grieving mother sat at arm's length from her life's greatest loss with only three members of the family, an aunt, an uncle, and a cousin, all from farmlands in Kansas. LaRana stood with Hannah and Isaiah. Jalen and Shelly stood nearby. Five of Willow's friends grouped well back of the burial site. A local preacher spoke a few last words then calmly shook the hands of those seated. Tears slowly trickled down the fraught face of Willow's mother.

LaRana still struggled with a sense of blame. She hung her head while the meager gathering began to disperse. Things she might have said or done to convince Willow of the danger taunted her thoughts. The mother's sobs grew louder. She clung harder to Hannah's arm. She attended a couple of family funerals in the past but was never close to the deceased.

Joined by Shelly and Jalen, they moved to within a few yards till family embraces ended. With the crowd all but gone, the visiting family walked toward the car. Willow's mother slowly rose and placed a hand on the casket. Few condolences had been given. Hannah and LaRana eased around the chairs to meet Willow's mother. Her aura of hopelessness tore at LaRana's heart. The grief on her face and the sorrow in her eyes loudly proclaimed her life had also just ended. With words hard to come by, they both gave a consoling embrace.

"Willow mentioned your name a few times. She said you were a little different. I also believe you are different, not to my eyes, but to my heart. You are the only classmate to talk to me. For that, I am very grateful."

"Mrs. Fontane, this is Shelly Strade and her son, Jalen. If there is anything we can do to help, please let us know," said Hannah.

"Pleased to meet you Mrs. Strade and Jalen. Thank you very much for coming."

LaRana was at a loss for words till remembering those of her mother. "We'll come by to see how you are doing in a few days if that's okay."

"I don't want to bother you, but yes, I would like your company."

A light drizzle began to fall. Hannah and LaRana stepped several yards back but stayed till the cemetery emptied. They quietly left as the devastated mother arrived to her family. Only those waiting to inter the deceased remained.

LaRana stopped by the Escort. Glancing back at the burial site, she shivered at the haunting vision of the casket disappearing into the ground. Hannah calmly placed a hand on her damp shoulder.

"What do you think Mrs. Fontane needs most at a time like this?"

LaRana pictured the bereaved mother, the tears, the mental anguish, the long days of loneliness. Her reply came quickly, an answer transcending the material.

"A friend."

"Exactly. When we visit, maybe we can help by letting her know she has at least two friends and, who knows, maybe a lot of potential friends."

LaRana's face lit up. "Wow, Mom, that's a great idea! It's my guess she'll be alone after tomorrow…and probably depressed. I would love to go with you…not that you need me, but I did have a connection with Willow…sorta."

Hannah's face glowed with pride. "I couldn't think of a better person to help with the visit. I believe it would be a very good after school activity. I'm off in two days. How about then?"

"I'm in!"

With both settled in the seat, LaRana's mind began to toss. Watching the casket disappear brought conflicting thoughts. She recalled the preacher's oft-used references to heaven and hell, religious words relegated to the mystical. New questions arose. Was this the end of existence or is there more? Does a realm exist other than what is seen or touched, something far beyond the comprehension of human intellect? She held a staunch belief life ended here. Now, she wasn't so sure.

Missives Four

Esul,

You are as wretched as wretched gets. Your master is the father of lies, and you certainly have learned his deceitful schemes. There is nothing below your contemptible influence. We may have lost Willow, but it will only intensify efforts to bring others to the Light.

Our Father's Word is filled with warnings of your diabolical methods. We will never lessen our efforts to reach our Master's creation, covering the planet with the great news of our Savior, and providing access to the necessities of life. If we had more time with Willow, a better fate may have been hers.

And in case you missed it, LaRana regretted she didn't try harder to turn Willow from the ill-conceived rendezvous. She had genuine feelings for someone else. I know you hate to see a human grow past selfishness to consider the welfare of others. LaRana is moving toward us, little by little. Her disbelief in our realms is being questioned. She is beginning to realize there might be an existence after physical death.

She is also beginning to see the evil you spawn. It is our hope she will soon seek her Savior. Her prayer will be heard, and no one who sincerely seeks my Lord will be disregarded. I know you sense this in her. Sorry if that disturbs you.

Hannah has grown even more. She is beginning to look to our Master for answers to life's problems, most of which can be laid at Escar's feet. As Paul taught the precious souls at Ephesus those many years ago, my Lord teaches humans in this segment of time. Adorning the whole armor of God along with the magnificent attributes of love for others will protect her from your evil intent.

I see you are testing Jalen. I'm sure you noticed his candid shame of a wayward deed. He discovered a great character trait in a man he admired, a man who accepted his declaration of genuine regret and relegated it to the past, putting it out of memory much in the manner my Master does. Sometimes, a keen awareness of wrong and the value of forgiveness can foster a staunch desire to turn in a different direction.

You used a troubled soul to get to Jalen, but look what happened. Jalen stood for what is right even in the face of danger. Sorry your little ploy backfired. Jalen is learning life occurs outside of himself, something I know draws your ire.

While it grieves us we couldn't reach Willow and may lose others, more humans are looking to us for answers, even the Answer. We truly enjoy second chances. Hannah realized she just received one. More humans are getting wise to your heinous ways. They are beginning to see what my Master offers may well be a balm for life's woes, or might I better say, the woes you devise. I am certain you see this happening.

What say you, demon?

Jariel

*****

Jariel,

I read considerable distress in your missive. You appear to be groping for a way to win. My master doesn't need to lie. He just convinces humans of something that may not be true. Just like me, you see. I don't make people eat. I do nothing but merely set the table. Willow was simply drawn to the food we prepared. Since she didn't take advantage of the table your Master sets, she chose ours as multitudes before her. And you must agree, the table we set is quite appealing, overwhelming even. Most humans simply do not have the character or fortitude to turn down our sumptuous fare.

How naïve she was to think tragedy couldn't happen to her. Isn't it amazing how we arrange such volatile circumstances by connecting evil intent and blind trust? I simply define their puny lives by heartaches, regret, wars, hatred, greed, lust, apathy, desire for adoration, and the list goes on and on. As long as we keep human eyes turned inward, to eliminate rational thought, neither you nor your Master can prevail against us.

LaRana's compassionate reaction was briefly concerning, but it quickly passed. Misfortune might need to be much closer. Not that I will lay a hand on her so to speak. She may require a good reason to once again believe she can't win at life, but is indelibly doomed by circumstance.

Her struggle for relevance will shatter and collapse as shards of glass from lofty cathedrals. Her prayers will eventually be spawned by fear, a petition for help in time of need, a plea for understanding, temporal and lacking depth.

Not exactly what you prefer.

Jalen's incident was simply to determine if he would buckle in the face of danger. I categorically despised to see him stand up to my temptation, but I am just getting started on him. Just watch what happens when doubt hits him like a sudden storm. I just need to get a little closer to home. Maybe his father can help our efforts since he is not pleased with his son.

Try not to be too dismayed at my confidence. Get used to it. I will garner all the eternal souls for whom we contend. There is little you can do to stop me. We are getting quite excited about their arrival. I will personally greet them at our wide gate.

I know I sound like a braggart, but I just can't help it. I'm so good at what I do, and I will do all to keep these typical humans from your realm. I will prevail!

Esul

5

Glimpse of Eternity

A mild winter neared a long-awaited spring. Jalen finally saw graduation in sight while LaRana relished her last junior semester. Friendships grew closer, Jalen with LaRana, and Hannah and Shelly with each other and the church, and most noticeably, Hannah with Isaiah Johnson.

Shortly after noon on a vivid Saturday, they peacefully relaxed on an old, wooden bench at Salarin Lake. A pleasant warm breeze drifted across the water, serving notice spring's enchantment was at the doorstep.

They exchanged friendly greetings with others passing by. Small talk mixed with laughter for nearly an hour till Hannah became silent for several moments. She stared at the gentle, meandering waves with small whitecaps leisurely lapping across the lake. She finally leaned back and brought forth a matter pondered for several weeks.

"Isaiah, each Sunday, I've heard the preacher...and you...talk about baptism. I watched others do it while yet understanding why. I had always written it off as some strange ritual devised by religious folks, but now it's different. I keep thinking about one sentence... among many others...that Jesus said. "He that believes and is baptized shall be saved." I've spent most of my life looking to be saved, partly from a cruel world, but mostly from myself. Why is this baptism thing so important?"

Isaiah scooted to the front of the bench and looked straight at her with eyes deep and alive. His intense aura made obvious his passion for spiritual matters. A warm smile welcomed the question.

"One thing among others embodying our existence is the concept of choice. It's the thing we do most in our lives. Eve was the first to confront it in Eden. As most of us, she made a poor one. Choice can bring joy or sorrow, smiles or tears, life or death. At the beginning, the Creator breathed into Adam, and he became a living soul, not a temporary fleshly entity, but a living, eternal soul. This shell we call a body will someday be gone, but our soul will not. It will return to the spiritual realm of God where we will give an account of our life here.

Since He created us as spiritually eternal beings, He and Satan have wrestled for the souls of mortals, for yours and mine. Be assured that even now, they are locked in battle for our eternal destiny. While God's authority was mighty, Satan had a strong grasp on the power of death. God chose Jesus to be the One to break that grasp. In much the same manner as He ascended from the dead, we also can…not the physical body, but the eternal spiritual entity within us."

"That has puzzled me. Why a need for Jesus? Surely, if God has power to create all this, He could find something, or someone, else."

"That once had me scratching my head. God wanted us to know how much He loved us, His prized creation. Just think for a moment. What is most precious to you?"

"That's easy. LaRana."

"Indeed, and well said. Could you give her up to die for anybody you can think of?"

"No way. Not a chance."

"Now, think of God. Though all-powerful, He has feelings and emotions just as we do. He sacrificed His only created Son for all of us, whether good or evil, regardless of physical or cultural differences. Can love get any greater than that?"

"No, I guess not. I doubt any human could do the same."

"After great suffering, Jesus willingly died on the cross for the sins of the world, past, present, and future. This was His primary purpose. He was entombed but rose thus overcoming the destroyer's hold on death. That one simple step from the tomb, no more than an instant in the vastness of time, is the greatest dividing line in the history of the universe. Before that step there was only death, a spiritual death, a potential eternity of misery. After that step there was life, spiritual life, a potential eternity of bliss. The water in a baptistry, a pool, or even this lake symbolizes the tomb of Christ. As he entered His tomb, we enter ours. As he stepped from His tomb to a peaceful eternal existence, we step from ours to a peaceful eternal existence assuming we follow His precepts and keep Him first."

"I guess I think too much from the reality around me. LaRana and I live day by day. I'm struggling to grasp the concept of a spiritual eternity. Tomorrow is about as far as my mind allows me to think. Yet it all sounds so…right and beautiful. I just needed to hear it again…from you."

"We all ponder about tomorrow, what we should do, where we are going, all the things that occupy our lives. But a day will come for all of us when there will be no tomorrow, at least in this realm. Just as we prepare for winter or retirement, we also prepare for the day of no tomorrow, the day when we change realms. The only question remaining is in which realm will our soul reside? Remember when He created us in His image? That certainly includes making us eternal beings just as He is. He doesn't force us to either eternal realm. He allows us to choose. Without doubt, the vast majority of us humans choose Satan's realm. When you decide to become my sister in Christ, just let me know. I can't think of anything that would thrill me more."

Hannah gently leaned back, gazing at the lake. The bright sun and gentle breeze sent twinkling diamonds dancing across the surface. Thoughts of the past mingled with those of the present. She glanced at Isaiah, envisioning an opening door but unsure how to pass through, or even if she should.

"Thank you. I'm still sorting things out. Since we began going to church, LaRana seems less moody and more settled…for lack of a better word. She is beginning to feel the pain and sorrow of others. After Willow's tragedy last fall, she has spent a lot of time thinking. You and others have opened up a whole new concept of caring, of love. To say the least, you all have been quite a shock to our perception of life."

Isaiah nodded with a genial smile. "Now there you go! Can't get anything by you! You're already getting the picture!"

"Say now! Speaking of pictures! When do I get to see the pics you took on our trip to Shadow Rock Gardens?"

"Well, let me think for a moment. Hmm, well how about… tonight? We'll have an evening at the movies, as it were. I'll pop some corn and make a pitcher of my famous sweet tea."

"Pop some corn? Pop some corn? Mercy sakes! You make your famous tea, and I will bring the food. Pop some corn indeed. Well, maybe after you try my beef tip stew."

"I can hardly wait. There may be other things we can talk about."

Hannah looked longingly into Isaiah's eyes then softly spoke. "Now what other things could they be?"

"Oh, I don't know. I'll think of something."

They shared a hearty laugh then rose and strode arm in arm down the sunlit path. They frequently exchanged glances with words unspoken, revealing an inner connection shedding light on Shelly's precarious past, a past where the stranglehold of failure once stubborn, now gradually began to weaken.

Dark thoughts and deep regret of callous mistakes slowly gave way to welcome hopes for better days to come. Her life, once consumed by the coarse and selfish, now discovered the giving and caring. She deemed the difference immeasurable, especially for LaRana.

The pleasant evening spent with Isaiah brought both enjoyment and deep thought. Isaiah couldn't get enough of the beef stew. Between the two, only a little remained for LaRana.

With night quickly aging, Hannah took Isaiah's hand. "Thank you for the good evening. Your sweet tea was great."

"Well, I could say a lot for your beef tip stew, but the fact it's nearly all gone speaks for itself. It was delicious. Tell LaRana I'm sorry I got a little greedy."

"I will. And… I will strongly think of your, ah, intriguing vision of our future."

"I surely hope so. I don't want to think about not being with you."

With dishes done and hugs exchanged, she gently eased her hand from Isaiah's. Thoughts gently swirled while ushering the Escort toward home. She began to grasp the possibility of a relationship once pictured when a dreamy-eyed teenager but lost in the agonizing ordeal with Allon. Pestering thoughts still haunted. Would Isaiah take a similar path as Allon? Would bricks of trust so neatly stacked come crumbling down? Would LaRana accept a new environment? Could sufficient attention be given to both? A host of thoughts, some of joy and some of dread swirled in her mind and heart. She decided to quickly strive toward desired events.

She quietly entered the house, still glowing from the evening's pleasant moments. LaRana sat at the kitchen table, deep in thought with her usual tapping pencil, trying to finish a difficult English assignment.

"Well, did you have a good evening with Isaiah, oops… I mean Mr. Johnson?"

"Oh, ha, ha. It went…well…okay."

"Okay? Merely…okay? I try not to read other people's thoughts very often, but you seem to be spending more time with…uh, Mr. Johnson. Could you, just maybe, be having a thought…that I, just maybe, should be aware of?"

"Oh, LaRana. Don't be silly. We enjoy each other's company and that's all. He is just…nice to be around."

"Hmmm. Okey dokey. Just wondering," replied LaRana, slightly raising a brow.

They shared a laugh and spent what little remained of the evening working on LaRana's assignment. At nearly eleven thirty, Hannah pronounced the session finished and time to close the day. With a quick hug and good night kiss, LaRana headed for her room while Hannah finished washing the few dishes remaining.

With all now quiet, Hannah restlessly lay in bed, staring at the ceiling. Spinning thoughts kept eyes open. Hopes and desires, long ago sent to the archives of youthful memories, were resurrected. Could she once again open her heart? Isaiah was real, a man in whom she could trust. She welcomed the vision of an oft-desired home life for herself and LaRana. Such a notion hadn't entered her thoughts for many years. At 1:30 a.m., she was still weighing pluses and minuses in the possible turn in life. She fretted she might be doting on the pluses while neglecting the minuses. With no solution reached, she finally drifted off to sleep.

A spectacular Sunday sunrise sent glorious rays streaming through the window. Hannah stepped to the porch to behold the new day. The southern breeze came no more than a whisper. Birds sang incessantly as if in competition. Billowy clouds softly rested beneath a brilliant blue sky. For years, she could see only one path, one fraught with danger. Now, two paths were visible, one familiar, one unknown yet inviting.

Midmorning was cool but sunny. With pressing thoughts whirling, she herded the old car toward the church building. LaRana talked often, but Hannah had little to say. LaRana finally noticed her thoughts were elsewhere. Memories of past moments of silence came to mind, stinging memories of new unwanted circumstances life continually wrought. She couldn't help but remember tough situations when Hannah had something heavy on her mind. None of those worked out very well.

"Anything wrong, Mom? You're sure quiet and spooky this morning."

"Oh, no, no. I'm just thinking about…about…a very important matter, one that's been on my mind lately. Let's just say my vision has gained considerable clarity the past few weeks."

"What do you mean?"

"Oh, you'll see…maybe."

"Well, it must be quite a secret. I also find it odd these… matters…pop up after an evening with Mr. Johnson. I'm itching with curiosity about this…matter. I must say, you have me in deep suspense."

Hannah parked in the crowded lot. Her eyes lit up when Isaiah strode down the sidewalk. He paused when they waved and headed his way. Hannah felt the pull of two forces—one desiring a sought-for step forward, and one a reluctant step back to the closet of misery.

"Now, isn't my timing impeccable? May I possibly escort you two lovely ladies this fair morning?"

"We would consider that a pleasure," said Hannah with a radiant smile.

Isaiah leaned over and spoke lowly. "And I sure look forward to popping the question."

LaRana froze in her tracks. *Popping the question? Popping the question! Oh, my, she's surely not going to get married, not...today...not here...in front of everybody!*

LaRana paused then briskly caught up and walked close behind her mother who now stepped spritely, hooking her arm into Isaiah's. Never had she seen her so cheerful. Possible reasons flooded her mind. She began putting pieces together, and all added up to one likely conclusion.

Something is going to happen between these two this morning. She must be getting married...but it can't be getting married. But...maybe it can. No...it can't be. She would have told me. I just know she would have told me... I think.

When they opened the door, Amelia, Ashlynn, Bridgette, Katelyn, and Jessica, the Fab Five so decreed by LaRana, ambushed her with wide eyes and usual smiles. A new girl was with them, tall and slender with long, lightly colored hair.

"LaRana, this is Cheyenne. She just moved here last week. Cheyenne, LaRana."

"Glad to meet you, Cheyenne."

"Same here."

They headed for class with the girls talking ninety miles an hour. LaRana glanced back, watching Hannah and Isaiah walk down the hall. They were close, real close. It was obvious something was afoot. She wanted to follow them on the sly to find out what was going on, but zealous friends tugged her arm. Between the girls, her mother and Isaiah, she surmised a lot of something was going on.

Bridgette shuffled around Ashlynn. "Hey, LaRana, Cheyenne's a good singer, and she came up with a rad idea. She thought it would be cool to have a concert here. Mr. Cook said it could be done. We could advertise it, maybe open it up to the community. The dudes could help us…if we pound on 'em enough. What do you think?"

"I think it would really be neat, but I'm not sure about me. I've never been a part of a concert. I might freak out."

Jessica flipped her hand. "Ah, with your cool voice, you'd sound good even if you shook in your shoes."

"So you in?" queried Katelyn.

"Well, uh, yeah, I guess so, if I can hide behind somebody."

"Too bad, I done got that place. We thought you'd dig it," said Amelia. "We want to start practice as soon as we get everybody on board."

"Okay. I'll, uh, be there when I can."

"Sweet," exclaimed Bridgette. "Now all we have to do is convince the guys. That alone could be a monumental task."

The girls chatted excitedly as they headed for class with LaRana quietly bringing up the rear. Ashlynn paused till LaRana caught up.

"I've sorta been watching you at school. You seem to have some fine motor skills. Would you like to come to the archery range and give it a go? I would love to see you bend a bow."

"Well, I…uh…maybe. I haven't held a bow since I was about five. One of our neighbors had this little bow with these cute little arrows that…well… I…uh… I actually haven't shot a real bow."

"Wanna give it a go some day?"

"Sure, why not, as long as you promise not to laugh."

"I promise. I bet you'll do better than you think. I see a touch of fire in your eyes. I'll get with you on a day we both can go."

"I'm game, I guess. Thanks for the invite."

With fist-bumps exchanged, Ashlynn sped up to the other girls. LaRana shrugged her shoulders and put the concert and archery invitation on the back burner. Curiosity of her mother's strange behavior returned. She tried to think what was going on but only one came answer to mind.

She's getting married. I know she's getting married, and she wouldn't tell me.

Bible classes slowly passed, allowing time for LaRana's anxiety to grow on what big event was about to unfold, if there was a big event. Comments from the discussion leader and her classmates were half heard, pushed out by thoughts of a coming change. Would it be for the better or worse? She struggled to think better when worse is all she ever knew.

The singing was uplifting as usual. The preacher stepped quickly to the podium as usual. LaRana glanced at Hannah whose face was stoic yet beaming at the same time. Isaiah snuggly held her hand.

Now, I'm completely baffled. I've never seen her like this. I bet the preacher is going to make an announcement about Mom and Isaiah.

The preacher followed his customary routine, no announcement and no surprises. The sermon was short and thought provoking but seemed an eternity to LaRana. Anticipation piqued, but nothing out of the ordinary ensued. Suddenly, as he gave his usual invitation, Hannah put her hand on LaRana's arm and warmly smiled.

"I love you."

She stepped into the aisle with Isaiah right behind her. They proudly walked to the front then turned and stood together, eye to eye, hand in hand. LaRana froze, her mouth agape.

"Oh, my goodness, my goodness, my goodness. They are getting married. Oh, my goodness. Why didn't she tell me? She said she would, but here she is! Just as big as all outdoors!"

As the congregation sat down, Isaiah stood with Hannah at his side.

"Hannah Lester has come forward this morning to put on the Lord in baptism. We all have grown to dearly love both she and LaRana. There is no greater decision to be made than that of becoming a child of God."

He turned and gazed directly into beaming eyes. "Hannah, do you believe Jesus Christ is the Son of God?"

"I do, I surely do."

"Great! I never tire of hearing that."

He motioned for a lady who took Hannah toward a room adjoining the baptistry. LaRana was shocked. She sat mesmerized, trying to balance a solid sense of pride with mixed thoughts on peculiar rituals. A glance around the auditorium found beaming faces and unknown whispers. She managed a forced grin and sat as quiet as possible. Ashlynn and Amelia smiled and gave her a gentle pat on the back. She returned a slight grin then cringed back into the seat.

Why is she doing this? This is a great place and all, but this baptism stuff is just plain weird. This could be embarrassing. At least she's not getting married without telling me.

As a cheerful song came to an end, Hannah appeared in the baptistry with Isaiah. The crowd grew deathly silent. The only sound LaRana could hear was the thundering beat of her own heart. Isaiah broke the stillness.

"Hannah, I baptize you in the name of Jesus Christ for the remission of sins."

As she went under the water, LaRana's breath hitched. Her eyes widened. When Hannah came up, she exchanged a long embrace with Isaiah while a deafening roar came from the crowd. LaRana recalled previous baptisms, but this time the crowd seemed much louder. Excitement was infectious with singing breaking out from wall to wall, unrestrained, joyful voices from faces aglow. The music swirled around the auditorium as if directed by angels. Though still somewhat mystified, she had an odd tinge of delight. She wanted to both jump for joy and crawl under the seat.

Several minutes passed before Hannah returned. She gleefully motioned LaRana to her side. LaRana sheepishly pointed to herself then whispered, "Me"? Her mother motioned several times with a little more animation before LaRana moved. She meekly inched by people who gladly let her pass. When she reached the front, Hannah put an arm around her shoulders and pointed to her eyes.

"Vision."

LaRana half-heartedly smiled then kept it for the people who shook her hand and hugged her as well as her mother. She peeked around those near and discovered many more patiently waiting their turn.

Oh my goodness! We're gonna be here forever!

An elderly lady with a walking cane inched forward, stopping by LaRana. "Isn't this wonderful! Your mother is such a nice lady. Oh, I do hope to see you follow her."

"Thanks, I, uh, I, uh, I am, uh…thanks."

Though unable to grasp all that was happening, LaRana saw her mother as never before. She was graciously happy, ecstatic even. Hugs and handshakes came from all, black, Hispanic, white, Native American. It didn't matter. It was like a barrier had been torn down, a blight of evil shattered by the light of good. She finally relaxed and soaked in the joy coming to her mother, seeing a dark door closing and another, brilliantly lit, opening for a glimpse of a future still eluding her comprehension.

With the last handshake, congratulations came to an end. Isaiah turned to Hannah and embraced her for what seemed quite lengthy to LaRana.

Now that's a long hug.

Thoughts were frightened mice running in all directions. She wasn't sure how to take all her eyes beheld. Conflicting environments and peculiar concepts wrestled for her favor. The distance between her two worlds had never been so wide.

The street held many consequences to decisions. She knew most of them.

The church was an enigma of emotions, of belief in the unseen, of actions strange to the reality of life. She struggled with most of them.

With congratulations finally coming to an end, the elated crowd slowly dispersed. Hannah stood with Isaiah while Shelly and Jalen waited near the door. After a round of final hugs, they headed for the parking lot. Hannah stepped much livelier than usual. A smile remained, a smile lighting her face. After watching Jalen's Jeep speeding away, LaRana ran to catch up with her mother and Isaiah. They exchanged few words, but the glint in Hannah's eyes spoke volumes.

Isaiah gave the new convert a final hug. He soon gained his car and drove away. Silence returned as Hannah and LaRana shut the doors to their ancient chariot. LaRana leaned back with a slight sigh, searching for words. Her uncertainty didn't go unnoticed.

"You seem a little unsure. Were you disappointed in what I did today?"

"Oh, no, Mom, no," came the muted answer with a slight touch of a fib. "It's uh…well… I mean…it seems like an odd thing to do.

We've seen others doing it, but I never believed you...uh...would. What's the big deal about baptism? I thought it was just a ritual the weird...uh... I mean, unusual Jesus people did. You know, kinda freaky."

"Do you think I'm crazy?"

"If being happy is crazy, then you were a raving lunatic. I have never seen you so loony... I mean happy. And all the other people there, you'd think they were meeting someone famous, not...that you're not...famous...with me, but it didn't seem to be a put-on. They seemed really thrilled, even hugging me! Wow! For a minute, I thought maybe I ought to jump in the water since you did."

"Keep your ears and heart open to what we're learning here. The time will come when you, and only you, will face the same choice I did. And you, and only you, must decide for yourself. It's odd how we hear something over and over but not grasp it. Be patient. You are growing. A time will come when your vision will be clear. The demons of doubt will nag and try to muddy what is real. Be ready for them. And remember, if and when you have any questions, I'm always here for you."

LaRana spoke little more as the worn vehicle puttered down the road. Thoughts on where reality ends and fantasy begins raced in all directions. Both blurred. Which was which?

Try as she might, she could not sort them out.

*****

Willow's demise left Jackknife sifting through a host of available girls, Sarona among them. A warm, Monday night found them cruising the strip, stopping twice for six-packs of cold beer. Jackknife was on the edge, gulping one after another.

"Hey, sure you don't want any more?"

"No, a couple is enough for me. Think maybe you've had enough?"

"Not a chance! I'm just getting to feel good. Give me the last can. I might stop for a few more. Probably smart you stop at two. You may need to drive."

Nearing midnight, he stopped again. He slightly tripped exiting his pickup. With awkward steps, he entered the convenience store, seeking another half-dozen. The store clerk, seeing his impaired condition, questioned the request, encouraging him to go home and sleep it off.

"Look, clown! I want a six-pack! Don't give me any lip!"

"Sorry, sir, I can't do that. You've had enough. You need to leave."

With angry, uncertain steps, he stomped back to the pickup. "That stupid clown! Questioning me! Questioning me! Telling me to leave! I'll show that bozo! He doesn't know who he's messing with!"

He reached under the seat, grasping a pistol, elastic headband, and a cloth sack. Sarona gasped. "Jackknife! What are you doing? Let's go! Let him be! Let's get out here! I want to go home!"

"No way, doll! Sit tight! I'll be back!"

With mask in place, he checked the pistol then staggered to the entry. Slightly tripping, he flung the door open. With two swift steps, he reached the counter, shoving the gun in the clerk's face.

"Okay, punk! I think you wanna gimme my six-pack!"

The clerk's eyes widened. With fear written on his face, he hustled to the cooler and returned as quickly as possible.

"Now, that's more like it. Open the register, clean out all the green, and stuff it in this nice little bag! I ain't gonna say it twice!"

The frightened clerk nervously gathered the cash, swiftly bagged it, and jumped back. Jackknife roughly grasped the take then tilted the gun to the clerk's right and fired, shattering the glass.

"Just lettin' ya know, dummy. If I see any fuzz, I'll be back! I won't miss the next time!"

Jackknife kicked the door open, stumbled to the pickup and tossed the bag on the seat. Sarona froze. Her face flushed with fear. She couldn't manage a word.

"He won't question me again! Hang on, babe, we gotta get outta here."

He slammed the pedal down, tires squealed as he left the lot and sped down the highway till disappearing down a dark side road. Sarona tried to be calm. Her heart raced. She glanced at Jackknife desperately wanting to go home. He slowed then stopped.

"What do ya think, babe? We got a pretty good haul." He suddenly became quiet then glared below a furrowed brow. "Be sure, sweet cheeks, be 'dead' sure you don't say anything to anybody. I wouldn't want to visit your house. Got it?"

Looking into piercing eyes, Sarona gulped. "Yes, uh, uh, okay, okay!"

"Good. I think we understand each other."

Jackknife eased down back roads then stopped three blocks behind Sarona's house. She quickly got out and promptly headed for home. Jackknife waved his gun outside the window.

"Remember! No one!"

Her heart pounded, she hastily nodded before turning to a little-used gravel trail. She silently disappeared into the darkness, quickening her steps. Panting hard, she arrived home, quietly opened the door and stepped in. Her heartbeat was a pounding drum. She swiftly shut the door. Feeling weak and trembling, she leaned against it, gasping for breath. Thoughts and scenarios swirled. Questions raced everywhere. Would he really kill her, kill her mom, or burn the house? Gathering as much composure as possible, she reluctantly went to the front room.

"Oh, bout time you got home. I was beginning to get concerned and a little angry. Everything okay?"

"Yeah, uh, yeah, everything's okay. Our ride was just a little longer than we thought. Uh, I'm bushed. I think I'll head for bed."

"Well, me to, now that your finally home. Listen, Sarona, I'm guessin' your still hanging out with bad company. If it don't stop, I'm gonna ground you for a long spell. We'll talk about it later. Now, get your fanny in bed!"

Sarona hurried to her room, shut the door, and plopped on the mattress. Tears desperately held now freely spilled. She quickly rose, frantically paced the room before collapsing on the bed only to rise and pace again. The past hour was a blur. She thought hard on the ordeal. Questions came and went. None were answered.

The morning sun rose to reddened eyes. Sarona slept little, wondering what the day would bring. She began doing menial chores:

cleaning a drawer, restacking quilts, anything to stay in the bedroom. Finally, the dreaded beckoning came loud and clear.

"Hey, you gonna sleep all day? Better git in here! Breakfast is on the table! You can do what you want with it!"

Sarona slowly came in and sat down. Her mother began washing dishes piled up from two days neglect. Sarona nervously nibbled at the food, leaving most uneaten. It didn't go unnoticed.

"What's with you this mornin'? Breakfast is usually your best meal. Oh, well, eat it or leave it. Don't make no difference to me."

"Sorry, Mom. I don't have much of an appetite."

"If you want somethin' else, you know where it is. I'm gonna catch the news."

Sarona toyed with the food, still trying to grasp what happened the night before. A crime committed, a robber, a shot fired, an unwitting accomplice, a steely threat, and a cloak of fear. What now? She gently pushed the bowl away.

"Sarona! Quick, git in here! Look at this!"

Sarona froze, guessing the reason for the urgent demand. Reluctantly, she stood well behind her mom as the newscaster spoke of the robbery. Her breath barely came.

'Surveillance shows the suspect racing from the convenience store on Dalton Avenue. He rushes to a red pickup with a possible accomplice in the seat. Close up shows what looks to be a young woman. The camera caught the pickup leaving at an angle to see all but the last two numbers of the license plate. Anyone having information about this crime should contact the local authorities. Now for the weather…'

"Sarona, didn't you get into a red pickup sorta like that last night?"

"Yes, Mom, but there's a lot of red pickups. It could have been anybody."

"Well, you better not be that anybody! Ain't sure how I could handle that!"

Sarona stayed in her room till midafternoon, pondering what to do. Options raced. None stayed. Shortly before three thirty a patrol car arrived. Sarona panicked, quickly leaning against a wall. A peek out the window found two policemen at the door.

She entertained running then lying but had confidence in neither. She sat on the bed's edge, waiting for the inevitable.

Sarona's mother took a deep breath and opened it. "What do you want?"

"Mrs. Audrey Jantzen?"

"Yeah, that's me."

"Is your daughter here?"

"Yeah."

"Could we see her, please?"

"Sarona! Cops here to see you! Better not be what I think it is!"

Sarona wiped away the last tear before coming to the door. "I'm Sarona."

"Do you know a Jackson Wells?"

"Uh, yes."

"Were you in his pickup last night?"

Sarona looked down then to her mother before loudly blurting, "Yes, but I didn't do anything! I was just riding in the pickup! I didn't know what he was going to do!"

"Sarona! What have you done? It was you! Why? Of all…"

"Mom, I'm sorry, but I really didn't do anything. Jackknife…"

"Mrs. Jantzen, we need to take your daughter to the station. You may come with us or on your own."

"I'll follow you."

"Mom…"

"Just shut up! Shut up! Don't talk to me! Go on with them!"

*****

Frequent showers and warmer air ushered in spring's beauty. LaRana spent considerable time volunteering after school at the local Girl Scout unit. She worked diligently, helping with programs and special events, even organizing a cookie baking and singing at the Pallon Ridge Rest Home with the Fab Five now becoming the Super Six with Cheyenne. She marveled how chatting for but a few minutes lifted the residents' spirits. A new sense of self-worth blossomed. She began to grasp the concept of doing right and doing her best. She heartily pursued those values with relentless effort and tireless hours.

But not today.

On a quiet Saturday afternoon, the moving sound of folk-rock music mixed with a touch of country held her attention. LaRana fluffed a pillow, stretched out on the well-worn couch, ready for a desired rest. She turned down the volume, nestled the pillow, and shut her eyes. With the sun slowly dropping in the west and six hours till Hannah came home, LaRana melted into a teenager's crash time. Comfortably snuggled under a warm throw, she drifted off.

Brrring.

Her eyes flew open. She glared at the interrupter. "Ah! Give me a break. Who can this be?"

She shut off the music and reluctantly reached for the cell but fumbled it to the floor. Grousing, she scrambled from the couch, recovered it then plopped back into the cushions. The voice on the other end was weak and broken.

"Sarona?"

A pause. She slowly rose and paced. A wrinkled brow rested over widening eyes.

"Sure…yes. Uh, I guess now is okay. Come on over."

Click. Silence. She stared at the phone; curious thoughts raced. "Hmm. Now that was really weird. She sounded like her world ended. I wonder what's bugging her? Well, so much for a peaceful evening."

Since Willow's tragedy, she spent little time with Sarona and Janene. Reasons for the call raced into mind but just as quickly left. Nearly thirty minutes passed till footsteps hit the porch. Still puzzled, LaRana hurried across the floor. The door barely opened when she was immediately embraced. Finally released, she stepped back. Sarona was noticeably nervous, her face full of despair. She tried to manufacture a smile, only to fail. She took three steps into the room then spun back to LaRana who barely shut the door.

"I'm in a bad situation! I don't know what to do! I made a really stupid mistake."

"Uh, how?"

"I cruised with Jackknife several days ago. All was cool till he got crazy drunk. He lost it trying to get a stupid beer at a convenience store. He robbed it and fired a shot. I was scared nearly senseless. To make it short, he was arrested and charged with armed robbery. The fuzz took me in as an accomplice, but Jackknife convinced them I wasn't involved. I got a little lucky. No jail for now, but I can't leave Pallon Ridge, I guess till the hearing at least."

"Wow! What was your Mom's reaction?"

"That's mainly the reason I called you. She's kicking me out. Said I was an adult, and she wasn't having a no-good daughter in her house. She gave me time to pack up and find somewhere else to live. I was, uh, hoping I could stay with you till I find a place."

"Only my mom can answer that. If for some reason you can't stay here, how are you going to find a place or even pay for it if you do?"

"I'll quit school then find a job of…some kind. Washing dishes, cleaning houses, working on a farm, whatever."

"You can't quit school! You just have a few months!"

"I don't see much of a choice. I messed up. Now, it's time to grow up."

"I'll ask Mom when she comes home. She's really creative at solving problems."

Sarona again wrapped arms around LaRana. "Oh, thank you! I knew I could count on you!"

LaRana patted her back with eyes finding the ceiling. *Oh my, what have I gotten myself into now?*

*****

Hannah came home at 11:30 p.m., looking forward to the bed as usual. Entering the family room, she found LaRana asleep on the couch. She shook her shoulder. LaRana twitched.

"What are doing sleeping on the couch? Boogeyman scare you?"

LaRana rubbed her eyes, quickly rising with a yawn. "Mom! Oh, glad you're home. I know it's late, but I couldn't wait till morning. I, uh, may ruin your day…again. A senior girl at school was involved in a crime situation. You remember the incident at the convenience store Monday? She was the one waiting in the pickup. She says she didn't do anything wrong…stupid, for sure, but not wrong. She's on probation or something like that. She came here and dropped a bomb. Her mother's booting her out of the house, giving her some time to find another place to live. She asked if she could stay here. I didn't know what to tell her, only that I would try to help. I thought you might know somewhere she could stay, at least till graduation."

"Well now, you do have some edgy acquaintances. What's her name?"

"Sarona Jantzen."

"Do you believe her?"

"For some reason, yes. She's made a lot of bad decisions, but I think there's some good inside. Wishful thinking? Maybe, but this could be the turning point in her life, one way or another. Is there any way she could stay here?"

"Well, I would like to say yes, but our rental agreement states no one but family can live here. I would ask the landlord if a few days would be okay, but that's about as good as we could do."

"Well, I fear she'll get mixed up with, uh, people who might take advantage of her. If we can't help her, well then, we just can't. I was just hoping we could help her solve the dilemma so she could graduate."

"Now hold on just a minute. Give me time to think. Midnight after work is not my best time. Let's sleep on it."

"Thanks, Mom. I didn't know where else to go."

"That's okay. Your heart is in the right place. I'll do my best, but no promises."

*****

Jalen helped LaRana over a small stream meandering down gentle slopes overseen by Talova Peak. The final traces of winter's snow pack gathered in bubbling rivulets racing to the lake below. A mountain shower quickly came and just as quickly left, leaving pleasantly fresh air. Spring flowers peeked through warming soil. A red squirrel dashed to the lower limb of a young tree then sat, twitching its tail, barking his annoyance at the intrusion.

"The air is cool. I should have had you bring a sweater," said Jalen, kicking a glob of mud from his shoe.

LaRana took a long sniff. "Cool, yes, and it has a nice aroma of pine and spruce. It seems so clean up here."

"That's for sure. I'd guess we're somewhere around 8,400 feet in altitude. The views of Pallon Ridge and beyond are great sights, and they only get better as we get higher. Hey, I've got an idea! Let's scale the peak. It's early afternoon, and it's not very difficult if we're careful. I've been on it several times. What do you think?"

"Are you sure? It looks pretty steep to me."

"Ah, we can make it. It's about forty, maybe fifty, minutes from here. But I guess being a girl, you might struggle to peak it."

Wham! LaRana's hands quickly hit her hips just long enough for one to be raised with a pointing finger. "Oh, yeah! Bring it on, buster. Being a girl! Being a girl! Ah, you sure can be aggravating at times."

Jalen laughed, grasped her hand, and bowed. "Atta girl! Let's go. I dare say, fair lass, you got this!"

Trees all but disappeared near 9,000 feet, and the trail turned noticeably upward, growing rougher with each switchback. The bald peak sat as the region's sentry at 9,323 feet.

LaRana's body grew heavy, but she kept plodding behind Jalen. Finally, with a deep groan, she paused and plopped down on a flat boulder. She leaned back, slowly stretching weary legs.

"Let me catch a breath. This is almost like work if it wasn't so beautiful up here."

Jalen sat next to her. "The higher we go, the thinner the air, the harder to breathe. Scaling the high peaks takes some acclamation. Just relax. We have enough time."

"Wow! We seem to be running out of…real estate," said LaRana. "It's like the sky is creeping in around us."

"There's isn't much room on the peak, but you'll get used to it…gradually."

"Thanks a lot. That's not very consoling."

A gentle but brief shower fell from scattered clouds slowly moving across the sky. A slight mist settled on the rocky trail, making it noticeably slicker. After several minutes of small talk and admiration of views, they resumed the trek upward. Jalen coached LaRana as she took the lead for the last hundred feet. She lowered to all four for the final rise. Trying to find a solid footing, she dislodged a sizeable rock, sending it tumbling by Jalen who swayed to the side.

"Oops! Sorry. You okay?"

"Yeah. However, one is enough if you don't mind."

With a turn around a large, embedded formation, they arrived at the top. Several moments passed till breathing slowly returned to normal.

"That wasn't too bad," said LaRana, sitting near the rim. "I think I could get used to this."

Jalen sat next to her. "Just as long as you're not the one dodging the boulders."

LaRana laughed and slapped his arm. "If Mom could only see me now. Well…it's probably better she can't. Wow, it sure is cool up here, isn't it?"

"Yeah, it's really a mind opener."

"No, I mean it's really, really cool, you know, like…colder."

"Oh, okay. I guess you're right."

He scooted near and gently put an arm around her shoulders. She nestled against his chest. "Hmm, that's much better. We're really high up. It's like we need to duck to avoid bumping the sky. I wonder how far we can see?"

"A very long way for sure."

"Hey, I just remembered something! When I was very young, Mom bought this neat little book showing two people going up a mountain to see the sunset. It was so cute. I recall thinking about being the girl in the book. And ta da, here I am."

The thinning clouds gently drifted away, leaving the sun to resume command of the sky. Two bald eagles soared high above then swooped toward the forest below. Their speed and grace spoke of nobility.

"Such majestic birds. I never tire of watching them." Jalen suddenly pointed to their left. "LaRana, look over there…a double rainbow!"

"Wow! That's beautiful, breathtaking. Think it's an omen or something? Uh, you know, like…two together…side by side in perfect harmony. Hey, I just remembered something else! That book also had a double rainbow! Two people going up a mountain and seeing a double rainbow! What a coincidence! Perchance an omen, dear chap?"

"I don't know. Maybe we should make it an omen. Tis altogether within reason, my lady, that just for us God has sent it. I fail to perceive any bloke nigh to say it isn't."

"Done, sire," declared LaRana emphatically. "Tis our rainbow. And…it does beg the question why? Maybe, just maybe, time will tell."

Jalen gave LaRana an extra hug. She melted in his arms. Both past and future seemed far in the distance. Time paused to savor the moment. The peace and beauty of the panoramic scene filled her senses. Jalen broke the calm with pointing fingers.

"This is quite a view. Look, there's the school. It's quite small from here. And over there is Salarin Lake resting like a dazzling diamond. Behind us is the national forest. It seems to run into the sky. The scenes here are good, but there are some peaks that rise well above Talova. The peaks going above 14,000 feet are really breathtaking, visually and literally. They're called, uh, duh, fourteeners. One of these days, we need to go to Uncompahgre Peak. It's a little over 14,300 feet. The trek to the top is nothing short of glorious. An early June to mid-July climb finds the wild columbine in full bloom, gracefully nestled around boulders and trickling streams. A sweeter aroma does not exist. Pleasant intoxication, I call it. Marmots and chipmunks scurry over the ground, at times pausing to check out intruders. Quite often, majestic elk herds graze the high meadows near timberline. Standing on the peak is breathtaking in more ways than one. Words fall short to describe the incredible views."

"Sounds exciting, romantic even. Just a minute, sire. I believe you did say 14,000 feet? You got to be kidding! How about taking a helicopter, or maybe a balloon?"

"Do I detect a trace of trepidation in my bonnie lass? Tis not like thee. Perchance you may with doubt be overcome?"

LaRana leaned back and stared at him for several moments. "Unkind sire, I do believe that in my stamina you have no confidence. But with stark honesty, I would have to give proper thought afore offering consent. However, I do surmise such an astonishing sight would it be."

"Indeed it is, among many adjectives. And when we get down, we'll zoom over to Mt. Elbert. It's over a hundred feet taller than Uncompahgre. It's the tallest in the entire Rocky Mountains of North America. If Uncompahgre rests on the top floor, Elbert is in the attic. We don't duck the sky. We're one with it. Standing on the peaks, it's nigh impossible not to believe in God. No one stands alone on those regal sentinels. And speaking of God, what do you make of all the things we're learning at church?"

"Well, I've seen a greater happiness in both of our mothers. Mom seems more content since her baptism. I've seen more smiles cross her face recently than in several years. She just beams at life. I'm still trying to find out how a dunk in water can change a person so much. I see her a little less these days since Mr. Johnson entered the picture. He's been a Godsend, so to speak. She seems ten years younger. What about you?"

"I'm still trying to put all the pieces together. Though my dad is still a selfish jerk, Mom seems to cope with it better, even putting an optimistic face on the situation. If God is so great, why can't he put our family back together? If He can create this beautiful view before us, why can't He move one human being? How what isn't seen interacts with what is simply baffles me. Prayer is way above my head, uh, also…so to speak. Yet I have made and renewed some good friendships. Our mothers may have been wise to take us to church after our little adventures."

LaRana slightly smirked then slapped his arm. "Whatever is going on, Mom has changed dramatically. There's a bounce to her step, radiance in her eyes. It's like magic. Isaiah has had a big part in that. She certainly has a thing about him, but I must say, he is a fine man. I'm guessing he would make a good stepfather.

As for me, I'm sorta like you, trying to figure all this out. For several years, I wanted to be just like everybody else, do what everybody else was doing, wear what everybody else wore, talked like everybody else talked, follow the fad, no matter what it was, anything to fit in, to belong. I nearly drove my mother crazy. Being around you and the girls at church has helped me determine to think for myself, to be myself, not some mindless puppet of society. Maybe that's one thing we have in common. We both like to dance to our own music.

My opinion of Jesus people has drastically changed from weird to admirable, from people to avoid to role models to look at. I don't know if all this could happen without a God. I've wondered if this relationship between people would be the same if the setting wasn't a church, not a result of belief in an almighty Creator. And yet, I see a genuine love that appears to have no boundaries. It's kinda like looking from this peak, nothing to mar our vision. Maybe someday, I'll understand. For now, the ride has been good, especially for Mom."

"Maybe our vision will be even better on Mt. Elbert," declared Jalen.

"I'd absolutely love it… I think. But don't get any notions on Everest. I got no hankerin' for it. By the way, how does it feel to be a short-timer in high school? What are your plans for the summer?"

Jalen turned his eyes to LaRana. "I'll miss high school a little, classmates and teachers. However, I'll especially miss it for the fact you will be there without me around for protection. You, I will miss a lot. I'm still hopeful for a baseball scholarship. It all depends on what I do the rest of the spring and early summer. Time is running short. I would like to play for State. I heard they might have scholarships yet available. I believe, or at least hope, the door is still open."

"Somehow, I know things will work out good for you. I've heard quite a bit about college life, and I also know there are a lot of pretty girls at State. I've been thinking how to keep your full attention on books and baseball and away from other…more…enticing distractions."

"Well, I could say that you might find some dudes next year while I'm slaving away over books. Maybe if you took up the bassoon, you might have less time to check out the guys."

LaRana pulled back then smacked his arm.

"You're impossible. For some reason, I feel good being around you. Beats me why. All you have on your mind is baseball, which, now that I think about it, may not be a bad thing."

They shared laughs with tender moments then took their fill of nature's marvels. LaRana leaned on Jalen with a slight shiver. Jalen gently stroked her shoulders. "Oh, while we're up here, I believe it might be a good time to give you this."

He reached in his pocket and pulled out a brilliant gold necklace holding a heart shaped gold locket with initials JS. "I thought you might need this when I'm absent, like this fall. It automatically repels any bloke trying to make a move on you."

LaRana slowly left his shoulder and stared nearly breathless while softly stroking the gift. "Oh, oh, Jalen! I don't know what… I can't imagine…oh, it's beautiful…it's perfect!"

With eyes beginning to mist, she placed her hand on his neck and quickly kissed him. "Here, put it on, put it on!"

"I would truly be honored, my lady. Tis a pleasure to be of aid to the fairest lass in the entire realm."

"Wow, I've never had anything like this. It's absolutely magnificent. Wherever I go, I will wear this. Tis for certain that on me it will stay. How can I ever thank thee, kind gent?"

"Well, at the current moment, my intellect it does escape, but I, in due time, may something strike upon."

LaRana thinly smiled and slapped his arm. "Let's head down. I can't wait to show this to Mom."

They started the descent as the slight breeze was interrupted by moments of strong gusts. Jalen led her down a difficult slant in the trail not far below the peak. He paused then glanced up when LaRana screamed. Her foot slipped, and she fell over the path's edge, sliding toward an unforgiving drop.

"Jalen! Help!"

Her frantic plea flew to his ears. He desperately grasped and latched onto her wrist. He skidded on loose rocks till finding solid footing.

"Hang on tight! Don't look down!"

She landed her foot on a jutting formation then tried to pull up. Jalen's grasp began to slip, but she managed to set her foot on lightly embedded rocks. She groaned deeply but again tensed when they broke away, plummeting to the vale below. She dangled in thin air for a few moments till Jalen moved her to another small protruding ledge. Her heart nearly burst from her chest. Death, never given a moment's thought, rushed in with open arms. She screamed in stark fear when her feet left the tenuous hold on slippery boulders. Jalen braced against the rim of the path and with all he could gather, gradually pulled her back to firm ground.

LaRana collapsed in his arms, sobbing and shaking. She grasped the necklace with both hands. Jalen was silent. He held her close till trembling gradually ebbed to shallow breathing. A glimpse of eternity drained emotions, bringing a sharp awareness of life's fragile balance.

Silent moments passed till Jalen quietly but gently spoke. "I thought I had lost…"

LaRana suddenly wrapped her arms around his neck, and with tears yet flowing, embraced him as if nothing else mattered. Breath came slow and full. She lay in his arms, staring across the vast expanse.

"I owe my life to you. I don't know what to say that would be enough. You not only have given me a cherished keepsake, but you have given me life itself."

"You don't have to say anything, but prudent 'twould be from this time hence you in advance inform me when you're going to slip."

Tension finally eased. She managed a slight laugh and slapped his arm.

"Would you kindly try the other arm? This one's getting a little sore."

She promptly slapped the other arm.

"What say we keep this incident low key? You know…like… it's our memory, ours alone, a memory I for one will cherish since… well…you're still alive."

"Well now, that's a strangely romantic thought, but I like it. No use in upsetting Mom. She may ban me from mountains."

They shared a laugh with a fist bump.

The descent went without further incident. Reaching timberline then down to an easier trail, they walked hand-in-hand through the quiet forest. LaRana began talking quickly, spending frayed nerves with numerous words. Jalen patiently listened till they arrived at the trailhead. He opened the Jeep's door for LaRana who suddenly paused.

"Um, when do you think we could go to those fourteeners?"

Missives Five

Jariel,

I must say you do appear determined to mount a fervent challenge. I may have taken our quarry for granted, a mind-set I will certainly change. My determination grows stronger when these petty humans find time in their puny lives to listen to your Master. I usually don't have to resort to strenuous measures to collect souls. While most are easy, I may need to get considerably closer for these.

I hate to admit it, but I am severely disappointed Hannah obeyed your Master. It infuriated me to see her so elated. She is getting too far from me. However, as you know, I always spend extra time with those who have chosen to follow Him. As many who are excited at the beginning, she will soon mellow and begin her slide into mediocrity and complacency.

Her journey on the path of righteousness will not be smooth. I will change her assurance to doubt, patience to anxiety, vision of the future from one of bliss to one of regret and misery. A little adversity will reveal her reservation that your Master is real. She will be dedicated at first, but as time passes, she will, at best, become just another average attender. You know how good I am at setting devotion to your Master way down on humans' priority lists. Putting Him first will become a chore too great.

I don't need to spend much effort with those who reject your Master and choose to live for self, or me, however you want to look at it. We have a place reserved for them. Hannah may have taken that first awful step to your realm, but she is still vulnerable. Any bump in the road, or even worse, will indeed plunge her into the chasm of despair and dark days. And it is possible I may have to get to her through LaRana.

We both are keenly aware how precious LaRana is to Hannah. If LaRana fails to grasp the reality of you and me, she will once again plummet into the chasm of doubt and failure. LaRana is beginning to understand the value in helping others, but that is a trait readily seen and felt. Bridging the gap from earthly values to belief in us will keep her in the mire of doubt. Ah, precious doubt…a pinnacle so hard to conquer. LaRana will be no exception. My success with her will crumble Hannah's newfound faith.

Were you a little, or maybe, a lot concerned over LaRana's wonderful misstep on the mountain? I almost had her again. I tried to keep her mind occupied with romantic thoughts, but by mere chance, Jalen had to interfere. She keeps slipping out of my hands, but it is just a matter of time before she is mine.

You do have one who has caused me grief. Isaiah. Escar had a hard battle with an Isaiah long ago before your Master became human. That didn't work out very well, but we have learned much since then, as you so aggravatingly know. This Isaiah is much like the old one, quite stubborn about his allegiance to the Creator. He has resisted us so long we have all but given up on him. That's not to say if he experiences some difficulty with his staunch faith, I won't be there. As I continually roam, I do at times find those who stray just a little from your Master. Much like a bird wandering from its nest.

Sorry to be brief, but I must get to work. I have several circumstances to arrange for these despicable souls.

Esul

*****

Esul,

We sadly watched you again connect evil intent with careless decisions. Sarona's poor judgment is a fitting example. Her future may be highly questionable but not yet determined. We know quite well your persistent efforts to gather anyone with misplaced motives. She may be heading to your realm, but we will not cease to help her find the path to ours.

I can't remember ever hearing you sound so desperate. Watching and listening to Hannah was highly satisfying. It's enthralling to hear our angels rejoicing over her. Such beautiful music they make. She has given great thought to your schemes and found them baseless and vain. You know of what I pen. She will only grow in strength as a follower of the Christ. I know you hate to hear such confidence, but I do so like bringing it to your attention. It almost makes me sad to see you in such a rage. Almost.

I heartened you took notice of our fine servant Isaiah. He's been a thorn in your cohorts' side of for a long time. You have desperately tried to shake his faith, to collect him, but it elates us to see him spurn your efforts. Just think how many he has led away from you to us. And just imagine if Hannah's feeling for Isaiah grows and they unite, what a force they will be. It's good when one partner in a marriage is faithful, but how powerful it is when both are committed to my Lord. I'm certain you spend a lot of fretful time thinking about it.

I thought you might be lurking about, so I helped Jalen keep his thoughts to stay close to LaRana. It's your persistent style to arrange danger. It didn't surprise me you would interfere with their hike up the mountain. I keep hoping to notice a hint of decency in you, but you never seem to entertain it. You most certainly are despicable, but I realize despicable is what you do.

I'm certain you saw Shelly's eyes light up when Hannah came to my Lord? She's getting stronger each day. It's hard to stop the love Shelly and Hannah have developed over a short period of time. It's just what my Master wants for His family. I know you see it. I can envision how incensed you get. You might save your anger for more frustrations ahead. I do like the mind-set and heart-set in these seekers of my Master.

I urge you to give up on these precious souls, but I realize you won't. Get ready for disappointment. And remember, I am always watching.

Jariel

6

A Chasm Widens

A sour mood rode to work with Roland. A heated argument with Shelly and Jalen on the previous evening still lay sour on his mind. Their church activities and Jalen's persistent infatuation with LaRana pushed emotions to the breaking point. For weeks, his job turned from enjoyable and friendly to virtually unbearable. As much as he tried to maintain a cordial atmosphere with co-workers, the four walls of home could not contain family troubles.

Usual jovial interactions had all but disappeared. He struggled to hold his temper while quietly going about his tasks. Mental peace was elusive. In his eyes, each glance from the workbench found co-workers whispering and glimpsing his way. Tension grew with each passing moment.

The cutting torch became a buffer from unwelcome comments. Gossip his son was getting close with a mixed-race girl was making the rounds. Some gave it little thought, but others had a different opinion, one he also held. Knowing the girl's character didn't matter, only her color, her heritage. He wondered for days when the needling would start. His silence was accompanied by a change in attitude. It didn't go unnoticed. Momentarily pausing the torch, another barb came his way.

"Hey, Roland, is Jalen still getting thick with the halfer? Wow, man, she'll be a strange addition to your family tree. I'm guessing there's some interesting conversations at home," chided Harmon, lightly scoffing.

Roland glared, aching to respond, but let it pass. He resumed his task, refusing to look up. Daily taunts tightened already frayed nerves, bringing a dread to go to work. His hands shook, and he missed the line. He quickly shut down the machine, realizing such errors were not well thought of. He corrected the gaff to near perfection then prepared to restart the cutter. Before he could, Freddy launched another stinging bolt.

"Maybe a halfer is all he can get, you know, considering he got run in last year. I bet the local gals won't give him the time of day. I don't think he could lower his sights anymore."

Roland briefly paused before starting the cutter, trying to ignore the goad, but the poison arrow hit its mark. Patience finally ran out. He angrily threw the switch and spun around. His face bore a rage within he could hold no longer.

"Look, I have problems like anybody else. None of you guys have perfect homes, perfect sons, or perfect daughters. I don't like what Jalen's doing, but I'll work it out just like you do. And I don't remember razzing you. It's best you let it be."

"Well, now, I guess we touched a nerve. Sorry about that. We just hate to see a pal losing contact at home. But if you want to make more of it," said Freddy, confronting Roland.

Roland quickly squared up to the agitator, clenching his fists. His eyes narrowed. He briefly paused then shoved the smaller antagonist. Freddy firmly stood his ground. Several tense moments passed till broken by a hand in the air.

"Ah, forget it," said Roland, turning back to his station.

Freddy shook his head while Harmon snickered as he walked to the water cooler. Roland began cutting another pipe as maddening thoughts swirled.

That boy. He's making my life miserable. Why can't he be like the other lads? Next, these goons will be digging me because he's going to church.

The day dragged on. Roland's wrath remained, refusing to lessen but continuing to grow. Frayed nerves danced on a razor's edge. Numerous glances at the slow-moving clock were finally rewarded when the hands landed on quitting time. He felt intense pressure to ease his woes, and with relief sorely needed, he knew just where to go.

*****

The church parking lot was nearly filled. A large Friday night crowd assembled for a concert the youth group finally arranged. Most were members with yet a sizeable number of visitors. Chatter, mixed with laughter, whirled around the neatly decorated auditorium till several girls and a few lads shuffled to their places in front of the spectators. Some stood on the floor while others stepped up on short platforms. After a brief silence, Mr. Cook moved in front of the noticeably nervous teenagers.

"My class has been working on a few songs, actually for quite a while now, and we thought this concert would be a good opportunity to see what they could do. I believe all but one of the boys managed to be here. While they might enjoy the idea of singing for you, I'm quite certain the sumptuous food our amazing ladies brought may have been a contributing factor for their presence."

A swooping reaction burst from the chorale. Eager singers endorsed the opinion with no reluctance. "Yeah! Right on! You got it! Amen, brother!"

"This concert was a brain child of Cheyenne who moved here a while back. So if anything goes wrong, the group says to blame her."

After laughter raced around the auditorium, the entire group pointed their fingers at Cheyenne till a singer by her side ruffled her hair while the others offered robust praise in unison, "Cheyenne! Cheyenne!"

The slightly self-conscious singer with a now reddish face heartily bowed to all.

"Bridgette and Jessica will perform a duet for us a little later. LaRana has given Bridgette the nickname of Pipes. We all agreed Pipes was quite appropriate as you will see, or better, as you will hear. And speaking of LaRana, she's been a welcome addition to our group. She has made the mixture of voices even more exciting. Jalen told me her voice really carries, especially when she gets high."

145

A murmur swept through the crowd. Glances with a chorus of whispers raced around the audience.

"Whoops. Sorry. That didn't come out quite right. I meant when she's up on our lofty peaks, her voice really carries. Uh, forgive me, LaRana, Jalen."

Two nodding heads brought hearty laughter till once again a measure of decorum settled in.

"We have a few lively spirituals along with some patriotic songs, and of course, a couple of romantics for both the young and, quite probably, the not so young."

Lights dimmed while several late arrivals hurried to seats. The cozy atmosphere prompted a few arms to wrap around shoulders.

"I'm really proud of this bunch, not only for their voices, but also for their eagerness and determination to learn about our Lord. They get a little weird at times, but they're growing spiritually. Ladies and gentlemen, our future."

With a wave of his arm, he turned attention to the singers.

They stood in sections, eager to get the show on the road. Animated excitement broke loose with a jolt. Precise harmony filled the hall with spectators in awe as song after song brought cheers and applause.

When the concert neared its end, Mr. Cook quickly stepped to the front. "We have two more songs I think you will enjoy. Pipes, Ashlynn, and Cheyenne are up next. Their selection is in honor of Cody and Elishah who are getting married in a couple of weeks. They have chosen Follow Me, a song from John Denver, as you all probably know. Ladies, do us the pleasure."

The room fell silent as the girls' enthralling voices perfectly blended, gently resting on each ear. With the last note, they bowed as hands clapped for several moments.

"For the last song, we have one all of us can take to heart. Katelyn, LaRana, and Jessica will join Pipes on You'll Never Walk Alone. We think you will enjoy it. The words are quite uplifting especially when we get a little down."

Applause slowly ebbed as the lights once again dimmed. The quartet stood side by side in a humming prelude. Melodious notes flawlessly joined, drifting over a silent audience. Emotions were touched while a few eyes misted. With the last note coming to rest, the lights came on, and the crowd stood for a hearty ovation. The chorale responded with bows and relieved faces.

"For all the singers and myself, we thank you for supporting our next generation and attending our concert. After Roy gives thanks for the food, please come up and let these young men and women know how you liked the music."

With the prayer's amen, the room came alive with handshakes and appreciations. Shelly glowed with pride. She heartily gave Jalen and LaRana a hug. Hannah met her daughter's eyes then embraced her. The singers freely mixed with a grateful audience till the time-to-eat bell rang. Shelly shook several more hands before meeting Hannah at the back of the room.

"LaRana was awesome. I didn't realize she was so versatile. Her voice sounded even better than usual with the group."

"They did sound good together," replied Hannah emphatically. "The kids here, especially Jessica, Ashlynn, Katelyn, Amelia, Cheyenne, and Bridgette, or I guess I should say Pipes, were great. I see why LaRana calls them the Super Six. I believe even I could sound decent singing with Pipes. The last song touched the hearts of all. Wow, what a quartet. All the young ladies here have really been good for LaRana. She has changed a lot, definitely for the better. Even though she enjoys her new friends, she's still uncertain about spiritual matters. We talk about church, but she still struggles with some things. Being visually different has always troubled her. Now being different by going to church has been a little hard to accept. Her connection is mainly social, but that's an enormous step in the right direction, especially since the connection is mostly with these girls and, of course, Jalen."

Shelly lowered her voice. "Jalen and I feel we have found a more enjoyable direction, but the atmosphere at home still needs some work. Roland is somewhat at odds with us being involved with our church family. He's been on quite a roller coaster, sullen at times and belligerent at times. It may seem odd, but we walk on pins and needles when he's home."

Hannah gently rested a hand on her shoulder. "I certainly understand from my experience. However, I often think of the old saying time can work wonders. Let's hope your enthusiasm eventually rubs off on him."

With food consumed and visiting done, the large crowd dwindled till only a few remained. Shelly and Jalen drove home with the joyful occasion still fresh.

"Looks like we had a little shower this evening. The cool air is quite refreshing. You sang quite well. They all did. I see why Pipes is thinking about a major in music. Wow, now that's a voice! And you were right… LaRana's voice is subtle but captivating. I wish your dad could hear you all sing. Maybe he'll be in a good mood tonight. As hard as it may seem, we have to stay optimistic."

"Thanks, Mom. LaRana is quite a girl, or should I say…young woman. She has grown up a lot this past year. Dad? Who knows? He hasn't had much good to say for quite a stretch."

"Well, I think you've also grown a lot. I believe you're answering my question." She glanced at Jalen with a proud smile. A quick fist bump declared they were on the same page.

The drive across town was spent recapping the evening's enjoyment. Caution grew as they neared the garage, each silently hoping the church activity would not cause a conflict. Jalen brought the Jeep to a stop, closed the garage door, and warily got out. An ominous stillness met their arrival. Roland usually had the TV loud enough to hear from the garage, but no sound was heard. Jalen wondered what waited inside. He had an idea but held it. He couldn't shake a strange feeling all was not well.

Shelly's sense held the same. "I didn't see any lights on. Your dad must be in bed already, but it's awfully early for him to hit the sack."

They cautiously entered, uncertain of the next few moments. Jalen turned on the lights to nothing but silence.

"Roland!" queried Shelly. "Roland!" Silence remained. She turned to Jalen with eyes of despair. Her shoulders sagged. "You don't suppose…?"

*****

"Hey, Roland. No hard feelings about this morning," said Harmon. "I shouldn't be shooting my mouth off so much, especially to a buddy. I was out of line. Your problems are your problems. You don't need me to butt in. Here, this beer's on me, pal."

"Thanks. Sorry I lost it. I was, and still am, uptight about the situation with Jalen. I just don't know what gets into that boy's head. He's at the police station one day, at the church the next. He's dating your niece one day, the halfer the next. He's at that church again tonight, singing like some momma's boy. At least the church thing has kept him out of trouble. I swear, I want to shake the snot out of him sometimes."

"Well, I know you gotta hate the halfer deal. I sure would. I don't know what I'd do if my son had a hankerin' for one. Take an extra drink, and maybe you can drown it. See ya at work."

Harmon slapped Roland's back then headed for the door, briefly stopping by a few rather loud patrons. Roland spent little time downing the token peace offering.

Nearly two hours passed with few customers remaining, mostly regulars sitting at the bar. He tried to hear conversations, but canned music muffled the words. Persistent striking of pool balls and player voices occasionally broke the muted rumble. Roland sat alone at a small table in a dimly lit corner. Several cigarette butts lay crushed in the tray. Smoke leisurely rose, becoming a wispy cloud of despair softly hovering above the table. The numbing of beer felt good till thoughts of Jalen and LaRana revived his anxiety. An urge to talk to someone arose. With no one around, he chose the glass at hand.

"Why is that boy doing all this stupid stuff?" he mumbled. "Everybody stares at me like I should be pitied. I don't want any pity. Shelly hasn't helped any at all. What kind of sissy have we raised? Why can't he be a real man like the other lads? Dumb kid!"

He grew louder, churning in his own world, and a few patrons, bellied to the bar, turned in a chorus of laughter. Roland grumbled, aching to scream, but he didn't want to be a spectacle.

Another brew seemed the right remedy.

He wanted Jalen to be like him, to work in the mill, to marry a local, and to drink with him. An inward anger burned over time, and little by little, he pushed him further away, ashamed at his failure, painfully regretting his son travelled a far different path than he desired.

Another beer.

In his view, Shelly's return to church was a rejection of him. Her incessant talk of discovered friends, new and old, roiled inside. He grappled with spurs of selfishness, fruits of neglect, and coldness of a growing distance between himself and Shelly. She's to blame for this mess, he reasoned. She could help get Jalen in line with his thinking if she had a mind to, but she wouldn't. He was alone, reeling in the pit of denial. Thoughts of Shelly's betrayal stirred his now groggy mind. He needed an answer for his torment. The nearest one rested on the table.

Another beer.

Wallowing in self-pity, his wrath and misery passed through too many brews. His head drooped, and he fumbled with a cigarette. He jerked his hand back as a finger hit the lit end. The manager came to the table and placed a hand on his shoulder. Roland looked up with glassy eyes.

"Wha' ya wan'?"

"I think you've had enough for tonight, Roland. It's getting late. Maybe you'd better head on home. Need someone to drive you?"

Roland swirled a hand in the smoky air. "Nah. I kin make it on my own. I don' need no rotten 'elp from nobody. Hah, jus' maybe my son 'll show up 'n see me 'ome. Fat chance o' dat. He'll neber be a man. He's mos' likely singin' dem li'l ditties wid dat haffer at dat lousy schursh. It don' make no sense. Jus' be glad yer son ain' no momma's boy."

He toddled through the door, slightly stumbled on the deck's edge, and lumbered to the parking lot with clumsy, uncertain steps. A light drizzle added to misery. He lifted the keys from a pocket only to drop them near the pickup. Stooping to retrieve them, he cursed then fell. With some exertion, he managed to find the vehicle's seat. Sluggishly driving home, he muttered to nobody, fighting each small turn in the road. An oncoming car swerved and blared its horn as he crossed the centerline.

"Ah, shub up, ya bloomin' idiot! I ain' gonna hit ya."

The challenging drive did nothing to sober him. Anger at everything grew with each uncertain mile. He still weaved as he entered the garage, slightly scraping the side of the pickup. He tumbled from the seat, falling to a knee on the floor. With some difficulty, he regained his feet, continuing to mumble till finally staggering into the house. Shelly and Jalen sat near the fireplace conversing about the evening's concert. Roland slightly tripped as he entered the room, knocking a cup from the table.

"Well, the schursh goers ha' come 'ome. I can't figger wha' you do wid dem Jesus freaks. You sure ain't 'ome much, 'n I'm gittin' midey tired of it. It's all yer fault, Shelly, all yers. You dun tuk this boy 'way from me, pushin' him into more school, more ball games, and dat lousy schursh. And…he goes and messes wid a haffer jus' to shame me."

Shelly sprang from the chair, took a step, and held out her hand. "Oh, Roland. Let me help you. You're about to fall."

"I don' need no 'elp! I kin make it on my own. You 'n the panny wais' can go on to bed. I'm gonna git me anudder beer…like a real man."

"I think you've had more than enough. This isn't helping any of us. You can't go on like this!"

"Helpin'? Wha' 'bout you? All yer helpin' is makin' a ninny outta Jalen. The guys are buggin' me 'bout him datin' the haffer, and gittin' run in. I ain' gonna take it no more. Yooou hear me, woman! I ain' gonna…pud up wid it! You dun gone and…and made a mess ou' of everthin'."

"Shut up! Stop talking to Mom like that!" demanded Jalen, leaping from the sofa with his own anger rising.

Shelly set a hand on Jalen's shoulder. "Easy…easy. Just…settle down. Let me take care of this."

She reached for Roland's arm. "I think it's better if we all went to bed. We're not getting anywhere tonight. I'll help you to the bedroom."

Reeling to the side, Roland slapped her hand then shoved her to the floor. Before he could gather his balance, Jalen sprang from the end of the table and sent a fist across his chin. Roland crumpled in a heap. Jalen jumped on him, ready to land another blow when Shelly caught his arm.

"That's enough, Jalen! No more. I'm okay. I'm…okay. Leave him on the floor. It's a good place to sleep it off."

Jalen glanced at Shelly then glared back at Roland. "If you ever do that again, I'll kill you! Do you hear me? I'll kill you!"

Roland's eyes floated aimlessly. With a low moan, consciousness fled. Jalen slowly stood and embraced Shelly whose face was ghostly white. His eyes didn't flinch; his words didn't waver. He wrapped his arms around Shelly then eased back and looked straight into her eyes.

"I mean it. If he ever again lays a hand on you, I'll kill him, come what may."

Shelly lost strength and wilted in Jalen's arms. Tears freely flowed. The chasm between Jalen and Roland had widened to the breaking point.

Too wide.

All she hoped would come to pass now dimmed as a setting sun. The sense of loss swept over her. She shook uncontrollably, solaced only by the arms holding her.

*****

A warm, windless Saturday morning found LaRana immersed in a biology assignment. Her eyes hardly left the textbook for nearly an hour. Finally, with a deep breath, she leaned back on the sofa. With a couple of minutes of rest, she returned to the book only to be interrupted by the phone.

"LaRana speaking… Oh, hello Ashlynn…when…this morning? Uh, well…yeah, I guess I could go. I definitely could use a break. Hold a sec."

She gently lowered the phone. "Mom, would it be okay if I went with Ashlynn to the archery range?"

"Sure, just remember, we're going to Jalen's game tonight."

"Yeah, I can go…what time?… That's good. I'll be ready."

LaRana rushed to finish the assignment. Less than twenty minutes after closing the book, Ashlynn and her grandparents pulled into the driveway. LaRana hurried down the steps, soon settling in the back seat.

"Thanks for the invite. I'll try not to embarrass myself. Now, you do realize I ain't Robin Hood…or even a very distant relative."

"That's okay. Everybody has to start somewhere. I brought all the gear we need. I just hope you enjoy it."

"I wouldn't mind coming to one of your meets. Let me know when one comes up, and I'll try to be there."

"Sure will! I can use all the support I can get!"

With a few miles covered and pleasant talk exchanged, they soon stood by a row of stations several yards from an array of brightly colored targets. LaRana paused, wide eyed and opened mouth.

"Wow! These things are small! You can actually hit these things? I was looking for something…like…the side of a barn."

"They are intimidating when first beginning, but you'll get the hang of it. We'll start at twenty yards."

Ashlynn covered a few of the basics then demonstrated the process. She hit the target with three arrows, all within a foot of the eye. LaRana's eyes widened.

"Wow, are you serious? You got to be kidding! There's no way I can do that."

"Well, maybe not to start. Try not to get too discouraged. It takes a lot of practice to gain confidence. Here, give it a go. Just let the arrow go. Don't try to make it go."

Ashlynn handed LaRana the bow with a couple of pointers then stepped back. With visible tension, the beginner let one fly only to miss by several feet.

"Ahh, that was terrible. Let me try again."

"Just relax. Focus on the center. Try hard not to push the bow toward the target. Keep the left arm steady as you release your fingers. They will move back some after the release."

LaRana let two more fly, each a little closer.

"Better! You'll get this!"

She pulled again, and the arrow careened off the target. The next arrow stuck in the left edge.

"Bazoom! I finally hit it! I could get to liking this!"

"I thought you would be a quick learner. Now, let's see how close you can get to the eye. Pull it a few more times and challenge yourself."

LaRana sent two more. One hit near the edge. One missed by less than a foot. For nearly five minutes, she sent arrows to the target. Several found it. Misses were fewer.

Ashlynn nodded her approval. "Hey, very good! Now, the chips are down. The pressure is on. You have one more arrow to hit the eye—only this time, the eye is a lethal varmint, maybe a killer beast just waiting to pounce. When the pressure mounts, when it seems all will be lost if you miss, take emotions and anxiety to zero. Be completely calm and don't rush the release."

LaRana took a long, deep breath. She tried to stop the tremble in her left arm. She couldn't. She lowered the bow, took a slow breath, staring at the target. Her eyes narrowed as she again set the bow. Within three seconds, she released the missile. It hit slightly over nine inches from the eye.

"Yes!" screamed Ashlynn. "Great shot!"

"Oh, my goodness! I didn't think I had a chance to do that. Beginner's luck for sure. Thanks a ton! Now, it's your turn. See if you can put an arrow inside of mine."

Ashlynn accepted the challenge with a nod. "You've set a good hit, but I'll try to beat it."

Ashlynn methodically set an arrow and let it fly. It hit two inches off the eye. She quickly released another, hitting the eye's edge. A third was calmly set and released. It centered the eye.

"Wow! I stand in complete awe!"

"Well, I've sent a few more than you. However, I recall my first pulls. They were not as close as yours. Just remember, when all seems lost, and you have only one more shot, be calm, think clearly, anxiety to zero, and trust."

"Thanks. I may try to get better at this, although I can't imagine ever being good enough to make the team."

"You'll have the summer to get better. I'll let you know when I practice. Maybe you can go with me."

"I might just do that. It sure is challenging."

*****

With little time to spare, LaRana arrived at the stadium where Jalen was playing in a tournament championship game. Life smoothly unfolded before her eyes. She heartened to watch her mother change from a sense of despair to an aura of hope, from agony of looking back to joy of looking forward, from resolve of failure to hopeful anticipation.

Her own life slowly settled. Willow's death and Sarona's plight led to serious thought on who she was and where she was going. She grew closer to Jalen, a friend who bravely stood up for her, who convinced her a mixed ancestry wasn't a collar of shame. Interaction at church brought a better understanding of how real friends acted. It set her on a solid platform of both decency and vision for the future.

The game was close when Jalen came to the plate in the bottom of the ninth with two on, two outs, and two runs down. With crossed fingers, she whispered, "Come on. Come on." Stillness shattered at the crack of the bat. Jalen's game-winning drive flew over the left field fence. Along with most of the crowd, she leaped from her seat and loudly cheered. The team celebration lingered till the stands finally began to empty.

She patiently waited with Shelly near the parking lot while several pumped-up spectators congratulated Jalen as he walked by the lower railing of the stands. A young lad waited with his mother near the third base exit. Excitement lit his face; eyes sparkled above a wide grin. He ran to Jalen with arms high. Jalen knelt, accepting his hug.

"Thank you. What's your name?"

"DeShawn."

"Well, DeShawn, do you play baseball?"

"Yeah…when I got a glove. I play second base, sometimes left field."

After a hand slap, DeShawn started back to his mother. Jalen took a step to leave then paused, turning back to his admirer.

"Hey, DeShawn! Come here a minute."

He looked at his mother who nodded. He ran back, his face carrying a puzzled expression.

Jalen held out his glove. "Here, this is yours. It may be a little big, but you'll grow into it. Practice a lot, and you could become a star. Don't let anyone say you can't do it. I think you will, and I hope to come and see you play in a couple of years."

The boy's eyes widened, and a smile ran across his face. With a hearty thank you, he reached up, gave Jalen a long hug then sped off, holding his cherished gift. Watching him run, he saw himself at that age. DeShawn proudly showed his mother the glove. She lifted her eyes to Jalen, touched her heart and pointed to him. Jalen nodded with a deep breath and misty eyes. He turned to leave the field when one more tribute came from an elderly man still seated near the far end of the stands.

"Great hit! I bet your pop is proud of you," came his well-intentioned declaration.

Jalen's eyes met Shelly's. Nothing was said till he turned to the man. "Thanks, I'm sure he is."

He enjoyed waving to fans, but his heroic achievement was dampened by the absence of his father. Although in anger, he had spoken of killing him, he still held hope Roland would utter a long-lost word in a tone of sincerity and love. He also knew such hope had no legs. Shelly caught the frown. She quickly changed to the moment at hand.

"Nice dinger, I believe you guys call it. You've really been playing good. Did you see any college coaches?"

Jalen shoved woes aside and returned to the thrill of the evening. "I think at least three were here. It's quite possible my chance for a scholarship is yet alive. Who knows, maybe dreams can still come true."

They neared the Jeep with Jalen's words still warm. He suddenly stopped, his heart raced. Two men casually approached. Jalen quickly noticed their attire. They shook Jalen's hand then those of Shelly and LaRana. The older man gave a notebook to the younger. Jalen's anxiety mixed with anticipation, and he could barely get his breath.

"My name is Byron Stafford. This is assistant coach, Gary Stone. I've heard a lot about you. I assume this is your mother, and let me guess, a very supportive lady friend."

"Yes, sir. This is my perfect mother, Shelly, and my amazing girlfriend, LaRana."

"It's a pleasure to meet you both. We won't keep you long. I wanted you to know our staff has been watching your progress for the past year, and we strongly believe you would be a good fit for our program. One of your past coaches, Mike Monroe, gave you an excellent recommendation concerning your character and work ethic. Have you ever thought about playing for State?"

Jalen's thoughts raced back to hours spent dreaming of wearing a Bear uniform, running the bases in a Bear uniform, making a great play in a Bear uniform. He tried to calm his nerves. His reply vaguely inferred the list of seekers was lengthy.

"Yes, sir. State has been my, uh…first choice for some time."

Coach Stafford turned to Shelly who tried to keep emotions in check. "How do you feel about State, Mrs. Strade? I was looking to meet your husband as well, but I'm hoping you both hold the same opinion. We always prefer the decision be agreeable to all."

"My husband, Roland, was…unable to be here tonight. I'm sure he will welcome your interest in Jalen. As for me, I don't know much about college sports, but I also couldn't think of a better school."

"Well, thank you. It's good to hear that. Jalen, your SAT and academic records are good. We'll send you scholarship details within a few weeks. After you've studied them carefully, we'll set a meeting to do the signing and schedule a tour of the campus, assuming you agree to the offer. It's been a pleasure to meet all of you. Please give Mr. Strade my regards."

"Thank you, Mr. Stafford. I certainly appreciate your interest. I will try hard not to disappoint."

"I'm sure you will. Have a fine evening. We look forward to seeing you in the near future."

Jalen stood frozen to the ground till the coaches were out of sight. He turned to Shelly whose wide eyes matched LaRana's. Yet both paled to the excitement on Jalen's face.

"Can you believe it? A scholarship to State! A Bear. I'm going to be a Bear!" With exuberance running over, he hugged Shelly hard, a little too hard.

"Oh!" she exclaimed.

"Oops, sorry, I got a little carried away."

Shelly brushed her sleeve. "Whew, now that's a bear hug. Ah, well, it just, sorta came out."

He hugged LaRana then lifted her and spun around.

"This wouldn't have happened without you two, especially you, Mom. You've helped me attain my dreams ever since I can remember. I'll certainly do my best to make you proud."

"Well, you've already got a good start on that."

Jalen looked a little puzzled till offering a slight grin. "Must be the question again. I'll try to finish it someday. I believe this would be a good time for a celebration. We're going for a bite at the Frosty Treat. Why don't you come with us?"

Unsure of Roland's condition, Shelly chose to let them revel on their own. *Maybe I can get him into a better mood before Jalen returns.* She proudly smiled with a quick embrace.

"I'll pass this time. I should get on home. I don't want your… well… I just need to go. I probably need to fix a late supper. You two go and celebrate. I'll tell your dad the good news. Don't stay out too late. I'll see you at home."

Jalen paused for only a moment. Thoughts of the clash with Roland resurfaced, and he agonized he would become violent when he wasn't there. He watched Shelly disappear around the stands, wishing her troubles would come to an end. LaRana slid her arm around Jalen's with both spritely walking toward the Jeep.

"Well, sire, it does appear you have found the end of thy current noble quest. Perchance, dear chap, you just might entertain, let's say, a new quest of gallant purpose. In the meantime, quite proud to be on your arm is this lass. Tis my guess there be a sizable assembly of other fair lasses who cheerfully with me would change places."

"Perchance that be so, my lady, but tis my ardent belief the one who there now resides shall properly suffice."

Hand slaps and hearty laughs.

Jalen walked tall around the end of the protective net, still astounded over his good game and scholarship offer. Several spectators offered congratulations while they strode through the lot. He walked on air, his head swimming in elation at reaching a childhood goal. For the moment, he thrust the thoughts of a distant father to the back of his mind. This was a time to celebrate the beginning of a new page in life.

As he turned onto the highway, he began talking rapidly, giving LaRana a pitch-by-pitch account as if she hadn't been there. LaRana quietly sat, patiently listening, realizing this probably would not be the last replay of a ballgame.

"I put myself in game winning situations nearly every time I played in our yard at about age nine. I had a feeling I was going to come to the plate in an important situation. I just didn't know what inning it would be. Wow, the bottom of the ninth. It doesn't get more thrilling than that!"

The replay gradually wound down, but Jalen was yet in high gear about the best night he could remember.

"Hey, I'm starved. How about you?" With LaRana's nod, he glanced at the dash clock. "Uh oh, we'd better step on it. Paul will be closing before long."

The traffic light turned green, and anxious to get to the Frosty Treat, he hit the pedal. His account of the game and meeting with Coach Stafford resumed in high gear as he entered the intersection, unaware of a van speeding out of control from the street to the left. In the beat of a heart, a flash of light was quickly followed by an ear-splitting impact on the driver's door sending the Jeep careening sideways across the street, crashing into a utility pole.

Glass lay like scattered diamonds. Cars screeched to a stop. Several onlookers rushed to the scene, some gasping in wonder, some in stony silence.

LaRana slowly regained her senses. She felt a sharp pain in her shoulder and gently stretched back. Through faintly blurred vision, she saw Jalen slumped over the wheel. A red flow ran freely from the back of his head. She wiped blood from her face, not knowing if it was hers or Jalen's. She gently touched his shoulder only to find it damp. He didn't move. Clutching the door handle, she screamed for help till a bystander yanked it open.

"Are you okay, lady? It's probably better you don't move. An ambulance will be here soon. Try to relax."

She leaned back, suddenly feeling queasy in her stomach. Shadowy figures slowly moved, voices muffled. Several tried to open the driver's door, but it was smashed into the seat, stuck tight. Blood splatters dotted the few broken pieces of window remaining. Jalen had yet to move, his face lying tilted in the air bag.

LaRana gently turned her head. Vision slowly cleared as reality began to set in. "Somebody help Jalen. Please! Help him!"

Her plea raced around the intersection till a bystander eased her way through the growing crowd and approached the Jeep. She gently placed a hand on LaRana's shoulder.

"The police and ambulance will be here soon. I know it's hard, but try to relax. What's your name?"

"LaRana. Please help Jalen!"

"Someone's coming shortly to help him. Gently lean back and take a few deep breaths. Good…that's better. LaRana. That's a captivating name, a classy one. Try to relax. Try to rest your head. Help will be here before long."

LaRana leaned back to the headrest and managed a frail smile, calmly conversing for several minutes. Her legs felt weak; heartbeats came slower. With clammy skin and closing lids, she became oblivious to everything. Voices began to wane. Time slowed as memories of the past and visions of the future ran together. On the edge of reality and consciousness, she turned to Jalen with a quiet but imploring voice.

"Come back. Come back."

Another voice interrupted her quiet desire. "Step away, please. Step away. Move back."

She opened her eyes to the blinking of patrol car lights. An officer looked in. "Ma'am, can you understand me?"

LaRana gradually turned her head. A vision of the past teased her thoughts.

Another officer. Another badge.

This time the badge was welcome.

"Yes, sir. Don't…bother with me. Please help… Jalen. He's… he's hurt real bad."

The sound of saw to metal loudly screeched till the driver's door fell to the side. Immediately, two paramedics gently eased Jalen from the seat, carefully placing him on a gurney. LaRana caught glances they exchanged. Their unspoken words were loud and clear. Within moments, Jalen silently laid in the back of the ambulance.

An attendant came to LaRana's side and helped her from the wreck. She stood on wobbly legs but managed to trudge toward the back of the ambulance where attendants started to close the rear door. LaRana held up her hand then grabbed the door.

"Stop! I'm goin…with him. I'll give you…information as we go."

An attendant held up his hand. "Another unit is on the way. You need to wait for it."

"Now that's all well and good, but I'm accepting your gracious offer to go with Jalen. I can give you whatever…stuff you need."

The EMT's glanced at each other then helped her inside. She gazed in disbelief as Jalen's head was gently wrapped. The blood flow slowed to a trickle, but she knew he lost a lot, maybe too much. She became dizzy and tilted to the side. An EMT placed a cool towel on her forehead and a bandage on a slender cut on her chin. Feeling weak, she mumbled thanks before leaning back and closing her eyes.

Thoughts, both distant and near, teased her memory. Visions of pleasant times spent with Jalen were vivid till chased by his ashen, death-laden face. This moment was all that mattered. She stared at his body lying motionless, wishing he would awaken or make a movement, any movement.

Still he remained.

She shut her eyes, pondering a myriad of joyful occasions with Jalen. Suddenly, among the attendant's voices came a dreaded sound. Her eyes flew open when a long, shallow breath said he was fading, drifting away as an ebbing sea. The monitor's lines were short and inconsistent, and beeps began to slow till an unbroken sound said he was gone.

An EMT felt his pulse then quickly moved his hands to Jalen's chest. Several pumps failed to change the line. LaRana could barely breathe as she pleadingly stared at the monitor. Time abruptly halted. A tear rolled down her cheek, followed by several more. A second attendant began CPR and finally broke the flat line. LaRana held her breath till the beeps returned, slightly erratic but there. She eased back with but little strength remaining. The attendants worked swiftly but carefully. One motioned to the head wound and softly spoke. LaRana couldn't hear all the words but knew what was said. They finally stemmed the flow and placed another fresh wrap around his head, but exchanged glances revealed their thoughts.

"We have a pulse, weak but stable."

"At least for now. We need to get him to ER as soon as possible. The pressure on his brain must be quite…"

A glance at LaRana finished his declaration.

Her pulse raced while the siren, yet blaring, now grew distant, echoing in the canyon of anguish. She gently shut her eyes, recalling days of joy now drifting far in the past. A vividly clear vision of Jalen on Talova Peak grew dim, slowly flowing away. She reeled in a void. Roads ran in all directions but went nowhere. Jalen's smiling face crossed her vision but quickly gave way to the blood-soaked head lying before her. She gently held then stroked the necklace. While still a cherished connection, it now seemed a bridge between life and death.

The beeps again slowed. Barely able to breathe, she stared at the monitors, trying to ignore a burning question, but it wouldn't go away. Was this the last ride?

A lifetime of expectation collapsed to a few seconds of fleeting hope.

Missives Six

Esul,

You are quite the master of devious, enticing a young man to drive laced with ill devised concoctions. I'm sure your hand was somehow involved in Jalen's misfortune. We are quite concerned about losing him, but how much inner strength remains is yet to be determined. We believe it is sufficient to deny your desire. You may think such trials will change the direction he and LaRana have embarked on, but you will be proven wrong. My Master's vision of hope and life will see them through any stumbling blocks you place before them. This event will only strengthen their resolve.

Your zeal to employ mind-distorting potions has created considerable chaos and death. You have deluded humans to believe their sordid innovations can be used anytime, anywhere. While your power of deception is quite formidable, we will overcome your treachery. Whether he remains or passes, Jalen has set in motion circumstances that could unite the family and maybe a host of others.

Sewing discord in the Strade family may bring a temporary sense of victory, but it will not last. Shelly's resolve is strong. She will find a way to overcome your diabolical efforts.

Humans often plummet to the bottom of torment and misery before looking to us for answers. You actually may have helped Roland reach that point. His fate is not yet sealed.

I'm certain you think Jalen's choice to physically stop Roland will turn him from growing toward us, but you may be mistaken. I believe Shelly's strength and Jalen's desire to see Roland become a true father will turn him away from you.

While you work tirelessly on killing hope in those who walk the earth, it is that very hope, the great anticipation of a better temporal life mixed with forward looking to an eternity of bliss, that prevails for those who sincerely seek it.

You have been very successful in deluding minds, clouding vision, and belittling a sense of what is right. However, devious demon, you cannot always prevent our light from scattering your darkness. You cannot prevent all of God's creation from seeking the truth.

While I can only imagine the glee at the turmoil you have spawned, be certain the seed we planted will not be prevented from sprouting. The Word going forth from my Father's mouth will not return to Him void. Though you have spread your darkened shadows and sent your spears, I have endless faith those for whom we contend will reject your master.

Jariel

*****

Jariel,

Do I perceive anxiety in your tone? I do enjoy the angst you must now feel. I find it quite amusing to use the creative talents of these paltry beings to set up circumstances of bedlam and chaos.

I could hardly contain my pleasure at Roland's over-indulgence in that masterful brew. We thoroughly enjoyed seeing young Jalen resort to violence. I'm quite certain the family didn't grow any closer together. On the contrary, they will only get farther apart.

You must agree our marvelous swill can tear a family asunder. Whatever you try to bring them to your concept of life, I need only to make their own destructive devices irresistible, thus plunging them into our vision of existence.

Watching that van hit Jalen's vehicle was truly gratifying. You know I wasn't the driver. I only helped a young man think he had to have the concoction within his reach. It was quite amusing to see him try to drive with a mind distorted and eyes blurred. I am so proud of that lovely leaf. It's just strong enough to serve our purposes.

It's such a shame that Jalen lies near death. You spoke as if he was going to recover. Might you be slightly delusional? The end of his life is forthcoming. We expect a last heartbeat at any moment. We're already preparing his place in our cozy abode. I can barely contain an eagerness to see him in our realm. The spirit of my master hovers over him as you read this missive, but this you already realize. Is that a worrisome frown on your face? I can only hope so. That pleasant little incident will surely lead to several rejections of your Master who has promised a better life.

Those humans do not possess the vision we do. As I have proclaimed many times, if I can keep their sight on the temporal, I can all but seal their fate. Such will be the case with LaRana. How sad another step to rise above her past will be pulled from under her. She already has difficulty grasping your Master's concept of life. When Jalen passes, any hope you had for her will be gone. Losing him will widen the road to our rapidly growing collection.

In all this glee, there is one who is beginning to grasp the reality of your Master far too much… Hannah. As you know, I just can't let her freely sail to your realm. We will see how strong her conviction is. You know me, if there is a chink in someone's armor, I will find it. Be assured, white robe, I will usher her back to past failures.

Let's be blatantly real. The Strades are falling apart, Jalen nears our abode with every passing second, and LaRana's frail vision of your Master is about to disappear. I fail to comprehend how you cope with so many setbacks at one time? Sorry for all your trepidation, but the outcome is already in sight.

Esul

7

Stubborn

The delicate surgery took an hour and a half on the clock but an eternity for Shelly. She nervously paced the floor with hope frantically wrestling despair. Roland quietly sat near the door. His unbroken gaze appeared to hold deep thoughts, but she couldn't tell of what or for whom. While his body was within a few feet, his mind was miles away.

With the regular ICU full, Jalen was assigned a room straight across the hall from the nurses' station. Though well equipped for close observation, the eerie quietness felt cold to Shelly, a coldness carrying the relentless aura of death. She tried fervently to stay hopeful but thoughts doggedly leaned in another direction. She continued wearing out the floor while Roland melted into the chair.

Tension tightened when two nurses carefully wheeled Jalen into the room. Roland rose and stood by Shelly who watched with fretful eyes while they hooked him to the monitor and checked the IV drip. Shelly's nerves knotted. She silently groaned. Jalen lay motionless with breath barely noticeable. Deeply desired beeps came too far apart to raise any anticipation of recovery. Anxiety piqued while she desperately hung onto each one, inwardly pleading for another. She eagerly sought comforting vital signs. The monitors stubbornly persisted to give her none. The room became silent with nothing heard but the rustling of linens, soft whispers of two nurses, and uneven beeping of a struggling heart.

Shelly glanced at Roland. He spoke not a word. The gulf was intact. The vision of his altercation with Jalen refused to go away. Though unsettled by what his mind held, what may rest in his heart troubled her more.

Unable to restrain fear, Shelly silently eased behind the nurses while they quietly adjusted hoses. The extensive surgery left nothing but unanswered questions, slow beeps, and a well-wrapped bandage. Fleeting thoughts raced from the dire present to a bleak and uncertain future. She wondered how life could be so cruel. Jalen just received a major goal, an open door to dreams, now closed in one horrific moment.

The slow and slightly irregular beeping, unwanted yet urgently desired, created an atmosphere setting her nerves on edge. He lay unconscious next to a stand with a clear bag slowly dripping a host of prayers through thin tubes.

Roland returned to pacing the room, now dangling somewhere between angry and concerned. LaRana and Hannah anxiously stood but a step beyond the door. The nurses finished their tasks and offered encouragement with pleasant smiles.

"He's resting peacefully. We're carefully watching his vitals. The surgeon will be here shortly. Let us know if you need anything, anything at all. We're right across the hall."

The nurses quietly left the room leaving Shelly standing next to the delight of her life. Images of past joys and struggles slowly moved through her mind, keeping time with the monitor. Occasional erratic beeping chased her eyes from the motionless joy now facing a challenge to survive.

Roland calmly walked to the foot of the bed. He said nothing but stared with mixed emotions. Taunting thoughts meandered, some of concern, some of regret. His face revealed neither profound worry nor meager annoyance.

"I'm sorry, Shelly. I guess bad things can happen to anyone. I was hoping this God you all think so much of would help, but He sure is taking his time. I guess Pallon Ridge must be a hard place to find. For what it's worth, Isaiah Johnson wanted you to know he was praying in the chapel."

Shelly turned and stared for several moments, gazing into Roland's face. He caught her look and dropped his head. She took a slow breath, wondering if the heart of the man she married had hardened beyond return. Entertaining thoughts her mate of many years had yet to embrace her only added to the trial lying at her side.

"Isaiah's a good man, a caring man. I thought he might come."

"Are you saying I'm not a caring man?" blurted Roland, deeply frowning. "I care as much as anybody."

His words knifed through her soul. Had Roland's real state of mind finally been revealed? Her eyes were piercing yet dejected, her voice carrying a deepening despair. Though his body was at arm's length, his heart was miles away.

"As much?"

Roland started a retort but kept silent. His eyes turned to Jalen, eyes holding an aura of disappointment, but Shelly could not tell for whom. She tried to stay strong with what energy remained.

"I don't think you know how much he loves you, how much he wants you to be proud of him. It nearly broke his heart when he hit you. He felt the gulf between had become so wide neither could reach the other. Tears replaced anger. He wasn't able to find sleep for hours. His childhood adoration for you has all but disappeared."

"Well, what I did was wrong. I can see why he did it. I hoped it would stay in our house. Oh, the Lester woman and her daughter are still outside. I thought maybe…they would not come, that maybe the accident would…uh…dampen this infatuation."

The urge to scream was all but unbearable. Though her legs quivered, she stood like a sentinel, fighting to lash out at blatant prejudice. The gravity of the situation held her wrath, but heartache continued to grow. She urgently searched for a reply when the surgeon knocked on the door then entered.

"Hello, Mr. and Mrs. Strade. I'm Dr. Malone. The surgery went as well as could be expected. He lost a lot of blood. The cranial area was slightly compromised, but we're quite optimistic our efforts will be successful. We can't say at the moment the extent of damage that may have occurred. We will carefully monitor his progress. The survival rate for similar injuries is not high, and motor skills and speech may be affected. However, we believe he is strong to have made it this far. Having said that, it's going to be tedious for a while, but with that firm constitution, his chances are better. You might thank Someone higher than us he has survived so far."

Shelly paused, waiting for Roland to respond. He didn't. "Thank you, Dr. Malone. We appreciate your candor along with your effort and concern for our son."

"I know the coma is upsetting, but it's probably for the best at this point. These injuries are hard to predict, but I believe your devotion will be beneficial. If attention is needed, the nurses and Dr. Watson will be here for the night. I'll check on him tomorrow. Are there any questions you might have?"

"None that can be quickly answered," said Shelly. "Please accept our thanks for all you've done."

"The staff here is exceptional. They will keep close tabs on his progress."

With an assuring smile, he shook hands with both and left the room. The sound of the closing door ushered them back to the moment's uncertainty. They stood silently over the bed till Roland shrugged his shoulders and took a deep breath.

"It seems we have a long wait in our path. All we can do is hope for the best."

Shelly didn't look up, keenly aware her emotions were challenged from two sides. One needed removed.

"I'll stay with Jalen. You should go home and get some rest. I'll let you know if the night...doesn't go well."

Roland nodded with a hand on Shelly's shoulder. "Call me if anything happens."

Shelly nearly collapsed at the quick reply. She hoped he would determine to stay with her, to travel the uncertain road with her, to provide comfort to her. Her legs nearly gave way at the sound of the shutting door, not only to the room, but also to a harmonious home and a loving mate to share it with. The emotion most dreaded overwhelmed her.

Alone.

Though others who cared were not far away, it still felt as if the hospital was empty, the town empty, and above all, her heart empty, abandoned by the one she longed to be her strength, her sanctuary in the storm. Marooned on the island of sorrow, she held the bed rail to avoid knees from buckling. Her thoughts turned to the One in whom she beseeched to see Jalen through the surgery.

"Lord, I'm not worthy to call on You, but I request my son be spared. Whether from the doctors' hands or Your hands, I plead for his life. I also pray for patience with Roland. I don't know if I can bear losing both my son and my mate. Please grant me forgiveness and mercy."

Though appreciating the surgeon's candid assessment, his words "the survival rate has not been high" kept doggedly repeating. While staring at her motionless joy, two rays of light quietly entered. Hannah and LaRana eased across the room and stood one to each side. Two arms softly wrapped her shoulders. Nothing was said, but volumes were spoken. Love and care, given in silence, eased the tension. Her body quivered and eyes misted as Hannah helped her to a chair.

"Thank you. I really needed comforting arms. I could think of only one better than yours."

Hannah looked into her ashen face and troubled eyes then gently touched her shoulder. "I understand."

Shelly wanted to say more but could not summon the words. She was heartened at the solace and care of a precious friend.

Alone, she spent a rainy Sunday morning agonizing over irregular moments with an obstinate monitor. Time managed to discover a way to pass slower. Jalen moved but a little, mostly muscle tics and mournful spasms. A few friends from church stopped by. Shelly, not yet ready for visitors, gave a brief update before returning to Jalen. She set Monday evening for visitation, assuming all would go well. Roland arrived shortly after noon. A calmer aura rested on his face and in his eyes. The slight change was enough to lift Shelly's hopes.

LaRana spent the afternoon at the hospital, talking with Shelly, avoiding Roland, and working on assignments. Her presence helped time pass quicker. Evening came with no change in Jalen. Roland patted Shelly's shoulder then left. Shelly thought it a positive sign, one deeply needed.

Hannah began the night shift, leaving LaRana and Shelly to oversee progress till her first break at nine. She and LaRana spent most of her short rest with Shelly. Talking was brief as each watched and listened to Jalen and the monitors.

"Can I stay with him, at least for a while, or maybe…the night?" came a strong question out of the blue.

Hannah started to reply but realized the question was not to her. LaRana's query lifted Shelly's spirit. Her nod came with a smile.

"If your mother agrees, it's fine with me."

"If you don't think she'll be in the way, I guess it'll be okay… but, young lady, leave time to get ready for school. I would gladly stay, but as you can tell, I'm still on the clock. I will definitely check in during my breaks. If you need anything, send LaRana to find me. I'll be on the fourth floor."

Several silent moments passed after Hannah departed. Shelly found it comforting to have someone to talk with, even if not the one so desperately desired.

"Thank you for staying, LaRana. I gather you're already aware that Jalen has been quite taken by you. Finally, when it comes to girls, I think he made a wise choice. I've grown to be very proud of you. It's heartening how you help others, especially Hannah. You could not have a better mother. Of all my friends, she is without doubt the dearest."

LaRana smiled and began to answer, but Jalen slowly groaned as if deeply pained. She was at his side in an eye's blink. With a strong desire to ease his pain, she slowly reached but didn't know where to touch him. She pulled back and nervously wrung her hands, uncertain what to do.

Shelly understood her anguish. "He's done that several times. Frustrating, isn't it…so badly wanting to relieve the agony but can't?"

"I wish I could do something for him. I feel so…so…helpless."

"I found it comforting to stroke his forehead, at least what part isn't bandaged. I don't know if it helped him, but it helped me."

"You don't mind?"

"Not at all. Somehow, I believe he'll know it's you. Wishful thinking? Maybe, but who knows, maybe not. I'll grasp for anything at the moment."

LaRana gently moved her hand down his cheeks and over what forehead wasn't bandaged. His hands were cool to the touch, but his head was warm, quite warm. She decided that was good since she couldn't cope with it not being.

"Mrs. Strade, I'll be glad to stay for a while. Maybe you could get some rest on that cozy bed. I'll wake you if there's a change."

"Well, I'm not sure. Thanks for offering, but I think maybe I should…"

She suddenly caught her words, sensing a glowing light emerging. Knowing sleep would be elusive, she put a hand on LaRana's shoulder.

"On second thought, I'll just do that. Jalen seems to be in good hands. Let me know…when…he wakes up."

Shelly slipped off her shoes, stretched out, and pulled the sheet over her legs. A peaceful feeling gently flowed over her. She closed her eyes and prayed, not only for Jalen's healing, but also thankfulness for LaRana's presence. The bed eased tension, but her eyes would not stay closed.

Only slow uneven beeps interrupted the deafening stillness till a melody, whispery but clear, drifted through the room. LaRana softly sang while gently stroking Jalen's head. Shelly relaxed and calmly listened. The soothing voice ushered her into a shallow sleep.

Time continued to creep. LaRana ever so gently kept stroking Jalen's head. In the unsettling stillness, she meekly prayed. "I don't much about You, but I do believe You exist… I think. I don't know how You help people, but if You can, or will, please help Jalen. He's one of the good guys. I'm pretty sure he believes in You."

LaRana pulled a chair to the bedside and leaned back. She wondered why Roland didn't stay. Maybe he had to leave for some reason, she decided. His sullen look as he left the room was another gaze of rejection. Thoughts of his rude countenance brought back memories of her father. It was the same hateful look that broke her heart on the night he died. She had forgotten many things of early childhood, but

Allon's last day on earth remained vividly clear. His callous passing by without a touch or a smile continued to haunt her deepest memories. She was just beginning to understand his neglect was not her fault.

Hannah stopped in shortly before 2:00 a.m. LaRana put a finger to her mouth to maintain the quietness. Hannah paused, glanced at Shelly then smiled and nodded. Her conversation with LaRana held an aura of warmth and care. She lightly brushed her hair, gazed into her eyes, and whispered.

"I'm very proud of you, proud to be your mother. What you're doing is right, for Shelly and Jalen. When...he comes out of the coma, it will, perhaps, be partially due to your gentle care."

LaRana felt good at the declaration. Grasping the concept of love and concern for others, turning vision from inward to outward, brought a warm feeling. New ground was being trod, bringing a greater sense of self-worth.

Shelly had been awake since Hannah arrived. After listening to a pleased mother, she slowly rose. "Thanks for the nap, LaRana. And I agree with your mom. An inward passion to help others is one of the greatest qualities. You may be the one to put him back on his feet, heartily alive as before."

"I can certainly agree with that. Uh, I guess I better go now. Breaks seem to pass so quickly. I'll see you at the end of my shift. If LaRana needs to be out of the room for any reason, don't hesitate to send her, or if necessary...drag her out."

"Thanks again. I believe one thing is certain. She may be the one needed most in this room. I'm not sure I could survive this without both of you."

After another quick visit by Hannah and a nurse check at five in the morning, Shelly and LaRana engaged in small talk to help pass the time. Only random deviations in the monitor's rhythm interrupted the gentle peace. LaRana held her breath at each fluctuation. The dimly lit room became her inner world. Everything else seemed distant and unimportant. Fresh memories and dreams of the future remained outside the walls, reserved for recall at another time, whether for joy or sorrow. Time and space were reduced to only the moment and room at hand.

The clock crept to a few minutes after seven in the morning with LaRana still at Jalen's side. Shelly returned from a needed refreshing and proudly stood by LaRana, listening to the tireless yet heartening beeping till two nurses entered.

"Time to check everything out," said the older nurse. "The night went well, but we still have a way to go. Maybe you should get some breakfast while we tidy up in here."

"Sounds good to me," came another voice from the door. "I believe both of you could use a good meal."

"Well, you may be right, Hannah. I need to call Roland first."

Hannah and LaRana waited in the hall till Shelly emerged from the room. She was less tense, and a slight smile graced her face. LaRana thought her noble to cover the dreaded fear of the unknown, standing emotionally alone on the threshold of the door to a broken heart.

"I feel rested for…whatever happens. Roland is taking off work. He'll be here sometime this morning. He's bringing a change of clothes and a couple of things I need. Thanks for staying with Jalen, LaRana."

"Wouldn't have it any other way. I'll need a little time to freshen up for school, but I can definitely wait till breakfast is over."

They walked briskly to the cafeteria and soon sat down to a good meal. Hannah offered a calming prayer. Shelly mused on her new lease on life, rising from the depths of desperation, without God and lost, to joyfully returning thanks. Shelly had been there for her when times were bleak. Now, the generosity was returned.

I believe that's the way it's supposed to be.

"How can I thank both of you? You've been so gracious. I don't know how long before he…comes out of the coma. You don't have to stay here. I'm sure you both have a lot to do."

"I will be here as much as I can," said Hannah. "I work the night shift again so I will need to get some rest."

"I will be here, period," said LaRana emphatically. "I want to be here if…oops, scratch that, my bad…when…he wakes up."

Hannah leaned toward Shelly and whispered. "See, I told you she was stubborn."

Shelly didn't want to burden LaRana, but she saw devotion in her eyes and heard it in her tone. She surmised maybe two healings were taking place, one of physical and one of spiritual.

"It may be a while before he revives, but hopefully we'll all be here," said Shelly, patting LaRana's hand. "Go with your mother. I don't want you wearing yourself out. I'll see you back here at say, four."

"I'll be here right after school, no later than three thirty. Of that you can be certain."

*****

Routine filled Monday morning. Changes in Jalen were small, some promising and some depressing. At midmorning, Roland sat in the ICU waiting room wrestling with various conflicting thoughts. He and Shelly had met with the doctor several minutes earlier. The report Jalen lost some ground in the last few hours still rested on his ears.

Hannah took Shelly to the cafeteria, leaving Roland to wrestle with his demons. Self-pity churned his mind. He grappled with doubt and anger at nearly everything and everyone except himself. He deplored his existence, uncertain of anything. Isaiah entered the room, breaking his stupor.

"How's Jalen doing, Mr. Strade?"

Roland clenched his teeth, rolling his eyes, barely looking his way. Isaiah was the last person he wanted to see. "About the same, I guess. The report wasn't the best."

"How are you doing?"

Roland looked past the room, past the town, to the edge of existence, drowning in confusion. "I really don't know."

"You have a marvelous family. I keep hoping you would come to church services with them."

"I'm not much on religion. Can't see how it helps, especially with this."

"Oh, you don't think God is aware of Jalen's plight?"

Roland spun around, glaring at the unwelcome visitor with a stern voice. "Look, Mr. Johnson! I know you mean well, but I don't believe there is a God!"

"I see. My, aren't those machines hooked to Jalen really something. I wonder how those came to be? Any idea?"

Roland could hardly contain his irritation. Whatever he needed or wanted, a God talk wasn't it. He also didn't want to create a scene. He paused for a few moments then turned with a frown.

"Well, it stands to reason smart minds designed them."

"Oh, I agree, smart minds, indeed. As I reason, quite intelligent. It makes a person wonder how the smart minds were made?"

"Plenty of study and research for sure."

"You certainly got that right. It takes someone with capacity for design to make these wonderful machines. Yes, design is such a marvelous concept."

Isaiah reached into his pocket and laid the contents on the table. "I happen to have a few pieces of metal. I would like to have a nice pocketknife made from these pieces. How do you think it could be done? Could I just leave them on this table with hope that someday they will somehow get together and become that knife?"

Roland tensed, laboring to hold a rising temper. He burned to tell Isaiah to leave but stayed his annoyance. "Don't be ridiculous. I suppose someone who knows what he's doing could make it for you."

"I agree again. It takes a skilled designer to make a nice, precisely functioning pocketknife. Maybe you could do it, being a master welder. What about us? Did some material lay like these pieces then eventually come together to form a human?"

Roland teetered on the edge, strongly desiring to get in the visitor's face. Without turning, he rashly replied, "You can be insulting, you know that? Sure, we have design. That doesn't mean some almighty being did it. We just happened."

"Then does it not stand to reason this pocketknife could just… happen from these pieces? We are no more a product of circumstance and accident than a knife coming from these pieces without a high degree of design. Can you think of anything in this universe that doesn't show a measure of design?"

"Well, no, but I'm not the smartest guy in the world. Science says there isn't a God, and that's good enough for me."

"I hear that. Science certainly can be very persuasive. A lot of people use science as a reason to place God in the realm of myth. However, science actually proves there is a God. Please allow me. If nothing is all that ever existed, then there would be nothing still today. Something can't come from nothing. Agreed?"

"Yeah, I guess so. I ain't stupid!"

"It only stands to reason that something of unimaginable creative powers existed. Something must have been eternal or else nothing would be here. It's only logical that whatever is eternal is the creator of what isn't.

Now, think deep for a minute. Only two things exist: mind and matter. Everything in the universe can be found under these two. Can you think of anything else?"

"Uh…no. Not off the top of my head, but there's a lot I don't know."

"Science says that matter and the energy it produces cannot be created or destroyed, only altered. If matter cannot create matter, then matter cannot be eternal. That leaves only mind. And though we cannot comprehend how, we know, by the process of elimination that indeed, mind is the eternal factor."

"So I guess you're saying the eternal mind is God."

"I will leave you to ponder if there is any other conclusion. Thanks for listening to me carry on. Sorry if I bothered you. I know you're dealing with a difficult situation. If you would, keep the metal pieces till tomorrow then do with them what you will. And for what it's worth, which I believe is a lot, I'm praying for you, Shelly, and Jalen. If you need anything, feel free to let me know."

Roland half-heartedly nodded, relieved an unwelcome visit was over. Isaiah left the room leaving Roland with meandering thoughts and a few pieces of metal. For several moments, he glared at the pieces then angrily shoved them aside. He rose and gazed out the window where an image of a man stared back. The image appeared lost and hollow, surrounded by questions but holding no answers. An opening door broke his near trance.

Shelly came in with uncertain eyes. Roland's gaze held the same. Little was said as they walked toward Jalen's room. They paused when a nurse met them at the door.

"Any change?" asked Shelly, desperately hoping for any positive sign.

"He's resting peacefully at the moment."

Shelly graciously thanked her with an uncomfortable feeling that the question was not answered, at least not in a manner so desired.

Not a good sign.

They entered with doubting expectations overtaking the optimistic. Shelly felt the longer the coma, the less the chance of normal recovery, or even recovery at all. The worst scenario doggedly crowded out the desired. They silently stood by the bed. Jalen moved ever so slight, barely more than a twitch, and uttered a slow groan. Shelly grasped his hand and held it carefully. Roland put a hand on Shelly's shoulder. She heartened at the touch of each hand. For an instant, a long-lost connection returned, a sense of oneness not felt in years.

"What will we do if Jalen…comes out of the coma but can't function?" said Roland, once again with little thought.

Shelly looked him straight in the face, wondering why the question arose, why an answer would be necessary. "We'll love him just as much as before. The condition of body and mind doesn't determine what resides in the heart."

"It means a lot of things will need to change. I believe you're prepared. I hope I can handle it."

Shelly wasn't sure how he meant it but decided it leaned toward consideration for Jalen's welfare regardless of the circumstance. Anything positive was good even if she had to fabricate it. Her thoughts turned to others.

"It was nice that Isaiah came again. Did he have anything to say?"

"Oh, yeah! I'm sure you can guess. God stuff. He had this little game he played with some pieces of metal, a simple trick, but pretty deep at the same time. I really wanted to tell him to shut up, but I didn't want to make a scene. I've done enough of that. I just let him talk. Maybe it made him feel good."

"Thanks for listening. He's just trying to do his best. Can you get some of the chores done around the house this morning? I'll let you know when there's a change. I'm sure there'll be a lot of visitors this evening."

"Sure, give me a call if you need anything, or if there's any change. I'll be back later in the afternoon."

Roland patted her shoulder then gently hugged her. "Try and get some rest. This evening may be quite long."

Well timed. Felt good. She wasn't sure where it came from. She wanted to believe from the heart, but it came nonetheless. She at least regarded it a spirit lifter.

Early afternoon crept by. Shelly's thoughts were tumbleweeds in a prairie wind. Loosing emotional connection to Roland was pain enough. Losing her only son would push her over the precipice. Doubt barreled through a widening portal while hope stuck in a dwindling one.

Will he be able to function, to walk, to talk, to reason, to ever strive for his dreams, to lead a normal life? Will he even live? Surely, a God that brought him this far would not allow him to die...would He? I don't even know how God answers prayers. Some say the answer to many prayers is no. No! I'm not sure how to handle that.

Time slowly passed. Shelly nodded, trying to stay awake, when startled by the opening door. She heartened to see LaRana coming through it. She glanced at the clock: 3:28. They quietly conversed between intervals of silence and stroking Jalen's forehead. His somewhat ashen color unnerved each, but neither spoke of it. A sudden groan came with a spike in the monitor. His breathing became fitful. The door burst open, and two nurses rushed in. Backing away, Shelly reached for LaRana's hand, and each stood speechless, unable to move. Was this the end? Was it over?

The monitor's erratic pattern lessened at the end of several unsettling seconds. Calm was finally restored, but two hearts continued to race.

"Thanks for coming so fast," said Shelly. "I wasn't sure he… he…" She couldn't finish her thoughts.

"That's what we're here for. He's stable for now. He appears to be a pretty tough guy," said the taller. "We want you to know all of us here are in this with you, heart and soul."

Shelly smiled and placed a hand on the shoulder of each. "Thanks again. You have been ever so pleasant."

With the nurses gone, Shelly sat down with her head in her hands. She gently leaned back, looking directly at LaRana. "I don't know how many more of these sudden changes I can take. I do know this…you're being here has greatly helped me get through them."

"Thinking about what's swirling in my mind, I can't imagine what you must be going through. If there's anything else…"

"There's nothing any of us can do that I'm aware of. Continue to pray is all that comes to mind. You've been a rock for me. Not only have you showed me your concern but also your character."

Hand in hand, they looked in each other's eyes. Common desires were exchanged with no words spoken.

Late afternoon eased into early evening. Shelly and LaRana lost track of time. The room became a void, nothing moving, no sense of the past or thought of the morrow. The wheels of time came to a halt, waiting for Jalen to go in one direction or another.

A host of people came for the visitation, several school personnel, many from the church, and more than a few from the community. Jalen's coach and teammates came as one, filling up the room. Hannah cheerfully spent her first break greeting visitors as they entered. LaRana's heart leaped when the Super Six came in. She motioned them to the side, wasting no time in bringing them up to the moment. Shelly and Roland kept busy taking turns giving regards for coming and reports on Jalen's condition. While wearisome to repeat the same words, time quickly passed. Shelly heartened when Mike Monroe stepped through the door. His countenance brought a welcome moment of relief. She realized his apprehension was the same as his friendship.

Genuine.

The outpouring of support ended at nearly nine thirty when Isaiah left followed shortly by Roland. Only Shelly and LaRana remained till Hannah returned.

"Well, how did the rest of the visitation go?"

"I was a little astonished. Quite a few came. Most I knew, but some I didn't. They were quite gracious in expressing their concern. LaRana, bless her heart, was an absolute jewel, helped the evening go much smoother."

They started to return to Jalen when the waiting room door again opened. LaRana was pleasantly surprised to see a familiar lady come in.

"Mrs. Fontane! How good to see you. I believe you've met Mrs. Strade at...on a previous occasion. And I trust you remember my mother Hannah."

"Yes, I remember Hannah, if I may, at Willow's funeral and a few days after. I have not forgotten the care you, Hannah, and Shelly showed me. I remember the visit not only to see what I needed but also to actually help me on a few occasions...and to invite me to church. No one else came to visit. I couldn't stay home when I had a chance to return the kindness."

Mrs. Fontane's breath slightly halted. "I'm not much on prayer, but I will pray for all of you, especially Jalen. I am still trying to find peace. It's quite elusive. I'm not sure it will ever change. I certainly hope you do not...lose...your son, Shelly."

LaRana heartily hugged the yet grieving visitor. Shelly and Hannah followed with the same. Shelly kept her hands on Mrs. Fontane's shoulders. "Thank you so much. Your visit means a lot to me. I couldn't comprehend what you went through, but I'm beginning to understand."

Hannah put words into action. "I would be honored if you would let me pick you up to go to church with me and LaRana this coming Sunday. I once was quite skeptical when a...good friend took us. It was a life changer. Would you do me the honor?"

"Well, I...might do that. I don't mingle well with people, but I probably need to get out somewhere."

"Great! I'll pick you up at nine thirty. I think you'll find it quite uplifting."

With Hannah going back to work and final goodbyes to Mrs. Fontane, Shelly and LaRana returned to the ICU, finding Jalen resting peacefully. The monitor's beeping promptly returned them to the uncertain trial. Shelly was visibly exhausted and laid down for a shallow rest at nearly twelve. With LaRana sitting near, she drifted into the deepest sleep since the ordeal began.

The clock turned one in the morning with LaRana nodding at Jalen's side. She woke with a start, silently scolded herself, then quietly talked to him about anything that came to mind: hiking to mountain peaks, her precious necklace, baseball, even fishing, which she knew absolutely nothing about. That didn't matter. She had to talk, and she had to sing. Her song, usually given from her chords, now came from her heart.

Another uneventful hour crawled by, then another. Only Hannah's short stops interrupted the routine. Glances at the clock then back to the monitor found little change in each. LaRana continued to sing and stroke his head.

At a little after five, she stood, yawned, and stretched.

Suddenly, a groan, a moving arm.

LaRana froze, peering into Jalen's face. His eyelids fluttered then opened. They stared at each other, speechless for several moments. LaRana wanted to alert Shelly, wanted to talk to Jalen, wanted to call the nurse, wanted to yell to the world, but couldn't manage a word.

Jalen slowly closed then again opened his eyes and spoke around the mouthpiece. "Nith...zong."

"Mrs. Strade! Jalen's awake!"

Shelly's eyes flew open. She sprang from the bed, nearly sprawling to the floor. "Jalen, can you see me? Can you hear me?"

Jalen slowly nodded.

A nurse promptly came to the room. With a beaming smile, she gingerly removed the mouthpiece. "We can do without this at least for the moment. Well, it's good to see you awake, young man. We began to think you were going to sleep the spring away."

After careful fussing with tubes and machines, she turned to Shelly. "Talk to him, but don't let him try to get up. Let's take it a little at a time. Dr. Malone will be here before too long."

Most of Jalen's words came weak but coherent. Processing communication was delayed; pieces drifted but slowly came together.

"What is she…talking about? I remember…uh, I remember getting hit but nothing…after that. It was…um…tonight, after… the game. And ooh, I have…quite a headache."

"You have been here for nearly three days," said Shelly with a touch of joy mixed with relief.

"Three days. Three…days? What? How can…that be? I've missed… I think…the Canyon River game."

Shelly and LaRana turned to each other, widely grinning. Shelly put a hand on Jalen's shoulder. "Yes, yes you did, but what you almost lost, but thankfully kept, is probably a little more important."

Jalen started to rise but fell back. "Wow, I really…have…a mean headache."

"You just keep yourself down, do you hear me! And don't be messing with that bandage!" scolded LaRana. "The nurse said a little at a time. Besides, you're still hooked up. Try that again, and you got me to deal with."

A pall fell over the room for several seconds. Shelly couldn't help but smile. Jalen frowned. Nothing more was said about getting up.

The nurses came in, checking the monitors and tubes. They put the mouthpiece back then left smiling with thumbs up. An hour passed when Dr. Malone knocked on the door then entered.

"Well, I see you decided to wake up. It's about time. We thought you might not waken for a day or maybe a day and a half, tops. Your injury was quite severe. I imagine you have a headache. I'm always optimistic, but I did have some concerns on the delay. Good thing you're tough, though maybe not quite as tough as these two fine ladies."

Shelly grasped the doctor's hand. "I can't thank you enough. You have brightened our sky once again."

"We would like to take all the credit, but we can't. Seeing the severity of the injury, I was quite concerned he might not pull through. I was told a lot of people used our chapel. Perhaps most of the credit should be given to Somebody else. I may have just been the instrument. I'll stop by later in the day. With some strict instructions, he might possibly be able to go home in a few days. He will need some therapy to see if all is well. We'll see how the rest of the day goes."

"Thank you. Money doesn't seem enough to repay you."

"Well, how about getting me a ticket to a baseball game when he's ready to play. I've heard a lot about him."

"That's a deal," said Shelly with a wide smile. "I'll try to get you the best seat."

Dr. Malone worked with Jalen for several moments. "Hope you don't mind if I come to a game."

Jalen muttered around the mouthpiece. "I…'ould be…'onored."

"You'll need to stay with the mouthpiece, off and on for a little while, to see how you progress. I would say try to relax, but I'm guessing these two will see to that. The headache should lessen in a few hours, but I'll order something for it. I believe you'll be ready to sit up by then."

With a pat on Jalen's shoulder, he left the room leaving two ecstatic ladies behind. Shelly snapped her fingers. "I need to call your dad. He'll be glad you're awake."

"Oh, my, I completely forgot. Mom wanted to know when he awoke," declared LaRana suddenly. "Excuse me, and you stay put, sire. Perchance you even entertain the thought of getting up, forget it, or your lass will blow her stack."

Jalen grunted with a thumb up.

LaRana returned within fifteen minutes and stood near Jalen. Roland arrived shortly after eight in the morning. He met Shelly with a soft kiss on her cheek, a greeting common in long years past but now felt warm. She couldn't remember the last one.

"Thanks for calling," he said in a much kinder tone.

He said good morning to LaRana with a smile nearly causing Shelly's jaw to drop. He then turned to Jalen. Rambling, soul-searching thoughts, entertained overnight, became words.

"It's good to see your eyes again, Jalen. Your accident has caused me to think a lot. I never properly apologized for my...indiscretion. I'm really sorry it all happened. I bet you'll be on your feet in no time. I believe you still have some games to play."

Jalen fumbled with the mouthpiece then removed it. "Uh... thanks. I'll be home soon, I think, if I can ever get by...these two."

Missives Seven

Jariel,

You are receiving some fortunate breaks. I was extremely confident Jalen was ours. Did about all I could under the circumstances. That van should have sent him to our realm. We were prepared to receive his spirit. It infuriates me to think my prey will believe in prayers to your Master. Enjoy your temporary victory. I am quite certain we will get another chance. As you are keenly aware, we have many more enticements to lure these simple-minded humans.

I perceive you are gloating about this momentary setback, but I'll do my best to make it short-lived. I envision situations to profoundly test any faith these hapless beings place in your Master. You are acutely aware of our tenacity to prevail.

LaRana and Jalen seem of interest to all. Maybe working on them a little more will set the stage for rejection of your efforts. Unfortunately, Jalen may recover, but he has yet to seriously consider you. LaRana still has conflicting thoughts, and that's all I need. If something untoward befalls her, the others could lose their shallow faith in your Master.

I really don't look forward to your reply, but even losers must have something of which to boast. You may deem Jalen's ordeal contemptible, but I certainly am not ready to concede anything. Enjoy your little victory for now. It will not last long.

Esul

*****

Esul,

My, your failure to end Jalen's life outside my Master must have really upset you. Our Creator's gift of prayer has surely caused you untold grief. There are times prayers are answered differently than humans desire, but He always has the interests of the sincere in mind. I also realize such answers have caused some to fall away and turn to your charms, but not this time. The extreme events you so precisely orchestrated have failed at least for now. May I be so bold as to inform you of your ill-begotten effort?

First, Jalen still lives. I believe you thought his demise would drive a stake into the hearts of those in his life. We won't know that answer since he so persistently clung to life with some help from Shelly, LaRana, a competent physician… and my Master. Remember, He hears. Jalen's near fatal accident will surely give him pause to reflect on how he survived and bring him to think deeply on the power of faith.

Secondly, LaRana prayed, granted with some uncertainty, but she sought divine help. That will be sufficient for a continued search for her Savior. Your desperate efforts to gather Jalen and LaRana have just met the resolve we like to see, along with serious consideration of the existence and power of our Master.

And in case you ignored a meeting we set in motion, take note of Roland. Our admirable servant, Isaiah, combined compassion with courage to speak with him about the Creator. While Roland's defenses are thick and his eyes blind, Isaiah was able to give him reason to contemplate us. Maybe you had better reconsider your confidence he would never give us a second thought.

All in all, I would say your appalling effort has failed to divide those for whom we vie. In fact, if anything, you have set the atmosphere for a uniting of minds and maybe hearts. Such may cause you serious dismay, indeed. I certainly am aware you will try more extreme circumstances to win, but I am determined to see them fail.

Jariel

8

Unexpected

Hannah shuffled about the kitchen, gleefully humming a tune, thoroughly enjoying a peaceful but rare Friday night at home. The longed-for evening with LaRana was a time to rejoice and celebrate with a baked delight. A sweet aroma wafted through the house, serving notice a fresh delicacy had left the oven.

"Do you want ice cream on your apple pie?"

"Sure, why not? It's just a few more calories. Wow, that pie smells good. Maybe you should get off every Friday night."

While patiently waiting, LaRana's thoughts moved elsewhere, turning back to a friend's plight. With a sumptuous treat on the way, she didn't want to throw water on a great evening, but a desire to resolve a dilemma resurrected.

"Mom, do you have a minute?"

Hannah set the platter of delight on the table next to LaRana. "Sure, always for you. What's on your mind?"

"With Jalen's accident, we haven't had much of a chance to think about Sarona's situation. She told me today the hearing went about as expected. It seems she's off the hook, at least for now. Apparently, her mother hasn't mellowed. According to Sarona, she hardly would look at her. She's been staying with a girl named Janene. Her mother told Sarona she needed to find somewhere else in a couple of weeks at the outside. Any ideas?"

"I checked with our landlord. She couldn't allow it for some liability and financial reasons. True or not, we must honor it. Does she have any new options?"

"Sorta, but they're very risky. It's my guess she'd be going from trouble to more trouble. She did mention a relative, an uncle I believe, in Alaska of all places. Seems he may be the only option she's got."

"Whoa! I didn't say we should give up. This isn't a small matter. At least give me the weekend to think. Maybe something will turn up."

LaRana leaped from the sofa and wrapped grateful arms around her neck. "Oh, Mom, thank you, thank you. I knew you would try to help."

"Now look, young lady. I'm not a miracle worker, and these situations rarely turn out very well. The best I can do is check around. Now, you dig into this pie before the ice cream melts."

Saturday morning found Hannah pacing the floor, recalling a friend in her teen years faced with a similar predicament. A few possibilities crossed her mind. She wasn't optimistic about any of them. Running out of sound options, another avenue arose, one intruding on a treasured friendship. With a touch of anxiety, she took a deep breath and picked up the phone.

"Hello, Isaiah, I need to see you. Can you meet me at the Frosty Treat? I really could use a cup of coffee."

She paused, waiting for a hopeful reply. "No, there's nothing wrong with me or LaRana. It's...well, something private. Oh, yes... coffee with cream. If Ashlynn's there, she'll know."

Shortly after nine, she passed through Frosty Treat's doors with no small measure of apprehension. Paul leaned on the counter discussing a fishing lure with a customer while Karen hoisted a tray of food toward a party of four. The intellectual assembly of seasoned minds held down their usual location, sipping coffee and heartily recalling days of yore and current events deemed worthy of conversation. Ashlynn, beaming as usual, waved then turned to take an order. The teen's contagious smile lifted her spirits.

Several patrons greeted her with cheerful hellos. A few she saw visiting Shelly at the hospital. She recalled her first entry to the restaurant when she felt like an outsider, a spectacle for gossip. She also recalled how wrong she was.

Isaiah sat by the window in a sunlit booth. He motioned her over where a steamy cup of coffee waited her arrival.

"With cream, I believe."

"You got it. Thanks."

"Well, I had a little help from Ashlynn. What else besides coffee do you have in mind? Something private can mean a lot of things."

Hannah scanned the café as if assuring privacy then lowered her voice. "Well, this one is really important. LaRana told me about one of her senior classmates who had a run in with the law. I, uh, assume you're aware of the incident at the convenience store a few weeks ago. An acquaintance of LaRana's was with the perp. She's been cleared of any wrongdoing, but her mother kicked her out. We're trying to find a place for her to live, at least till graduation. Since you know about everybody and every agency in Pallon Ridge, I thought you might have a suggestion, and… I just had a bad feeling I'm abusing our relationship by asking."

"Oh, don't feel that way. I believe in helping anyone who makes mistakes. I've made my own. We actually have a group of middle agers who are dedicated to helping people who find themselves in tough situations. I don't recall such a circumstance as this, but they've tackled a few hard ones. They're a dedicated bunch. Driven, you might say. They thrive on results. Would you meet them with me?"

"Sure, I would be glad to. Amazing! You never cease to astonish me. Thank you, Isaiah. You may be a Godsend for this young lady. Should I bring LaRana?"

"Now, don't celebrate yet. And yes, LaRana should be there. I'm sure she knows her better than we do. This is a serious consideration for all concerned. Let's pray about it now. I find prayer a good start to any endeavor."

They held hands and Isaiah petitioned the Lord to oversee the challenging effort. Hannah was astounded at his devotion and faith in God. To all she had learned about him, one pearl of character always glowed brightly.

There was nothing phony about Isaiah.

*****

Time swiftly passed. Early spring was warmly welcome. Pulling a morning shift was unusual, even surprising, but Hannah didn't mind. Sunlight rushing through hospital windows brought a welcome change from paler glows of street lamps. It also allowed pleasure of evening time, especially for LaRana and Isaiah. Only moans from patients in pain or unable to get any rest interrupted the silent halls.

Another rinse of the mop, another basket emptied, another bed made. Hannah drew satisfaction from doing a job as skillfully as possible. She organized the oft-menial chores and accomplished them timely and efficiently. Other than accepting a task and giving her all, she kept one overriding thought.

It paid the bills.

She saw the despair and heard the agony of those painfully recovering from, or preparing for, surgery, and of those whose remaining days would be spent at the hospital. Brightening the moments of the stressed became a driving force. Helping others brought a sense of achievement, usually simple, yet oddly profound, immeasurable. Giving the unfortunate and suffering a temporary joy brought a deep, inward sense of worth, a state of mind previously known only with LaRana.

Early afternoon found her cleaning a room in Extended Care. Some rooms were empty. Others held patients desperately struggling with serious life-threatening issues. Groaning filled with agony tore at her heart. Within the section's chorus of moans came a familiar voice, feebly drifting across the hall.

"Miss Hannah, can you...hear me? Miss Hannah, Miss Hannah, do you have...a moment?"

Hannah hurriedly tucked in a clean sheet and bagged the used. "Just a minute, Mrs. Frazier. I'll be there shortly."

She fluffed then placed a pillow on the well-made bed. She hastily crossed the hall where an elderly woman lay hooked to a slow but consistently beeping monitor. The room was bleak. One vase of somewhat wilted flowers, brought by an old but considerate neighbor, offered the only brightness. Hannah wondered if loneliness brought her to the brink of death as much as a failing heart.

"What can I do for you, young lady?"

"I feel…a little weary. I sure would like to hear…one of your stories again. Could you…tell me the one 'bout you and your cousin… you know, the one where you'uns got chased…by that mama bear."

Mrs. Frazier's eyes desperately pleaded for someone to spend time with. Hannah sat by the bed, surmising her remaining days were few. Alone she laid, no family visitors, and few friends to come and pass the time. All that remained was the sound of someone's voice, a gentle voice sending memories back to carefree days of an innocent age. A sound saying someone cared, a sound walking by her side on the bridge from the known to the hoped for. Hannah deeply felt the patient's desperate desires and offered her free time to provide comfort.

"I go on break in ten minutes. I'll be back. You can be sure of it."

"Thank you, Miss Hannah. I…can always…count on you."

She returned as promised, pulling a chair bedside. A weak smile and a shaky hand greeted her arrival. The patient's face was ashy, but her eyes were bright and grateful.

"I'm sorry to bother you, Miss Hannah, but I do like…your company and your stories. They remind me…of when I was…but a small girl."

"Never you mind, young lady. Talking with you is a pure pleasure. I haven't seen your family come in. Do they live near Pallon Ridge?"

"No, I'm…all that's left. I came…from Texas four years ago. I…wasn't able…to get out very often. Didn't have…much of a… chance to make…new friends."

"Well, I hope you don't mind me calling you a good friend. I've heard you pray. You certainly lifted my spirits. Let's see now…oh yes, me and my cousin Asia. Now what a strange coincidence, I just happen to recall a few more things about that ornery ol' bear."

For several minutes, the distraught patient absorbed Hannah's words, often mixed with labored chuckles and dancing eyes. She kept her gnarled and slightly cold fingers calmly lying in the storyteller's gentle hand. Hannah occasionally paused, interrupted by short coughs and spasms of pain. She patiently but helplessly waited, unable to ease the physical misery. She finished the story as Mrs. Frazier's eyes half shut over short erratic breaths.

"Thank you... Miss Hannah. You...made...me...you...made..."

Her declaration grew weaker, and the monitor became erratic. Two nurses rushed in as the line went flat. One quickly tried CPR with no response. Several more attempts proved unsuccessful. Hannah stepped back with sorrow oozing from her eyes. One nurse quickly paged a physician; the other kept pumping her chest. In less than a minute, a doctor rushed to the bedside, but his efforts failed. The room grew eerily quiet till the doctor whispered to the nurses.

Hannah stared at the lifeless body; no more pain, no more anguish. A thin smile reflected contentment that her near constant misery finally ended. Asking then receiving permission, Hannah wiped away the patient's tears. A calm aura now rested on her face. She thanked the nurses and physician then left the room with both a sense of loss and a warm feeling that Mrs. Frazier's last moments were not spent alone.

Eternal thoughts walked with her down the hall. Though grateful to help in the last moments of a lonely life, she wondered what waited for Mrs. Frazier as she entered the timeless; when for most the thought of "what's next" had but one answer. The query remaining chased all others.

Was she a child of God?

It suddenly dawned, a door opening wide, a light beaming through the minutia of life, chasing a host of pursuits to the shadows of irrelevance, leaving the only important question when a person departs this world.

Am I a child of God?

Not who will be getting the house, not who will take care of uncle Bill, not when granddaughter Joan will marry the high school math teacher.

Nothing else.

The quantity and value of possessions, the pride and vanity of achievement, all took a backseat to the eternal query.

Am I a child of God?

Temporal goals and plans, oft-considered life's priorities, suddenly lessened. The achievement and status of today woefully paled against the infinite tomorrows. How she stood with her Creator rose to a sharper focus. She recognized the value of her own steps taken to personally answer that question. Her enlightenment quickly changed to a solitary thought.

LaRana!

A new determination was formed. Among all the things she couldn't give, there was one resting in her hands. Her daughter would know the answer to that question when she passed. She walked down the hall with a mixture of sadness and illumination.

She entered the laundry room where a co-worker looked up from folded sheets. "Oh, hello, Hannah. Hope it's been quiet on the floor."

"All was usual till Mrs. Frazier passed away."

"Sorry to hear that. She was quite pleasant. Oh, before I forget it. Mrs. Belton requested your presence in her office when your shift is done."

"Did she say what for?"

"Nope. Ain't got a clue. Just said for you to see her. Nothin' else I'm aware of."

Hannah's thoughts completely turned around, incessantly rambling till her shift ended. Would the meeting be an offering for regular hours with a possible raise, or would it be for something less desirable? After all, in her mind, such meetings usually didn't end very well. Leave all our cares with the Lord said the preacher. With no one else in mind, she decided to do just that, come what may.

The clock's hand finally reached quitting time. Still suspicious of the purpose, she briskly walked to the elevator. Pestering unknowns wavered between anticipation and dread. Questions and curiosity accompanied anxiety. A sudden thought something bad happened chased all others. *Is LaRana okay?* To soothe her wonder, she rationalized.

It must not be LaRana. She would have sought me and told me herself. No, it must be something else. But if it isn't...? Oh, my, I may need a little help with this, Lord.

The elevator door could not open quickly enough. Hannah hurried down the hall, forcing a smile to oncoming staff and visitors. She stopped at the administrator's door; a glance upward sought divine comfort. She hastily stepped inside then paused, trying to regain some measure of poise. She tried but failed to calm a growing fear. An attractive secretary looked up from her computer.

"Hello, Mrs. Lester. Mrs. Belton is expecting you." She tapped the intercom. "Mrs. Belton, Mrs. Lester is here."

Hannah nodded and smiled, walking less than composed toward the door, unsure how she would leave. She hesitated, took a deep breath then entered. Mrs. Belton rose and motioned toward a chair. A warm smile graced the administrator's face, a smile saying something unwanted was about to happen.

"We haven't had much of a chance to talk with each other since you began with us. I'll take the blame for that. I've heard a lot about you. All good." She hesitated, taking a deep breath. "First, let me say your work here has been exceptional."

Hannah's heart sank at "has been." The words were anything but new. Once again, the guillotine's blade hovered over her head. Once again, haunting visions of the past raced in, unraveling emotions. The now memorized questions, "what job next" and "what town next," flooded her mind, drowning out all other thoughts.

"Due to the new, reduced budget, we had to trim three positions. Unfortunately, yours was one. Your end of employment date will be three weeks from today. I'm so sorry for this action, and I wish you only the best in the future. I trust your work ethic and friendly personality will quickly help you find a new position. Feel free to use me as a reference. If our budget changes for the better or a position comes open, I would gladly rehire you if you were available and so desired to work with us again."

Hannah slowly gained her feet, shaken but undaunted. She knew the routine by heart. She firmly grasped an offered hand and managed a smile. Her sweet yet strong character rose above the torment within.

"Thank you very much for allowing me to work here. I can only hope my effort has been satisfactory. I counted it a real pleasure working for you, your staff, and most importantly, our patients."

With somewhat awkward goodbyes exchanged, she calmly left the room. She nodded farewell to the secretary then gained the sanctuary of the corridor, trying to chase a host of whirling demons. She stumbled slightly, bracing against the wall. Breath came quick and short. Once again, doubt raised its ugly head. Since coming to Pallon Ridge, hadn't she done all the right things, worked odd hours to pay bills, attended church, become a child of God? She vividly recalled LaRana's question of years gone by when Allon walked out.

'Mommy, did I do something wrong?'

She realized the query came from an innocent four-year-old, yet she couldn't help but entertain the same question. Uncertainty pounded on the fabric of her faith, taunting, and refusing to leave. The road to stability, recently paved with anticipation, took a sharp turn.

Unexpected.

What do I do now? What about LaRana? At least she's safe. Why would God allow this? What will everybody say? I'm a new Christian. Life is supposed to be better. Maybe I'm not good enough. Why does He hate me?

She suddenly understood that questions of a desired cherished relationship were not confined to four-year-olds.

She slowly ambled down the hall, wondering what comes next. Thoughts raced in all directions but went nowhere. She left the hospital to find a late afternoon sun brightly shining in a vivid blue sky. The few billowy white clouds, often calming, became stifling, seeming to gather close around her. Or was it the shattered confidence, the dreaded loss of a long-desired, stable relationship, the disappointment of religious expectations? The blatant fear of uncertain tomorrows joined hands with the whys of today.

Her steps grew heavy near the concrete path to the parking lot, the same path and the same parking lot as twice before. The only difference was the location. Visions of a settled future gave way to dark memories of a troubled past. She softly spoke to no one but a meandering breeze.

"Is this how it's going to be? Continually climbing the walls of despair only to slide down. And LaRana? How do I provide for LaRana? I must find a way, somehow. Why, oh why? Just as everything was going...going...oh, how could this happen?"

She quietly sat for several minutes in the old Escort. A variety of people leisurely traversed the sidewalks with visually carefree smiles. A touch of jealousy crept in. She finally departed, trying to grasp the gravity of the circumstance. Nearing Salarin Lake she suddenly turned into the park at the lake's edge. She desired time alone, time to think. Her steps ventured to the bench where she often relaxed with Isaiah, making memories hopefully for a lifetime. Those memories, yet close, now seemed destined to reside in the closet alongside those of years gone by. She stared at a rush of gust-blown whitecaps sweeping across the water till disappearing. Such would be the destiny of her aspirations.

Isaiah seemed farther away, just outside of arms' reach. Would what they had together dim and fade away in the chasm of despair? Was it all real or just an illusion that came for a short visit only to swiftly vanish?

What will he think of me? Another failure? I've lost a job, and now will probably lose a...hoped for future. How am I going to make it?

"I know," she impulsively blurted to the lake's gently drifting waves, "maybe I can get unemployment for a while, then welfare. Easy to get, easy to keep, they say. Perhaps, at least, I can get LaRana through her junior year in high school."

With a hastily formed plan in tow, she started the car only to suddenly hesitate.

"But then what?"

Missives Eight

Esul,

I surmise you are delighted with Hannah's misfortune. I have no reservation your wicked mind was somehow involved. You spare no angle to cause agony and uncertainty in my Master's creation.

You may reason Hannah will lose her faith, but she will prove you wrong, demon. Your assumption of weakness is erroneous. She has greater resistance than you presume. Her thirst for the truth, though now being tested, will keep her vision turned toward our realm. She will perceive the roadblocks you so cleverly devise. With help from her newly found family, she will meet the challenge of your devious schemes.

I know you didn't overlook the joy she brought to those in distress at the hospital. She's finding the value of serving others in need, the inner peace that comes from easing the anguish of the suffering. You may have placed doubt in her mind, but you cannot erase the kindness in her heart.

You surely noticed how Hannah and Isaiah are drawing closer. Might that cause you any grief? She is learning what my Master spoke so much about when He walked this earth, loving others as herself. And now, Hannah is beginning to comprehend that Christian is not a title to wear but a lifestyle to live.

I reveled the moment she suddenly grasped the big picture of life. While your efforts try to keep humans wrapped up in the temporary and immediate, she caught a glimpse of eternity in the passing of one our believers. All the things occupying the minds of mankind are insignificant compared to the question she came to understand, the question you try to hide from unsuspecting souls.

Hannah is sorting out life's priorities. She is determined to answer that question in favor of us, not only for herself but also for LaRana. Sorry, but your task just became more difficult. So enjoy yourself for the moment. It will come to an end.

Jariel

*****

Jariel,

Well now, desperate angel, how did you like that magnificent turn of events? Hannah's moment of revelation was followed by another failure. It allowed doubt to marvelously return. I was profoundly elated, a masterful stroke of genius if I might say.

Hannah's awareness of that vital question will soon fade along with hopes of finding peace. She will give in to her fate of failure, and of course, LaRana will diminish with her. I do so enjoy seeing humans strive to reach the Light only to fall back into a struggle with life. At the pleasure of bragging, I am quite good at keeping vision short and selfish.

It is my ardent desire to get into humans' heads. A weak, defenseless mind allows me entrance. I like to fill it with a lot of clutter and confusion. It's such a great place to sow the seeds

of destruction. Poor Hannah. She thought her life
was finally on the mend. Look what one bump in
the road can lead to. I believe she is about to give
up the pursuit of life.

You are keenly aware how I despise thoughts
of self-worth and self-reliance. I am much more
comfortable with concepts of self-failure. She has
a stunning case of it. And now, she's teetering
on the edge and heading for the abyss. Splendid
indeed.

You seem to be so defensive. Is it that you
cannot stand my little victories, my small con-
quests that so often build to the big one, another
collection of pitiful souls? This one wasn't too
hard. If someone at the hospital had to go, why
not make it the newcomer to town? It's so common in the human world. Why, you might ask?
I have found stirring up partiality and prejudice
can lead many souls our way. You must agree.
I've been doing it successfully for as long as I can
remember.

Hannah will get depressed, and lonely, and
desperate, and I won't go on. LaRana has nothing
to fall back on but her past. How do think that
will work out? Your effort to bring the Lesters and
the Strades into a relationship with your Master's
servants is like a row of dominos. Hannah will
fall, followed by LaRana, followed by Jalen, followed by Shelly, and I already have Roland well
on the way.

As for her newly found family, I can hardly
contain my amusement. She isn't, let's say, "one of
their own." She's no more than a Hannah-come-
lately. I know nearly all in that appalling congregation of annoying ingrates have overcome prejudice to embrace the different, but those were

close people, long-time friends, neighbors even. Now Hannah and LaRana might be given some pity but little else. Then, it's hit the road again, ah yes, the magnificent one-way road to us.

Are you troubled about my methods of collection? Don't rejoice if at times you thwart a few. I've got many more, some gently persuasive, some rather direct, and some just plain frightening, though I find them humorous.

It's been so long, even beyond recall, since I had a greater desire to garner a soul more than LaRana. Seeing her try to turn life toward something meaningful has made me all the more determined to gather her. It has become an obsession.

Well, let's watch them all fall, one by one. And fall they will, hopefully soon. I need to pick up the pace. There are others warranting my attention.

Esul

9

Mama

The last rays of evening slowly disappeared leaving the end of twilight with but a wisp of breeze. Hannah fretfully sat on the sofa, again mired in the quandary of failure. The darkness of life joined the darkness of night. Her heart was breaking with hopes hanging on a thread. Nearly two years had passed since breaking the news of moving to LaRana, news met with nothing more than a shoulder shrug. This time would be harder. LaRana was overcoming the past, finding trust in new friends.

Though a prayer left her lips, it was offered with no small degree of reservation, fighting a gnawing doubt any ear would receive it. After all, she surmised, the path of mistakes was far too long to expect anything else. The demons returned, mocking and pulling her toward despair. She rose and paced the room before stopping at the window, desperately trying to conceive a positive thought. None came. She continued to wallow in failure till the dwindling light brought street lamps to life. She trudged back to the sofa and quietly sat in the growing darkness. The door's opening and shutting broke the eerie silence. LaRana cautiously stepped passed the entry.

"Mom, I'm home… Mom? You here?"

"In here."

LaRana entered and turned on the light. She quietly set a folder on the table with an inquisitive look. "Why are you sitting here in the dark? Is something the matter? Are you okay?"

"Sit down, LaRana. We need to talk."

LaRana's cheerful countenance immediately fell. She recalled similar words from previous occasions and wondered what drastic news was coming this time. She plopped down in the chair, peering at the despondency in her mother's face.

Words welled in Hannah's throat. The daunting task of bringing them to her lips proved more difficult than imagined. LaRana rose from her chair and gently sat next to her. A bewildered frown rested on her face. She slightly wrung her hands, patiently waiting on what was already feared.

Hannah knew the words by heart. They were a memorized discourse, worn and despised, waiting in the wings for recall. Having tasted the joy of bliss and renewed hope for life, she found them difficult to once again utter.

"LaRana, I lost my job today. I'll be out of work in three weeks." She paused, unable to immediately find any more words.

LaRana leaned back with a jolt. "Again? Oh…sorry, Mom. I shouldn't have said that. What are we going to do? I don't want to leave Pallon Ridge. We're just getting our feet on the ground. I've found some good friends and a school I like. I really want to finish here."

"I know… I know. Don't say anything to anybody about this for now. We'll try to think of something, but if not, we may need to move back to Alabama."

"I'll get a job. I can work after school, maybe at McDonalds… or Sonic. Maybe Paul would give me a job. I can work with Ashlynn. Amelia is working at the Lake Side restaurant. Maybe they'll give me a job. I'll wash dishes or whatever to help us stay here."

"For now, you need to focus on your studies. You've made straight A's since we came here, and I want you do the same this semester and next year. You might qualify for academic scholarships. We need those to help with college. You also are helping a lot of needy people, which is of no little importance. I will find a way to support us, whether here or…somewhere else if need be. Remember this one thing. Trust the Lord no matter what the situation is. When all seems gone, trust in Him. He will help. We may not be able to see how, but we must have faith that He is able."

As soon as the words were out, Hannah knew they were right, just maybe not for them. She felt lessened asking LaRana to trust in the Lord while strongly challenged to do so. A desire to place full faith in her Creator could not dislodge the nagging thorn of an irresistible destiny, a fate sealed in youth, a fate repelling all efforts to die. As hard as she tried, she couldn't see any light ahead.

LaRana's upbeat mood suddenly changed. A quick trip to the past invited anger to overcome reason. She leaped to her feet, and her voice bounced off the walls.

"No, this isn't right. I'm not going back to where we were! There's nothing there for me...for us. I thought things were supposed to work out now that you're one of them. Is this what happens to Christians? I don't know how to trust in somebody I can't see or even understand. Probably just as well. This revered God seems to pick and choose the ones He caters to. We must have been left off the list! No! I won't do it! I won't go back!"

LaRana burst into tears, dashed around the sofa, and ran to her room. A slamming door hauntingly echoed till a heavy pall descended. Hannah rose and started to follow only to stop and lean weakly on the wall. Her breath came short and quick. With sudden silence, the room became a tomb with shrinking walls and no front door, only one in the back, one she despised to again open.

She regained the sofa, leaned back, and shut her eyes. Visions slowly appeared, visions of the past thought buried, each one more haunting than the one before. Allon's glaring face was etched in disdain without so much as a twitch. He walked quickly by with a shrug of cold shoulders. Her mother, feverishly working in the garden, gave her a hasty glance, wiped her brow and continued hoeing. A very young LaRana quietly sitting on the ground, returned her gaze through desolate eyes. She tried to grasp any measure of self-respect, but visions kept repeating till well after midnight when she finally fell into a shallow sleep.

A rising sun found her still lying on the sofa, staring at the ceiling, searching frantically for answers, for direction. With solutions yet elusive, she settled on prayer.

"Lord, I don't know how or even if You hear prayers of someone new, but we need to find a way to stay here. This is the first time I have had real hope for LaRana. I know I'm not worthy to ask for anything, but I'm at a loss on what to do. I feel the sting of another failure. Am I doomed to repeat my past? I know I will lose LaRana if she returns to…old habits. If You are there, please help."

She quietly arose, desperately trying to believe the mental words just uttered. The present was hidden by visions of bygone days, haunting shadows of a worn shanty barely providing shelter, dreams of rising above eyes of prejudice and ashes of poverty. Now the path was eerily lit, leading back to a crypt of misery.

Doubt settled in with a vengeance.

Saturday seemed an eternity. LaRana was subdued, falling into mood swings, some with stony silence, most consumed with rage. Hannah became cautious, withdrawn, unwilling to confide in anyone.

Sunday arrived with dread to attend church. She and LaRana skipped Bible study but came to the worship service. Both minds were filled with uncertainty. One harbored resentment, the other confusion.

The back door opened wide.

Hannah solemnly sat by Isaiah as the crowd quickly gathered, her normal bright aura now dimmed by fear of rejection. A host of people passed down the aisle. She knew most by name. So many. She suddenly realized more people were closer to her now than any time in the past, and yet they now appeared to be moving away, slowly ebbing into shadows. She also knew she was the one moving from them.

Isaiah noticed a change. "Anything bothering you? We missed you in class."

"No, nothing. Just…got around a little late this morning," came a fib.

"You seem both to be here and somewhere else."

Hannah glanced at everything and everybody but Isaiah. "I'm sorry, but… I… I just have some personal things I need to work out. I'm sure everything will be okay."

Isaiah moved to look straight at her. "Is it something I can help with?"

Hannah lowered her eyes and whispered. "No. No. I will take care of…things. You needn't worry about me."

She stared at the cross looming over the auditorium, a cross promising hope now seemed no more than a historical symbol. She mentally reached to touch it, but desperate efforts fell short. A picture of Jesus wearing a crown of thorns hung on the wall to her right. His eyes, usually encompassing the entire crowd, now looked straight at her, through her, as if peering beyond the physical. She shifted her gaze, feeling considerably smaller. Her trembling hand found Isaiah's arm while distressing words desperately tried to remain unspoken. A declaration, struggling to stay hidden, was given wings.

"I do want you to know that if, for some reason, we can't stay in Pallon Ridge, I will cherish the time spent with you."

Isaiah was stunned. He looked all around then drew closer with words barely audible. "What? Are you leaving?"

Hannah grasped to pull back the announcement but could only offer a meager response. "I certainly hope not. I shouldn't have said anything, especially during this moment. It just…came out. Please ignore me. I believe it's time to start services."

The song leader's voice ended the exchange. Isaiah's face held an aura of sadness. He paused further inquiry, allowing her space to sort out apparent dilemmas.

With services ended, Hannah threw Isaiah a shallow smile, no words, no embrace. Hannah's silence bore a determination to keep her demons inside. Parting for the morning was cordial but strained. She closed the door to the old Escort and to those who were near, to anyone who might reject her for another failure. LaRana quickly buckled in. Hannah eased the car from the lot, leaving puzzled and concerned friends. For several blocks, silence was a third passenger.

"Did anybody ask you anything?" said Hannah, sharply piercing the stillness.

"Nope, and I didn't say anything. Nobody knows but you and me. Wouldn't do much good anyway. Maybe going back is the life we're supposed to live. It was too good to be true to think we could fit in with these people, to rise above those we sought to get away from. I guess this is the other shoe."

"We're not gone yet. Something will turn up. I can get unemployment for several weeks or maybe even several months. We have to get you through the spring semester here. Surely, I can find something by then."

"Mom, I love ya, but I don't have much faith in people helping. I'm still going to look for work even if I have to quit school."

Hannah swerved to the shoulder, screeching to a halt. "No! You will not quit school! You are not going to be another me! You have to make it out! You just have to! Only at last resort will we leave Pallon Ridge. We haven't come this far to turn back. I may not be a very good provider, but I want you to make it above all else."

"Well, help will need to come from somewhere. I don't see much around."

No more was said. Hannah wrestled with anger then disappointment. Every path of possibility ran directly to a "road closed" sign. The remaining distance home was driven in silence.

Hannah spent much of Monday morning carefully pouring over help wanted ads, but nothing popped off the pages. She met with several businesses but couldn't quality for anything. Numerous phone calls proved futile. Several shops put her name on a list. She knew what that meant. Frustration engulfed her, refusing to let go.

Finally home, though well spent, she nervously paced, fighting imminent defeat. Doubt smiled, resolve crumbled. With nothing but rejection for the day's efforts, she plopped into a chair, her body and mind drained of everything but hopelessness.

Jalen arrived to pick up LaRana in late afternoon. Her normal bubbly enthusiasm was noticeably missing. Quickly leaving, she was silent, donning the garment of anger.

Hannah noticed her demeanor as she approached the door. "LaRana..."

"Back later!"

The sound of the slamming door was the same heard trying to walk through the many found open. She quietly sat, pondering thoughts till the silence grew too loud. The room closed in, ominous and suffocating. She quickly grabbed her purse and headed for the lake, seeking warm thoughts to chase the cold. None came.

She parked the car then dejectedly walked toward the bench holding a host of pleasant memories, hopeful anticipation of a stable future. She strolled along a bed of large rocks surrounding a glorious flower arrangement when she met another couple walking arm in arm. Vividly recalling the tender feeling of Isaiah's entwined with hers, she gently stroked her arms, one of possibly forever and another of soon to be gone.

She reached the bench and sat alone, staring over clear water barely rippling in the gentle breeze. Several others calmly walked by and offered a hearty greeting. A few couples ambled down the path, gleefully chatting amidst chuckles of mirth. A haunting dread arose that she would soon relegate such pleasure to the canyon of memory. She returned their pleasantries with a mix of friendliness and jealousy. Consoling thoughts doggedly tried knocking down numerous daggers hurling at self-respect.

They could not.

Failure was firmly attached, dragging along, waiting to crush every effort to rise above the sting of past woes. Afternoon shadows grew long as the sun sank toward the horizon, sending stunning rays of red and orange across the heavens. Weary eyes grew heavy then closed as she leaned back. With silence drowning out pleasant sounds, a voice from years long past dropped from a darkening sky. For a moment, everything around disappeared, leaving only a vision of her mother standing over her with hands on hips.

"Now you jes' pick yerself up, Hannah girl. Don' ya even think 'bout quittin'. No slackers here, li'l lady. Ya gonna bring up my gran'daughter right! If'n ya can work, ya work. That's the way I done brung ya up. As long as yer able to fend for yerself, do it. If all ya can git is sloppin' hogs, then slop hogs. Don' put yer life or LaRana's in the clutch o' dependin' on somebody else. Others'll be glad to help if'n ya git to where ya cain't make it. Don' say there ain't no way. There's al'ays a way. Ya jus' have to stick with it till ya done find it. Now, git off 'a this here bench, lift yer head up, and git crackin'."

A flock of geese rose from the lake as if startled by the blatant dressing-down. Hannah's eyes sprung open. She watched them gracefully glide across the water, taking Mama's last words with them. She couldn't help but smile at the sternness of her face when she spoke. The pleasant sound of birds singing in the tree above returned. She rose and set a quick pace for the parking lot. A new resolve, yet shaky, began to dim the clouds of gloom. She prayed nearly all the way home, trying to chase doubt with assurance her Master would hear the urgent prayer of a desperate mother, a battle yet a standstill at best. Besides, she reckoned, Mama was not one to mess with.

She found the living room nearly dark, but a faint light appeared from LaRana's slightly open door. She eased in and found her lying dejectedly on the bed.

"I wondered where you went," said LaRana. "I wanted to tell you how sorry I am to get so mad. I was thinking only of myself. Bet you been out lookin'. Any luck?"

"Apology accepted. I also believe I was doing the same," she smiled, sitting down at LaRana's side. "I need to talk with you. First, we are not leaving Pallon Ridge! We made it this far from desperation, and we're not going back."

LaRana's eyes widened, a look of surprise covered her face. She quickly sat up. "That's great! Where did you find work?"

"Well, I haven't just yet, but I will...somehow I will. I'm not relying only on my ability this time. I do believe my Lord will help me."

"Oh," said LaRana with markedly dampened enthusiasm and dropping eyes. "I just thought...maybe you..."

Hannah desperately tried to maintain faith, to keep a firm resolve charging ahead. "I really believe the Lord will not turn from our prayers. I'm guessing you have prayed about this, haven't you?"

"Well, uh, I, uh...not really...well...sorta maybe."

"Sorta? Well, just maybe He also hears sorta prayers at times."

"How are you going to find work?"

"I've hit about every business in town, but I'll hit 'em all if that's what it takes. Flip burgers, wash dishes, do maid work, whatever, maybe even slop hogs."

"Slop hogs?"

"Well…uh…never mind. There must be something out there for us. I have a good feeling."

"You have a good feeling? Well, I guess that beats a bad feeling. Where are you going to start?"

"Where I should have in the first place, at church. I believe we have a large family willing to help, not necessarily with money but with prayer and maybe helping us search. Besides, they know more people and possible job openings than we could ever know. Just think, LaRana, do you get the sense your friends at church would help you if they could?"

"Well, uh, yes, but your task is most likely a little tougher than anything I would need."

"Oh, I don't know about that. We never know the trials to be faced, trials that disregard age or status. Who can tell? Even you may face a more severe situation than looking for a job. Think of Jalen. Was his ordeal not of a higher magnitude than ours? Did he have friends like you to lend all the help possible, including prayer?"

LaRana thought momentarily then shrugged. "I suppose you're right, but life and death, that's a rare situation."

"That may be so, but what do you think Jalen would do if you needed help in a desperate situation…like…having to move? Do you think he would be glad to give it?"

"I don't know. I haven't given it any thought."

She put a hand on LaRana's shoulder. "Would you want him to help?"

LaRana lowered her head then just as quickly looked up. "Yes, Mom. I really would. In fact, except for you, he would be the first I would want to help."

"Well, I believe the same about our church family. I'm now their sister, a 'blood' relative. I would try to do anything for them, and I believe they would do the same for us."

"They're cool people, but that's based on the good times. And remember, we're black and half black. I also believe what happens during the bad times tells the greater story."

"As do I, and I believe color doesn't matter to them. I also think their vision goes beyond color. It goes to what's in the heart."

"Now, that would be different. I hope you're right."

"Yeah, I hope I'm right...no...no... I am right! I believe God answers prayers other than those of life and death. Our friends, our brothers and sisters at church seem eager to let God work through them. I'm going to call Isaiah. He should be the first to know. What say we meet him at the Frosty Treat? It's only a little after eight. I could use one of Paul's renowned shakes. A walk in the early night would be nice."

"I was going to ask if I could go with Jalen to the mall. He wants to look for some items he thinks he 'desperately' needs for college as if he was going to start classes tomorrow. He hasn't even graduated yet. I told him an early start to prepare is good, but now is a little bizarre. Well, anyway, he could pick me up at the Frosty Treat."

"Sounds good. You call Jalen and I'll call Isaiah to see if he can come this evening."

A light, evening breeze cooled the day's heat as Hannah and LaRana doggedly labored to overcome pessimism, gleefully chatting on the way to a place of good food and good people. Hannah again wrestled with the decision to seek help from others. She felt considerably diminished to take advantage of her relationship with Isaiah but kept her feet moving. LaRana thought it a great time to ask a few questions.

"Mom, why would you want to tell Isaiah first?"

"I could ask you the same about Jalen."

"Now, Mom, that didn't answer my question. Why Isaiah?"

"He knows me better than anyone else besides you. I do believe he has an interest in...my, uh...my...um...welfare. For some reason, I think he would want to be the first to try to help."

"When are you two getting married?"

Hannah stumbled and dropped her pocketbook. She quickly gathered herself, picked it up, and nervously brushed it off.

"Getting married! Who said anything about getting married? Land's sakes, child, I haven't thought about...uh...well... I haven't thought much about...uh...well, I guess it has crossed my mind. But it probably hasn't crossed his. So don't you go and get any notions about us getting married. Besides, I would certainly check with you if…uh…such a situation came up."

"Oh, that's nice. I appreciate that."

"Now…ah, since you mentioned it, what do you think?"

"About what?"

"Getting married…to Isaiah."

"So should I assume the situation has come up?"

"No, of course not, but say the situation did come up?"

"Maybe I should wait till the situation does come up."

"You're probably right…since that's what I said. But maybe just a little idea, you know, in case the situation comes up…just a little."

"Ah, I think I'll wait till the situation comes up a lot."

"Okay. That's okay," came the reply with a gentle nod. No more was said as they turned onto the sidewalk at the Frosty Treat. Awkward seconds quietly passed till she suddenly stopped and turned to LaRana. Her words were wrapped in a near pleading sigh.

"Oh, come on, give me a hint at least. We're in this together. I really want to know, and I think you really know I really want to know."

LaRana gave her a quick hug. "I lean toward the feeling he would make a good stepfather. But…just remember, if the situation comes up a lot, you gotta check with me first. Agreed?"

"Agreed."

They walked across the parking lot, sharing a moment of laughter. Jalen patiently waited, leaning against the Jeep's fender. LaRana gave Hannah a peck on the cheek. It was only a quick peck but one she needed.

"I'll be back by ten or so."

"Make it closer to ten than so. Good to see you, Jalen. Hope you're doing well. You seem to be getting stronger every day. How's the noggin?"

"Great. Finally, I can resume more strenuous activities in a few days if doc gives me the green light."

"LaRana told me you got a job at the Fitness Center. How's that going?"

"Super! I only get about fifteen hours a week, but it helps. I do some rehab there, so it's convenient."

"Sounds good. Have fun and be careful."

Jalen gave a thumbs-up, and soon, with the Jeep leaving the parking lot, Hannah reached for the handle of Frosty Treat's door. Several patrons sat and cheerfully chatted. Karen gave a quick wave. Ashlynn was her customary bubbly self, offering her usual smile as she passed by the entry. A new girl was with her, a young lady whose eyes lit up the room, whose smile was warm to a fault.

"Mrs. Lester, I believe you know Cheyenne. One of our girls had to quit. She's shadowing me to learn the ropes. I'm hoping she gets the job."

"How could I not know? One of the Super Six. I also hope you get the job. You have a good trainer."

"Thank you, Mrs. Lester. Just trying to keep up with Ashlynn is my first task."

"I sure can understand that. She's quite a chore to stay up with. I'm waiting on a gentleman. Could you come back when he arrives?"

"Sure. We'll be on the lookout for… Mr. Johnson."

"Can't get anything past you."

She watched them go to another customer. *Paul is really good to help students. The world needs more like him. Hmmm, perhaps LaRana…*

While her thought was good, she shelved it to the back of her mind to be recalled if needed. *Well, maybe this summer or senior year.*

She looked across the room and spotted an empty booth in a quiet corner. She wove around tables, receiving several hellos and friendly smiles. She nodded, returning the same.

She approached the booth when a sudden thought crossed her mind. *Am I being too brash, too imposing on Isaiah? Will he be offended? Am I again taking advantage of a friendship?*

"No! Get away from me, Satan!" she blurted a little too loudly.

A few glanced with puzzled looks. She felt a warm rush on her face. She recalled the moment of decision to become a Christian and the love freely offered by her new family. Second thoughts were pushed aside.

I believe this is the way it's supposed to be.

Nearly ten minutes passed before Isaiah arrived. He looked around the room till Ashlynn pointed her way. After a few greetings and back pats, he slid into the booth.

"Good evening. It's always a pleasure to see you, Hannah. I look forward to cozy atmospheres with you. This restaurant sure meets that."

"I know we usually sit by the south window, but I preferred this booth tonight. Is that okay?"

"Well, the waitress may be confused, but certainly. I consider any place with you is just fine."

A blush.

Ashlynn returned to the booth with her usual courteous smile and Cheyenne by her side. "Seems you found a new booth. Cheyenne will be waiting on you. She's ready to swim on her own."

Isaiah beamed. "It's nice to see you again, Cheyenne. You couldn't have found a better restaurant to work at."

"Thank you, Mr. Johnson. I think I'm at the right place."

"I'll go and let her solo on you two," said Ashlynn with a nod.

"Don't mind at all," came Isaiah's reply. "We'll try to be easy."

With Ashlynn going to another table, Cheyenne calmly asked, "What can I get for you two tonight?"

"A strawberry shake," said Shelly.

"Make that two," added Isaiah.

"Two strawberry shakes coming up." Cheyenne dotted the order pad and left with a smile.

They watched her leave, gracefully moving around tables, checking on patrons. Isaiah nodded his approval.

"Paul and Karen are great people. They are so good to help students get a start in a work setting. At least one of them is always here in the evening and weekends. Paul at sundry times heads for the river or lake or wherever there's a puddle big enough to get a lure in. Notice the display of fishing items. Now, just how many food establishments carry fishing gear? I've gone with him a couple of times. He catches fish no matter what. If he can't catch 'em, they probably can't be caught. Sure puts me to shame."

Hannah managed a slight smile through other, more pressing thoughts. Isaiah folded a hand under his chin. He looked into Hannah's eyes but said nothing for several moments. He noticed a hesitation, a nervousness seen only once before.

"It's a pure pleasure to again be in your company, but I sense there's something bothering you. I noticed it at church."

Hannah finally settled on getting straight to the point. "The reason I mentioned the possibility of leaving Pallon Ridge is... I lost my job at the hospital. It appears a cutback got me. I inquired at several businesses with no luck. I wore the phone out with the same result. I considered going back to where we came from and picking up my old job, but with a not so gentle voice from the past and a leap of faith, I determined to stay here if any way possible. LaRana is doing quite well in school, and she's around other friends I don't worry about."

She slightly dropped her eyes. "And of course, I thought of leaving my church family here...and, leaving you."

Isaiah fell silent for but a few seconds. He reached for her hand.

"I'm glad you decided to stay. No, I am thrilled you decided to stay. If I may be so bold, I have thought of you more than just a sister in Christ, which I know is most important. I look forward to every time we can get together, to walk the park, to sit side by side in church, to go on recreational trips, or to hold your hand across a table like this. I had resolved such feelings were gone forever. And... now... I hope I haven't offended you."

Tears welled. "On the contrary. As you, I've had thoughts of a... relationship. You not only have brightened this evening but many days before. Most have been pleasant, some have been cautious. I didn't want LaRana to get hurt again, but also I didn't want to get hurt again. You've been a breath of fresh air in my stale life. You've led us to a family we've never experienced. Our lives are so much richer. It's mostly due to you, although I must throw a few kudos to Shelly and Jalen Strade."

"A couple of fine people for sure."

"And you all have led me to Christ Who has given my life purpose, Who has given me direction, Who has given me a chance at eternal life. I understand now whereas before I was blind and selfish. But you, Isaiah Johnson, you have made this life bright and helped me gain the possibility of a future for LaRana. For that, I can never repay you."

"For my part, I hope our relationship has grown past owing and repaying. It is my desire we draw closer together, and who knows, maybe I will luck out and fool you into thinking I'm a good catch."

Hannah smiled. "I would like that. I want you to know all about me and my past, warts and all."

"I thank the Lord daily for such an exquisite lady coming into my life. I do hope to get to know you, warts and all. Oh! I just thought of something! Our congregation's secretary, Shirley, has submitted her retirement notice. Her final day will be in…a little less than three weeks. Would you be interested?"

Hannah's eyes widened. "Why, yes, yes I certainly would. What qualifications are needed?"

"Some computer and organizational skills, ability to get along with people of various personalities, keeping record of programs like our day school, answering phone calls, paying bills, putting up with hard-headed teachers like me, and this, that, and the other."

"I'm a little short on computer skills, but I'm usually a fast learner. I believe I can handle this, that, and the other."

"I'll talk with the elders. If they're interested, they'll want to meet with you. I can't promise anything, but at least it's a start."

"Do you think I may be infringing on other members? Will my, uh, heritage be a problem?"

"Some others may be interested, but you'll be considered no more or no less than anyone else. And no, we don't judge others by color or heritage. There are Christians all over this very diverse planet. We are the same in the eyes of our Creator, as we are in our own eyes."

"Well, that's good enough for me. We haven't been here very long, and I don't want to cause any bad feelings."

"I can't imagine anyone thinking ill of you. But I will check on other possibilities in case someone else gets the position."

"I am certainly willing to do whatever it takes, either at the church or somewhere else. Thank you, so much. How can I ever repay...oops...sorry."

With shakes finished, they parted, each with a mission to do. Hannah chose to walk home with relief and thankfulness. She wasn't sure about the secretary's position, but just the thought of others, precious others, might be willing to help lifted her spirits. She envisioned Mama peering down from the starry sky, smiling below eyes aglow with pride. She could hear her pleased voice, *"See, didn' I done tell ya."*

Lord, thanks for hearing my request, and thanks for Isaiah...and Mama. You have been good to me. I hope I don't disappoint You.

*****

The mall was unusually crowded for a weekday evening. Several teenagers strolled the corridor. A host of parents with young children drifted store to store looking for gadgets, clothes, and sundry items students deem necessary to pass time, to look better, or more precisely, impress their fellow students. Jalen and LaRana walked hand in hand through several outlets looking for items, some of similar purpose.

Though she tried to have faith in her mother getting a new job, LaRana wanted to tell Jalen about the possibility of moving. She kept looking for the right time but couldn't find it. As usual, she was enthralled at being with Jalen no matter the place. Setting distressing thoughts aside, she returned to the enjoyment at hand. LaRana was not bashful in giving opinions on Jalen's somewhat bewildering choices.

"Just exactly what do you need a dart board for? Let me guess. It's a guy thing. Clothes, I can understand. New phone, I can understand. I can even see a football, but a Wiffle ball and a Frisbee? Those, I can't understand. I thought only children played with such toys."

"LaRana, you're a doll, but we guys gotta have some fun time, considering all the long, tedious, boring hours we spend studying, slaving over books as if there was no tomorrow."

"Yeah, right."

"And just think about it. There won't be any extra time for say…girls."

"Hmm. I sure would like to believe you, but I know dudes better than that. There usually is little time for anything but girls. However, I want you to know I trust you without reservation. In fact, I trust you so much I'm going to gather a cast of spies at State to watch your every move. So a book, a bat, a Wiffle ball, or even a stupid Frisbee is all you better have in your hands."

"Hey, how about some Chicky Chunks? I'm a little hungry, and Chicky Chunks is one of my favorites."

"Let me see: baseball, Wiffle ball, Frisbees, and food. Yep, we're about to get your free time covered. And I can't imagine you ever being a little hungry."

While waiting in line, they set aside ideas on Jalen's needs and wants, choosing to ponder summer plans, where to go and what to do. The line slowly moved, testing Jalen's patience. They finally arrived at the counter and voiced their orders.

LaRana stepped forward. "A five-chunk with sweet tea, please."

Jalen followed. "A ten-chunk combo, five extra chunks and a large Dr. Pepper."

LaRana smacked his arm. "That's fifteen chunks!"

"I know. I know. Just thought we didn't have enough time for a large order."

LaRana started to reply till lifting her eyes to the heavens, smacking his arm again.

With food in hand, they meandered around full tables searching for one empty. They stood for but a moment then spotted a couple leaving a two-seater on the far side. They picked up the pace and arrived at the table a few seconds ahead of another searching couple. The table was not far from the main entry, providing a clear view of a wide variety of people, those coming and those going. Some they observed with mutual approval, while others left them with a total loss for words. After finishing a tasty meal, they sipped on sodas and talked of days past and days to come.

"You know I'm really going to miss you," said LaRana wistfully. "I still vividly remember you lying in that hospital bed, not knowing if you were going to make it. I even prayed, unsure whether there was anyone to really pray to. It did puzzle me a bit that you made it…not that I didn't want you to make it…but that you did maybe, uh, partly, because of my prayer. And then I thought, since your mom prayed, and Isaiah prayed, and Mom prayed, and everybody at church prayed, my prayer wasn't so important after all."

"I don't know a lot about the Answerer of prayers, but I do know about those who offered them. Your prayer thrilled me the most, even if unknowing, and unsure. I'm convinced He heard your prayer, and who knows, maybe your prayer was the difference. It's for certain I've been granted more time on this earth. Spending time with you has only made me more thankful to Him. I guess I'm becoming more of a believer each day. I assume He answers my prayers because here you sit, nagging me about Wiffle balls and Frisbees. What more could a guy ask for?"

A smack on the arm. A few heads turned.

"I'm really going to miss you. I might need help finding my locker next fall, and my knight in shining armor won't be around."

"Considering all the dudes who'll try to move in on me, I may have to cut class and show up that day to make sure they know to back off."

Another smack on the arm. A few more heads turned.

Jalen looked straight into LaRana's eyes. "As I once said, you got the best of both parents, and I think you are the most beautiful lass I have ever seen. There's a line in another John Denver song that says, 'The time I spend all by myself, I mostly spend with you.' My feelings are similar. I may often be alone, but I will not be by myself. You'll always be at my side regardless of the distance between us. Wherever I am, there you will be…only, be sure to run fast if I happen to be on the baseball field."

Another smack on the arm. Several more heads turned.

"I'm really, really going to miss you. It's going to be a long senior year. I can't imagine walking down the hall and not seeing you, or walking by the field, knowing you're not there. I'm hoping dreams of what could be will get me through lonely days and nights."

"I trust you'll keep going to church. I'm beginning to understand some of this Christian stuff, and I believe it's real. I just haven't figured what parts yet. Without the unlikely connection between our moms, we wouldn't be here. Our only lasting memory would be the vision at the police station."

"Yeah, what a drag that would be."

"During the off season, I'll be here every weekend possible. Two days with you is better than none. Besides, I need the rest of the time to throw Wiffle balls."

She reached over the table. Heads turned from all around. She offered onlookers a wry grin then promptly smacked his arm.

"Well, we better head for home," said Jalen leaving his seat.

"Yeah, the clock's probably heading toward Mom's so," she replied, rising.

Jalen glanced toward Chicky Chunks. "Uh, do you think there's enough time to get another five-combo? I may not get back here for three or four days."

LaRana's eyes bulged, her jaw dropped. A glance around revealed anticipating faces. She shrugged her shoulders, wryly smiled, and promptly slapped his arm. A chorus of cheers rang loud.

The clock stood a little before ten when they finally strolled toward the parking lot. LaRana held Jalen's free hand while he gripped a sack of chunks plus two bags in the other. Tender words and adoring eyes were exchanged on the lengthy walk to the Jeep. LaRana felt secure with Jalen, safe from not only physical harm but also mental anguish. She looked forward to the remaining days of spring then summer, till the day Jalen would be off to college.

She hadn't mentioned the situation with Shelly's job search. She decided to leave it to a higher Power.

Missives Nine

Jariel,

I presume you're reading this missive with considerable pleasure. I really abhor saying it, but I will. Orchestrating a mother's voice to Hannah was well thought out. As a reminder, I have made many of your Master's creation forget about the idea of self-reliance. Untold numbers have chosen to let someone else be responsible for their lives while they indulge in things that bring them unwittingly to me. Most indulgences, for certain, you do not approve of. What's eternal life to someone who doesn't want to follow your Master? Besides, the self-centered and mentally blind refuse to acknowledge the existence of you or me.

It can't get any better than that.

I'm very disappointed in Hannah. She was resolved to return to the past until that Isaiah came forth. He has become a considerable annoyance. He possesses a disturbing quality of inspiring humans with concepts such as nobility, honor, respect, forgiveness, sincerity, justice, and of all things, love. I find it quite easy to get unsuspecting souls to embrace my words like greed, selfishness, disloyal, vain, uncivil, complacent, and denial. He seems to reject anything we throw at him. However, this is a just a temporary setback.

You may surmise our battle is over. Think again. You know me better. I use a variety of ways to carry out my desires. As we roam the earth, we often find agents with unusual talents. You are aware how much suffering those of ill intent can summon, how much rejection of your desired precepts they bring forth, and how influential unbelievers can be.

I also find it refreshing how unfortunate events can destroy those either young in the faith or still not of the faith. You have made great progress with Hannah, LaRana, Shelly, and Jalen. It appears only Roland still drifts to my collection. Of this, I take personal exception. All I can say is beware. I often find it necessary to tease the thoughts of those with a strange view of life. It may take more than a wayward van to gather my desire. And be mindful, Jalen is going to college where we have many who wallow in the dark side of life. As I have said before, I will not rest until my craving is satisfied.

And do not be remiss to remember how I have warped minds of rulers, magnified hatred in numbers untold, destroyed a sense of decency, set up oppressive governments, torn down the noble, toyed with the minds of the weak and selfish, ripped asunder your Master's flock, and seared the hearts of multitudes. Pardon my boast, but with such lofty achievements, I simply cannot allow five trivial souls to escape my grasp.

So while you bask in the glow of good news, just remember, when things seem at their brightest, unusual things can happen. Yes indeed, very untoward things can come forth to shatter even the strongest of your believers. When your shield is taken away, when those who follow your Master see His protections gone, they will reject you, even curse you. We have seen it many times through the centuries, have we not? It is my speculation such a rejection is forthcoming once again.

So don't be surprised at what may transpire. Tables have been set, and desires have been accepted. I eagerly watch for my plan to unfold. If all goes as I foresee, I will collect all for whom we vie.

Esul

*****

Esul,

I would misspeak if I said I didn't take pleasure in Hannah's determination to provide for her family. I also revel in her perception of brothers and sisters in Christ. She is beginning to understand the beauty and grace of a life led by my Master. Gaining wisdom and assurance not only helps her but also her daughter. After all, LaRana is the one we both sought to collect, and she is the one who is on the cusp of active belief in the Creator and His Son. You know this, and I surmise it drives you to utter frustration.

Shelly has grown in her Christian walk. Jalen is also putting the pieces together, and they're beginning to make sense. He overcame your van and will overcome anything else you contrive. Roland yet remains an enigma, but we'll not give up. Sometimes, seeds sown take time to sprout.

As I have said before, you cannot prevent the Word of my Lord from going forth, and it shall not return to Him empty. It shall accomplish what He purposes, and it shall prosper those who gladly receive it. You may plant a thorn, but He shall raise a mighty oak.

You have many more souls in your realm, but you will not succeed with those whose hearts are filled with His Word. You have no power over the Savior. You lost that when He rose from the tomb. Therefore, you cannot prevent eternal life in our realm for those who understand and find wisdom and truth.

Hannah has long been a target of your vile attempts, but she has found the avenue of escape. She is beginning to comprehend the beauty and peacefulness in my Master's concept of life.

I'm intensely aware you have no dearth of evil schemes, but you can do nothing to those who truly follow my Master. I know of your diabolical efforts to shatter the faith of these precious souls, but it will be for naught. The power of my Master will hold forth.

Jariel

10

The Joining

The warm afternoon brought a slight southern breeze, a good day to meander around a beautiful setting. Hannah and Isaiah walked hand in hand, strolling among various beds of brightly colored spring flowers. Her life had brightened and confidence strengthened since finding a way to remain in Pallon Ridge. Glances at the past gave way to visions of the future. She could not recall a happier and more contented time.

"It's a wonderful day to be at Millander's Garden. And placing it by the lake was a wise choice. Maybe the clock will pause to better enjoy it. The flowers are so radiant and bursting with color."

"It's an amazing place, indeed," said Isaiah. "Its designer was inspired by Shaw's Gardens in St. Louis. No matter the time, except maybe for a spell in winter, seasonal flowers are always beautiful. I particularly like the section of wildflowers. The blending of aromas is so pure and sweet I can almost taste it. And just look at these majestic trees, ancient sentinels of noble character. They seem to hover over their realm as if protecting it."

"I couldn't agree more. It is a romantic setting," said Hannah, suddenly blushing at the choice of words.

"Yes, it is. Oh, by the way, how is the job training going? Any thoughts of backing out?"

"Not a chance. I love it, thanks to you again. It's only been a few days, but I'm already getting the hang of the computer. The elders, deacons, and members, especially Shirley, have been very encouraging. She's very patient and helpful to get me through so many tasks. I certainly enjoy the day care program where I get to mingle with bright, innocent young uns, as Mama would say. The Lord has blessed me in so many ways. I had always considered church people somewhat strange at best, but my brothers and sisters here are anything but strange. They're loving, caring, and so willing to help."

"I heartily agree. What would the world be like if all had the same decency and nobility? We sure wouldn't need so many prisons, and maybe the news would contain more stories of honorable and selfless deeds."

Gentle swirls of cool air accompanied the gentle stroll. They soon arrived at their favorite bench, the bench of Mama's unforgettable voice. The late afternoon sun's rays spread across the lake while several purple martins soared high then swooped down in a regal glide. The breeze fell to but a whisper while the sky rested over clouds softer than eider's down. Isaiah gently cradled Hannah's head with an arm on the back of the bench. Moments passed in silence.

"Isn't this a magnificent afternoon," said Hannah in a near whisper. "I feel like the trees, the flowers, the birds, and everything else are watching us, trying their best to impress."

"Yes, it's so quiet, and the lake seems to be kneeling to the sky," replied Isaiah, raising his arm from its rest. "Well, since we're speaking of kneeling…"

He rose from the bench then knelt to one knee, gently holding her hand. Hannah's breath came to a halt. Isaiah's eyes were brighter than the sun's gleam on the water. Two couples started to pass but paused for the perceived occasion.

"I cannot think of a better time to ask you to be my wife."

Hannah was overwhelmed. Sudden thoughts of LaRana were flashing beacons. *Oh…the situation has come up a lot, and I don't have time to tell her. What should I do?* Her eyes welled above her silence. She mentally crossed her fingers. *LaRana will surely understand.* As various thoughts spent time to whirl, Isaiah's countenance began to fade.

"I'm really sorry if I offended you, but I just had to ask."

Hannah cleared her throat and rather nervously stroked her hair. "Isaiah Johnson, I would be honored to be your wife. I remember the first time I held your hand. It was no more than a handshake, but I tingled like an awe-struck teenager. That simple touch has rested there ever since. I have grown to admire and love you greatly. No better man could I ask for."

He reached in his pocket and lifted out an ornate box. "I never thought I would give a ring to anyone. I hope you like it, and it fits. If it doesn't, I can take it back to the five and dime and get another."

A slap on the arm.

"Isaiah, it's beautiful, it fits perfect. It feels much better than… uh, never mind. I absolutely love it."

The bystanders heartily applauded, offering their hands for congratulatory shakes. Hannah and Isaiah were ecstatic, enthusiastically obliging. When the observers moved on, they sat back on the bench basking in the radiance of a long-desired occasion.

They embraced in the early evening's glow, together as one, sharing joys and memories of the past year. With the sun gracefully dropping toward the horizon, they slowly walked arm in arm down the sidewalk, now a soft cloud under Hannah's feet. The ride home was filled with excitement and quickly thought plans on whom to perform the ceremony, where it would be, and when. The only question with a ready answer was why. Love took care of that.

They lingered by Hannah's house as twilight drew to a close. After one more embrace and one more kiss, Isaiah drove away. Hannah gleefully watched till the car disappeared around the corner. She recalled a similar vision with Allon. The difference now was impulse replaced by maturity, infatuation replaced by love, rational thoughts of a contented future instead of sporadic moments of excitement that faded in the passing of time.

Her faith brought a keen understanding of life, Who gave it, and how it should be lived. She saw the path to peace, a path lessening the burden of guilt and failure.

She briskly walked up the steps, anxious to tell LaRana but a little fretful about her agreement. "The situation…she said. Let her know when it comes up…she said. Lord above, I sure hope this goes well."

With one more deep breath, she hastily turned the knob. LaRana sprawled on the sofa, deeply engrossed in a book. She stretched with a long yawn. Hannah gently shut the door. LaRana glanced over her shoulder then sat up.

"Well, about time you got home. I thought maybe you got lost. Let me guess. I'm gonna say…out with Isaiah."

"Can't fool you these days," came the reply with a beaming smile. She gently sat down with nervous hands in her lap. "LaRana, remember that, um…situation we talked about, the one concerning me and Isaiah? Well, it came up. What do you think I should do?"

LaRana dropped the book, her eyes lit up. "Did it come up a little or a lot?"

"A lot."

"Well, I'm certainly glad you waited for my opinion."

"Uh…well, um…anyway, what do you think I should I do?"

LaRana scooted across the sofa and threw her arms around her neck. "Oh, Mom, I think you should say yes. Say yes! You two were meant for each other. You won't find anyone better than Mr. Johnson."

"When do you think I should give him an answer?"

"When? When? Now! I love you, Mom, but you ain't getting any younger. Please don't take that wrong. Say yes before he changes his mind."

Hannah slowly reached into her pocket and revealed the ring, waving it with a smile. "Well, I'm glad you feel that way. I was a little worried since I already told him yes."

"Ya-hoooo!" shouted LaRana, leaping from the sofa, grabbing Hannah's hands as they quickly stood. With a smile from ear to ear, LaRana started a twirl. "You deserve a good man. I'm so happy for you. When's the wedding? Where's it going to be?"

"Well, we couldn't plan that out till I got your okay. I'm very glad you approve."

"You bet I approve!" A sudden cloud fell over LaRana's face. "Oh, oh, there's no one to give the bride away. Who can we ask to give the bride away? Grandpa would if he was alive. Maybe Shelly?"

"Oh, I've already found the perfect person for that chore."

"Good. Who is it?"

"You."

"Me? Seriously? Oh my, I couldn't... I wouldn't... I don't know..."

"Nonsense. I've never had anyone else in mind. It was always you. Whenever I thought about getting married again, which was very rare, it was you I wanted to give me away, but only if I can return the honor."

"I'll do the best I can, but it's going to be quite a while for the return."

"Well, it had better be! That's good enough, besides 'I do' is all you have to say."

"Aw, I can handle that... I think. And you most certainly can give me away...in marriage, I mean...not...just...give me away, although, I guess I tempted you to do just that several times."

"Never gave it a thought, young lady. Never. You have always been and will be my shining star."

Hannah quietly sat on the sofa with Rana clutched in her arms. Her mind raced back to LaRana's younger years, a time of innocence and gentle embraces. She held her joy as if once again she was four years old.

LaRana glanced up, proudly smiling. "Mom, you did good. Real good."

*****

Hannah found it difficult to slow her beating heart. The noon wedding was held at the lake in front of the oft-used bench, the bench changing life's corridor from despair of the past to anticipation of the future, the bench where Mama dressed her down, clearing a bewildered head. The scenic ceremony was held with songs from the Super Six, birds richly chirping from low branches, and young children tossing flowers around the couple as they walked arm in arm to face the preacher. Jalen and Shelly stood with LaRana who nervously, but admirably, gave her mother away.

The ceremony was picturesque but brief. With the crowning kiss, the rather large gathering offered congratulations before departing. Soon, only LaRana, the Strades, and the newly formed Johnsons remained.

Shelly proudly held Hannah's hand. "You two have a great trip. San Antonio has a lot to see. Enjoy the Riverwalk and Alamo. We'll take care of everything here."

"LaRana can stay by herself, but please check on her each evening. We'll just be gone for four days."

"Oh, Mom, I can take care of myself. After all, I'll soon be a senior."

"I know, I know, but it will ease my mind."

"We'll do that," assured Shelly. "If need be, she can stay at our house, or I can go to yours. In any case, she is going to have supper with us each evening, and there is no argument about it."

Jalen glanced at her with a slight frown; a subtle caution that such an arrangement might not be well received. Shelly's return smile said she understood. It also said it was the right thing to do.

Hannah looked straight at Shelly. Perceptive eyes said she realized her demons. "That's kind of you, but I sure don't want to cause any...uh, well, that really won't be necessary. Just check each evening."

"Nonsense. I look forward to having a daughter for a few days."

With goodbye waves exchanged, the newlyweds headed south for a long desired, memorable honeymoon. As the car left the lot, LaRana had a sudden sense of loneliness.

The chosen length of separation from her mother had never been so long. She rode home with the Strades in near silence.

LaRana passed the late afternoon with mixed feelings, pondering the changes unfolding. Jalen's presence helped ease the apprehension. Early evening found her sitting at the Strade table. The food was good, the atmosphere cool. Roland, nearly oblivious to her presence, didn't create a scene. Sundown's rays had all but gone when Jalen and Shelly drove their grateful but perplexed guest home. Roland's silent disrespect, though never brought forth in words, rested on three faces.

LaRana was keenly aware she was a burden, the center of an awkward situation. "That was a great supper, Mrs. Strade, but I don't want to cause you any stress. I can take care of myself for a few days."

"Don't even think about it, young lady. I wouldn't have it any other way. Jalen will pick you up at six sharp tomorrow evening."

They stood on the sidewalk while the sun's fading lit the street lamps. LaRana hugged both, thanking them for supper and a ride home. With a final goodbye wave, the Strades disappeared around the corner. She walked toward the steps, suddenly feeling a leap of tension. Hannah had never been more than a few hours away no matter where they were. She stopped near the door, finding nerves beginning to tighten. With no one to confide in, she chose the house.

"Well, just you and me. I think we'll get along just fine, although you look bigger and…uh, a little darker. Get ready for a lot of music. I'm definitely going to need some noise."

She slowly entered, recalling oft felt desires to be independent, to make her own decisions. With careful hesitation, she took the final step in, suddenly feeling alone, even empty. The room's stark bleakness stoked her anxiety. Though her mother rapidly moved farther away, she seemed closer. It quickly dawned that a house was warmed not solely by a machine but also by love and assurance.

A tense hour slowly passed. Loneliness crept in with the growing darkness. Mom was always there when needed. Now, her absence was unnerving. She gazed at the walls, usually warm and embracing, now cold and desolate. With the slim aura of twilight gone, she slightly shuddered and turned on the lights. A sudden urge to talk to someone swept over her. In the midst of solitude, she was the only one available.

"Don't get so uptight, girl. It's the same walls, same furniture, same…everything but Mom. Get a grip. You're old enough to handle this. It's only four days."

Reading would calm jumpy nerves she reasoned. Her unfinished novel laid on the light stand. She reached for it only to see

Hannah's Bible resting nearby. A strange need to read it swept over her. She pulled a throw over her legs and opened the book. Her hand was on the Twenty-third Psalm.

"Looks like a good place to start."

She read the psalm and several passages then tossed it on the sofa. It fell open and revealed a highlighted verse. "That was weird. What's this? Must be something Mom wanted to remember."

She again held the Bible and slowly read. "Whenever I am afraid, I will trust in You. I will praise His word. In God, I have put my trust. I will not fear. What can flesh do to me?"

She turned the book upside down, keeping the place, then gently put it down. Odd notions slyly arose. The room fell deafening quiet. The passage leaped from the page and swirled around her.

"How odd that verse popped up. Great! That's all I needed. I should have left it alone. Maybe she's worried about her trip, concerned about something bad happening."

All thoughts left but one, a sudden fear for her mother. A car wreck, a robbery, a shooting, everything disastrous came to mind. She calmly paced, trying to shake negative scenarios. She swiftly thought of Jalen, school, charity work, and mountains. All faded in the face of the passage. "Whenever I am afraid…"

"Mom must have been afraid at times. I hope nothing bad happens. Lord, if You watch over such things, keep her safe. I couldn't bear losing her. Maybe I should call her. Oh, don't be so stupid, LaRana. She just left a few hours ago. Besides, she said she would call each evening."

She spent a few minutes singing to break the eerie silence when the phone loudly rang, causing an anxious start. She reached for it, but her hand stopped and began to slightly tremble. The worst was imagined.

"Oh, what if this is someone telling me Mom and Isaiah had a wreck!"

With a still quivering hand, she slowly picked up her mother's cell. She sighed deeply and leaned back on the sofa.

"Oh, hi Mom. I'm so glad you called…you're where? Wow, Mr. Johnson must drive pretty fast…me? I'm…doing great. Glad you're okay…uh…sure, I guess I can do that. Don't worry so much. I'll get it done. There's what in the fridge…oh, okay. Great, thanks. I miss you. Enjoy the trip…love you too. Oh, by the way, thanks for leaving your cell. Oh, also, by the way…call whenever you want to, or… maybe even sometimes…when you don't want to."

The telephonic relief lasted for but a few minutes till her mind again turned to worry. She found a few grapes to nibble before nervously pacing the floor. The last grape went down when the phone rang. She thought it odd not wanting the phone to ring yet anxiously hoping it does.

"Oh, hello, Mrs. Strade… I'm doing just fine… I can't think of anything I need tonight. I just got off the phone with Mom. She's doing great. I'll see you sometime tomorrow…thanks for calling, and uh, thanks again for supper. It was really good."

She gently laid the phone down, again fretting about Hannah and Isaiah. *What would I do without her?* she thought. *Where would I go?* she thought. "Ahh, what's the matter with you, dummy? Quit acting so stupid! They're going to be okay!"

Dusk stepped aside for evening's peaceful yet unsettling calm. She grew restless. Alone. The eerie silence was deafening. For several agonizing minutes, she sat in solitude listening to, then singing with, her favorite songs. The sound of her voice put little more than a dent in the loneliness.

She tired of singing and turned off the music. Noises, unnoticed on routine nights, were loud and foreboding. She twitched at a rap on the window, thinking a shadowy form suddenly disappeared. A gust of moaning wind swept across the yard. She eased to the window and raised it higher, not knowing what to expect, only that it must be an evil of some kind.

Nothing.

A pack of coyotes began howling in the distance, prompting a vigorous reply by the neighbor's dogs. She stared deep into the sinister darkness where shadows of evil dashed everywhere. She couldn't shut the window fast enough. Racing back to the chair, she reached for the novel with still unsteady hands.

"LaRana! Get back to reality! Don't be a dufus! They're going to be just fine. You're going to be seeing space aliens before long! It's just a normal night…well, almost normal."

She nervously sat, read a few pages then slammed the book closed. She leaped to her feet, slowly paced the room, singing to relax till stopping suddenly by the end table. An anxious reach for the phone fell short.

"Gads, LaRana. What in the world are you doing? Jalen would think you're quite a wimp. Don't be so stupid!"

She plopped on the sofa, nestled in, and gently stroked her necklace. She finally settled down, grabbed her book, and began to read. Halfway through the second chapter, anxiety returned with a vengeance. With a good measure of annoyance, she closed it then scrambled to her feet.

"I gotta do something. I need to take a walk. A shake at the Frosty Treat sounds real good." She glanced at the clock. "Nine twenty-seven. I should have enough time."

The night breeze was only slight but cool. She pulled a light sweater around her shoulders and briskly walked down the dimly lit street. She thought it slightly odd no one was on the sidewalk or cruising the street as usual. An eerie quietness suddenly fell. She started around the corner when a man stepped out of the darkness, blocking her path. Below the shadowy light, she beheld a face, a face seen once before. Memory flashed and breath nearly stopped.

Willow's iPad!

*****

Jalen propped a leg over a chair arm while holding a rather thick novel. His head healed quicker than expected on the inside, but his hair had yet to fully cover surgical marks. He looked forward to getting back to competition the following week. Shelly calmly sat on the couch pondering the day's memorable event.

"Well, give me your opinion of the wedding. How do you think LaRana handled her part?"

Jalen slightly shrugged his shoulders but kept his eyes on the page. "It was nice. I know she was worried she would mess up just saying 'I do.'"

"Well, I thought it was absolutely beautiful. I was so proud of Hannah. She's had a tough life. She deserved a new beginning. Isaiah is one of the finest gentlemen I have ever met. They seem a perfect match for each other."

"I appreciate your invitation, or maybe imperative, that LaRana have supper with us each night. I doubt she's been very far from Hannah in her entire life. Besides, I think she likes our company. Dad, to his credit, stayed cool. That helped."

"Well, thanks, Son. I just hope she will come over each night."

Shelly rearranged the newspaper then rose and headed for the kitchen when spotting a stack of envelopes on the cabinet. "Oh, here's the mail. I got so wrapped up in the wedding and dinner I forgot to get it. At least, Roland didn't. Let's see if 'the' letter came."

Jalen tossed the book aside and sprung to his feet. "Yeah! If you don't mind, you look through it. Your luck is better than mine."

"Ah, let's see now. Electric bill...trash...trash...a notice from the bank...trash, aha...a letter from Coach Stafford!"

She held it in the air, waved it with a victorious smile then handed it to Jalen who quickly opened it. He read a few lines then looked up with a beaming face. "We got it! We got it!"

"Not so loud. We don't want to wake your dad. He had to work a couple hours overtime, and he was worn out. Let's sit down, and you can read it to me."

Shelly's face glowed with pride listening to her elated but anxious son read the letter. She lightly cheered while Jalen covered each point of the scholarship. They shared a few laughs at some of the pleasantly surprising details.

Shelly spun in a victory whirl. "Tuition, housing, and...uh, other stuff. This is too good to be true. The Lord certainly has blessed us."

"Yeah, I couldn't ask for more. Wow, it came a little late. I thought maybe Coach Stafford changed his mind. He's set a meeting at the college, uh, let's see…two weeks from next Monday if we accept the offer."

"Well, you've thought about this for years. Are you certain this is what you want?"

"Now, Mom, what do you think? I would have signed for less. This package is a beast…uh… I mean it's really good. It…ah…covers, I would guess, about three-fourths of my expenses, maybe more. I can work some in the off season to help with the rest."

"We can tell your dad tomorrow morning. I'm sure he'll be proud of you."

Jalen frowned and steadily peered at the letter, trying to balance great news with painful reality. "I'm not going to hold my breath. He'll probably be glad to see me gone."

"Oh, now, try to be a little more patient. He's been dealing with some conflicting thoughts. He can't yet understand why we haven't quit going to church. And he told me he hadn't had a beer since you, uh, came to my aid. Forgiveness may be difficult, but it can also be powerful. Say, it's not too late. I bet LaRana's still up. I believe she would appreciate a call…and the company. What do you think?"

"Great idea! She was really curious what the terms would be."

"Remember, she's using Hannah's phone."

"Got it."

Jalen shuffled to the end table. Tapping his fingers on the desk, he held the phone for several rings. "No answer. Hmm, maybe I hit the wrong number."

A second call fared no better. Jalen slowly set the phone down. He tried to appear unconcerned but failed. He stared at the phone, deep in thought.

"She's probably in the shower or gone for a walk, most likely to the Frosty Treat. She likes a late evening shake. But I think I'll drive over just to make sure she's okay."

"Good idea. At least we'll know for certain. I'll stay up. Call me when you get there. Maybe she's a little scared or lonely. If so, try to bring her here. I believe Hannah would understand."

"Yeah, but I bet she'll be more stubborn than scared. But just to be safe, I'm gonna check on her. Be back in a little while."

He couldn't get the Jeep out of the garage quick enough. He hit a red light at nearly every intersection. He tapped the steering wheel as short delays turned to eons, feeding a growing anxiety. Usually cool-headed, he grew nervous. Reasons came from every angle but comfort from none. He pulled into a motel parking lot and called again. He let it ring several times.

No answer.

His mind ran from the reasonable to the unthinkable. He drove by the church and recalled enjoyable times spent with friends, especially LaRana. He spotted Paul sweeping the Frosty Treat floor as he turned down a wide street. Still anxious, he spoke to himself.

"He's still open. I bet LaRana's there."

He quickly pulled into the parking lot. Throwing open the door, he sprang from the Jeep and dashed to the entry. Only three customers remained. None was LaRana. He struggled to regain composure.

"Paul, did LaRana come in here tonight? Have you seen her?"

"No, she hasn't been here. Is there, uh, something wrong? You seem a little out of sorts."

Jalen realized he was somewhat keyed up. He took a deep breath. "Just trying to find out where she is. She sorta likes playing games with me, and I most likely fell for it."

"Well, I'll be here for a little while longer if you need anything."

"Thanks, Paul."

He hurried to the Jeep, raced for three blocks then turned down the now familiar street. His heart calmed to see the lights' glow in the window.

"Well, that's a relief. She'll have some crazy reason for not answering. I think I'll tell her I was just in the area and decided to drop in. Can't let her get one up one me."

He turned into the narrow driveway, stilled the engine, and scrambled from the Jeep, looking all around. It was spooky quiet. He hurried across the walk and knocked on the door once then again, then again, louder.

"LaRana, come on. Let me in. It's a little late for playing jokes."

No answer.

He cautiously opened the door and eased inside, unsure what would be found. The living room was empty. He quickly moved from room to room but to no avail. His heart began to race.

"Something's not right," he whispered, breaking the deafening quiet, still hoping she was toying with him. "Surely, she's not out on a walk this late. Hiding maybe?"

He upped the volume, shattering the stillness. "LaRana! Come on! I know you're here! Nice joke, but it's getting a little old!"

Only a slight echo replied.

He spotted Hannah's phone resting on the table, recalling she left it for LaRana. Confusion grew. "She wouldn't leave without a cell. She has to be here somewhere."

He began another search when the cell rang. He raced back into the room, quickly raising it to his ear. *Maybe it's her.*

"Hello, LaRana?"

"Who's this?" came a strong but muffled voice.

"I'm Jalen Strade. Who are you?"

"Put Hannah Lester on the phone now!"

"She's not here. She's…out of town."

"Don't mess with me, jerk! Put her on the phone!"

"Look, buddy, she's not here. What do you want?"

"Tell her I'll call at noon tomorrow. Do not fail! Here me good! Do not fail!"

"Who are you?" demanded Jalen. "Hello! Hello!"

Silence.

Missives Ten

Esul,

It's my guess Hannah's union with Isaiah must have been quite a shock for you. They will become a powerful force for my Master. I would say more in my delight, but your loathsome scheme to influence an abductor's heart has caused us considerable angst. Your heinous ability to give wings to evil intent has brought no small degree of anxiety. This one may well be your most diabolic. We remember when your master tried to take control of our Master. He repelled you, and we believe LaRana will do the same.

We are keenly aware that the number of hearts opened to you has dramatically increased, but I am determined you will not add these precious souls to your collection, no matter from where you attack. Unfortunately, enticing humans with deceit and love of money are successful ploys. Your master brought about the demise of Judas, Ananias, and Sapphira in the days of old by entering their hearts. Many more have been lost with such treachery. We do not underestimate your ability to influence.

I detest admitting it, but seeing LaRana in the hands of one of your vilest minions has me somewhat worried. Our efforts have overcome similar obstacles, but regrettably, even this will be an agonizing challenge.

There are untold numbers of humans whose hearts you have corrupted. For those we mourn. Your evil runs deep and has no boundaries. Using a cruel agent to get to LaRana is typical of your abhorrent wiles. I am determined to see you fail even though you have that vile soul firmly in hand to do your will. There is no way for me to influence him, but there is a host of humans who will do everything possible to assure LaRana's safety. You have on occasion made oversights. We are trusting you have again, and if so, we will find it. Whether or not it helps with LaRana's plight is yet to be seen.

I perceive you have misjudged LaRana and Hannah. They are growing stronger in our Creator's teachings. They will not allow you! Try as you might, you will fail! The intent of my Lord will come to pass!

Jariel

*****

Jariel,

Well, now, I didn't mean to cause such panic. Why would you be amazed at the depth I would go to win? I was taken aback by Hannah's appalling action. You have done well. She and Isaiah might be great influences for your Master. Thus, it stands to reason, does it not, that I must destroy her newly found walk. I have too much invested in this battle to let your hoped-for victory go unchallenged.

They will be strong for you, or maybe not. Hannah is still a babe in your Master. I have danced all around her, but I deemed it crucial to take a much firmer grasp of her emotions. When I have taken away her most prized treasure, she will leave your Master, or become insignificant in His kingdom.

LaRana was getting a little too far from my reach. I just needed someone with, let's say, a kindred mind to draw her back. Oh, I just had a thought. She still isn't fully convinced you and I even exist. No wonder she hasn't acknowledged your Master. I'm so sorry. But as you are keenly aware, I often stray from the truth.

Before my ruthless and obedient slave completes his chore, she will belittle your Master even if he has compassion and spares her life. However, chances of that are all but nonexistent. She will beg for mercy, and we both know how much mercy my puppet gives. And just think, LaRana's death will emotionally destroy Hannah, Jalen will reject your Master's way of life, and Shelly will wallow in the throes of doubt for the rest of her days, and Roland, good old Roland, will plug along as usual. Ah, the dominos, how pleasant they fall.

You put up an admirable effort, but LaRana is mine! They all are mine! Of that, you can be certain! I will do whatever it takes to deny you this victory!

Esul

11

Hand of Evil

Jalen angrily tossed the phone on the table. "Crazy punks. Probably a prank, but it's not very funny. Yet…what if it isn't?"

He grasped his phone, quickly punched the buttons, and paced the room. "Mom, LaRana's not here, and I took a strange call, somebody wanting to talk to Hannah. His voice was strange. This doesn't smell very good. I'm going to call the police. I'll try to get them to contact Officer Monroe. Come as soon as you can. I'll wait here."

Twenty minutes passed, an eternity to Jalen. Shelly turned the corner and parked on the street. She quickly exited and crossed the lawn. Her expression bore a mixture of puzzlement and fear. She gave Jalen a quick hug as two squad cars stopped behind his Jeep. Jalen hastened his steps to the cruisers. He breathed a sigh of relief at the sight of Mike Monroe. The seasoned officer noticed Jalen's anxiety.

"Relax now, settle down. Tell me what happened. Take your time and remember details, even small ones."

Jalen took a deep breath and related events leading him to LaRana's house. He stressed the gravity of the call. His nerves frayed more at each detail. Visions of LaRana on Talova Peak, at the Frosty Treat, at school, at church, all tried to squeeze between the moment's words.

"I'm probably thinking the worst, but nothing else seems possible. LaRana would not leave the house open if she left for any length of time…" he paused in thought. "Unless she would go to the Frosty

244

Treat, maybe. But Paul was getting ready to close when I came by, and he said he hadn't seen her."

Mike's demeanor didn't change. "Let's go inside. I want to check the phone and look through the house."

Quickly entering the house, Jalen handed him the phone. Mike's expression was not optimistic. "We can check the call, but if his intent is ill, he's using a throwaway most likely."

He quickly entered the number but only silence returned. With a slight headshake, he placed it back on the table. "Just as I figured."

They covered each room and found nothing out of place till Mike spied the Bible.

"When we finish reading, don't we normally close the book?"

"I usually would, unless, maybe, I was just pausing for some reason," said Jalen, deep in thought.

"That may be true yet it could mean something else. Sully, go to the Frosty Treat and see if Paul had anyone unusual or suspicious come in tonight."

Suspense sharpened at Sully's quick departure. Mike slowly turned back to Jalen. "What else can you tell me about the call?"

"The voice was muffled, definitely male, and just as definitely demanding. Oh, I almost forgot, he also said he would call her at noon tomorrow. I may be wrong, but I don't believe this is a prank. I think some sicko moron has abducted her. I can't get the incident with Willow out of my mind. It makes me wonder if this could be the same creep?"

"We haven't covered all possibilities, but I definitely wouldn't rule that out. The Willow tragedy was unusual for Pallon Ridge, and now LaRana. It's a thought we hate to consider, but we have to. If it is the same person, we won't have a lot of time to put the pieces together. It seems, at least, we have till tomorrow. I need to contact Mrs. Johnson. Can you reach her, Mrs. Strade?"

"I have to call Isaiah's phone," nodded Shelly already punching the buttons. The phone rang several times, testing Shelly's patience.

"Come on Hannah. Tap it…come on…tap it…tap… Hannah! This is Shelly!" Realizing her angst, she tried to calm her voice. "We have a situation causing us concern. Officer Monroe wants to talk with you."

She handed Mike the phone then quickly stepped aside. She could no longer keep her composure. Her eyes filled then flowed with tears. Jalen quickly embraced her, trying to soothe her fears when a sudden rush of anger mixed with growing anxiety struck hard.

"How can this be?" she blurted through clenched teeth. "Who would want to hurt LaRana?"

"I don't know, Mom, but we have to find her. We just have to. I'd like to meet this scumbag. If he harms LaRana..."

Mike placed the phone on the table. "They're on the way back. Hopefully, this is just a sick joke, but we need to proceed as though she's been taken. If Sully comes up empty, we'll issue an Amber Alert. There's nothing else you can do now, Mrs. Strade. If it's okay with you, Jalen could help us for a little while. We'll take care of the premises. Tomorrow, we most likely will learn the demands if this is an abduction."

Jalen put his arm around Shelly. "Mom, go home and try to get some rest. Maybe it's all going to work out."

"You take care of yourself. Call if you find her, no matter the time."

The next few minutes were spent again going over the house and outer premises. Nothing was found. Sully returned with a headshake.

"Nothing unusual."

Jalen remembered the account of Willow's murder. There was no call, no ransom sought, nothing was known but the vile deed. Maybe, he guessed, just maybe, this would be different. He reached for straws, juggling fear, anger, and hope. With all the turmoil in mind, he hung onto one thought. The call must mean she is still alive. He also knew the thought was born more of desire than rationale.

"Sir, I respectfully ask if I can stay here in case she returns, or we get another call. I won't sleep no matter where I'm at anyway."

"Since this may be a crime scene, you need to go home." Mike suddenly paused in thought. "You say she likes to walk to the Frosty Treat in the evening. What say we take the same walk tonight? We might find someone still up who may have seen her."

"Great idea! Need to cover all bases...ah, sorry."

"Sully, secure the premises, but don't put anything on the street. Head back and start the process. I'll call if I need you."

Mike again looked the house over, hoping to find something missed. "I don't see anything out of the ordinary. Let's try to follow her steps."

They left with flashlights in hand and headed toward the Frosty Treat. The first several houses were dark. Dim streetlights created a haunting appearance, giving Jalen unsettling thoughts.

They soon found a house with a light on, and a gentleman taking his dog out to do its thing. The searchers abruptly stepped from the shadows, startling the man.

"Hey! Who are you?"

Mike lowered his light. "Sir, I'm Officer Monroe from the police department. We need to know if you saw a young woman walking past here this evening?"

"Oh, sorry. Well, let me think," came the reply. He rubbed his chin while tugging the leash. "Nola! Sit! Ah...yes, I'd guess somewhere around nine thirty...could have been later. Really wasn't paying much attention to time. Seemed like a young lady."

"Did you notice anything unusual?"

"No...no, can't say as I did. She was walking rather fast, but that's not unusual, especially at night. It seems a lot more bad stuff happens after dark than it used to."

"Thank you, sir. We appreciate your help. Sorry to bother you."

"That's quite okay. Always willing to help the law."

They carefully moved down the street but found no more windows lit. Querying two residents in the second block drew a blank. The declaration from the dog owner still pounded in Jalen's ears.

"I bet that was her," he said with both excitement and despair.

"If it was her, then we need to find what happened between here and Paul's. Let's move on and see if anyone else is still up."

They began to turn the corner when Jalen spotted an object lying on the ground, slightly reflecting the street lamp.

"What's this?"

He reached down and slowly lifted a gold necklace with JS on it. His heart raced, his mind leaped to unwanted conclusions.

"Did you find something?" queried Mike.

Tears welled in Jalen's eyes. He longingly stared at the necklace, pondering the only reason for it being there. He held it up. "This is her necklace! She wouldn't take it off for anything! Whatever happened, happened right here!"

"It sure looks that way," replied Mike, reaching for an envelope. "Put it in here. Though not likely, we might get a partial print off of it. I'll call and get this area secured for the night. We need to check with at least these two houses and maybe that small one to see if anyone saw her past this point. Sometimes it's a little hard to get a cooperative person this time of night."

Mike's call took little more than a minute. Jalen leaned against the pole, trying to envision the likely ill deed. He pictured her joy at receiving the necklace till thoughts of what may have happened started dragging him down.

"Well, let's take that house first," said Mike, pointing to his left. "We might as well wake them up since this area will be secured with some noise."

Residents of three houses were surprised and willing to cooperate, but all queries were negative. No one had seen LaRana.

"I'm quite certain she would not voluntarily get into a car," said Mike. "Whatever happened, it was quick. Let's head back. At least, we seem to have the site of an apparent abduction. We'll take Hannah's phone and gather at the station tomorrow morning. We can try to isolate the call, but I doubt we'll have enough time to peg it."

Jalen, still shaken, looked straight at the officer. "Mr. Monroe, I can't thank you enough for what you're doing?"

Mike smiled. "Just my job, Jalen, just my job. However, I may have a greater tie to this situation than most, so it's good to have nice people to work with. Emphasis on 'work with.'"

"I got it. Other than killing the creep, I promise not to mess up a thing."

Mike managed a knowing grin. "I hear you, but let's work on this together."

*****

Hannah fidgeted with her watchband then Isaiah's phone, hoping for the call saying all was well. Isaiah pushed the speed limit and then some, adding his silent prayers to those shared in voice. Shortly before nine thirty in the morning, they arrived at the station and parked near a squad car. Other than the staff parking lot, only a few regular cars could be seen. She took a deep breath, relieved the incident apparently had not been leaked. The last thing needed was a crowd of onlookers. She put a hand on Isaiah's arm, leaning back against the seat. Their eyes met. Words unspoken were understood.

Isaiah came to her side and opened the door. Hannah eased from the seat, gazing at the front door, wishing LaRana would come bouncing out to greet them, smiling and saying everything was all right.

Come on, LaRana. Come on.

Shut the door remained.

Isaiah held her hand. "Let's trust in the Lord. He'll see us through this trial."

Hannah managed a slight smile through trembling lips. The recent entry into a new life was yet fragile. *Trust the Lord. Trust the Lord. I know I should, but how? What can He do? Miracles are not part of my world.*

"I'm trying, Isaiah, really trying, but I'm struggling with why. Everything was going so smooth. I thought life would be better. Do all Christians get tested like this?"

"I'm quite certain evil doesn't check on someone's spiritual belief. The epitome of wickedness most definitely is not a respecter of persons. There is one thing for sure. The eternal author of nightmares uses all his power to separate us from trust in the Lord, to drive us to doubt. His malevolence has no boundaries. He wants us to question our faith."

"I'll try to stay strong, but right now, I'm afraid he's winning."

They met Shelly and Jalen with consoling hugs. Hannah gazed at anxious faces. Her breath froze. She tried to control emotions but couldn't. Shelly wrapped consoling arms around her till the trembling eased. With little said, they went inside.

The morning crawled, spent with what happened, the what ifs, and what to dos. A few more officers arrived, some local, some state. Hannah anxiously paced the floor, waiting for the dreaded call. Chatter fell to near silence at eleven thirty. Time crept at a snail's pace. The room became a subdued chamber for the angry, the anxious, and the fearful.

Several curious people passed by the station. A look of wonder rested on their faces, a look saying something odd must be happening. Jalen nervously watched from a window, choosing to remain inside. He hoped the situation could be kept quiet.

Continual glances raced to the cell lying on the table, a simple phone now the center of attention. While dreading the call, not receiving it meant something happened to LaRana, something no one wanted to consider.

"Can we trace the call?" asked Shelly, shattering the stony silence.

"We thought about that last night. We can obtain the number and the approximate area. The perp will give us a drop off site, but it could be miles away from LaRana," replied Mike reluctantly. "The best we can do for the moment is just record the call. It's my guess we're dealing with someone who has given careful consideration to details."

The clock slowly inched toward noon. The room became deathly quiet. As stated and nearly to the minute, the phone rang—to some a sound of hope, to others an echoing death knell. Eyes darted as the dreaded, but longed for, moment had come. The ringing phone answered one question all held inside.

LaRana must still be alive.

Hannah had an odd sense of relief. Her hand shook as she grasped the phone. Her uncertain voice was as strong as she could make it.

"This is Hannah Johnson."

"The new Mrs. Johnson, I presume. LaRana informed me this morning you just got married. Congratulations. I say that so you know I have the pleasure of her company. Here, say hello."

"Mom! Please help! I'm…"

"LaRana! LaRana!"

The voice quickly changed. "See, she's okay…for now. Oh, also tell Officer Monroe hello for me. I believe he's there with you. Oh, good luck tracing the call. I'll be brief. I want exactly two hundred thousand in hundreds placed on the old bench at the intersection of old Mine Road and the Hixson Trail by 1:00 p.m. tomorrow. I'm trying to be nice by giving you time. Make it real money. I know the difference. One person, one vehicle, one case. If I see anything or anyone else, LaRana is dead. If there's a tracer on the case, LaRana is dead. If anyone tries to follow the case, LaRana is dead. Do you understand? LaRana is dead!"

"But I can't…hello…hello!"

Sully looked up, shaking his head. "Blocked somehow."

Hannah dropped the phone and burst into tears. She took a shaky step, helplessly collapsing into Isaiah's arms.

Missives Eleven

Jariel,

I know you must be in the throes of despair. I assume you realize by now I have no boundaries when gathering souls. You might as well get ready for the next challenge. Your feeble efforts on this one has failed. You know the heart and mind of my servant. I will soon welcome LaRana to our cozy realm. I surmise this will be a devastating loss for you. And just think what this will spawn. It will certainly set the rest of the souls on the wide road to our abode. All I can say is, may your luck be even worse next time.

Esul

*****

Esul,

You are as vile as any demon I have contended with. Yes, we are highly uneasy with the turn of events. However, we never concede until the spirit leaves the body. You may have these souls in sight, but we will not lessen our efforts to derail your gathering. Strong hearts can at times overcome even your most heinous efforts. We shall see who prevails.

Jariel

12

Fur Ball

Night slowly crept toward sunrise, stubbornly hanging on to the chill of mountain air. Eerie beams from a three-quarter moon squeezed through the cabin's slender cracks, lightly streaking the haunting darkness. A steel pole with attached cord rose between a primitive toilet and a small cot. At the other end of the cord was a desperate figure whose frantic cries were swallowed by deep canyons and lofty hills.

The evening walk toward the Frosty Treat seemed a lifetime ago. A multitude of thoughts on what comes next teased LaRana's mind till finally settling to one…death, a gruesome death. The surroundings dread and her abductor's history brought an explosion of emotions. She vented dire frustrations on the only source available.

"Is this what I get for trying to learn about You? I thought You took care of Your followers! Maybe I'm just a nobody to You! I'm going to church. I'm hanging around with Your people. I've even been reading the Bible, and this is what I get? This Christian stuff ain't got much to it! Oh, yeah, follow Jesus and things will be better they say. Can You see where I am? Well, things ain't better! In fact, they couldn't be any worse! I came from a life nobody would want to a life that looked good…at least on the surface. I guess I was wrong. It looks like 'dead' wrong!"

Anger erupted. She angrily kicked a small stool into the cot, smashed a nearly empty cracker box, and yanked the cord as hard as she could before crumpling against the wall. She rose to her knees then pounded the floor, shaking with rage till resuming her wrath.

"Where are You if You exist? Don't You help? All those Bible stories and lofty sermons, what use are they? I tried to become like Christian people, but I guess I wasn't good enough. Did I do something bad? Am I too ugly? Maybe You are just a myth!"

LaRana was alone except for an unconcerned mouse feverishly scouting for food. She eased across the floor, sat down, and leaned against the pole. Her weary eyes were half-shut as thoughts again ran to the night before, a simple walk for a peach shake, a pleasant evening with a wisp of breeze and soothing sounds of night. The serene evening became a haunting nightmare. Reality swiftly fled at the sight of Dawson. She vaguely remembered being grasped, gagged, blindfolded, shoved into a van, and riding over rugged terrain till fear numbed any sense of presence.

"And where am I now, little fur ball?" she implored the mouse with emotions nearly spent. "If only you could talk."

Night's gloomy darkness slowly vanished with the sun's rising. Unknown critters wakened with incessant chatter, chasing the unnerving stillness. She stepped to the cord's length and peered through the cracks in the wall. Nothing moved but feathery shafts of knee-high grass softly swaying in the wisp of wind. Dark shadows of overhanging trees created an eerie appearance. She whirled around and screamed in frustration. The startled mouse scooted near the cot and rose on its hind feet.

"You've got to get a grip, LaRana," she scolded herself through gritted teeth. "Think! Think! Here I am, somewhere between God and a mouse. Where do I start to get out of this?"

She searched for anything to cut the cord, peering into every nook and cranny the cord's length allowed. The effort was futile. Out of options, she plopped down on the cot and stared at the floor, following each step of the rodent. It found a small ort then rested on its hindquarters, lifting the find with both front feet. As it began to chew the morsel, it sat on its haunches and gave the appearance of being in prayer.

"Prayer! You can't be serious!" she vigorously declared. "I don't even know if He exists, but If He does, I don't think I'm on His... worthy to listen to list. But I once prayed for a friend, a good friend, and he recovered from a bad accident. Of course, other people, really good people, also prayed. I always felt it was their prayers God answered. After all, they may be close enough to Him to be on speed dial. I'm guessing everybody knows I'm gone by now or soon will know. I hope they're praying extra hard. My little voice may not help much. Hey, who knows, maybe yours will be heard. But you know what, little fur ball? Mom said to trust in the Lord no matter what. Since no matter what is where I am, I think I'll give it a try."

She knelt a few feet from the mouse. It didn't move but continued to gnaw on the ort, leisurely watching with no sign of fear.

"Lord, sorry for ranting. I'm...uh, in a little bind here. There are just some things I don't understand. It seems You're taking care of this little rodent, and though I may not be as much in Your sight, could You help me? I know my prayer pales to others whose faith in You is...uh...stronger. If there's some way You can help me out of this jam, I certainly would welcome it. If You can't, I understand. If I don't make it, please help Mom and Isaiah have a great rest of their lives. They deserve it. And since I'm asking, help Jalen reach his goals. He's a really good guy." She again eyed the mouse. "Oh, and thanks for the fur ball."

She painfully moved to the cot, trying hard to relax and ponder her abductor's next move. She didn't like the choices. Though feeling alone, she took some solace her captor was not there. Trying to find answers, she flipped her hands in frustration, sending the mouse dashing to a pile of wood. It wriggled its nose then hunkered down, keeping its eyes fixed on LaRana. The rodent appeared to sense she intended no harm.

"I bet a lot of people will be scurrying around, sorta like you, trying to find me. It's good to see people who care about other people. Though, I'm guessing you wouldn't know about that. Everybody and everything's out to do away with you. I thought my mother was the only one who cared for me, but you know what, fur ball, I was wrong. I found a bunch of people who treated me like...like a friend, or a daughter, no less, or a sister maybe. What do you think? Will somebody find us? Will we get out of here alive?"

The mouse wiggled its nose and squeaked twice.

"What...you hope so? Yeah, me too. I know one thing, it had better be soon. I doubt time is much of a friend. In fact, for the moment at least, I guess you're the nearest friend I got."

The morning slowly crept till the sound of an ATV broke the near stillness. A peek through the cracks brought a shudder. With the engine silenced and sound of footsteps, LaRana cringed against the pole. Dawson entered, tossing a couple of boxes on the table.

"Well, it's about time to give Mrs. Lester a call. We'll see how much she wants you back."

"Leave her alone! She just got married! She's not even there!"

"Oh, let me guess...to Isaiah Johnson, I presume. I knew they were close, and I can assure you, she's in Pallon Ridge. Now, dear LaRana, that does change things a bit. I can up the price for you. It's about time for a nice little ultimatum."

He unpacked the boxes, looked at his watch then tapped the cell. A devious smile crossed his face. "The new Mrs. Johnson, I presume. LaRana informed me this morning you just got married. I say that so you know I have the pleasure of her company. Here, say hello."

"Mom! Please help! I'm...!"

Dawson pulled the phone back then pushed her into a pile of wood. Dazed, she lay still, barely able to move. Only a few seconds passed till Dawson killed the call. He leisurely drew near his captive, calmly kneeling down.

"Sorry for being so discourteous. Just making sure your stay isn't interrupted by anybody. I believe I left you enough food for the night. I may return this evening, but if not, I'll see you tomorrow if all goes well. I hope for your sake, it does. But if it doesn't, I wouldn't have but one choice."

His demonic laugh sent chills racing. With a gentle pat on her head, he rose then left. The ATV's ebbing sound brought a longed-for stillness. Yet in pain, she rose and lay on the cot. Tears flowed from dreaded thoughts. Mentally and physically spent, she found a shallow sleep for close to an hour till the silence was rudely broken.

Unnerving sounds of animals unknown swirled from all directions, some pleasant, some menacing. Suddenly came the sound of claws raking across the planks. Startled, she eased to the wall and peeked through the slats. Her breath hitched. She lurched back. A large grizzly nosed around, sniffing at the scent of food.

LaRana's heartbeat seemed far too loud. The scratching became a pounding. She cringed at the sound of a board cracking. She could stand it no longer. With fear at its peak, desperation burst forth. She frantically screamed with all she had, grabbed a small piece of wood, and pounded on the wall time and time again. The bear abruptly stood straight up with a loud growl before hustling away in a huff. LaRana plopped on the cot, spent of strength and emotion. She closed her eyes and lay quietly for more than an hour till peeps from the mouse stirred her awake.

The creepy yet calming silence returned. She sat then stood and paced only to sit for a few short breaths then swiftly rise to pace again. Time crept, nobody came, neither abductor nor rescuer, neither demon nor angel. She occasionally talked with the mouse, nodded in and out of futile attempts at sleep, snacked at the meager supply of food, and sought a way of escape. Nearing early evening, she still found no answers, no options.

With night approaching, the unnerving silence returned. Sleep came fitfully. She tried thinking of pleasant things, memories of good times spent with her mother, with Jalen, with the girls at church. The moment's despondency quickly squelched any attempt to find hope. She trembled intensely at repulsive thoughts of Dawson's mere presence, his nauseating closeness. She imagined Willow's last few minutes, trying to picture the tragedy. Her heart quickened at the horror of the vision.

Darkness fell till the spring moon graced the sky. The whispery breeze slowly died leaving a ghostly stillness and no sign of Dawson or anybody. Perhaps, she conjectured, he left her there and wouldn't return. She tried to console herself with that thought, but it had little conviction. Her scenarios dwelt only on Dawson's return or nobody finding her. Reaching no other outcome, she agonizingly chose the latter.

Night spent its moonlit hours, and the morning's bright sun thrust its rays between the wall's thin cracks. The peculiar rodent returned, scurrying around the floor in search of orts, hopefully appearing overnight.

LaRana gently grasped a cracker and tossed it toward the mouse. With several squeaks, it quickly picked up the gift, keeping its eyes on the donor. LaRana toyed with her roommate, flipping her hand to see if it would scamper away. It remained with nothing moving but paunchy, little jaws. She held out another ort in her hand, teasing the mouse to claim it. The eager rodent came straight to her, eased the ort from her hand, and promptly stood on its haunches, beginning its usual gnawing ritual.

LaRana leaned against the pole, cradled her head in cupped hands, and closed her eyes. Weariness, driven by fear and helplessness, swept over her. She sat as still as the mouse till a noise sent the rodent scurrying to cover. An ATV's engine faintly hummed then grew louder till suddenly stopping. A few seconds of silence was interrupted by the sound of footsteps.

Oh, please! Let it be the right one.

*****

The tormenting night brought the day Hannah dreaded. She sat at a table, surrounded by a host of people trying to solve the quickly developing, gruesome tragedy. Roland quietly sat alone at the back of the room, seemingly untouched by the imminent disaster, yet oddly compelled to be there. He spoke little, immersed in battle with his own demons.

An overwhelming sense of desperation could not be hidden. Each knew victims of abduction had, at best, a slim chance of survival. Hannah frantically wrestled to find answers but could not grasp an encouraging thought. Would he kill her, and what would he do before he killed her?

LaRana is dead. LaRana is dead. LaRana is dead.

The abductor's last words pierced her heart, overshadowing the declaration Jesus is the Light of life. Those words, comforting in the calm setting of church, seemed distant and hollow in the midst of real life. Though desperately searching, she couldn't see a glimmer of hope. The overwhelming enormity of the ransom crushed her spirits.

"There's no way I can get that kind of money," came her quaking voice.

"We're working on that," Mike firmly replied. "A couple of our staff is trying to put it together. The bank is willing to help. How much, we don't know. We'll get a call back, hopefully before too long, yea or nay."

Isaiah pocketed his phone. His face held a slight radiance. "The church will gather a considerable amount. There's no doubt a daunting task lies before us. We must set a goal of LaRana's safe return and work confidently toward it. While we mortals are limited to what is possible, our Lord isn't. He should be the centerpiece of this effort. I have faith we shall rise above this poor excuse of humanity."

Hannah tried to absorb his confident words. She ached for him to be right, but above a strained smile, her despondent eyes revealed a raging battle between faith and doubt, between reality and fantasy. While Isaiah stood on solid ground, she was sinking in sand. He placed an assuring hand over hers. Although his touch felt good, haunting possibilities refused to ease.

"I'm really trying hard to have the faith you hold, but my track record seems to be getting in the way," she said just above a whisper.

"Isaiah's right," said Shelly, getting to her feet. "With just us, this may seem impossible, but with God, all things are possible. We all, or nearly all, have heard or read those words many times without need for deep thought. But now, evil is testing our faith. We now walk on the same water Peter tried to walk. Unlike Peter, let's keep our eyes on the One who can turn impossible to possible."

Isaiah nodded and lifted a hand toward her. "Well spoken."

Jalen was taken by his mother's declaration. He rose and embraced her but said nothing. His face said he understood, but his mind was less hopeful.

Far less.

Mike offered his approval. "Such stout-hearted faith. Let's try to keep it. We have a good gathering of mortal heads here, but there's certainly room for one more, and who knows, He might be the One to help us get through this ordeal."

Shortly before eleven, the phone rang. An avalanche of silence hit the room. Eyes darted from face to face. Everyone dreaded any ill news on LaRana. Mike took the call. After several anxious moments, he gently lowered the phone, looking up with a smile.

"The ransom demand has been met."

A jubilant chatter broke the gloom. Hand slaps and fist bumps raced around the room. Wonder fell upon each face with no one more overwhelmed than Hannah.

"How did that happen so fast, or even at all?"

Mike shook his head. "It beats all I ever heard of. The bank was generous, your church was quite generous, but we were still short. The old saying 'news travels fast in a small town' must be true. People came from all around to push us over the top. Pallon Ridge surely stood up for one of its own today."

Hannah was stunned, never thinking she would hear those words spoken about LaRana or her. *One of its own! One of its own! Me? LaRana? I can only hope I get to tell her about this.*

"I don't know what to say. How could I ever thank them properly or repay the debt?"

"I don't think they did this expecting any return but LaRana," said Mike. "Maybe you'll have an opportunity someday, not only by voice but helping when one of theirs meets a dire situation."

Hannah's face finally bore a hint of optimism. She glanced at Isaiah sitting across the room. He pointed upward and nodded.

"With God."

Hannah relaxed till lifted spirits were once again challenged. Her mind still held the thought that even with the demand met, LaRana's return was highly uncertain. Would the abductor panic? Would he find a way to take the money and still end her life? After all, if he were Willow's killer, he would have no qualms about doing the same to LaRana. The ransom's euphoria slowly melted in the wake of the ultimate heartbreak.

*****

The door flew open. LaRana's breath paused, her heart fearfully leaped. It was neither savior nor angel. There was no hand to keep her from falling. No words of joy to chase unrelenting terror. No elation at being found. Instead of a knight in shining armor came a demon from the dark, a gruesome creator of nightmares.

Dawson tossed a sack near the stove then came toward his captive. LaRana cringed back, overcome by his presence. The mouse scampered under an old chair at the back of the room.

"Well, now, my lovely LaRana. I apologize for the poor accommodations, but it does have one thing in its favor…solitude…no one around for miles and miles. But I guess you're already aware of that."

He stood above her and ran his hand over her face then across her shoulders. "Ah, fair LaRana, try to relax. Not that it matters much to me, but it will be easier for you. Maybe you should pray real hard to your God. You see, I know more about you than you think. Among other places, I watched you go to church, wasting time with belief in some fictitious God. Besides, I don't think your so-called Deity will hear you in this place. Eventually, someone may find you, but…well, you know."

The words sent a shiver down her spine. She tried to appear brash, fearless even, not wanting to allow him any sense of satisfaction. She summoned a steely gaze, one born not of confidence but desperation. Her pointed words came strong yet wrapped in a hollow conviction.

"You won't do anything to me. I'm getting out of this dump. Since you didn't kill me, you must have demanded a ransom. It will be paid, and I'll be rid of you."

Dawson calmly leaned over her. His soft declaration landed hard. "Oh, to be sure, a ransom will be paid, but I will give some thought about what to do with you. Will I kill you? Well… I'm not sure. I have yet to make up my mind. The ransom will not save you, but my, uh, compassion may. You are so beautiful. I would rather take you with me, but that causes complications. You'll just have to wait."

"Why did you kill Willow?" blurted LaRana, grasping for anything to put off the inevitable.

"Willow? Willow? Oh, yes, I remember Willow…feisty, sexy, and dumb as a rock. She wanted to be adored like so many these days. It was easy to get into her mind. She was made for me. I had money at the time, and I knew I wouldn't get any green for her so I simply couldn't let her live. You, on the other hand, have beauty and brains, and hopefully, enough friends to pony up. I just happen to need money at the moment or we would not be talking now. I would like to find a way to keep you alive, but that's a hard chore. It brings so many problems. I must survive. So many more need my attention. You understand, you must understand."

LaRana struggled to find hopeful words. "Once the ransom is paid, you'll have no choice but to let me go! Besides, they know your name. They will find out who you are."

Dawson laughed; his face turned stern and livid. "My name? Do you think this is my first time? Now, LaRana, you're brighter than that. Let me see. I used Ervin on the first one, Garrison on the second, and Dawson on dear Willow. I think you're smart enough to know I would never use my real name. Sorry to disappoint you, but I don't have to let you go. I have this routine down to a science. The three before you would tell you so, but unfortunately, they can't. As soon as my, uh, banker…gets the money, I'll be right here to determine your destiny. Sorry, no promises."

With a chilling laugh, he grasped a pair of binoculars and left. The door slammed shut along with her possibilities. She wilted into the cot. Slender hopes collapsed. Tears profusely flowed. Her reddened eyes followed the mouse racing to his spot on the stack of wood. She tried to summon a desperate prayer, but quivering lips refused its passage. There in the confines of a shattered heart it remained.

The drone of the ATV slowly waned, ushering in a strangely desired solitude. She tried to put the returning sound from her mind, but it relentlessly endured.

Lord, I've run out of words. Hope is gone. I am completely in Your hands.

She leaned back on the bed, drained of strength. She mulled over the next step, to find an open door, an escape from here to anywhere, to devise a way to survive.

She drew a blank.

The mouse scampered toward the cot, rose to its hind feet, and loudly squeaked, breaking the maddening silence.

"Thanks, fur ball. Thanks for staying here with me. I know you would help if you could. I guess if I can't have those I love around when I…uh, well, you will have to do."

*****

Operations ran full speed. Hannah found the hubbub of activity impressive yet daunting. The euphoria of meeting the ransom gave way to discussion of available options. The gravity of the situation grew more intense. The chair's cushion filled with needles. She clung to Isaiah's strong yet gentle hand to keep from collapsing.

Intense efforts to collect the ransom sent news of the abduction racing through the city. A small yet growing crowd gathered outside, turning the near silence into a constant but muted buzzing. A few officers kept the curious at a distance.

The room swarmed with activity. Local officers mingled with state patrolmen in strategy and information sharing. Mike Monroe engaged in tense discussion with three state troopers near a diagram. Shelly and Isaiah sat at a corner table with Hannah whose nerves had worn to a nub. Jalen quietly stood by the window, staring deep in thought. He pondered circumstances, played out scenarios, and devised plans of his own, all with no small measure of wrath. Mike motioned for a gathering near an oft-viewed map.

"We don't like the perp's instructions. He's researched his location well. It's quite certain an accomplice will make the pickup. We can also be sure he'll be watching for any deviations. Till we find out differently, we must assume we're dealing with Willow's killer which makes the success of our plan even more vital."

Hannah moaned. Isaiah grasped her hand and looked into grief-swollen eyes, eyes exuding visions of looming failure, of life's purpose fading into obscurity. The abductor's loathsome voice again rose, tormenting, relentless, tearing at hopes perilously dangling over a bottomless void.

LaRana is dead! LaRana is dead!

She held her head in her hands. "Shut up! Shut up! Leave me alone!"

A room full of heads turned. Isaiah pulled her to his shoulder, wrapping her in comforting arms. "Let's go to a quieter place for a while. These gentlemen will keep us informed of what's going on."

Mike hesitated till Isaiah and Hannah left the room "I think we all see the stakes at hand. Let's get this done." He paused again to regain thoughts. "We can't trust him to make the exchange. However, we must follow the instructions and come up with a way to recover LaRana. We can't be caught anywhere near the drop off. If anyone is seen…well, we just can't be there."

"Do you think she's still alive?" asked Roland from across the room. "He's given us no assurance of it."

Jalen was surprised yet wary. Was his silence broken by an unspoken desire for her death or a sincere interest in her survival? Unsure of the reason, he remained silent.

"We know she was alive yesterday," replied Mike. "Now is anybody's guess, but all we can do is proceed on that assumption. Undercover troopers are manning as many roads in the county as possible. She could be held nearby or miles from here. The bulk of our efforts will be after the drop is made."

"What about the satellite image? Are we able to get a picture of this drop spot?" asked a trooper. "That would let us trail the bagman."

"Sully's working on that, but time isn't on our side, and I'm not sure our capacity is sufficient," replied Mike momentarily pausing. "We gave the feds the particulars. We just have to wait and see if they can make it happen."

Mike paced the room while officers and troopers quietly discussed possibilities. His normal tolerance was being tested. What seemed hours was but a few minutes when Sully set the phone down.

"They'll try to get the image of the drop area, but it will take some time, maybe more than we have."

Mike grew visibly upset. His patience boiled over. "So all we can do is sit here and wait till long after the perp is gone! We have no way of knowing which way he will go, what mode of transportation he has, or more importantly, where we can even locate LaRana! Search the maps for any remote structure within a ten-mile radius of the drop site!"

Jalen calmly paced as various ideas were offered then dropped. He continued to listen while considering other possibilities. Sit and wait were words he didn't want to hear. He suddenly stopped listening. A light came on, a very dangerous light: one without significant risk. While ideas were exchanged, he quietly left the room and made his way down the hall to the receptionist.

"Pardon me, ma'am. Charell, I believe. I'm working with Officer Monroe on this situation. He's busy with the troopers. I don't want to interrupt. I have to leave for now, but in case I find out anything, I would need to call him. Would you happen to have his cell number?"

The nattily dressed lady said nothing for several seconds. "Well, normally I wouldn't give it out, but I think he would trust you, especially at a time like this. I wouldn't want to be partially responsible for the victim's demise."

"Thank you, ma'am. Thank you, very much. I believe we all have a part in this situation, including you. Who knows? You may be the reason she survives."

With the number in his pocket, Jalen swiftly stepped down the hall with a staunch determination. His pace quickened with a plan gradually coming together.

Maybe I didn't roam these hills and mountains for nothing. An army can't go along the trail, but I can. If I can get to the ridge above the drop off without being seen, I can inform Mike where the bagman is heading. It sure would narrow the territory.

He returned to the bustle of activity. "Mr. Monroe, I need to go home for a bit. I should be back before too long."

Mike waved, barely looking up from the table.

Jalen eased over to Shelly. "Mom, I'll, uh, be gone for just a while. I think I'm beginning to get a little rank. A good shower seems in order."

Though deceit nagged, ideas and actions quickly began forming. He drove home somewhat concerned of his deception, but impulse and anger kept him going. He stopped in front of the garage. With nerves gradually tightening, he flung the door open. Anxiety rose, thoughts became words nobody heard.

"Man, everybody's going to be furious for doing this, but I just can't stand around and do nothing. I just have to pull this off and help find where the jerk's holding her."

He grabbed the gas can, quickly filled the tank while shuffling much of his self-assumed responsibility to the ATV. "Listen up, Nellie, it's all up to you. You gotta get me there on time, no sputterin', no conkin' out. I need nothing but your best."

With his cell safely tucked away, he kicked Nellie in gear and sped down a back road leading to an old, partially overgrown trail nobody used. He knew exactly where it went.

*****

"Okay! We're getting a satellite visual," blurted Sully, raising jubilant hands. "They'll set us up to receive images with a minute target. We're looking at a short delay and maybe a scratchy video. It probably won't be perfect, but it should help even the playing field."

Isaiah and Hannah returned. The hopefully good news lifted their spirits. Several officers gathered around the monitor.

"Good going, Sully. Try to get the site of the drop off. This will at least give us a fighting chance," said Mike, glancing toward Hannah. "Keep the visual wide enough to see which direction the bagman comes from and direction he leaves."

With a little quicker step, he sat down by Hannah. "I don't know if our tracking the perp will be enough, but it sure does give us a better chance to...rescue LaRana."

"Thank you. At this point, I'll grasp for anything that keeps her alive."

Mike rose then paced the floor waiting for the images to come through. Sully broke the near silence. "We got a visual!"

A round of cheers filled the room. Mike moved back to the monitor. "Has Jalen got back yet? I'd like him to see this. Widen the scope a little more."

Sully adjusted the visual, silently gazing at the monitor. He leaned forward with a frown. "Now what's this? We have a biker appearing to be headed toward the drop off!"

Mike peered at the speeder. The visual wasn't perfectly clear, but he knew the biker. "Jalen! Blast it! What is that lad thinking? He's going to mess up the whole plan! He's putting LaRana's life in severe jeopardy! What in creation is he thinking about? Our chances of a successful recovery have all but disappeared!"

He suddenly remembered Hannah was nearby. "I'm sorry for the outburst Mrs. Johnson, but Jalen has taken a potentially disastrous risk. Let's just all hope and pray he doesn't get LaRana and himself killed."

Shelly gathered all the poise she could. "I'm sorry, Officer Monroe. I know he's a little impulsive, but he does know these mountains. I believe his motives are correct, and I have faith he can do what he set out to do. He may have thought this was the only way to save LaRana. With that said, uh, you might give him a call if you can."

Hannah stood up and didn't waver. In light of the seemingly impossible, she tried to be positive. "I can't be certain he's doing the right thing, but I do know he's concerned with LaRana's life as much, and maybe more, than anyone in this room. Yes, I could be condemning if LaRana doesn't make it, but I couldn't lay the blame on Jalen. His heart is in the right place. All we can hope for is that his head is there also."

For several moments, the room fell quiet till a few muted whispers drifted from the officers and troopers. Mike's demeanor was measured.

"Well, I suppose we view things from a different perspective. I can understand yours, but I hope you understand ours. The money is not important. LaRana's safe return is our only concern. Regardless, the die is cast, the odds are not favorable, but…maybe your faith can at least be of comfort. We'll try to act on any info without due risk. It seems all we can do for now is what Mrs. Johnson said."

*****

The rough, narrow trail wound through the old-growth forest. Jalen held Nellie tight as she bounced over rocks and limbs. At a little over twenty minutes from Pallon Ridge, he slid to a stop in a small clearing, took the phone in hand, and checked reception.

Still there.

He guessed everybody might be wondering his whereabouts. He also presumed Mike would be the first to realize where he was if satellite images were available. He wondered how his brash deed would be accepted. A second thought said it was probably better not to know.

He crept over a few large rocks on the descent of a ravine then sped up a steep rise toward the intersection. The trail ran around a deep gorge to a ledge well hidden by a veil of small, leafy trees nearly three hundred and sixty feet atop a plunging slope to the old station's wide, somewhat rocky lot sparsely covered by knee-high weeds. Rotting trunks and bushy shrubs offered a broken but sufficient view. He shut Nellie down, listening to the sudden silence. He once again checked reception. Three bars, a smiling nod, a look at his watch: 12:53.

He repeatedly peered through binoculars till a Jeep pulled up to an old, rickety bench. The driver got out, set the case on the bench, then quickly regained the driver's seat and drove away. One pm came and went. Jalen grew concerned. It was time. He punched the number.

"Officer Monroe, this is Jalen. I… I…yeah, I know, I know… let me explain. What… I might be charged? I'll do my best to not jeopardize the mission, but I just couldn't sit and wait for the satellite. Oh, you got it working…great! I'm above the old station…as I guess you know. I figured I could find out where the bagman headed after the pickup, thought it might speed things up a bit. I know… I know…but I couldn't see any other option. I can see the case. It's a few minutes past the deadline and no sign of anyone. I hope I haven't been made. There's no…wait…an ATV is coming. Hold a sec. Do you see him?… Good. That's cool!"

A well-worn four-wheeler raced toward the old bench. Its rider, with face covered except for eyes, leaped off, quickly opened the case, carefully scanned it front and back, felt all around inside then just as quickly closed it. He glanced around the area while holding a phone to his ear. His message was brief. With a hasty remount, and the case secured, he sped from the station to an obscure trail across the clearing and disappeared while another on-looker, on the far side of the hill, lowered a pair of binoculars, wryly smirking.

"Perfect! Now, back to my dear LaRana."

Jalen carefully watched the bagman's direction then raised the cell. "He's on the move up the old Elk Horn Trail. It's really rough and forks into three smaller trails in a few miles. I can follow him on the Gorge trail. It's rougher but shorter. I can get to the trailhead before he does and see where he goes from there."

He paused then replied. "I'm sorry, Officer Monroe, I know you're angry, but I can't duck out now. Yeah, I know… I know… I'll be careful. Just trying to back up the satellite. You should see the trail he takes. It's all up to you now…what's that? The…monitor went down! We need it up! We could easily lose any location! I hear you… yeah, I know, I know."

Jalen slid the cell in his shirt pocket, pondering options. He could think of only one. He gunned Nellie and bounded down the slope to an overgrown intersection. He ended a few hundred feet of smooth terrain, abruptly turned, and sped down a rough road to another trail rising to a long ridge.

With a little more luck, I can get to the fork before he does.

He gave no thought to safety only speed. He slid around a sharp swale only to meet an old stump. Nellie tilted onto two wheels, sending Jalen sprawling from the seat. Both man and machine came to rest against a clump of scraggly junipers leaving Jalen nestled in several broken but sturdy limbs. He deeply groaned, laboring to regain his feet. He felt a slight knot on his head, a few scratches, and a bruised shoulder. Nellie lay on her side with only two fender dents. With a quick pull, Jalen set her on all four.

Once again in the seat, he reached for the cell, but found only an empty pocket. He leaped from Nellie, scanning the ground in a near panic for what seemed far too long. He nearly covered the entire area when the sun gleamed off the phone in a cluster of large rocks, lying like a corpse. He quickly yanked it from its rocky coffin and punched the numbers, frantically hoping for a sound. Nothing. With an angry declaration, he slung it into the woods.

His heart raced. Thoughts swirled. He crawled on Nellie, unsure of the next move. "Well, what do we do now, old girl?"

With a deep breath, he grasped the grips. "Yeah, me too. I can't think of anything else either. I don't see anyone around but us. We've gotta catch that scumbag, and I know just the place."

*****

"Sir, the monitor just went down!"

"Ah, that's all we needed! Keep trying to get it back!"

Mike impatiently watched Sully labor to regain a visual, again and again. Nothing. He had to find the trail leading to LaRana. Only one solution was available. With a slight grumble, he grabbed the phone and punched the numbers. No answer. He punched the numbers again. *Come on, Jalen. Come on!*

Nothing.

He lowered the phone and glanced around the room, a room filled with silence and wide eyes.

The operation came to a screeching halt.

*****

Jalen swiftly thrust the starter, bringing Nellie to life. He sprang down the path, slowed around several large rocks and jutting obstacles, spending time held so precious. Finally, he tossed caution aside and tore over the trail. Half buried rocks and scattered limbs often took all four wheels from the ground.

Vital minutes seemed eternal till he stopped above a widened area where the lower trail forked into three smaller paths. He shut Nellie down, waiting impatiently. Minutes crept by.

I hope I'm at the right place. He should be here before long. At least, Mike should be able to see him…but…what if he can't? Satellites can be erratic.

Time continued to pass. Anxiety leaped. Finally, the sound of an engine came through the trees, barely audible but getting louder. As hoped for, he spotted the ATV nearing the fork. He wiped his brow, took a long, slow breath, and gently patted his ride. Nagging thoughts whirled in his head.

What if the satellite isn't working? They won't see which trail he takes.

He sat motionless till the bagman slowed to a crawl directly below the ridge.

Oh, man! Should I do it? Maybe I… Nah, no way! Oh, well, I wish I could come up with a better idea!

He herded Nellie over rough terrain to a sparse ridge above the trail. "We're gonna need some more luck, old gal. I can't think of anything else to do. I hope we ain't messing things up. Be a jewel. Don't conk out on me now."

He gently eased to an opening leading straight down a severe slope. A descending thicket of small bushes on the left became a welcome barrier. He crept forward then twisted the throttle to full, descending in a storm of pebbles and dust. Nellie smashed broadside into the ATV, violently throwing its rider into a large unforgiving tree trunk. Nellie spun then turned over, sending Jalen whirling in the dirt. Undaunted, Jalen jumped to his feet and pounced on his query, painfully writhing on the ground.

The man cursed and screamed. "My leg! Oh, my leg! It's broken!"

"Yeah, and that ain't all that's gonna be broken if you don't tell me where you're going."

"I was just taking…a ride to see…the flora and fauna."

Jalen knelt and leaned on the man's right leg. A piercing scream echoed through the trees. He checked for weapons and found only a large, Bowie-type knife at the man's side. He flung it away then grabbed the man's collar.

"Where were you going?"

No answer.

Jalen placed a knee on the leg and twisted hard. The man's head jerked as he bellowed in anguish. Sweat oozed from his forehead as he gasped for breath. Jalen again grabbed the man's collar and pulled his head from the ground.

"Tell me where she is, or I'll tear your leg off!"

No answer.

Jalen grasped the leg and bent it upward. The man shrieked, putting a shaky hand on Jalen's arm.

"Stop! Stop! She's at…the cabin…near the…old Eagle Claw mine. I beg you, put my leg down!"

Jalen again twisted the leg. "Don't lie to me! I'll break it off!"

"I'm…not lying. She's there. Dead or alive… I don't know."

Jalen dropped the leg and rose. *Why didn't I think of that old cabin near the mine? It's nearly grown over with trees. They may not see it with the satellite. That's just about four miles off the Silver Bush trail.*

He quickly searched the grounds. Nothing. He menacingly stood over the man. "Where's your cell?"

"I don't have one."

"Yeah, you do! I saw you use it!

"Guess I lost it."

Jalen frisked him but found nothing. "Ahh, where is it? Hmm, just maybe…"

He rushed to the perp's four-wheeler. Luck was his. A cell rested in the box. In but a few moments, Jalen reached Mike. "I have the bagman out of commission. Sorry, I had no choice. I…uh…lost my cell. I'm on the fleabag's cell. He says LaRana's at the old ramshackle cabin above Eagle Claw mine. I'm not sure we can trust him, but he was at a…disadvantage. What should we do?"

"How do I know? Well, the perp was willing to cooperate for obvious reasons. I should have thought of that old shack. What do you want me to do?"

The conversation paused. Jalen grew anxious. Mike's answer was short and not heartily accepted.

"Stay here? A quiet approach sounds good, but nearly an hour is a long time! That doesn't sound so good. We have to get there quicker than that!"

Another pause. A grimace.

"Stay with the bagman! Okay, I'll stay with the dude, but you've got to get there quicker than an hour! If the creep has a timetable with this guy, he'll know something went wrong long before that!"

Another long pause. A headshake.

"If that's the best you can do, do better! I'll stay with this piece of dirt! Whatever you do, get there in time!"

Jalen again paced then sat on a rock across the small clearing from Nellie. The bagman's moaning interrupted his thoughts. Jalen mulled over the situation. One certain factor was clear; time was on the perp's side. A swift glance at his adversary found him grimacing and moaning.

"Stay with the bagman! Uh! Stay with the bagman, my eye. This dude ain't going anywhere. Fifty minutes! Sixty minutes! Maybe more! That's a long time—too long. The bozo may already suspect something's wrong by now. I can be there in less than fifteen minutes…to see what's happening. Yeah, yeah! There's just no way I can stay here!"

He slid off the rock and turned for Nellie. He stopped in his tracks. The man, favoring his right leg, stood with a sneaky smirk.

"You're not too hard to fool, punk. Sorry, but my leg has miraculously healed, a little sore but good enough to do you in. By the time anyone gets to the cabin, we'll be long gone. As for you, you'll never know."

Jalen glanced at the knife lying in front of Nellie. The man smiled, also spotting the blade.

"It seems we have the same idea."

They bolted at the same time, but the bagman was much closer. He grasped the knife and swished it across Jalen's arm, opening a slight gash. Jalen reeled backward and fell to the rocky ground, his mind grasping for what to do. With confident strides and slow waves of the blade, the man calmly approached.

"Sorry, loser, but I need to be on my way, and you're the only thing in it, but not for long."

Missives Twelve

Jariel,

Sorry to get back so soon, but I couldn't wait. As you see, my desire has worked out perfectly. LaRana will soon be mine, and Jalen will be with her. Such a disaster will destroy Hannah's already shaky faith. Shelly's faith will go up in a puff of smoke. The only one pleased will be Roland. He will get back to his selfish, inconsiderate normal.

Maybe you better move on to the next losing battle.

Esul

*****

Esul,

I must admit, I am quite distraught, but I never give up until the war is over. I never underestimate the power of my Master, no matter the circumstance. Even at the loss of LaRana and Jalen, Hannah and Shelly will find solace and strength. Jalen may fail, but your pawn has not yet prevailed. They are not yet in your hands, demon.

Jariel

13

Chances Are

LaRana wearily trembled then screamed till collapsing on the cot. She breathed heavily for several moments then rose, desperately yelling through cracks in the wall. Only silence answered. Her voice fell to a whisper. Exhausted, she crumpled to the floor.

She watched the mouse quietly creep from the pile of wood. It stopped, sitting on its haunches a few inches from her feet. LaRana gently tossed it a cracker chip. It didn't flinch. They're eyes met. Its nose wiggled. She slowly put her hand on the floor, palm up. With no reservation, the rodent crawled into it. Ever so carefully, she raised her hand to eye level. The mouse stared, squeaking with a nod. LaRana managed a slender smile while gently lowering her unusual friend. Without a sound, the mouse snapped up the chip before scooting back to the woodpile. Yet expecting her captor's return, she found a strange peace for whatever might happen.

She sat for nearly half an hour inwardly pleading for a rescuer, but the sound of an ATV shattered the thought. She tried to remain calm, to control emotions, but could not.

Dawson entered the cabin sporting a smug grin. Setting a carryall and binoculars on the table, he leaned on it with both hands for several seconds. With a sudden turn, he leisurely approached his captive, gently moving one hand through her hair while stroking her neck with a knife in the other hand. She could barely draw a breath, paralyzed by the nauseating scent of his closeness. Evil slinked within inches. Satan was upon her. Death's door opened wide.

Consumed by the moment, she was alone with no thought of the morrow or recall of the past. She leaned back, closed her eyes when suddenly appeared a vision of the mouse peering at eye level. The tension slowly eased. Her mind began to clear.

Dawson leisurely straightened. "Well now, my sweet little bird. How delightful to see you relax. See, I'm not so bad. Ruddy will be here shortly, but not here long. I'll soon have the money and time to decide what to do with you. I should have already disposed of you, but there's something about you so pleasantly different than the others. I actually wish we were of the same mind-set, but... I know such would be quite a leap for you. So I really would like to let you live. As I wrestle with options, make sure you don't do something stupid. That would only make the decision easier."

LaRana said nothing. Desperate thoughts on escape hastily came and passed. She shuddered when Dawson set the knife on the table. A chilling vision of Willow staring at a knife trembled her heart. He caught her gaze and slightly snickered.

"Does this bother you? This is one of my handy, little blades. I always liked the old western movies where the gunslinger notched his pistol with each kill. I have two marks on this hilt. This one here is Willow's. You may, or may not, be the third. A lot depends on how you treat me. All I want is for you to like me. Please understand. I really need someone to like me. I must have someone to like me!"

Dawson suddenly tensed. He peered out the window then down to his watch. He frowned, looked at LaRana then returned to the window. A slight scowl crossed his brow. His demeanor quickly turned from measured quietness to visible annoyance.

"Ruddy should have been here by now. For your sake, fair lady, I hope nothing's gone wrong. I can't have anything go wrong. No! Nothing! Nothing!"

He again paced the floor, mumbling and cursing. A few minutes seemed eternal. Dawson grew visibly stressed. LaRana's heart raced. His demeanor promptly changed. Anger found his eyes. Would he lose it? She knew too well that result. Notions quickly came then left with the same haste. The mouse peered from behind a stick of firewood. He bobbed his head then twitched his whiskers. LaRana took it as a good sign, unable to entertain any other meaning. Dawson saw the rodent and threw a can his way. The mouse darted back to hiding.

"Stupid mouse. I guess this old shack is full of 'em." His cold eyes glared at LaRana. "Well now, Ruddy being late is not good, not good at all. Something must have happened. This changes everything. I'm so sorry, but I must end our little visit and get out of here."

He carefully moved toward the knife. Her mind took a giant leap to the edge of eternity. She tried to scream but failed. She slumped against the pole, tense yet exhausted. Suddenly, the dreaded, yet welcome, hum of an ATV descended like a judge's gavel. The time had come. She lifted her eyes but spoke not a word. Nothing was left to say. Her forlorn gaze sent a final plea.

Dawson quickly moved to the window. His anger suddenly disappeared. "Ah, yes. It's about time. The old Suzuki draws near at last. I'd know that throaty sound anywhere. And there's good old Ruddy. He's kind a' crazy, but he's tough and loyal. He'll be gone soon, and then, my dear, and then…"

LaRana's faced grimaced, but tears didn't flow. None remained. Never had a few minutes seemed her last. Possibilities were gone. Time ran out. The mouse quietly came out of hiding. It gave a final squeak then stood still. With a frantic plea, she looked upward with only imploring eyes.

The ATV stilled. Sounds of footsteps on the porch echoed in the cabin. Suddenly, the door was thrust open. A lone figure burst in, catching Dawson by surprise.

Jalen.

With a determined glare, he motioned with Ruddy's dagger. "Get away from her! Move over there! Your days are over, scum!"

Dawson calmly eased toward the center of the room. His eyes narrowed, his slow movement measured. A smirk crept across his face.

LaRana shouted, "Jalen, he has a knife on the table!"

"Leave it be, or you'll feel this one!"

"Well now, if it isn't little boy Strade. I admire your spunk to get this far, but you are going to be disappointed. Now, I have to kill you both. Of course, I'll start with you. Dear LaRana can watch her brave but stupid rescuer meet a gory demise."

Dawson leaped for the knife. Jalen ran at him, but Dawson quickly stopped and spun around, catching Jalen with a violent backhand, sending him sprawling to the floor. In a heartbeat, Dawson was over him. He thrust his blade toward Jalen's chest, but it hit the floor when Jalen slammed a foot into his knee. Rolling to the side, he swiftly gained his feet.

Dawson pressed forward, slashing the blade. Jalen inched back with each swirl. He blocked a thrust and swirled his own knife. Dawson swung his arm and parried the thrust, sending Jalen's blade flying harmlessly across the floor. A quick stroke opened a shallow gash on Jalen's chest. Dawson laughed below wild but confident eyes.

"How does that feel, loser? You thought you could take me? I'll spill your blood all over the floor. Such a shame for poor LaRana to see you carved up like a piece of cheap meat."

Another stroke. Another gash. Blood ran over Jalen's shoulder. Dawson pressed closer, LaRana screamed. Jalen tripped near the woodpile and fell to the side.

Dawson stood over his prey. He slowly nodded with a smirk. "Not bad, clown, but we're done here. Say goodbye to your lovely lady."

He raised the blade and yelled. Jalen grasped an axe handle leaning against the woodpile. In the blink of an eye, he swung it at Dawson's legs, landing a solid blow on the side of his knee. Dawson stumbled to the side. Jalen shoved the handle into his stomach, sending his foe reeling backward, trying to catch his breath. Jalen scrambled to his feet as Dawson charged and brought a powerful thrust of the knife. Jalen blocked his arm then sent the handle into his chest. Dawson's breath fled, sending him to the floor in a heap, writhing in pain.

Jalen's breath came heavy and quick. He slightly stumbled then began cutting LaRana's cords. "You okay? Did he…?"

"No…but we…"

"Need to get out of here, fast! Yeah, I know!"

"I'm more than ready."

A final cut sent the cord to the floor, but Dawson quietly picked up his knife and eased to his feet. His eyes blazed with madness. With Jalen's attention to the cord, he silently approached. Without a word, he took a step and quickly raised the knife.

LaRana glanced over her rescuer's shoulder. "Jalen!"

Jalen quickly lurched to the side then slung the axe handle at Dawson's ankles, tripping him to the floor. Jalen sprung to his feet and quickly moved toward the door. He looked for anything to even the odds. He saw an old fireplace poker lying on the floor and made a lunge for it. He grasped the poker, but Dawson was over him.

Ashlynn's words leaped into LaRana's mind. "When all seems lost, and you have only one more shot, be calm, think clearly. Take emotions to zero."

Dawson reached down, grabbed Jalen's throat, and raised the blade. "I've had enough of you, hotshot!"

LaRana quickly stepped behind Dawson, with axe handle in hand, knowing the swing must be true.

It was.

Before the thrust was finished, LaRana smashed the axe handle on the back of his head. He stumbled to the side, glanced at LaRana with astonishment, crumpling to the floor.

Jalen slowly rose. "Wow, what a blow! I wasn't sure how to deal with that last thrust."

He scooted over and leaned against a pillar. LaRana quietly sat by him. "You are undoubtedly the bravest dude I ever met. However can I thank you?"

"Well, I believe you just did with that axe handle. Remind me to never make you mad." LaRana managed a wry grin, swiftly proceeding to faintly slap his arm.

Jalen took the cord from the bar and secured Dawson's arms behind his back then tied his feet together. He slowly calmed, gently leaning on the woodpile. For nearly half an hour, LaRana relaxed with her head on Jalen's arm till a noise from above broke the silence. Two helicopters landed nearby with troopers leaping out, quickly descending on the cabin. A chorus of footsteps tromped on the porch. Mike Monroe burst through the door, quickly scanning the room. Troopers were suddenly everywhere. Two stood over the still silent abductor. Mike sheathed his firearm, calling for medics as he helped Jalen and LaRana to chairs. With LaRana being attended to, Mike moved in front of Jalen with a stern look.

"What is it with you? You're helping me at the station one moment then racing through the hills a moment later! What about staying with the bagman? We lost the monitor for nearly thirty minutes. What about another call? But no…here you are, doing something stupid again. I thought you had learned better!"

"Well, uh, things got rather…complicated. I couldn't be sure the monitor was still alive, which I guess it wasn't. So I couldn't be sure you would make it in time or even get here at all. I could have called again, but I kept thinking about time. I could never forgive myself if we ran out of it."

"What happened to the bagman?"

"Well, um, that's a little embarrassing. I pulled this neat maneuver with ol' Nellie down a slope, knocking the dude off his ATV. I, uh, worked him over a little. I thought he had a broken leg, but he… uh…well…he didn't. He got the drop on me, but he wasn't very good at dodging rocks. It was just like gunning down a runner with a perfect throw to home plate. After connecting with a couple, he went down. I saw he wore jeans just about the same color as mine, so I took his jacket, hat, ATV, the case, and well, here we are. He's tow roped to a tree back at the fork's head."

"I should run you in for interfering with an official operation, but… I'll let you off this time. Just don't let it happen again. Do you realize the odds you could pull this off? You had only two, slim, and are you crazy? Probably doesn't matter. You would have tried anyway." He glanced at LaRana then back to Jalen. "Oh…by the way… nice going."

Mike ruffled his hair and turned to the troopers and medics. "Let's get this piece of work on a stretcher. Make sure to take care of LaRana…and this loose cannon. Bag all the evidence. And someone take care of the ransom. By the way, where is the ransom?"

"It's on the bagman's ATV. You can't miss it."

State troopers carefully searched then cleared the premises while medics finished with Jalen. He gently rose with a few groans. LaRana slyly approached, taking him by the good arm. They quietly stepped to the back of the cabin where she flung her arms around his neck, landing on his chest.

"Ahhh!"

"Oops, sorry. I, most gallant sire, don't know what to say other than you were out of your mind to try to rescue me. But oh, you certainly were a sight for hopeless eyes. That's twice you have saved me. How can I ever repay my noble knight?"

"Oh, fair lady, at a total loss I currently am. Perchance, a notion of grand extent in due time will regale my intellect."

Mike approached and handed LaRana a cell. "I believe there's a mighty worried lady waiting for news. I think you on the end of this phone would be the voice she wants to hear. Give her a call."

LaRana eagerly punched the numbers. Tears welled then oozed. "Mom, it's me. I'm okay. I'm safe. State troopers and medics are everywhere. Tell Shelly that Jalen is fine…wonderfully fine, except for a…scratch. We'll be back soon."

A pause.

"No, really, Mom, I'm okay, very okay! I'm anxious to see you. I love you, Mom, I love you…what? Okay." She handed the phone to Jalen. "Your mom."

"Hi, Mom… I'm great! Just a scratch as LaRana said. Not sure when we leave here, but we should see you all soon…thanks."

The ordeal's weight crashed down on LaRana, running headlong into the rapid rise of overwhelming joy. She sat on the cot while Jalen met with Mike and two troopers. The room was alive with activity. Elation finally fell to drained emotions. She stared at the floor.

Lord, thank You for doing…whatever You did to help me live. I will try my best to understand more about You.

She relaxed with a deep breath when another movement caught her attention. The mouse peeked from the woodpile with two squeaks and a wriggled nose. It suddenly dawned why a dumb, little mouse would unwittingly help keep her sanity. She glanced up with a nod and a smile then looked back at the rodent.

"Thanks, fur ball."

*****

The helicopters came to rest at the city airfield. LaRana and Jalen were placed in a police cruiser with Officer Monroe. They heartily welcomed the peace and quiet. Just above a mile from the Justice Center, they turned onto the highway. Mike suddenly interrupted the pleasant drive.

"I think you have some company, LaRana."

She leaned forward, gazing out the window. People were lined up on both sides of the road, holding hastily made signs and shouting in unison.

"LaRana! LaRana! LaRana!"

Arms fervently waved, cheers loudly raced as if a hero had returned. It seemed all of Pallon Ridge had come.

"I believe it's safe to say you are on the minds of a few people," said Mike. "I've never seen anything like this."

Jalen gazed awestruck. "Would you look at that? Absolutely amazing! Word certainly travels fast. It appears they're mighty happy to see you."

LaRana choked back tears. "Me? Why me? Most of them don't even know me! Why would they do this?"

Jalen gently eased back then ruffled her hair. "Oh, I'm not certain, but...maybe it's because you're one of their own, a Ridger as we say."

"But...how did so many even know of...this...thing?"

"Well, let's see. If one person got wind of the situation, then he or she told maybe a couple more who each told a couple more who started a phone relay, an online...well, you get the picture. I believe there's an expression 'news travels fast.' Apparently, yours was on steroids."

She rested her head on the back of the seat, closing her eyes. Visions of the past began to swirl, memories of being no more than an oddity, lonely moments when only her mother cared she existed. She dropped her head into her hands and softly cried, not of sorrow, but of illumination. A needed arm embraced her. Jalen's shoulder, bandages and all, never felt so good.

She gingerly leaned forward when the cruiser slowed near the station. Hannah, Isaiah, Shelly, and Roland stood in front of a jubilant host of people. Two news cameras perched on eager shoulders. Her heart began to race. Setting aside the pain, Jalen dashed around the van, dramatically opening the door with a wave of his hand. She slowly exited to a chorus of cheers.

LaRana fell into Hannah's arms. Tears ran from each, glorious drops of reunion. The crowd raucously applauded, chanting with fists raised in unison.

"LaRana! LaRana! LaRana!"

Shelly met Jalen with glowing eyes and a beaming face. Her embrace was filled with relief and pride. Roland stepped near and offered his hand.

"You did good, real good."

Jalen accepted with an odd smile in front of slight disappointment, glad his father was there, appreciated his words, yet still not hearing a long-desired word.

Mike and two troopers ushered them past inquisitive reporters to the station door. They walked down the hall where a quiet room awaited LaRana, now nearly sapped of energy. She collapsed on the sofa with Jalen at her side. She leaned her head back and closed her eyes, melting into the cushion's comfort.

Several silent minutes passed. Everyone gave LaRana time to spend the weariness of nearly three agonizing days. Mike was on one phone, a trooper on another. Hannah sat with Isaiah. Only the muted jubilation of the crowd broke the near stillness. A sudden motion from Mike ended the calls. A hush fell over the room. LaRana opened her eyes, took a few deep breaths, and sat up straight. She peered into calm faces. Hannah became the spokeswoman, calmly inquiring what all wanted to hear.

"Do you want to talk about it now or wait till later?"

LaRana quickly scanned the room then took a deep breath. "Well, if I have to do it sometime, I'm guessing now would be as good as any."

Hannah held up her hand. "Now, let's go one at a time, please. Officer Monroe, do you want to go first?"

"I think just listening would be good for now. I can complete the official report after things settle down."

"Shelly?"

"I'm in no hurry. I'm relishing the results. Details can come later. Besides, a lot of anxious questions wait down the hall and maybe outside. No use for LaRana to do this more than once."

Mike knelt beside the sofa. "Are you sure you want to do this? We can tell the reporters you would meet with them later."

LaRana momentarily thought before replying. She deeply wanted to go home and crash, but intense desire to return to regular life as quickly as possible won out.

"I'm at a total loss that so many people...uh, cared so much. For some reason, I feel compelled to tell my story, at least in part. Besides, I want to get this over and get back to some kind of normal. The quicker this is behind me, the better. A good shower often helps get rid of filth other than normal dirt, but I can wait another hour or so. Let's get this done."

Officer Monroe ushered Hannah and LaRana to a crowded meeting room where two TV cameramen stood behind fervent reporters with recorders in hand. She sat down with Hannah sitting next to her.

"What was the most strenuous part of your captivity?" asked a reporter in the second row.

"The silence. Not knowing what was going to happen. It was fertile soil to let my greatest fears grow."

"What was the most encouraging time?" came a query in the front row.

"Again, the silence. I figured the longer no one was there, the better my chance for someone finding me. That proved to be true, although the timing was a little tight. But I'm certainly not complaining."

Questions were asked and answers given till the query so powerfully engaging her thoughts was aired. "How did you manage to keep your composure, your wits?"

LaRana paused then slightly grinned. "First, let me say, I may never kill another mouse."

Eyes blinked, a few chuckles, and odd looks called for more.

"A mouse?"

"There was this little mouse that was so patient while I talked to it. Now, don't you all go and entertain the idea I'm crazy. I've already come to grips with that thought. That little critter seemed to know my plight, to sense my fear and desperation. He even talked to me frequently."

Puzzled eyes darted from face to face.

"It was in squeak language, of course, but it seemed to understand. And…it had no fear of me at all. It took a cracker from my fingers several times. I couldn't shoo it away. I even held it in my hand and lifted it to eye level. It's odd, but my nerves settled when it was near me. As I look back, the mouse may have been in my hand, but I believe I may have been in another Hand. The most vital reason, I truly believe, was prayer. To begin with, that mouse had no business hanging around a human, but it did. Was it from God? I don't know, but it certainly wasn't normal behavior for a mouse. It sure helped keep my sanity.

Secondly, I prayed often. Even though I was a doubter, I prayed. Notice the "was" a doubter? No longer. I always thought that…if God actually existed, He would only help those who sorta…catered to Him, the Jesus freaks, as I so mockingly called them. But on the way back, I couldn't get out of my mind that He helped me, a doubter, through a hopeless situation. It's also strange my last plea, sent with no words, came straight from my heart. How do I know? Well, I really don't know, but I didn't think about whether He was real or not. I only plead.

Thirdly, in a moment of do or die, an archery lesson flashed in my mind, a very valuable lesson from a very good friend, one that probably saved both me and Jalen.

And last, I knew some really good people were pulling for me, even praying for me. And it appears, more than I could imagine. So can I prove He heard? No, but there was that unusual mouse, and there came my gallant knight in not so shiny armor with all the troopers in the world, and here I am. That's enough for me. And oh, thanks to all in Pallon Ridge who cared and showed so much support for me. I would never have given thought to such an outpouring of concern."

LaRana stepped from the podium, peering into faces bathed in amazement. She felt a rush of relief mixed with renewed strength. Hannah concluded the session with courteous thanks. Reporters meandered toward the door, still chatting.

LaRana went back to the waiting room where Mike was smiling. "That was great! You couldn't have said it better."

Everybody in the room expressed the same sentiments, all but Hannah. Though she offered no words, her radiant smile and thankful eyes touched the pinnacle of pride and revealed the content of her heart. To LaRana, hers was the most powerful.

For nearly half an hour, law officials spoke to all involved, insuring details were correct and complete. With final questions answered, LaRana sighed with relief, ready to go home.

Hannah proudly walked with LaRana while Shelly motioned Jalen to her side. Her smug expression caught Jalen's attention. "I've kinda been wondering. Just how did your 'shower' go?"

"Ah, I…really apologize for that. If Officer Monroe knew what was in my mind, I would probably still be locked up. I hope you'll forgive me."

"Well, I guess I can this time. Actually, I would have had a heart attack if you had told me what was in your head."

They quietly walked down the hall when Charell approached. She congratulated LaRana and Hannah who graciously thanked her. As they continued on, Jalen lagged back till they turned the corner. He sped back to Charell.

"There's a major hero in this case, and I'm talking to her. Like I said, you may be the reason she survived. While you certainly deserve much more, all I can say is thanks, thanks, thanks."

"Well, I really appreciate that. It means a lot. However, if it's okay with you, let's…ah, keep it between ourselves."

"Done. One more thanks."

With handshakes finished, Jalen walked briskly around the corner, catching up as they approached the entry. Isaiah had a knowing smile, Shelly one of elation, and Hannah's carried the vastness of a mother's love. Jalen started to open the door then put one hand on LaRana's shoulder, smiling with the other hand to his ear.

"Uh, I believe there's a whole gaggle of people still outside eagerly desiring you give them a wave and a smile. After all, you're the biggest story to hit the Ridge, maybe ever. Perchance they strongly would desire to hear from their shining lass of honor. Dost thou have sufficient vim to give it a go, my lady?"

LaRana managed a slight grin and slapped his arm. "Well, sire, I suppose thou wilt not let me live it down if thy question I opt to decline."

Hannah started to speak, but LaRana raised her hand. "It's okay, Mom. I may well owe my life to not only those in this room, but to those outside also."

Hannah lowered her hand with a slight nod. "Okay, but keep it short, please. I'm guessing Jalen might like to get medical attention since I still see bandages."

"Gotcha."

"Jalen, would you kindly usher this lady to the masses that wait," said Mike with a wave to the door.

"My pleasure."

The crowd's muted talk leaped to a roar when LaRana appeared. Jalen raised his hand, and the cheerful din gradually diminished to a hush. LaRana silently stood, proudly scanning all who remained. Her heart began to race.

"I've spent a lot of time wondering why I didn't have many friends and when I would have. Now, as for my part, I see the best friends anyone could have standing not only in front of me but, more importantly, by me. I can never do enough to show my appreciation for your support during…the past few days. All I can say is thank you with all that is in me. I can truly say I came home to the best town on earth, Pallon Ridge."

The crowd burst into a roar and began to chant. "LaRana! LaRana! LaRana!"

No longer could she hold the tears. They flowed down to a grateful smile as Jalen led her to the van.

With a slight shake of his head, Mike opened the door. "Amazing. I've been doing this for quite a while, and I've never experienced anything like this. I just might come by some Sunday morning to... uh...see how you are doing. I'll get the final report tomorrow. We better get Jalen in the van and head for the hospital for proper attention. I can take you, your mom, and Mrs. Strade in the cruiser if you would like."

"No way! I've also been down this road before." LaRana's voice was noticeably forceful. "I'm going with him in the van, period!"

*****

Phone calls and well-wisher visits filled the week following LaRana's daring rescue. She became the face of the school environment. She vividly remembered the cutting remarks, the reproachful eyes, and the cruel rejection. Now, she couldn't walk the hall without smiles of welcome and back pats of acceptance.

After school on Friday, LaRana and Jalen quietly rested at her house. A small commotion caught their ears. A rather large group gathered in the yard, peering at the old house as if a monument. Sensing LaRana's uneasiness, Jalen performed another rescue, this time from the lingering curious. Quietly easing out the back door, he whisked her away for a peaceful walk at Salarin Lake. Reflections on the past and the now led to thoughts on the future. They were heartened to meet Isaiah on his customary trek around the lake's trails. With his usual smile, he joined their solitude on the windless evening.

"Well, it's nice seeing you two on such a pleasant day," said Isaiah, looking at LaRana while pausing to swipe a handkerchief across his forehead. "I trust you're fairing well?"

"A little quiet time really feels good," replied LaRana. "I'm still trying to figure out how so many people knew, or why they even cared, about my…ordeal. I was blown away by the all the people lining the streets when we returned."

"Your prayers didn't travel alone to our Lord. I'm guessing He had never received that many petitions in such a short time from Pallon Ridge. We opened the church for community prayer and many came. Your plight struck a spiritual chord."

LaRana grew deep in thought. "I guess it may have started with that little mouse, but yesterday, Jalen and I talked about…religious things. We both kinda felt the real and spiritual were two different worlds, like a mountaintop and a canyon."

Isaiah grinned. "That's one of the better comparisons I've heard."

LaRana leaned forward and spoke as if a door of understanding had opened. "But they're not separate! They're intertwined, each interacting with the other."

"Well now, perceptive indeed, you are. The spiritual works to make the physical serene and contenting as well as providing an avenue to continue."

"Continue? Continue what?"

"Life, my dear lady, life itself. Eternal life is not a fanciful concoction of man's intellect. Eternity is the dominion of God, and He created us to dwell in it. Remember when He said, 'Let Us make man in Our image?' He obviously wasn't referring to a temporal physical body. Without doubt, He made us to be eternal in a spiritual realm."

LaRana blushed. "I feel dumb I couldn't see that before, but it's all beginning to make sense. We talked about the odds of me being alive, you know, like the lottery on steroids. I can only speak for myself, but I simply must become one of His followers, His child as I've heard you say. Would you do me the honor… Dad?"

Tears seeped down Isaiah's cheeks to a wide smile. "I would be delighted and proud to baptize…my daughter."

LaRana threw her arms around Isaiah. He cried and laughed at the same time. The long-sought connection of a daughter to a father brought a lump to Jalen's throat. His own father came to mind, a father in name but not in heart, near but far away. His eyes misted at the scene of two finding a long elusive joy. His focus returned to the power of the moment.

"Is there room for two?"

Isaiah stepped toward Jalen and grasped his hand. "Most certainly! My, oh my, what a magnificent evening this turned out to be."

Two excited yet serene souls drove home below a brilliant sunset. A cluster of billowy clouds cradled a radiant sun putting a glint in LaRana's eyes.

"I heard how you nearly got into a fight on my first day at school here. It seems you're always taking up for me or coming to my rescue."

"When I first saw you, I knew you were lost, and I mean lost, like a goose in a hail storm. I figured you needed someone to take pity on you, and I just happened to be in the area, and…"

Two slaps on the…good arm.

*****

A few afternoon clouds meandered over Salarin Lake, unable to hinder a brilliant sun from spreading twinkling lights across the water. A few friends and family, somewhat normal for a baptism, surrounded Jalen and LaRana. Mike Monroe made an appearance, offering a hand to each before stepping a distance back.

Jalen was pleasantly surprised. "Wow, I wonder how he knew what was going on?"

Paul and Karen came by and offered congratulations. "To honor your ordeal and this event, we're treating you both to meals for a week. I think I speak for Pallon Ridge in saying we're proud of you both."

"Thanks, Paul, Karen. We will definitely take you up on that!" returned Jalen with a firm handshake.

"Same here," added LaRana. "Uh, I assume you're aware how much food this galoot can stow away."

"Oh, yeah," replied Karen, wryly. "I've ordered extra."

As Paul and Karen walked away, Jalen stood in awe. "Uh, what is going on? We thought everything had died down by now."

"You two are still in the hearts and minds of Pallon Ridge. With the way news travels, don't be surprised if a few more show up," said Isaiah with a trace of a smile.

LaRana spotted a familiar figure standing under a majestic pine. She vigorously waved, and a friend quickly walked toward her.

"Mom, there's Sarona!"

"Oh, yes! I nearly forgot! I haven't found the time to tell you. One of our couples at church agreed to let her live with them. She can finish school, and they'll help her map out a plan for the future."

"Wow! That's amazing. Is there no limit to the generosity of these people?"

"It's eye opening for sure."

Sarona hurried the last few steps, throwing her arms around LaRana. "Thank you for listening and helping me find a port in the storm. The Delsings are a super family. I guess I'll be seeing you in church. I don't know anything about this Christian stuff, but I think I'm gonna be learning, like it or not."

"If you don't mind taking my word, you're gonna like it. I'm so happy for you. You're going to do great, whatever you do."

The gathering began to grow, desiring to honor their local celebrities. People from various churches, people who didn't go to any church, business owners, service workers, students, and curious residents came to be part of the saga capturing statewide interest.

Jalen peered over the rapidly increasing audience, looking for one he thought might be there.

Roland was nowhere in sight.

He nervously paced in anticipation, hoping the gulf between could be breeched. Cars streamed into the parking area. The gathering of few became a gathering of many. LaRana's attention was also caught.

"Look at all these people. Why? There must be at least a hundred or maybe more. I'm getting a little antsy. What if I mess up, like falling, or having water go up my nose, or…something?"

Jalen was no less amazed. "Yeah, it sure is a little unnerving. It's just a couple of baptisms. But maybe it's for some bigger purpose, you know, like you. Who knows, you might even make it to the state newscast…again."

After finishing the sentence, he leaned toward her, holding out his arm.

Slap.

"Yeah, well, thanks a lot. I've had enough of that already."

The large group gathered blocked Jalen's view. Roland was nowhere to be seen. Shelly caught his anxiety.

"You know your dad. He doesn't like crowds. I wouldn't count on him showing up. But who knows, stranger things have happened."

The baptisms went off without a hitch. Jalen and LaRana emerged from the water to a thunderous ovation. They toweled off while most of those gathered departed, but a good number remained and formed a greeting line. Several younger kids, and a few adults, asked for signatures. His eyes misted when he saw Cesar and his family in the line followed by DeShawn and his mother.

Jalen had a mix of elation and sadness, a thrill of being a Christian with the pain of an alienating father. He fisted Cesar and his siblings then shook hands with their parents.

As they moved on, a woman approached with pleasant smile. Jalen welcomed her. "You have a great young man in DeShawn. If it's okay with you, I would like to take him to the batting cage someday."

"Anytime. Thank you for your interest in DeShawn. He often talks about you. He is so proud of his glove. Here's my phone number. I'm sure he would be quite excited to go. He wants to practice about every day."

"I can see that he has a great mother. I'll call soon."

After a parting hug, he scanned the line and spotted Roland walking toward him. He stood as if stunned. His heart leaped, a little in joy, a little in fear his father would make a scene.

A relaxed aura rested on his face, one not seen in years. He grasped Jalen with both arms. "Son, I'm so proud of you. I've been a thoughtless cad for too long. Maybe I can't make up for lost years, but I'm sure going to give it a try if you can find a way to forgive me."

Jalen burst into tears no less than Shelly who joined in a family embrace, an embrace sought for years. Lost in the moment's euphoria, he barely heard the thundering applause. They stood hand in hand with eyes shouting not only had two individuals been reborn but a family as well.

"And also, I want to hear more about this Jesus stuff you all are so stubbornly set on. But no promises."

He looked at Isaiah who stood a few paces away then reached in his pocket and took out a few pieces of metal.

"A…good friend…gave me these seemingly worthless pieces of metal. I actually threw them away twice, but something compelled me to get them back. They've caused me to do a lot of soul searching. Maybe this old, hard head can be softened. It's time for me to listen…something I haven't been too good at. I hope the walls don't fall down when I walk into the church building this Sunday."

He turned to LaRana. "I've said some unpleasant things about you. For that, I ask your forgiveness. I think Jalen's, uh, interest… in…oh, I just think you two make a great couple."

LaRana accepted a hand then hugged Roland whose eyes widened above a smile. "Thank you. I truly appreciate that."

Jalen straight-eyed Roland. "Thanks, Dad. You just made a perfect day better."

Amelia, Pipes, Bridgette, Katelyn, and Cheyenne eagerly surrounded LaRana, each trying to talk first.

One of the Super Six was missing. LaRana looked to her left then right. Ashlynn stood several yards away. LaRana raised both arms, emphatically motioning her to come. Ashlynn's piercing eyes, once recalled as a gaze of concern, now beamed as sparkling lights of approval. LaRana quickly moved toward Ashlynn. They heartily embraced then exchanged a fist bump.

"You might not be aware, but you're responsible for saving not just one but two lives," declared LaRana boldly.

"Ah, you had what it takes to act in a pinch."

"Yeah, right. Maybe now, but not before your…uh, lesson." They shared a laugh then hugged again.

Shelly took Jalen's arm and ambled away from the crowd. "I'm so proud of you, Son. My confidence and trust in you wavered for a few fleeting seconds when we drove home from the police station. I simply wanted you to think before you acted, to reason out the right and wrong. And I must say, you answered my question beyond my wildest dreams."

LaRana and Hannah walked to the shade of a tree. Hannah looked directly into LaRana's eyes. "We've had several memorable days, among a few others, since we came to Pallon Ridge. This is the best day yet. As I said a few times over the years, you are and always will be my shining star."

*****

With graduation over and warmer air of summer settling on Pallon Ridge, the cooler air of elevation swirled around Jalen and LaRana relaxing peacefully atop Talova Peak. A quickly passing shower left the air clean and fresh. A long, rumbling of thunder echoed through the valley below.

LaRana relaxed against a rock, softly fiddling with her necklace while scanning the panoramic view. "Wow, even better than before. It seems clearer now. Maybe getting some of the chaos out of life helped."

Jalen's thoughts sped backward. "I wonder what the chances were that we would be here, considering our first sight of each other?"

"As I heard someone say, slim and...are you crazy?" LaRana turned her head to the right. "Hey...look over there. Oh, my. I can't believe my eyes! What a glorious double rainbow!"

Jalen put his hands behind his head and leaned back. "Yeah, our spectacular omen has returned. Wonder what the chances are we would see this beautiful rainbow up here two straight times?"

"That's easy. There were two chances, slim and... God."

Missives Thirteen

Jariel,

Though it may elate you, I am deeply disturbed at the current outcome. I most certainly will take this turn of events with a great deal of annoyance. I worked quite hard for these two souls in particular, and the souls surrounding them in general. Be assured, I am not done with LaRana and Jalen yet. My task may now be quite difficult, but it is not impossible. I have gathered many who obeyed your Master, ones who were shallow in His faith, and those who couldn't stay the course. I will be watching for an opening.

As you well know, I will now go after them with all the weapons in my arsenal. Gaining an unbeliever is quite easy yet nothing spectacular, but snatching a believer from the hands of your Master is most gratifying. Doubt can still be sown in their hearts and minds, especially when life turns down. Mix cares of adulthood with a few trials, some minor, some major, and the barrier of doubt will again rise. Such a powerful recipe it is. They, like many, will think since they now belong to your Master, worries of life will be gone, and joy and prosperity will be their lot. You already know how those thoughts can be shattered. We constantly watch for those who drift away.

I will concede this temporary victory, but I will not rest until I claim all of your hapless converts. Jalen and LaRana may revel in their chosen path, but we will see if their shield of faith can withstand my fiery darts. Quenching them is quite the chore as you so keenly know. Their breastplate of righteousness is very thin at this point. I will not tarry to test its resilience.

While the temporary loss of LaRana and Jalen is greatly infuriating, the change of heart in Roland distresses me more. I was strongly confident he would break the Strade family and create permanent scars on Shelly and Jalen. Alas, my assessment was a little off. I despise losing the easy ones. He is yet to be yours, so expect to hear from me. Remember, the pull of the pub is very strong.

I am going to admit Hannah presented a real challenge. She is so steeped in self-initiative and braced by solid character that destroying her is going to be a tough battle. It rankles me to realize her staunch faith in the Savior is getting stronger. Connecting with Isaiah made my task quite difficult. I've never had any luck with him. Though I may flee for the time being, I will still watch for a crack in their armor. You know me, I may back off, but I never give up. Unfortunately, I perceive in you the same resolve.

And what is it with these puny humans? The support and prayers, the gathering of purpose, and the outpouring of care and concern, from those aggravating people of Pallon Ridge. They helped lay waste to one of my best plans, and now they see the power of petitioning your Master, and before long, many more will seek the path to Him.

My disappointments are growing.

Alas, my work never seems to be done. I hereby grant you this hopefully short-lived victory. I will with confidence move on to others. There's never a dearth of souls needed gathering. Unfortunately, I know you will revel in reply. I also know we will meet again on a fresh battle-field, and maybe I will sing the victory song.

So long for now, and may your successes be few.

Esul

*****

Esul,

I hope you don't mind if I rejoice along with the host of angels here. We began contending for two souls, and it grew to four. But look what has happened.

Not only have LaRana, Jalen, Hannah, and Shelly turned to our Master, but also Roland has decided to go to church, to see what those Jesus people are all about. Maybe it's needless to say, but you thought Roland would never believe in us. I have to admit, I too, had similar thoughts, but I continue to be amazed how powerful is my Lord's Word, especially when mixed with action.

I don't know why I sometimes doubt my Master's creation. Maybe it's because of the grief you cause with all your victories. After all, the apostle Paul not only disbelieved but also per-secuted my Father's children. We had serious doubts about him.

Mike Monroe has decided to find out what drives a group of people to be so decent, honest, and full of faith in a higher power. He was simply so wrapped up in his work he didn't look into the aspect of God. How ironic he taught so much to Jalen about temporal things that Jalen, by his faith and determination, might just lead him to seek eternal things.

And then there's Sarona, a hard-luck teenage loser in your mind and the minds of most humans. How heartening when LaRana and others saw her differently, not a person doomed to failure, not another soul relegated to the wishes of your servants, not someone to cross off the list. Now she has the chance to learn of us.

I have not lost sight of the fact you will continue to find openings in our converts' lives. While you sometimes may flee, you also are swift to return. I believe, however, these we won will be vigilant to keep you at bay.

Hold on a minute. It has just been brought to my attention that Jalen will be bringing Cesar to church. Also, just a reminder, Cesar is one of seven in his family. I also hear that DeShawn and his mother will be attending with Jalen. A heart of compassion cannot be denied. The number of humans who may seek our Lord through LaRana and Jalen is rapidly growing, all because your demonic efforts to collect LaRana failed.

I would love to see you pout and throw fits for the rest of eternity, but I know you better. I know you are moving on to others you may devour. When I become aware you are my adversary for another human soul, I will send you a missive. Now, until that time, I leave you with this one wish.

May your luck be even worse next time.

Jariel

About the Author

D. K. Barnes has served in various educational settings including public school math teacher and principal, educational services officer at a military installation, and church classes with both youth and adults. Now retired, he lives with his wife, Wanda, in Rolla, Missouri. Experiences with teens and adults have been both elating and heartbreaking. His perception of each outcome fueled the writing of *Missives*.